THE HOPE OF DRACONS

THE HOPE OF DRAGONS

A NOVEL

RACHEL A. GRECO

atmosphere press

For anyone overcome by the guilt of their mistakes.
You are forgiven and loved.

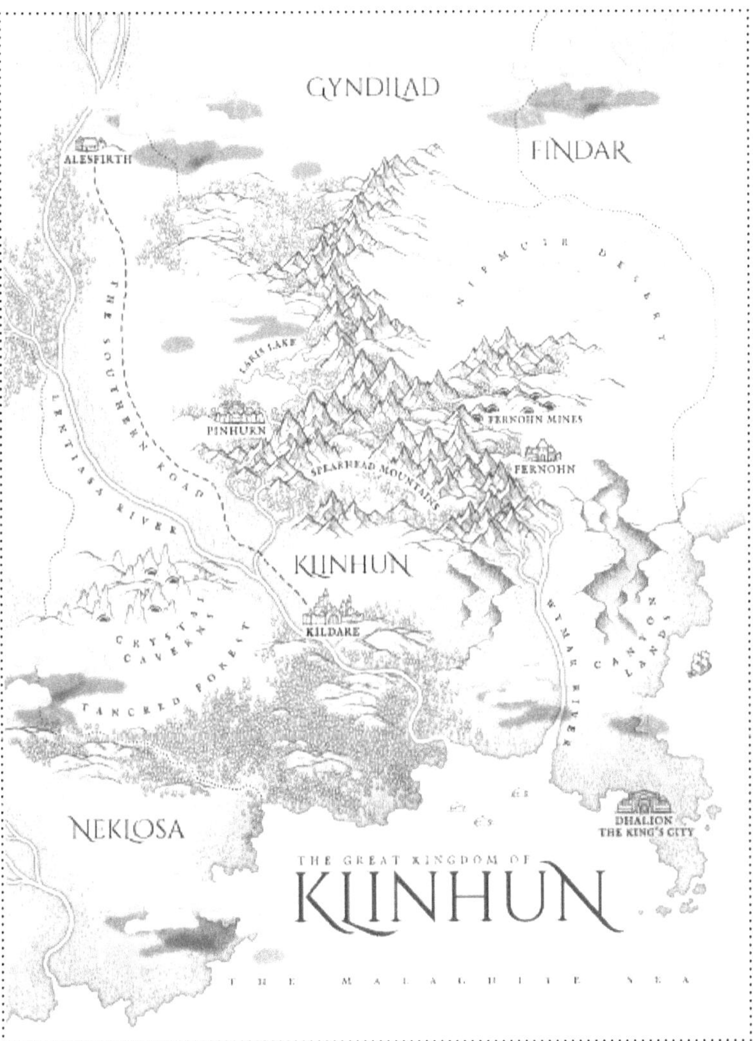

GYNDILAD
FINDAR
ALESFIRTH
NIPMOOR DESERT
THE SOUTHERN ROAD
LENTIARA RIVER
LARIS LAKE
PINHURN
FERNOHN MINES
FERNOHN
SPEARHEAD MOUNTAINS
KLINHUN
CRYSTAL CAVERNS
KILDARE
WINAR RIVER
CANAL
TANCRED FOREST
NEKLOSA
DHALION
THE KING'S CITY
THE GREAT KINGDOM OF
KLINHUN
THE MALACHITE SEA

Chapter One

Adelaide had died. Twice.

Once, when the Gyndilians had murdered her sister. Emma had been surrounded in desperate shouts and sticky crimson when so often she'd been surrounded by bright laughter and tender kindness. Her sister had faced the end alone—smoke, terror, and screams her only companions.

Perhaps her sister would still be alive if Adelaide hadn't left to buy leather. At least Emma wouldn't have died alone.

Adelaide knew Elias would still be alive if she hadn't begun the rebellion to overthrow him. Honorable Elias, her once enemy, prince, king, dragon, friend, had gazed up at her, his life draining away from the wound that Gunter, her best friend, had given him.

She'd been the one, though, to present that dagger to Gunter, to inflame him and the others with her fiery words.

And now Elias was gone forever, drifting alone in the sea, never to flash those stone-blue eyes on her, never to stretch his golden wings again, never to rule their kingdom justly.

Adelaide shivered. It was so cold in this cell without him, so quiet without his deep voice soaring into song. She shrunk into herself. *I'm so sorry, Elias.* He had healed her from her grief and prejudices, and she had rewarded him with death at the hand of her friend.

She clenched her legs tight to her chest, willing herself to shrink into nothing. If she couldn't have Emma's arms wrapped tight around her or Elias's cloak draped around her, then it would be better not to exist at all.

If only Elias had executed her for planning to overthrow him and his father instead of branding his own shoulder. Then he'd still be alive, uniting the dragons and humans, and Adelaide would be gone, unable to make any more mistakes.

Boots scuffed the tower's steps below, and Adelaide stood. It wasn't time for either of her meals; the sunlight slanting through the tiny window in her cell showed it to be early afternoon.

Berold's stubble-lined face came into view outside the room's barred door. He looked as if he'd aged ten years since Elias had died. Adelaide probably looked little better. The days since Elias's death seemed a lifetime—a lifetime of tears, regrets, and longings.

After her first flight as a dragon, she'd landed beside Elias' body. She hadn't been able to bear seeing him alone on the cliff, so, in her dragon form, she had gently placed him into the sea that he had loved so much. Perhaps it would carry him to Niclond, the land of dragons.

Then she had turned, painfully and unwillingly, back into a human.

Just as the glow of the transformation had dimmed, Berold had showed up and Cyr darted away.

"What have you done?" Berold had gazed at Elias's bobbing form as if a dagger had struck him as well.

Adelaide hadn't denied his accusation, and Berold had marched her here to this cell two days ago.

"Why did you do it?" Berold now asked, shaking the bars.

As much as Adelaide blamed herself for Elias's murder, she also blamed Gunter. "I already told you. My friend, Gunter, threw the dagger."

Berold stared at her. Then, his face scrunched up as if someone was stepping on his foot, he asked, "Why did you kill him? He took that burn for you. He loved you."

"I know. I know," Adelaide whispered, sinking to her knees.

As she had so often, she again watched the brand meant for her skin turn at the last moment and sear Elias's flesh by his own hand. She smelled the smoke and nauseating scent of his burned skin. She heard him answer Berold's astonishment at such an action by saying, "Because I love her," with the intensity of a dance.

Tears trickled down her dusty cheeks. "I did care for him." The realization had come too late, and now there was nothing she could do about it.

Berold looked past her at the wall, his face impassive. "We need him now more than ever."

Adelaide stood. "Why? What's happened?" For the first time since Elias's death, she thought of her parents and Odo back in Alesfirth.

Berold's gaze was an ice storm as he met her eyes. "Why should I tell you?"

"Because I care about this country."

"Then why did you kill our king?"

Adelaide closed her eyes. What was the point in arguing? Berold had never liked her and was clearly not going to remove the blame from her unless he saw proof. Proof that she didn't have.

"Because I was wrong and foolish." Adelaide hung her head, waiting for the axe to fall. She was not disappointed.

Emotionless, Berold said, "You are to hang at dawn."

Chapter Two

Cyr saw everything. He saw ants crisscrossing in the grass, people scurrying to and fro in the large stone nest below, and a squirrel puffing up its tail at the top of a tree. But he didn't see the one thing he wanted to: his mistress.

He didn't hear her whistle, nor could he smell her, since she had turned into a fire-flyer like Elias. Cyr didn't see him either—as a fire-flyer or a man—but he didn't expect to, because the last time Cyr had seen him, the man had smelled like death.

The hawk landed on a branch above the people darting about in the stone nest, weary from his search. He wondered why his mistress hadn't flown out of wherever she hid. But perhaps, like a fledgling, she didn't know how.

He had tried calling to her with his thoughts as he had done several times with the human-sometimes-fire-flyer Elias, but to no avail.

Movement out of the corner of Cyr's eye caught his attention. He opened his wings wide, soared on a draft, then landed on a branch of a sweet-smelling tree.

Ack! A sparrow squeaked, darting away.

Wait, Cyr said. *Have you seen a human girl with black feathers on her head?*

The sparrow disappeared into the forest's leafy clutches. Cyr considered giving chase, but that would just frighten the dim-witted creature more.

He turned his gaze to the grass far below. A bushy tail and two little ears stuck up. He dove and attacked the rabbit.

After devouring every scrap of the creature, Cyr flew high into the sunny sky. He then spiraled down toward the humans to look for his mistress, his heart hammering at their proximity. But the risk of getting caught would be worth it if he found her.

Adelaide would die in the morning. She had nothing left to spend on the thought after the storm of Elias's death and Gunter's betrayal. She wasn't surprised, for the punishment was deserved.

But it would have been nice to fly once more as a dragon, to lose herself in the salty taste of the ocean, the power of her silvery wings, the sound of the wind crooning her name, and the scents of evening sunlight and wild freshness as she had on her first flight after drinking the potion Elias had given her.

Mistress? Where are you?

Adelaide turned to the window. The thought was like a voice, but not quite. It was more internal like when Elias had spoken inside her mind as a dragon.

And then she remembered how Elias had communicated with Cyr in his mind. She didn't know if it would work while she was a human or even how it worked, but she longed for some friendly company in her last hours.

Cyr, is that you? I'm in here, she thought as loud as she could, imagining the hawk that she had healed.

A few moments later a familiar, dark-brown shape landed

on the windowsill, and Adelaide's dead heart warmed. But then it faltered again. What would he do when she died? She supposed he would then be truly free.

Mistress? Are you here? His voice was airy and somehow familiar.

Adelaide walked over to him. *Yes, I'm here.*

His amber gaze landed on her. *You look like a bird that's been fighting the wind all night.*

Adelaide rubbed her swollen eyes. *Well, Elias was just killed by my best friend, and I'm to hang at dawn.*

The fire-flyer is dead? I am much saddened to hear it. Cyr's wings dropped. *What does it mean to hang?*

It means the man who now rules this place is going to kill me in the morning. She sat down and picked up a piece of straw.

Then you must become a fire-flyer again and escape.

I don't know what will happen if I turn into a dragon in here. The room could collapse on me. Besides—she let the piece of straw float back onto the floor—*I deserve to die.*

Why?

Because I gave Gunter the dagger that he used to kill Elias, and I created the rebellion that overthrew him. It would be better for our kingdom if I was gone. Adelaide placed her head on her knees.

A soft, fluffy shape landed on her lap, but she refused to look at Cyr for fear she'd start sobbing.

Would it be better for your family if you were dead?

His words brought up blackberry-sweet memories: Adelaide chasing the chickens with Odo, talking with her mom as they made a pie for the festival, and her father's help—even after a long day in the fields—making a perch for Cyr when he was a fledgling.

Then she remembered Emma lying in the grave, pale as a fish's underbelly, and leaving her family in the middle of the night without any explanation. How much fear and worry had she caused her parents since she'd been gone?

What would they think of her when they heard about what she'd been doing and that she was a dragon now? Would they turn away in disgust or dread?

Yes, it would be better, Adelaide said.

I doubt that. But even so, didn't you make a promise to Elias before he died?

Why were birds so annoying? But Cyr was right; Adelaide had promised Elias to unite the dragons and humans. She glanced at the hawk's piercing eyes. *I'm the worst person to do that. I killed their king.*

Nay, that male with the silver weapon killed him. Cyr clicked his beak at her, and she flinched. *Elias believed you could do it, so you can. Besides, the sooner we get out of here, the better. It stinks.*

It was a little pathetic that Adelaide needed to be talked out of her despondency by her hawk. But Cyr was right about at least one thing: she had promised Elias to unite their two species, and she didn't want to let his memory down. Perhaps it could help make up for her failures.

Very well. I won't let Berold kill me in the morning. But in that case, I'll need the key for the door. She glanced at the barred entrance. *Do you think you can find it for me?*

What's a key?

After she explained, Cyr said, *I'll look.*

Adelaide folded her hands and stared at them. *And thanks for... well, convincing me to live.*

He rubbed his beak against her cheek. *Of course. Who else would I fly with?*

The sun set, casting Adelaide's cell in shadow. She pulled her cloak closer. Apparently, possessing the ability to turn into a dragon hadn't given her everlasting heat, although the fire from the potion still smoldered deep inside her.

She ate the stale bread and moldy cheese the guard had slid under the door. She wasn't hungry, but she had starved too many times to pass up a chance to eat.

The sound of flapping wings and the scent of sunlight and grass reached her. She glanced up.

Cyr squeezed through the bars and landed on her shoulder. *Is this the key?* He lifted one of his talons.

Adelaide opened her hand, and something cold and metallic dropped into it. She hoped it was the right one; she didn't have time to wait for Cyr to fly around the castle looking for another one.

Thanks, Cyr. Let's see if this works.

She inserted the key into the lock and tried twisting it. Nothing. The key remained stuck no matter how she twisted, fiddled, or groaned.

It's not the right key, Adelaide told Cyr. *Can you look for a different one? Maybe from someone inside this time?*

It'll be difficult not to be caught if I stay inside. I'll look around outside first.

Thank you. And hurry.

He flew away, leaving Adelaide alone. Again.

Now that she had chosen to escape and live, the walls of the cell seemed to press in on her. The shadows from the sinking sun writhed closer as if hoping to hold her until her execution.

Turning from them and her doubts about whether Cyr would find another key in time, Adelaide kept fiddling with the one she had until her hand ached.

Then she slipped it into her girdle and glanced out the window. The sun had fully set now, and a beam of moonlight fell across the floor, the same color as her dragon scales. The desire to be out there flying flared bright inside her.

Would this be the way she spent her last night alive, cooped up between walls of stone, longing for the wind in her face? Her parents wouldn't even know what had happened to her.

Hurry, Cyr, Adelaide urged as she paced across the room.

She tried not to think about what it felt like to hang and how it would pain her parents to lose another child.

Then there was a whoosh of wings, and Adelaide darted to the window where Cyr surveyed her with luminous eyes. *Did you find another one?*

Yes. I hope it works because those humans smell disgusting and are starting to suspect me.

Adelaide took the key from him, a heavier and thicker one than the previous key, and pushed it into the lock, holding her breath.

Chapter Three

Click. The lock opened, and Adelaide let out her breath. *Good. Now we can get out of here.*

I was already free.

You know what I mean. She slipped the key into her girdle.

The cell door opened onto a stairway lit by a guttering torch on the wall. Adelaide didn't see anyone, but men's voices resounded from somewhere below.

Let's go up, Adelaide thought to Cyr, who sat on her shoulder, and stepped onto the winding stone stairs.

Good idea. It's closer to the sky.

Adelaide and Cyr passed several more doors and flickering torches, but they didn't see or hear anyone. As tense as a hunted hare, Adelaide jumped when her foot knocked a pebble off the steps.

Faster, Cyr urged. *I smell fresh air.*

I'm going as fast as I can. But Adelaide smelled it too: air ripe with the scents of the sea, sap, smoke, and fish. It promised her a second chance, a chance to right her wrongs and discover what it meant to be a dragon. She quickened her pace, careful to stay quiet.

They soon arrived at the top of the stairs before a locked wooden door. The first key Cyr had given Adelaide opened it.

She stepped into a circular, tall room with a window dappling the straw floor in silvery moonlight. Something scuttled in the rafters above.

It smells much better up here. Cyr took off and landed on the windowsill. He turned back to Adelaide, his eyes reflecting the star-strung sky. *Let's fly.*

It's not so simple. Adelaide eyed the window halfway up the wall. She'd have to jump up to reach it. At least it didn't have any bars.

She wasn't sure how she would get out of the tower once she was up there; she had climbed too many stairs for it to be a safe height to jump from.

You just flew two days ago, Cyr said.

Yes, but do you see any wings on me now?

Cyr cocked his head as if looking for them.

I have to turn into a dragon, which would alert everyone where I am. We don't want people chasing us, especially angry, frightened people.

Adelaide surveyed the room again, looking for anything that could aid in her escape. Her gaze alit on a door to her left, smaller than the one they had entered. She placed her ear against it and heard the scuffing of boots and a man's voice saying, "It's chilly tonight. I wish we didn't have to be out here."

"Yes," another male voice answered. "But as you know, Dhalion needs all the eyes available with the threat of the Gyndilians looming. I don't know how Berold—"

Adelaide moved away from the door that must lead to the tower's parapet. She wouldn't be able to escape that way, and going back down would be giving up, which she had already resolved not to do.

So, it would have to be the window, then, where Cyr sat. She couldn't jump from it as a human, but perhaps as a dragon.

"It'll be just like climbing a tree," she told herself, although that wasn't much comfort. She had never liked heights, even when she'd climbed trees with Emma. That terror had vanished when she'd flown the other night. Hopefully, turning into a dragon had killed it for good.

Adelaide rebraided her hair, made sure the dagger that Berold had forgotten to look for in his grief wouldn't slip out of her girdle, and walked toward Cyr.

She hurled herself up the wall toward the window, arms reaching, and grasped nothing.

When she tried again, her hands seized the edge of the crumbling stone. With a grunt, she heaved herself up until she sat on the narrow ledge. Her head nearly hit the top of the window.

Adelaide looked out, then wished she hadn't. The grass was far, far below, and only with her new, sharp eyesight could she make it out. The trees in the forest looked like sticks, fragile and tiny. The castle wall loomed below and to her right, ready to crush her if she fell the wrong way.

She closed her eyes against an onslaught of dizziness. *This is not the same as climbing a tree. It's much worse.*

You look like a hatchling before its first flight, Cyr said from in front of her. *Do you need help?*

No, thanks. Adelaide grunted.

She thought about Elias thrusting the potion into her hand and asking her to unite their two species. He had picked her out of everyone in Klinhun. She would show him and everyone else—dragon and human—that his belief in her hadn't been misguided. She could do this. She *had* to do this.

She took a deep breath, opened her eyes, and leapt into the night.

Chapter Four

Gunter was weary. Weary of sleeping in the cold shadow of the mountains, of trying to ignore his Gyndilian captors' taunts, of gnawing on crusty bread. But most of all, he was weary of reliving those last few moments on the cliff where he had killed King Elias.

Sneaking into the castle had been surprisingly easy. Gunter and Baldwin, one of the Gyndilians who had accompanied him from Gyndilad to Dhalion, had dressed up like beggars while the other Gyndilians waited in the forest. Gunter told the castle guard a tragic story of thieves overpowering them and pleaded for justice.

After the guard consulted with a nearby knight, Gunter and Baldwin were let in under their watchful gazes.

Another man trotted off to find them some victuals and to make sure there was room in the stables to sleep. The knight stood nearby, watching them. At some motioning from Baldwin, Gunter spoke to the knight.

He couldn't remember what he had said. His hands hadn't

stopped shaking, and he'd thrust them into his trouser pockets before the man could notice.

While Gunter had prattled on, Baldwin stalked behind the knight and knocked him out with the hilt of his sword.

Gunter stared at the crumpled man while Baldwin grabbed his arm. "Come on, runt, before someone sees us."

They pushed the knight behind a cart, pulled their cloaks over their faces, and prowled around looking for King Elias. They didn't have long before the knight was found or he returned to consciousness.

"We might have to wait until nightfall and find some servants' clothes to gain access to the royal family's chambers," Baldwin muttered as they lurked by the stables while trying not to look like they were lurking. "We can't come back. Our story won't hold up a second time."

Gunter noticed movement out of the corner of his eye. He glanced over and saw a familiar profile walking on the other side of the stable.

He crept around the building toward the cliff to better see the person and caught his breath.

Could that be ...?

Yes, it was Adelaide. She was talking to a man with short brown hair who wore a crimson cloak stitched in gold. Gunter recognized him from Alesfirth as King Elias, his prey.

The sight of the man conversing with Adelaide made Gunter's head pound. Why did this man, who had taxed them until they starved and had done nothing to save Adelaide's sister, think that he could talk to Adelaide as if they were friends?

And why was Ade talking with him at all? Perhaps she was about to kill him. That was the only reason he could think of for his friend who hated nobility more than anyone he knew to be talking alone with a king.

Ade must have earned the king's trust on the way here and now would kill him. Relief bubbled inside him; he wouldn't have to do the deed after all.

But after several long moments, nothing happened. The two continued talking. What could Adelaide possibly have to say to a king that didn't end with the man stomping away in fury? Or dead?

"Do it now," Baldwin hissed beside Gunter, his hand on his sword hilt.

Gunter moved to the other side of the stable, making sure no one was looking. A horse from inside stamped its hoof, and Gunter almost yelled. Once his heart reentered his body, he peered around the stable.

The king's back now faced him.

Gunter pulled out the dagger Adelaide had given him, his hands shaking so much that he almost dropped it.

"Do it," Baldwin commanded from the shadows behind him.

Gunter's stomach crawled over itself. He was no murderer. But this was no ordinary man. This was the man who had caused his parents to go to bed hungry so he, Conrad, and Elysande could have enough to eat. The man who hadn't sent aid when their town was burning. Who bled them all dry for his greed and the sprawling castle towering over them.

Gunter grasped the weapon tighter. He would show Adelaide that he was just as brave as she, that he was worthy of her.

He stepped out from behind the building, stared at the middle of the king's red cloak, and threw the dagger with all his might, his eyes never leaving his target just as he'd practiced.

The king let out a groan and fell to the ground.

"You did it. Come on," Baldwin whispered, tugging on Gunter's cloak.

Then why didn't Gunter feel more elated, or at least relieved, as he stared at the crumpled form spilling blood onto the ground?

But then Adelaide did something that shocked Gunter more than his dagger striking the king.

She dropped beside King Elias, her eyes wide. Then she actually tried to stanch his blood.

What was going on? Killing or deposing the king had been Adelaide's desire ever since King Ganelon and Prince Elias had let her sister be murdered by the Gyndilians. And now she was trying to save the king? This was not the Adelaide he knew.

"Come on," Baldwin urged, but Gunter ignored him. His feet had become roots, holding him to the ground.

Adelaide leaned down to kiss King Elias, and Gunter clenched his hands. She began crying, making awful dying-animal sounds. Gunter had only seen her in this much pain when Emma had died, and he had never wanted to witness such anguish again.

This time, he had caused it. But why had the death of this man, the king, hurt her so much? Did she truly care so much for one of the nobility?

"Ade? Are you—"

Adelaide's scream for him to leave her alone ripped through Gunter, leaving shards of him on the grass.

He ached for her, but how dare she yell at him? He had risked his life to find her, had been kidnapped by the Gyndilians, and now had killed the very man she had wanted dead. And now she loathed him? It made no sense. Gunter wanted to shake her into answering his questions.

But Gunter was too fragile for such a confrontation, and so was Adelaide. Instead, he staggered away, barely conscious of Baldwin's grip on his arm.

It was that scream sheathed in loathing that kept Gunter awake at night and stirred him restless during the day. Surely Adelaide couldn't have loved—he winced at the word—King Elias.

The king must have manipulated her somehow, although Gunter had thought Ade would have seen through such tricks. But it was easier and less excruciating to believe that Adelaide had been manipulated than that she would choose an arrogant noble over Gunter. Was he so appalling?

He clenched his reins, and his horse tottered to a stop.

"So, you think you're in charge now, just because you killed the king of Klinhun?" Ligulf said from behind him, and the pig-squeal laugh of his brother, Leofric, followed.

Gunter urged his red roan forward. The men's teasing hadn't stopped after Gunter killed King Elias. In fact, it had increased, as if the men needed to remind themselves how superior they were by flinging insults at him.

At least Dunstan never taunted him. The quiet, large-eyed Gyndilian rarely spoke.

"Why can't I return home?" Gunter asked. He missed his mother's reassuring gaze, his father's dusty, windblown smell, his sister's bouncy laughter, and even the way Conrad would ruffle his hair.

He wondered if Conrad and the other members of the rebellion had reached Dhalion. They would probably return to Alesfirth now that Gunter had fulfilled their mission. And what was he getting for all his trouble? Nightmares and taunts.

"I already told you, runt," Baldwin said from the front of the group, "you're going back with us to Gyndilad and staying there until the deal is fulfilled and King Aethelmaer sets up his own king in Dhalion."

"What will I do in Gyndilad?"

Baldwin shrugged. "You won't be our problem then. The Master will decide."

The thought of standing again before the man who had held Gunter's life in his hands when he was first captured outside Alesfirth rose in his mind like a mountain lion about to pounce. His hands began to sweat. Would he ever escape the man's control?

"He could make you muck the horses' stalls," Leofric suggested.

"Or stand still while we shoot you for target practice," Ligulf joined in.

The brothers and Baldwin laughed; Gunter sucked in deep breaths to stop himself from heaving.

The group plodded by the Wymar River in silence; sparrows flitted about on the trees above them. Gunter envied their freedom and gaiety. He considered options for escape, but none were feasible.

"How much farther until Fernohn?" Ligulf asked a while later.

"Another two days or so if that man from Dhalion was correct," Dunstan said from behind Gunter.

"Two more days?" Ligulf complained. "I could use some ale and a bed."

"We won't be visiting a tavern," Dunstan said. "Drinking will only loosen your tongues, and we can't afford that when we're so close to the end of our mission."

Leofric spat to the side of his horse. "We can hold our ale better than that."

"Perhaps, but we need to reach Gyndilad as soon as possible with our news," Baldwin said. "We must attack Klinhun while the country is vulnerable." Baldwin looked at Gunter. "And it's all due to this fine Klinian here. You, runt, are on your way to making a good Gyndilian."

Gunter shuddered. "I'll never be a Gyndilian." He recalled the wet-hot blood, the wailing of children, and Ade's scream when the Gyndilians had attacked Alesfirth more than two years ago. Too many people—old and young—had been slain just so the Gyndilians could grab more land and power.

"I wouldn't say that." Baldwin's grin revealed rotting teeth. "Four days ago, you killed your own king."

That night, they camped under a grove of budding trees a few paces away from the Wymar River so as not to be spotted by other travelers or thieves.

The men were bundles of shadows beneath their blankets, their snores and the gurgling river the only sounds in the night. Dunstan, who had taken the first watch, was nowhere to be seen.

It was time to try to escape.

Gunter's stomach writhed like worms after a rainstorm as he grabbed his satchel and tiptoed through the forest.

"I can't let you leave." A shape materialized in front of him before he had taken five steps.

Gunter sighed. It hadn't been a well-thought-out escape, more like a desperate wish. He sat down on a boulder.

A breeze blew through the trees, and Gunter shuddered.

"Here." Dunstan retrieved a blanket from a satchel and handed it to him.

"Thanks." Gunter wrapped the blanket around him. Even though the days had warmed, the nights still bit, especially this close to the mountains. "Why are you nicer to me than the others?"

Dunstan settled on the ground across from him. "Because my head's not full of rocks."

For the first time in months, Gunter smiled.

"They hate everyone from Klinhun just because they're Klinians. But that's foolish. You're a man like me. You just happened to be born somewhere else."

"That makes sense. But the Gyndilians killed so many people in Alesfirth." Gunter gripped his blanket tighter as the screams and smoke returned.

"I know." Dunstan picked up a pine needle. "They shouldn't have attacked. I wasn't there, but I heard about it."

Gunter had begun to drift asleep when Dunstan asked, "Do you love her? That Ade girl?"

Gunter jerked up. "Don't say her name." Dunstan was part of the reason that Gunter might never see her again.

The Gyndilian looked up at him. "Sorry. You say her name frequently when you sleep."

"She was my best friend." Gunter had once dreamed of asking for her hand in marriage, but hadn't thought he deserved her. Now, with her shout echoing in his ears, he knew he didn't.

"It seems like she was more than that. I'm here if you ever want to discuss it." Dunstan nodded at him, then walked away.

Gunter stared after him, startled that a Gyndilian was treating him better than his best friend had.

Chapter Five

As Adelaide fell, she scrunched her eyes shut. The wind buffeted her, spinning her around and around. It was the same helpless, nauseous feeling she'd had when she'd watched the girl next door starve to death. She had been only five winters old.

Adelaide had given the girl some meat that Cyr had caught, but it hadn't been enough. They'd buried her in the spring a few months later.

Mistress, why aren't you flying?

Oh, yes. Adelaide didn't have to be battered by the wind. She was a dragon with wings of her own now.

She forced herself to remember the pulsing heat in her stomach and the beauty and freedom of flight.

A raging fire roared through her bones until she couldn't think about anything but the pain. And then the agony stopped as if the flames had been dumped with water.

Wings down, wings down! Cyr shouted into her mind.

Adelaide opened her eyes and wings just before she slammed

into the ground. She grimaced as she thrust her wings down, not used to their weight or awkward movement.

The motion shot her into the sky, straight to the glimmering stars. A roar of delight built in her chest. With the land splayed out below like a map and the wind now something that held her up not threw her about, her task to unite the dragons and humans didn't seem so impossible.

She felt as if she could fly forever, soaring past the stars to find Emma and Elias up there.

Adelaide swallowed her roar so she wouldn't wake up the castle and shot it out as heat instead. It was just sparks, but, hopefully, one day it would be a blaze.

Careful, Cyr squawked beside her. He was a small, yellow shape with green-tipped feathers, which would have confused her if she hadn't realized on her first flight that she had night vision. Apparently, only as a dragon. She guessed the colors had something to do with heat because the castle stones were a cool cobalt, but her legs pulsed a flaming red.

Why don't you have your wings all the time? Cyr landed somewhere on her neck, his touch as light as a leaf.

Adelaide tried to level out since she was now far enough above the castle that no one would recognize her as a dragon, but her wings caught a breeze, sending her up a few spans.

Cyr screeched. *You're worse than a fledgling. Just do what I do.*

He launched off and soared in front of her.

Adelaide tried to mirror Cyr's wing and tail movements, but hers were so much larger that she kept turning in circles, over-correcting herself.

Slower, and don't move your tail so much, Cyr said when he peeked back and noticed she wasn't doing well at following.

Adelaide wished Elias was there to teach her. How could she learn to be a dragon without him? The task seemed as impossible as making pie without flour. She'd been broken and narrow-sighted until he'd come along and healed her. She'd led all those people in the rebellion to possible death. What if she did the same for the dragons?

Flames raced through her bones, and Adelaide began to fall. Her limbs glowed like when she changed form. *Oh no. Not right now.*

Why are you burning like a fire? Cyr asked from where he hovered nearby.

Think about your dragon form, Adelaide told herself. She forced herself to think about her slick scales, spiked tail, and the talons curving from each foot.

The glow and pain vanished. Adelaide was still a dragon. For now.

She took a deep breath, trembling. *I think that's enough lessons for now,* she told Cyr. *I'm going to find Conrad and the others and let them know that I'm alright.*

Adelaide loathed the idea of returning to the castle so soon after escaping, but she couldn't leave Conrad and the others to a fate they didn't deserve. She would just have to be careful.

While drifting close to one of the towers to try to smell or hear Conrad, she almost ran into the spire. Cyr squawked.

Sorry, sorry, she said while twisting her tail and bringing her wing down. She whirled away, but then almost hit the other tower. She jerked up just in time.

I need to get out of this body before I kill myself, Adelaide thought to herself.

You just need to learn to control it better, Cyr said.

Well, Adelaide had *tried* to think the thought to herself. She'd have to practice that too.

Doubts rose like the Spearhead Mountains; would she ever become comfortable in this body?

Her skin began glowing again.

No. She was a dragon, and she could do it. She just had to think about Conrad. Where was he and the others?

She took another deep breath, only thinking about the scents she inhaled. A slightly rotten tang mixed with a resinous scent drifted by. She somehow knew the scent was worry.

Then the stones beneath her lit up like lightning, and she jerked back. *What was that?*

What? Cyr asked.

Those stones just lit up like a flash of lightning, Adelaide said, gesturing at the stone wall, now back to its normal bronze color.

I didn't see it.

How odd.

With no other clues to her friends' location, Adelaide decided to check the place behind the wall that had lit up.

After making sure no one was around, she landed on the dirt beside the castle. *I'm going inside as a human.*

Be careful. I don't want to have to go into that stinky stone nest again.

Adelaide gazed at Cyr as he glided away toward the castle. *You be careful too.*

She closed her eyes, thinking of her human form. The fire burned through her body, and when it flared so hot that she thought she must be lit up like a torch, the flames vanished.

Adelaide peeked around the corner and listened, missing her night vision and the strength of her body. But at least she didn't have to worry about falling to her death now.

Not seeing or hearing anything but the hooting of an owl, she crept around the stone wall, remaining in the shadows. She edged toward a door. It wasn't locked, but creaked loudly when she pushed it. She gritted her teeth, but no one came to investigate.

Inside, torches flickered on the walls, creating small domes of light. Adelaide stepped quickly and quietly, listening for any sign of people, especially her friends.

She heard a snore to her right and turned down a hall in that direction, hoping the sound came from a room where her friends resided.

The corridor ended at a simple wooden door guarded by

a knight who stood leaning against the wall beside it, snoring softly, his head lolling to the side. His ability to sleep in such a position amazed Adelaide. But then, he probably had a lot of practice.

She snuck closer, her eyes straying to a bronze key dangling from his waist. She leaned in, yanked the key loose, and took a quick step back. The guard moaned but didn't wake.

Adelaide let out a shaky breath, stole around him, and unlocked the door. She slipped inside, not daring to look back to see if the click of the door had woken the guard. She would know soon enough.

Chapter Six

The fire at the back of the room had dimmed to cinders. Sleeping bodies lay in the middle of the room on a pallet of straw and blankets, some snoring and others mumbling in their sleep. The sour smell of sweat and filth made Adelaide gag.

"Who's there?" A young boy whispered.

Adelaide crept closer. "Hubert, it's me, Adelaide. I need to talk to Conrad."

Two reflective eyes stared at her from under a blanket.

"It's urgent," she added.

The ten-winters-old boy turned and prodded a shape beside him. "Conrad, wake up. Adelaide's here."

The shadow groaned and sat up, rubbing his eyes. "Adelaide? How'd you get here?"

She sat down next to him and Hubert. Some of the other boys were waking and elbowing each other.

"I have much to tell you."

"Good, because we don't know anything. They've barely let us out to relieve ourselves."

Adelaide grimaced, adding that to her pile of mistakes.

"So, what's happening?" Conrad asked. "Where have you been?"

"What do you know?"

"We heard that King Elias died and that some people believed you killed him. We were only able to glean that much from the guards outside.

"King Elias was going to have the knights take us somewhere once he came back from speaking to you, but he never returned. And they're getting ready for a war with the Gyndilians."

Adelaide almost didn't hear the last part. Once again, she knelt beside Elias's body, trying to stanch the blood that kept flowing. Why wouldn't it stop?

"Adelaide, are you alright?" Conrad asked, leaning closer.

"It's true that King Elias is dead," she whispered, the words kidnapping the life out of her lungs. The elegant leather handle of the dagger Adelaide had stolen—Elias's own dagger—stuck out of his chest. How could someone who breathed fire and wore armor-hard scales die so easily?

"What happened?" Conrad reached out to touch her arm, and Adelaide flinched. How could she tell him the truth, that her actions had led his brother to kill the king?

Conrad's trusting eyes prodded hers. The same eyes that had watched her grow up alongside Gunter and had glared, squinted in suspicion, rolled in annoyance, and lit up at their antics.

Adelaide couldn't bear to see the truth fill them with confusion and then sorrow and perhaps anger at her—a mirror of her own heart. Yet how could she not tell Conrad? Wouldn't it be crueler if a stranger who didn't care about him told him the news? And he would find out; something like that couldn't be kept a secret forever.

Adelaide took several deep breaths past what felt like bags of barley sitting on her chest. "I'm sorry, Conrad, but he used the dagger I gave him to kill King Elias."

"Who?" Conrad asked, bewildered.

No one said anything. Adelaide was going to have to say his name, to twist the sword deeper into Conrad's heart.

She closed her eyes, seeing Gunter's perplexed face as she yelled at him to leave. "Gunter." His name was an ember that burned her all the way up.

"What?" Conrad asked, and the others exchanged confused whispers.

Adelaide wasn't surprised at their shock; she wouldn't have believed it either if she hadn't seen him do it herself. Although Gunter didn't lack passion and loyalty, he had never excelled in strength of heart.

Without looking at Conrad, Adelaide told him and the others what had happened, omitting the part about turning into a dragon. Instead, she concocted a false tale of stealing the guard's key while he gave her food and then knocked him out. That would be easier to believe.

"Gunter truly killed the king?" Disbelief coated Conrad's voice.

"Yes. I never thought he could do such a thing. And he probably wouldn't have if I hadn't started the rebellion and given him the dagger." Adelaide clenched her hands, vowing to make it up to Gunter somehow. If it wasn't too late.

Conrad laid a hand on her shoulder. "It's not your fault, Adelaide. Gunter's an adult and the only one to blame for his actions."

She couldn't meet his eyes as if, despite his words, she'd find the noose she deserved to see.

"Do you know where he is now?" Sayer asked, and Conrad's hand tightened on her shoulder.

"Nay. He left shortly after harming the king. Perhaps he returned to Alesfirth."

Conrad let go of Adelaide. "Perhaps. But he knows we were supposed to meet here."

After a moment, Sayer said, "So what do we do now?"

All the shadowed faces turned toward Adelaide. They still looked to her for leadership. Once, it had been like the weight of Cyr on her shoulder: uncomfortable and irritating at times but worth it.

Now it was like trying to juggle torches: dangerous and terrifying. For she now knew that her actions could scorch them. What if one of the boys turned out to be another Elias—stabbed and betrayed? Or worse, another Gunter—the stabber and betrayer?

This time, she wouldn't be asking them to fight for the freedom of peasants and their families but to fight for the freedom of all Klinhun alongside the creatures they believed had once destroyed their people. But she couldn't even tell them about the dragons because they wouldn't believe her, so she would also be lying to them.

If Adelaide hadn't made that preposterous promise to Elias and needed to make things right, she'd run out of here. But she couldn't; she *had* promised Elias. Besides, she couldn't leave her friends in this room to rot.

Adelaide hoped that if she dropped any of these torches—these boy's lives—only she would be injured.

She stood and asked, "Did the men from Pinhurn leave?"

"Yes," Aldy said. "The guards made them leave right away, and we haven't seen them since."

"Wish we had been treated like the king promised us," Talbot, a man a winter older than her, grumbled.

"It's Berold's fault you've been treated like this," Adelaide said.

Hubert yawned. "Who's Berold?"

"That knight who found us outside the tavern and took us to King Elias. He probably wanted us all to hang," Talbot said.

Silence shivered through the room.

"No one's going to hang." Adelaide placed her hand on Hubert's shoulder. He was only a few winters younger than her own brother.

"Still, once we get out of here, *if* we ever get out of here, we should teach that Berold a lesson." Talbot ripped up a piece of straw. "He's probably next in line for the throne and will treat his people just like King Ganelon did."

"We have bigger problems than Berold at the moment."

Adelaide turned to Conrad, who was staring at the coals. "What do you know about the impending war with the Gyndilians?"

He turned toward her. "Nothing specific. The guards just talk about how they could march into Klinhun anytime. When we see the knights on our way to the privy, they're always marching or practicing swordplay."

He went to a satchel against the wall. "I'm going to look for my brother. He won't be able to survive long in the wild by himself. And if he killed King Elias, we could use him in this fight."

Adelaide frowned. She was not going to lose another person from Alesfirth. Besides, Gunter's mistakes were hers to fix, not Conrad's. "No. If Gunter made it all the way from Alesfirth here on his own, then he can make the return journey fine. No, we can't worry about Gunter now."

Conrad opened his mouth to retort, but Adelaide held up a hand. "We can't spare you now, Conrad. You're the oldest one here and the best with a bow."

She turned to the others, too easily falling into the leader she'd been before the rebellion when a speech could rile them to cheers and action. They wouldn't like what she had to say now, and she didn't blame them. But their future and the future of Klinhun needed them.

Adelaide hoped that her words could inflame them one more time while also hating that she was going to use these boys again. They should be home spending the warm spring days with their families, not planning a war. But if they didn't, they might not have families to return to. "You must stay here and prepare to fight with the knights against the Gyndilians."

"What?" Sayer said too loud. The knight's snore outside the door stuttered, then droned on again.

"Fight with the people who want us dead? Are you the same Adelaide we knew in Alesfirth?" Rohesia, the other girl in the rebellion, scowled at her.

"That Berold would never let us join him." Talbot clenched his hands. "He'd sooner kill us than let us fight with him. We'd need to take him out first."

"We don't even know for sure if the Gyndilians are going to attack us," Everard said.

Adelaide sighed. She needed more sparks in her words, but the only kind she had was deep in her stomach.

She was no longer the woman who blindly called people to action; she now knew the consequences of such rashness, how they rippled like a stone thrown into a river, sometimes reaching all the way to the far bank.

"You can return to Alesfirth if you wish, but I know the Klinians will need you to fight. Either way, I can't stay here much longer," Adelaide said.

"Where are you going?" Conrad asked.

To Niclond, the dragons' home, if she could find it. She needed to persuade them to help her. Klinhun couldn't win a war against Gyndilad on its own, especially without a king. And putting a new human king on the throne would just continue the cycle of tyranny.

Adelaide couldn't tell Conrad any of this, though, so she merely said, "I must make a few errands to prepare for the war. I don't know how long they'll take, possibly through the summer."

No one probed for more details, either because they were too tired or knew she wouldn't give them. A few boys wiggled down into the straw, making themselves comfortable.

Adelaide leaned toward Conrad. "You must remain here and try to convince the others to stay and fight. And make sure they don't do anything rash, especially Talbot. He's always been violent. No matter how vile Berold is, we have bigger problems than him."

Conrad glanced at the blond-haired man who was rear-ranging his blankets with enough force to smother a fire, then nodded. "I will."

"If there's a war, you'll be needed here more than in Ales-firth."

"If they even let us fight." Conrad sighed. "I'll let everyone decide for themselves. And, Adelaide," he said and turned silver-bright eyes on her, "be careful."

Adelaide nodded. "I will. And I'm sorry, about Gunter. I never should have given him that dagger. I never should have—"

"Adelaide, stop. It's not your fault."

Dare she believe Conrad held no blame or anger for her? It was too dark to see the depths of his eyes.

"He made his decision and must face the consequences. I just hope he manages to get home safely."

"I'll look for him on my journeys," Adelaide said, though she wasn't sure what she'd do with him if she found him.

"Here." Conrad handed her an empty satchel and water-skin.

"Thanks."

The outside air eased something inside Adelaide. She snuck to the back of the building, thinking about the men's responses and what could happen if they stayed. Their unwillingness to push past their prejudice to fight with the knights against a common enemy did not bode well for how the rest of Klinhun would let go of a centuries-old hatred against dragons.

And what would the dragons do when she showed up on their island—supposing she could find it—and asked for their help? She was nobody to them; she couldn't even fly without changing back into a human. She wouldn't be surprised if they threw her out for not being a real dragon or killed her for trespassing.

A raven cawed somewhere nearby, and Adelaide pulled her

cloak tighter against a gust of wind. She scanned the turrets jutting into the sky as if Elias would soar down and make all her problems go away.

Her gaze caught on a tower with a kind of platform jutting out below its window. She remembered Elias pointing out the tallest tower near the far wall, telling her his room was located at the top because it was the easiest to fly out of without being seen.

The shadows around her suddenly didn't seem so dark, the breeze now just a promise of something better ahead. Elias had sat in that tower, had gazed out of those windows, had landed on that platform. He felt closer—just within reach—than he had since Adelaide had left him on the cliff.

She told herself he wouldn't be up there, but that didn't diminish the warmth spreading through her.

She was going up there to find answers about Niclond and where it might be, *not* to find pieces of Elias. But she didn't believe herself.

When she transformed, her heightened senses and heat vision felt like coming home. Thankfully, she didn't have any trouble flying up to the dragon-sized platform. But when she landed, the wood shuddered beneath her, and she almost slipped off. She dug in her talons and managed to stay on.

Adelaide turned back into a human, waited until her eyes adjusted, then pushed against the window. It swung open.

She hopped down into the room. To her right, against the wall, stood an ornate bed with billowing curtains. Somehow Adelaide didn't think the pallet was filled with straw like her family's.

A wardrobe sat against the far-left wall, and beside it was a table with a quill and ink bottle.

Adelaide had been a fool to be so eager to come up here. The room was just as bare and empty without Elias as Adelaide was. Even if sunlight had been streaming in through the windows or a fire had blazed in the hearth, without her prince and king, it would be dreary.

She touched the quill, trying to imagine Elias sitting at this table, writing letters to courtiers. But she couldn't. She could only see him riding Starflare down the Southern Road or sitting near a fire, trying to probe mysteries out of her.

Nevertheless, she was still tempted to pocket the quill or take one of the elaborate tunics in the wardrobe to keep Elias close; this was his home, and one of the last places he had been.

But she had hoarded Emma's cloak as if she could keep her sister with her after Emma's death, and it had done nothing but reminded her of Emma's absence.

Adelaide sighed as she fingered the gold embossing on one of his tunics. "Besides, your possessions are too fancy for me."

She shut the wardrobe on Elias's clothes stacked in neat piles. She needed to focus on the real reason she was here. To find something, preferably a map, to Niclond. But after searching through Elias's wardrobe, desk, and even between the coverlet, she gave up.

"Well, you didn't make this easy for me," Adelaide said, staring at his bed. She'd have to find directions to Niclond another way.

She left the lifeless room behind but knew that no matter how far or fast she flew, she couldn't escape the hollowness that Elias had left behind in her life.

Chapter Seven

The next morning, Adelaide asked Cyr, *Can you hunt for me?* It felt odd to ask him since she usually just flung up her arm and whistled a command.

He flew from the top of a pine tree onto her shoulder. *Why can't you? You're a fire-flyer now, yes?*

A dragon can't go stomping around Klinhun in the middle of the day. Someone would spot me and would try to kill or harm me.

Why?

Because Klinians hate dragons.

That's foolish. What have fire-flyers done to them?

Adelaide shrugged. *They believe dragons killed many of them, though they didn't.*

You would never do that.

She stroked Cyr's white chest feathers. *Thanks. Now, please hunt for me before I faint.* She whistled the high hunting note and thrust her arm into the air.

As Adelaide walked around listening for a stream to top off

her animal skin, she thought about how to find Niclond. The only people in Klinhun who knew the location were dead.

No, that wasn't true. She stopped at a base of a gangly oak tree. There was that man, the one whom Elias and his father had lived with before moving to Dhalion, the human-dragon messenger. What was his name? Manfred.

If anyone knew where Niclond was, Manfred would. He'd remained in contact with the dragons for years.

Gratefulness for something to do saturated Adelaide like a summer afternoon rain. She straightened her shoulders and looked for a stream with the confidence of the woman she'd been before Elias's death instead of the woman who couldn't even talk to her friend's brother while looking him in the eye.

At the stream, Adelaide was surprised that her reflection didn't show the hollowness left from Elias's death and Gunter's betrayal or the fire slumbering within.

Cyr dropped two dead hares at her feet. She skinned them and gave Cyr both stomachs, which he snapped up in two bites.

Adelaide grimaced. *That's disgusting.*

No, it's tasty. Don't you eat raw animals when you're a fire-flyer?

I've never eaten in that form. Hopefully, it won't bother me. Adelaide wondered whether she should make a fire or not to cook the hares. Berold and his guards would now be looking for her, and she'd rather eat raw meat than be stuck in that prison with only despair and a noose in her future.

But her dragon form would be more noticeable than a fire, and she needed to get some food into her stomach if she wanted to give herself the best chance to stay out of Berold's clutches. So, after asking Cyr to keep watch, Adelaide risked making a fire.

As she sat by the crackling flames and smoking meat, Adelaide thought of the many fires she had shared with Elias. The first one—the bonfire—had been at the Fire Festival, where Elias had first learned her name, ironically because of Gunter.

She had thought the elegantly dressed man was just another pompous noble. Had he truly first been drawn to her because he had seen her steal his dagger? The very thing that had come between them at the end?

The weapon at her back seemed to dig into her skin, and she stuffed it into her satchel.

After the bonfire, there had been the fire when Elias had taught her how to fish, a kindness, but odd because he hadn't known much about her at the time. That was when he had told her the story about the dragons' gift to the humans. She remembered how the story had caught her in its web, how senseless she'd thought he was for believing the tale.

Then there'd been the fire in the cave, where she'd mostly lived in shadowy nightmares and cold despair. Until she had told him about Emma, laying out her pain and sorrow like undressing her heart. He hadn't ridiculed and left her but had entrusted her with his true self: his dragon self.

And what had Adelaide done with that sweet vulnerability? Destroyed it. She and Gunter both.

She stuffed the rest of the rabbit meat into her mouth and turned her back on the fire.

Glancing up at Cyr on a branch, she asked, *Do you know of any cottages nearby?* Manfred's house had to be around here somewhere because he'd need to be near the castle to stay in contact with King Ganelon over the years. She also remembered Elias saying it was by a river.

Nay. He landed on her shoulder. *Do you have more meat?*

No, but I do have a job for you. I need you to fly over the trees and look for a cottage. It will probably be close to the Wymar River. Once you find it, return here so we can go together. Fly swiftly, and be careful. She ruffled his feathers.

I'm always careful. Besides, you're the one who was stuck in the stone nest.

Adelaide flicked his chest. *Yes, yes. Now, go.*

The entire time Cyr was gone, Adelaide strained her eyes and ears for any sight or sound of Berold or his men searching for her. Thankfully there was no sign of them, but Adelaide still longed to leave this spot.

When the sun bled into the sky, Cyr returned, and Adelaide sighed in relief. *Well?*

The human nest isn't far, not more than a hundred wing-beats.

Then why did it take you so long to find it and return?

I flew in the wrong direction at first.

Oh. Well, good work finding it. She tossed him several pieces of the cooked rabbit, and he gulped them down.

Did it look like anyone lived there?

Smoke came out of the hole in the top.

Good. Now we must wait until dark.

Why? Cyr gazed at her with his unblinking amber eyes.

Because I'm going to fly, and—

Klinians hate fire-flyers, and you don't want to die, Cyr finished.

Adelaide nodded. *Yes.*

She put on her cloak and grabbed her satchel. She walked deeper into the forest, wanting to put as much distance between herself and the castle as possible before transforming.

Even though Adelaide had flown just last night, she already yearned to do so again, to be untethered to this world. Yet she also cringed at the thought of her human body plummeting to the ground without warning.

But she had no choice, and her skin longed for release.

It began raining as they soared off toward Manfred's house. Cyr whistled in irritation, but Adelaide didn't mind. She could still see perfectly despite the steady rain, and the fire in her stomach kept her warm.

She followed Cyr easily, his feathery form a mix of blue, green, and orange above the trees. She focused solely on him and the hiss of raindrops as they hit her warm scales and didn't have trouble keeping her shape.

When Cyr indicated the location of Manfred's house, Adelaide drifted over and glanced down at a small clearing in the trees.

The Wymar River, a soft blue in her night vision, rushed along grassy banks as if trying to escape the pattering rain. The scents of muddy water and sweet grass clung to her nose, and she could hear the splash of raindrops hitting the river's surface even over the rumble of the water.

On their side of the river sat a wooden cottage with smoke curling from the chimney. This was the place Elias had learned to be human.

Adelaide's heart clenched, and her tail snapped close to her body. She wished he had been the one to bring her here.

Then flames licked at her scales, and they glowed. *Not again.*

Chapter Eight

Adelaide dove down into the foliage behind Manfred's house before she could turn back into a human, knocking over a few trees with her tail and legs.

She opened her wings, slicing some branches, and splashed herself with rainwater. Then she was on the ground, her talons sinking deep into the mud.

The landing had been noisy and messy, but at least she was still alive and still a dragon. The glow had stopped.

I've never seen anything land so badly, Cyr said from beside her.

Well, I've only done it twice and only have a hawk to instruct me. Adelaide shook some sticks and leaves off her back. After rotating her silvery wings, she folded them tight to her sides. Would she ever grow used to this body?

It then proceeded to transform without her willing it to. She sighed. Perhaps the potion Elias had given her was faulty, but she didn't truly believe that. It was all her, unable to focus and embrace her dragon side, which she didn't know how to do.

The rain slapped her with cold fingers, and she couldn't build a fire to keep warm because of the wetness, nor could she transform again in case Manfred or someone else found her in the morning.

So, Adelaide wrapped her cloak around her and curled up on some soggy leaves, Cyr standing guard above her.

Adelaide was more tired when she woke than when she had gone to sleep. The rain had drenched her within a few moments, and she had been unable to find a comfortable position on the sharp rocks.

She stretched, picked twigs out of her clothes, and slipped the dagger into the girdle at her waist just in case. She tried to cover up the enormous five-clawed prints in the mud from the night before with the scattered leaves from the storm.

Adelaide didn't see Cyr; he was probably hunting.

She made her way through the forest toward Manfred's hut. Birds chittered overhead, as glad as she was that the rain had stopped, and the sun had risen.

Adelaide paused, realizing that she was listening to the birds' actual conversation. She shouldn't have been surprised; if she could communicate with Cyr now, of course she could with other birds.

No one answered the cottage door when Adelaide knocked. She turned to the river that writhed like a caught snake, thrashing against its swollen banks.

As Adelaide meandered beside the house, she tried to picture a young Elias here but failed. She could only see him as a man.

Against the wall of the cottage leaned a shed filled with planting tools. A garden stood to the right of the shed, and a few ripe strawberries peeked out. Her stomach gnawed. Surely the man wouldn't miss a few.

As Adelaide reached toward a plump strawberry, Cyr's voice burst into her mind, *There's a human behind you.*

Adelaide spun, her hand automatically reaching for the dagger at her waist.

A stoop-shouldered man with white-tinged red hair and beard walked out of the trees by the river toward the cottage. He held a fishing pole in one hand and a satchel of what smelled like fish in the other.

Adelaide walked toward him, wondering what to say. She'd been more concerned about finding him than what she'd say if and when they met.

Cyr landed on her shoulder, and she took a deep breath. At least she wasn't alone.

The man glanced up and narrowed evening-sky eyes at her. His beard badly needed a trim. "Who are you and why are you at my house?"

"I'm Adelaide."

And I am? Cyr prodded.

"And this is Cyr, my hawk." She gestured at him, who eyed the man as if sizing up prey.

The man took a step forward. "What are you doing at my home?" He shot a look at the garden patch behind Adelaide, then at her satchel.

"I need your help if you're Manfred."

"That depends on what kind of help you need."

It was as good as an admission. Now all Adelaide had to do was convince him to help her. That wouldn't be easy, considering his scowling face and that he thought her a thief.

What would Elias have thought of this first meeting? He had spoken of Manfred with fondness, and when Adelaide first arrived on Manfred's property, she had attempted to steal from him. Perhaps it was better that Elias wasn't there.

"So, what kind of help do you need?" Manfred prodded.

Adelaide decided honesty was the best approach. "It has to do with dragons and the former king and prince."

"Dragons?" The man took a sharp breath. "They're long gone."

"Yes, that's my problem. I need to find them."

The man turned and climbed up onto the porch. "I'm sorry, but I can't help you."

He didn't sound sorry. He shut the door behind him with a solid thunk.

Adelaide hadn't come all this way to be turned aside so easily. She dashed up the steps and tugged on the door. It didn't budge, so she pounded on it. "Please, sir. If you are indeed Manfred, then Elias trusted you. He cared about you, and for some reason, he trusted me too. He showed me who he was and asked me to unite the dragons and humans."

Her fist smarting, she stopped hitting the door and leaned her head against it, bone-weary. "Elias told me about how he learned to be a human prince here. He said that you taught him how to ride a horse and catch fish. He's a good teacher. He taught me to fish, though I wasn't very good at it."

The door swung open, and Adelaide stumbled.

"He told you all that?" Manfred asked, frowning at her.

She nodded. "Please, sir. Gyndilad could invade Klinhun at any time, and we have no hope of defeating them by ourselves. Our neighboring countries won't help. They never have before. So, we need the dragons' assistance, and Elias told me that you helped him and his father when they first arrived here. Won't you help the people they cared so much about?"

Manfred shuffled his muddy boots, muttering to himself, then said, "Very well. I'll hear what you have to say, and after that I'll decide whether to help you or not. Come inside."

Chapter Nine

Adelaide followed Manfred into a one-room cottage that smelled of wood smoke, leather, and fish guts. A table and chairs sat in front of a blazing fire. Against the wall on the other side of the room was a bed stuffed with straw and covered with a cotton blanket. It was smaller than the one her family had shared, but just as tidy.

"Sit by the fire so you can dry out," Manfred said. "And in case you hadn't figured it out yet, I am Manfred." He dumped the fish onto the table and skinned them.

The boards creaked beneath Adelaide as she pulled one of the chairs closer to the fire.

Cyr landed on the back of a chair farther away from the hearth.

Manfred frowned at him. "Make sure that bird doesn't make a mess on the floor."

Adelaide mentally relayed the message to Cyr, who wondered why not. She didn't bother explaining human politeness and cleanliness. *Just don't do it. We need him to like us.*

"He's a marvelous bird," Manfred said, gazing at Cyr.

"Yes, he is," Adelaide agreed. She took off her cloak and laid it beside the fire, then spread her hands over the flames, luxuriating in the crackling warmth.

"So, how did you know Prince Elias?" Manfred asked.

"I met him at the Fire Festival in Alesfirth, where I'm from."

"Alesfirth?" The man's bushy eyebrows raised. "That's quite a distance away. How'd you end up here?"

"It's a long story."

"I'm a good listener."

While Manfred cooked the fish and some potatoes, Adelaide summarized her tale, keeping the parts of Emma, Elias's love for her, and how she could turn into a dragon to herself.

When she had finished, her eyes were wet, and the meal was ready. Speaking of Elias had stung, like walking over sun-warmed stones. But it had been good too, the pain ripping off old skin to make room for new, pink flesh to grow.

Now, though, she just felt exhausted and wished for nothing more than to see Elias and apologize for how horribly she'd treated him. Re-living the events had reminded her how kind and generous he'd been, when all she'd done was threaten him and run away.

"My, my," Manfred said with wide eyes as he gazed across the table at Adelaide, who had sat there while Manfred cooked.

A steaming plate of white fish and potatocs sat bcforc hcr. Ravenous, she grabbed a chunk of fish. Cyr squawked behind her, and she tossed him a piece.

The fish reminded her of the white sea bass dish Elias had given her at the castle, and she almost choked on the ale Manfred handed her in an attempt to chase the searing memories away.

"Much has happened since I last saw Elias." Manfred ate one of the potatoes, his gaze seeing more than just the forest out of the open windows.

Cyr rubbed his head on Adelaide's shoulder, but she was

too famished to hand over more food. A moment later he flew out the window.

"I haven't seen Elias since before the Fire Festival, when he left for Alesfirth." Manfred met her gaze. "I've grown old since then. These bones don't take to the cold like they used to."

He glanced at his muscled arms speckled with brown spots like bruises on an apple. "And then, of course, King Ganelon died. I wanted to go to his funeral, but my mare had an injured leg, and I couldn't make it that far on my own feet."

Adelaide had a sick feeling that Manfred hadn't registered the fact that Elias had died. She hadn't lingered on that part of the story; it was still a bleeding wound. Would it ever heal? Did she even want it to?

"Manfred, did you catch what I said about Prince Elias? He's ... gone," she squeezed out.

The man stared at his food. "Yes, I heard you. It's just not something I care to think about." He picked up a piece of fish and looked out the window.

Adelaide wondered which memory of Elias he was lost in. Teaching him how to fish as Elias had taught her? Showing him how to work a small boat? Or perhaps watching as the boy harvested strawberries from the same garden that Adelaide had almost stolen from?

"He would have made an excellent king." Manfred glanced at her. "You said you knew the man who killed him?"

Adelaide squeezed a potato so hard that it mushed out of her fingers onto the table. "Unfortunately. He was in my rebellion."

Manfred sighed. "You'd think dragons would be invulnerable to things like daggers and poison and such, and for the most part they are, but not in their human form. It has always astonished me how Ganelon and Elias gave that up and so many other things to be humans even though the humans hate them."

He rubbed a hand through his beard. "It was an impossible task to begin with anyway. Poor Elias." He breathed out what sounded like all the air in his lungs. "He broke this table once, actually." Manfred gestured to the oak table before them.

"Truly?" Adelaide asked. This was what she was truly hungry for, insights into Elias's past. "How?"

Manfred smiled. "It was in the first few months after he and Ganelon arrived. We were all sitting here for the evening meal, and Elias was mad that he couldn't eat outside in his dragon form. But they had to learn proper human behavior.

"Elias hadn't yet learned to control his more finicky human emotions and turned into a dragon right here. When he did, he popped off this piece here." Manfred tapped a section of the table near the edge where a faint seam zigzagged from his finger to the far corner.

"Oh, my." Adelaide couldn't picture Elias that angry; he'd always kept whatever emotions he felt controlled around her.

"It took me a good while to fix the table. Thankfully Ganelon and Elias helped."

Manfred popped a piece of fish in his mouth and wiped his hands on his tunic. "Elias was a good lad, always curious about everything. He broke several of my planting tools too, trying to understand how they worked, but I didn't mind. It was nice to have company about, especially a young lad.

"He always boasted to the chickadees and any other bird that would listen how much faster he could fly, and a few times he even turned into his dragon form to race them. That always panicked your father and I since he could've been spotted. It's a good thing I live so far from everyone."

Manfred shook his head, grinning. "It took him a long time to learn to fish. He always grew impatient and tried to grab them with his hands. That, of course, never worked out well." He laughed, and Adelaide smiled.

"He was good at it by the time he taught me." Adelaide remembered Elias's steady hands and careful instructions.

Manfred nodded. "He fished with me later when he would come visit. I'm glad he finally learned some patience."

He continued eating, and Adelaide contemplated sharing some of her own stories with him, but her memories were her last fragments of Elias, and she held them tight, afraid they might disintegrate if shared.

She regretfully turned the conversation to the reason for her visit. "So, do you know where Niclond is?"

"Niclond?" Manfred glanced up at her. "Not exactly. It's somewhere southeast of Dhalion out in the ocean. It's not too far, probably only a few days away by dragon flight. Why?"

Adelaide blinked. She had lived her whole life in a country that lay only a few days away from the dragons' land? Why hadn't Elias mentioned how close it was? "I need to speak to the dragons. As I said, we need their help, and Klinhun will never have a truly just and good king without them."

Manfred began shaking his head before she had finished speaking. "It's too dangerous. They don't even know that Elias and Ganelon were here. They'd probably attack you before you even opened your mouth. They won't be as tame as Ganelon or Elias, who spent years learning how to be human."

Adelaide fiddled with the fish bones on her plate. "Perhaps, but we need them. We have no king, and we're on the brink of war with Gyndilad. It's the only chance we have to defeat the Gyndilians. And I promised Elias that I would try."

Manfred shrugged. "Go if you must, but I'm too old for such matters."

"So, you know nothing more about the dragons or where they live?"

"Nay."

Adelaide probed some more about Manfred's knowledge, but soon realized that he either knew nothing else or was an exceptional liar. She gave up and listened to his tales about Elias and his father, which she drank in like a plant soaking up sunlight.

When Manfred placed more wood on the fire, Adelaide realized the light outside was fading.

Cyr? She called in her mind. *Where are you?*

I was taking a nap. His thoughts came from the direction of the river. *You humans talk too much.*

Manfred spoke before Adelaide could respond. "Elias didn't have an end to his life befitting a dragon prince, did he?"

Adelaide's warm, contented mood from Manfred's stories faded, ice wrapping around her. "No, he didn't," she whispered.

Manfred sank further into his chair, his gaze on the flickering flames. "That's tragic. At least Ganelon wasn't in any pain when he died."

Adelaide frowned. "How do you know that?"

Manfred's forehead creased as if deciding something, his blue eyes mere shadows in the glare of the fading light. "Because I killed him."

Chapter Ten

Gunter glanced behind him. Again. As if King Elias had risen from the dead and was stalking him, ready to gut Gunter like he had killed the king. Or, just as unlikely, Adelaide would come running after Gunter, begging him to return home.

What was she doing now that her precious king was dead? Did she miss or think of Gunter at all?

"Keep moving," Baldwin said, yanking on Gunter's horse's reins, causing him to almost fall off. "We'll never get there with you gawking at everything."

Dunstan nodded at Gunter as he rode by. They hadn't talked much since Gunter's failed escape attempt, but they had shared a few knowing looks. It was comforting to know that one of his captors didn't want to use him for archery practice.

The group traveled in the shade of the Spearhead Mountains, which thrust up on their left like fingers clawing at the sky. Most of the snow had melted, revealing hairy patches of evergreens, but a few white spots remained on the rocky tops and in the valleys where the sun didn't reach.

To their right rolled hills of grass so green that Gunter was tempted to jump off and roll around in it. The violet, white, and golden wildflowers sprinkled through the meadow reminded him of his mother and sister. In the spring, they would pick flowers and place them around the house to liven up the plain brown walls. Well, his mother would decorate while Elysande would skip about, weaving handfuls of blooms into tiaras and trying to put them on her father's and brothers' heads.

Gunter squared his shoulders as if preparing to dig into a hard, bare patch of earth. He would do all he could to see his family again and return to them as someone they could be proud of instead of just Raymond's short middle child or Conrad's younger brother.

Nay, he would be the one who got rid of the unjust king and escaped the Gyndilians. Never mind that he didn't know how to escape them yet.

That evening, they camped at the base of a mountain, and the cool spring air caused him to pull his cloak close. "How much farther until we reach Gyndilad?" He took a chunk of venison from Dunstan.

"Tomorrow or the day after if we keep up the pace." Baldwin picked his teeth with a fingernail the same yellow color as his molars. "Getting excited to see the Master again, eh?"

"Um, not quite." Gunter's stomach roiled at the thought of his life again being in the hands of the man who loathed Klinians and had ordered so many of them to die. Gunter didn't want to think of the pain the man could cause him.

He stared at his venison; it looked as appetizing as old leather.

"I can't wait till we leave this cursed country." Leofric stretched his hands in front of the fire. "I still can't believe how that female innkeeper treated us in Fernohn like we were about to rob her. Why would we want to rob a filthy, poor hag like her? Why do they even let females work here? Their place is in the home." He shook his head in disgust.

"Aye. And did you see how shabby the town was? Parts of it were burned and others falling apart. They should take better care of their property. We're lucky nothing caved in on us while we were there," Ligulf said.

Dunstan added a few logs to the fire and sparks flew into a sky as colorful as the fields of wildflowers they'd passed through. "If you recall, that woman mentioned there had recently been a mining accident and fire. Probably not all the towns here look like that. Dhalion sure didn't."

"No, they don't," Gunter agreed. "Alesfirth didn't look that bad before you destroyed half of it. And it's not the peasants' fault that the nobles and king used the country's resources on gathering as much wealth as possible instead of fixing the villages."

Baldwin surveyed Gunter. "That's why King Aethelmaer needs to take over this pitiful country and make it bright and shiny again like one of your coins. It shouldn't be too difficult for him without a king."

Gunter's cheeks flamed. "We're not pitiful, and—"

"King Aethelmaer and the Master will teach these Klinians respect and obedience," Leofric agreed, and Ligulf nodded.

Gunter wanted to pummel the three of them, but he was no match for their strength. "Why do you hate Klinians so much?" *He* had a good reason for hating *them*, but he had never understood why they wanted to invade Klinhun.

Baldwin chuckled. "Besides the obvious?"

"Which is?"

"Our king hates them, and he wants the best for us, so we should hate them too. He has our fealty," Ligulf said, spraying bits of meat everywhere.

"And there's that whole dragon thing." Leofric waved a hand in the air.

"What dragon thing?" Gunter asked.

"Leofric means that period of time when dragons sup-posedly ruled alongside the people of Klinhun and protected them, which most of the Gyndilians believe is hogwash," Dunstan clarified.

Gunter didn't know if he believed dragons had lived in Klinhun, but it didn't matter. They were either all dead or gone far away now.

Leofric pointed his half-eaten rib at Gunter. "Your country thinks you're invincible because of your past. But the dragons never did anything worthy of songs. And there could have been dragons ruling in Gyndilad for all we know."

Gunter doubted that because none of the tales mentioned dragons living anywhere else. If the creatures had existed, it would have been impossible to hide such a thing.

Baldwin joined in the discussion. "There was also that surprise attack on Neikhurn, one of our southern cities, by Klinhun about fifty years ago, where hundreds of our men died. Mayhap even a thousand." He took a sip from his animal skin. "And Klinhun came to the defense of Neklosa against us when we crossed the Schneick River during the Battle of the Mulhurs."

Gunter knew Klinhun and Gyndilad had been fighting on and off for decades but didn't know any specifics. He tossed a chunk of fat into the fire; it hissed and turned coal black. "That doesn't sound too bad to me."

He could feel Baldwin's gaze searing him. "That's because you're not a Gyndilian. We've always been enemies, and we always will be."

"That's fine with me," Gunter murmured.

Once the men drifted to sleep, Gunter went over to where Dunstan was sharpening his sword. The sound of stone on metal was loud in the night.

"You don't hate Klinians," Gunter said, trying to sound nonchalant.

"Nay. Some seek to do good and some to do bad, just like people in Gyndilad."

"Then why can't you let me leave? I can hit you or something so that it looks like you fought me."

Dunstan looked at Gunter and smiled. "You look like you have some muscle, but do you honestly think they'll believe that the runt defeated me?" He raised an eyebrow.

Gunter's hopes, rising like an injured bird, fell again. Dunstan was right; he was stronger, and he'd had formal training. "No."

"Besides, I have to obey my orders. If I don't, well, I don't want anything to happen to my wife." His hand gripped the whetstone tighter.

"You have a wife?" Gunter shouldn't have been surprised; Dunstan was only a few winters older than him. Still, it was difficult imagining the man living a normal life.

Dunstan nodded. "Her name's Ailith. And I have a little girl, Elgiva." His eyes warmed. "I'm able to provide for them by working for the Master. If I fail too severely, he could imprison me, and Ailith and Elgiva would starve."

"Ah," Gunter said. He understood what it was like to live one moment to another, working under someone else's orders with no way out.

"And for the most part, I like my job," Dunstan continued. "The Master might not be the kindest man, especially to Klinians, but he cares for Gyndilad and is an excellent strategist."

"Do you know him well?"

Dunstan put down the whetstone and examined his blade. "No. He keeps mostly to himself. He is a master with the sword, though." He glanced up at Gunter. "It might not be such a bad thing if Gyndilad takes over Klinhun."

"Now you sound like them." Gunter nodded at the snoring men.

"Well, from hearing about this rebellion of yours, the king was fairly lousy." Dunstan sheathed his sword.

"And King Aethelmaer would make everything better?"

Dunstan shrugged. "He might. He wants the best for his people."

"That's what every king says," Gunter muttered, "but they

hardly ever mean it."

"I wouldn't be too anxious."

"About what?"

"About what will happen to you in Gyndilad," Dunstan said. "You've proven your worth. It's not likely the Master will kill you. He'll probably train you to fight for King Aethelmaer."

Gunter scowled. "I won't attack my friends and family. I'd rather die."

Dunstan gazed at him long and hard, the sorrow in his eyes deeper than the sky. "You might be able to choose that. But think carefully before deciding."

◆ ◆ ◆

The men were as happy as fully fed wolves the next day, as if they could smell Gyndilad on the other side of the valley they climbed through.

"I'm going to drink three mugs of ale," Ligulf announced.

"I'm going to give my girl a good, long kiss," Leofric said.

"And you smell so bad that she'll toss you in with the pigs where you belong," Ligulf told him, laughing.

Leofric trotted closer to his brother and swung at him, but Ligulf ducked.

"We still have a long way until we reach the Master's camp, so don't let your thoughts get muddled," Dunstan warned from behind.

After ascending the valley, they came upon a stone fort rooted on the top of a hill in the shadow of a mountain. Yellow and blue Klinian flags on the roof snapped in the breeze, and knights paced along the fort's circular top, holding long bows. Sunlight glinted hard and bright on their armor, blazing into Gunter's eyes.

One of the knights called down at them, "State your name and business."

"This fort is all that stands between us and home," Baldwin whispered, a fierce smile on his face.

"Surely you're not going to attack them." Gunter squinted up at the still forms of the Klinians. Perhaps if he cried out, the knights could defend themselves and help him escape.

But before Gunter could say anything, Ligulf stuffed a cloth into his mouth and someone else bound his hands behind his back. Gunter squirmed, but it only earned him a punch to the gut that knocked all the air out of him.

Dunstan held Gunter's horse, his gaze on the knights in the fort who were still firing questions at them. Soon they'd be firing weapons.

"It would be foolish to attack them since they outnumber us. We'll leave that to King Aethelmaer's army," Baldwin whispered. "We're just keeping you silent so you don't get any foolish ideas." He tightened Gunter's bonds so they cut his skin; he cried out into his gag.

The Klinian knights were now aiming loaded bows at them.

"Let's ride, men!" Baldwin grabbed Gunter's reins and kicked his own horse into a gallop. As Gunter's horse raced after the others, he was thrown back, but managed to hold on.

An arrow twanged over his head, and he flinched.

The Klinian knights continued shooting at them, and someone was emerging from a door on the ground, but it was too late.

The men were already galloping past, fleeing like a flock of spooked birds.

The fort faded in the distance, as well as Gunter's chances of returning home.

His unknown fate loomed higher than the mountains, approaching nearer with every hoofbeat.

Chapter Eleven

Adelaide jumped up, knocking over her chair, and pointed her dagger at Manfred's neck. "Say that again."

He lifted his hands. "I killed King Ganelon. It was a painless death. I used berries and leaves from the yew tree."

"That doesn't matter. You still took his life." Adelaide's voice and hand shook. "Why would you do such a thing? I thought you said you were his friend."

"I am. I was. That's why I did it." Manfred's voice took on a pleading note. "When I visited him after the Fire Festival, I saw that he was dying. The human body he inhabited was making him sick and weak. He was in pain."

Manfred rubbed his face as if trying to scour the memories away. "I couldn't let him live like that."

"Why not?"

"I had seen him as a dragon, powerful and free, and now he was dying before my eyes, unable to move without pain. He deserved to die quickly and painlessly."

"But not at your timing. He had a son and people he loved."

Adelaide thrust the dagger closer to Manfred's neck, remembering Elias's moan and rainstorm of tears when he had realized that his father had died.

Elias hadn't been able to say goodbye to his father, hadn't even known he was sick because he'd been following her all over the country as she stole his horse and needed him to rescue her over and over again.

Although it was Manfred's neck that she pointed the dagger at, she now wanted to thrust it at her own. But the only way to make it up to Elias was to keep his promise.

She lowered the weapon and stuffed it out of sight, but Manfred kept talking as if still on the edge of life. "He was going to die anyway. I saw it in his eyes. I gave him what he needed: a peaceful ending. And I realized that now isn't a good time for the dragons to come. It would be disastrous. Humans would try to kill them, and then the dragons would fight to defend themselves, inadvertently destroying everyone until there's no one left in Klinhun."

"And when would be a good time for them to come?" Adelaide asked. "When the Gyndilians have ruined our homes and broken apart our families? When the nobles have succeeded in pushing the peasants into the mud at their feet?"

Manfred shook his head. "The dragons are powerful, it's true. And Ganelon and Elias were good, but they were just two people, two dragons.

"If dragons came now, especially with Ganelon and Elias dead, there would be a war. The humans hate them too much. They've been blinded by the twisted tales of the past." He stared at the table. "Nay, things should stay as they are. A human king will rise up and take charge."

"And fill his pockets with the hard-earned toil of the peasants like all the rest if Gyndilad doesn't take over first," Adelaide said without her usual fervor. Her insides were all scooped out; Manfred reminded her too much of herself.

"I'm leaving." She called to Cyr in her mind.

"You can't go now. It's late." Manfred gestured at the darkness claiming the windows.

Adelaide grabbed her satchel. "I don't mind sleeping outside."

"At least let me give you some food."

"I have enough, thank you." It was a lie, but Cyr could hunt for her, and she needed to get out now before she broke into a thousand fragments all over Manfred's table.

Cyr landed on her shoulder. *Are we going to fly now?*

Adelaide shook her head. She didn't have enough control of herself and was much too tired.

When the trees blocked Manfred's cottage from sight, Adelaide said, *That man killed Elias's father.*

Cyr clicked his beak in surprise. *Why?*

Adelaide related to him what Manfred had told her, reminding the hawk who King Ganelon was, since she didn't know how much he knew about human affairs.

When she finished, Cyr rubbed his beak against Adelaide's hand where she sat on a patch of grass. *I mourn that Elias didn't have his father for the last few months of his life. He was a good flyer, and his father was probably even better.*

I'm sure, though I never saw King Ganelon fly. She had never even met him, the man who had impacted Elias the most. She'd never known what he thought of her or how much Elias resembled him. And she never would.

Her eyes smarting, Adelaide turned her back on Manfred's mistakes and a hunger that could never be filled.

Are you ready to return to Dhalion? Adelaide asked Cyr the next morning as he tore into a squirrel.

The place where I rescued you from the stone nest?

In more ways than one. It was humbling and frustrating that she once thought she never needed anyone's help and now seemed to need it all the time. *Yes. According to Manfred, the island of Niclond is southeast of there.*

And you're sure these fire-flyers won't eat us?

No, but Elias wanted me to speak to them, which means he thought they'd listen. Hopefully, once they know he and I were friends, they won't harm us.

Cyr measured her, then went back to finishing his squirrel. *If you believe it to be so, then I do. I'm with you wherever you go.*

Unexpected tears rose in Adelaide's eyes. What was going on? Ever since the night on the cliff when Elias had died, she'd become as emotional as Emma.

She reached out and rubbed Cyr's head. *Thanks. That means a lot.*

I wouldn't be able to fly without you. He rubbed his beak on his talons. *Now where is this Nic-lond, land of the fire-fly-ers?*

I'm not sure. We'll have to fly around until we find it. She gulped as she saw herself plummeting as a human into the sea.

I could ask one of those annoying white birds if they've seen it.

Cyr, you think every bird is annoying.

Except hawks. We are the smartest of all birds.

No doubt. You can ask when we reach Dhalion. The thought of going near to the place where she had been held captive made her hands sweat and her stomach roll over, but there was no other option. It lay between them and the sea. They would keep to the trees as much as possible.

Come on. Adelaide walked deeper into the newly awak-ened forest in the direction of the King's City.

Cyr landed on her shoulder. *And you can't fly because it's daylight, correct?*

Correct. When Adelaide thought about flying, her heart leapt as if trying to take her with it, the fire in her stomach burned hotter, and her skin tightened as if turning into scales.

But then she recalled the out-of-control dizziness as she fell, the blurred trees rushing closer and closer, and Cyr's panic that mirrored hers, and the longing to fly dissolved.

I'll go look for danger, Cyr said as he soared past the trees into the sunny spring sky.

Adelaide watched his ease and confidence as if it was something she could reach out and snag for herself. She should be grateful for the ability to transform at all. But telling herself something was different than making it so.

When the evening music began—crickets chirping, frogs croaking, birds whistling their last tunes—Cyr landed on Adelaide's shoulder. *The big nest of humans you call Dhalion is nearby.*

Good. Adelaide's feet hurt, and her stomach rumbled.

You should know that male humans are walking around on the cliff by the giant stone nest where you were held captive. Someone with too-shiny feathers is making loud sounds at them.

Adelaide frowned, trying to understand Cyr's words. The knights must be training for war. She wondered if Conrad and the others had listened to her and joined the preparations, if Berold had let them.

Hopefully Berold was the one with chainmail (or, as Cyr put it, too-shiny feathers), barking orders at the men, which meant that he wasn't searching for her. Although she supposed he could have ordered others to look for her. But she couldn't hide out in the woods; she had to prepare for a journey over the sea.

She turned to Cyr and told him to get as many squirrels and rabbits as he could for their journey.

I guess I'll try to hunt too. Adelaide wasn't enthusiastic about the idea; if it turned out like her attempts to fly, it wouldn't go well.

Very well. I'll meet you here soon. Cyr darted into the twilight.

Adelaide placed her satchel beneath a bush, closed her eyes, and transformed.

The scents of spruce, sap, salt, baked bread, and freshly washed strawberries accosted her. Despite how hungry she was, the smell of fresh bread and fruit didn't tempt her. A more delicious scent lingered nearby.

She opened her eyes and peered through the trees where, in her heat vision, an orange-hued deer grazed, oblivious to the danger nearby.

Adelaide instinctively opened her wings. One of them sliced through a tree branch, sending it crashing to the forest floor. The deer bounded away.

Her body screamed at her to take to the sky where she had the advantage, but she was too close to Dhalion, so she closed her wings.

She took a few steps toward where the deer had fled, her clawed feet noiseless on the pine-needle-strewn floor. But her tail was a different matter. It hit a tree, and the sharp spikes cut through it easily, sending it down with a crash.

Adelaide tried to stop her tail from moving so much, but she couldn't completely keep it from twitching. The barbed end got stuck in a massive oak when she focused back to the front. She pulled forward, and her tail came out. But the momentum drove her forward into a boulder, which groaned under her weight.

The boulder cracked, and a few pieces fell onto her head and back. It would have given her a headache as a human, but now she hardly felt it.

Of all the apples! Every animal within fifty paces would have heard that racket and fled. If she couldn't even hunt for herself, how did she expect to bring peace between the dragons and humans? She shrank under the weight, as small as she'd felt when the women had belittled her for being a peasant back in Kildare.

Elias had given the potion to the wrong person. Her body

shrank as if it wanted to match the image in her mind. All the dragons on Niclond would laugh at her.

When Adelaide returned to the spot where she had placed her satchel, Cyr stood on the ground, his wings spread over his catch: two rabbits, three squirrels, and five chipmunks.

He closed his wings when he noticed her and asked, *Where's your prey?*

Adelaide grabbed her satchel. *I don't have any.*

As you said, you have only been a fire-flyer for a few days, and you have no one to teach you. It will come with practice.

For not being very perceptive about human details, he was about her moods. *We need to reach the cliff before sunrise, and I'm walking there.*

This time Cyr didn't ask why, for which she was grateful.

Once Adelaide loaded all the animals into her satchel, she walked down toward the city. She stayed in the trees and kept the road that led from the castle to the city on her left. It was the same road she had walked up with Elias and Berold when Berold had accused her of wanting to overthrow and kill Elias. That had only been a few days ago, but felt like ages.

On top of the cliff opposite the castle, she followed the roar of the sea to the place where the forest thinned. Waves slammed against the rocks below with enough force to knock a dragon unconscious, then they lurched away, trying to suck the rocks out with them.

The water was as black as the night sky except where the moon, half-hidden by a cloud, reflected against the surface, melting the black into a silver brighter and more powerful than that of her wings.

Instead of being awed by the sea's vastness as she had when she first saw it, she now felt overwhelmed. How could she find anything in that plain of never-ending water? How could she remain a dragon long enough without drowning? She was just one human—a mere bubble in the limitless ocean.

She clutched her satchel to her chest, fighting the temptation to flee and leave Klinhun and the dragons to their fate.

Everyone else could; why not her? But she knew why. She had chosen to change the course of her country and had damaged lives in the process. Now she must set it right.

I'm going to find one of those white birds to ask directions to this Niclond place, Cyr said before soaring away.

Adelaide peered past the city to where the castle sat on the higher cliff across from her. She couldn't hear anything over the crashing of the waves below or see anything but the brown stone fortress. She'd have to take Cyr's word that there were men up there training.

While Adelaide refilled her animal skin from a spring, a bank of dense fog rolled in from the sea and sat heavy on the cliff. It would make perfect cover.

Cyr returned, landing on her shoulder. *I found one of the white birds and told him where we were. He flies slowly but should be here soon. He knows the way.*

While they waited, Adelaide tried not to think about what might happen if her body transformed over the sea and how the dragons would respond to her appearance on their island.

A few moments later, something landed at her feet.

That's him, Cyr said.

A white bird, smaller than the hawk, with an orange beak, shook out its feathers and gazed at them with shiny black eyes. *Forgive my lateness. Is this your human? She smells of dirt and smoke.*

I'm Adelaide. What are you called?

She speaks! The seagull hopped backward.

Of course she does. She's a fire-flyer, Cyr said.

The seagull shuffled his wings. *So good to meet you, fire-flyer. You looked like a human, so I didn't know. So sorry. I'm Featherflies, by the way.*

Featherflies. That's an odd name, Adelaide said.

He puffed out his chest. *My mother gave it to me the first time I flew. I had the most beautiful feathers of my—*

So, you know the way to the land where the dragons live?

Adelaide interrupted. *You can take us there?*

Yes. I've been there many times. There's lots of delicious fish around there, especially the bright blue ones. I first heard of the place from my nest mate's brother, who got blown there once in a storm. He showed me how to get there because I'm his...

He talks a lot, like a sparrow, Cyr explained to Adelaide alone.

Yes. It would be a long trip. *Featherflies, how long does it take to reach the island?*

The bird stopped mid-sentence. *Three to four passings of the sun if the wind is at your tail feathers.*

That was closer than Adelaide had expected. She took a deep breath. They had to leave sometime, and the fog would keep them well concealed until they were out of sight of land. *Let's go.*

Featherflies screeched. *In this weather?*

Yes.

But it will be hard to see, and the wind ...

Adelaide leaned closer to him. *This is very important. You can either come with us willingly, or Cyr can pull you along with us unwillingly. The choice is yours.*

Cyr eyed the smaller bird and snapped his beak.

Featherflies hopped away from him. *Fine, fine. I'll do it.*

Good. Adelaide transformed, focusing on the strength of her muscles and the embers in her stomach and how right they felt.

You truly are a fire-flyer, Featherflies squawked, shuffling backward so quickly that he almost toppled over.

Adelaide picked up her satchel with a talon. *Go ahead, Featherflies, show us the way. And if you lead us somewhere besides Niclond, I will eat you.*

The seagull flapped off the cliff into the miasma. Cyr followed, keeping a wary eye on the bird.

Adelaide stared after them, but the fog soon swallowed them up.

Are you coming? Cyr asked.

She took a deep breath, letting the air fill her chest, and held it before releasing it. As she did, she surged off the cliff.

Chapter Twelve

Adelaide hadn't plummeted to her death yet. She hadn't even felt the warm glow threaten to melt her scales. She was too annoyed with Featherflies's nonstop chatter to think about what may or may not await her in Niclond.

He'd told them all about his family, about his first journey across the sea and how he'd almost drowned in a storm, which would have been interesting if he hadn't broken off in the middle of it to expound on how terrible it was to fly in a thunderstorm. Then he reminisced for what felt like half the night on his favorite kinds of fish.

A better name for the seagull would be Chitter-Chatter. Cyr kept looking at the seagull murderously too.

The sun rose and burned all the fog and when Klinhun disappeared behind the travelers, Adelaide and the birds were left alone in the never-ending expanse of rippling blue.

As the sun continued to climb, Adelaide's wings ached with each beat. Her tail down to the tip of her snout felt as stiff and rigid as rock. Her muscles were as flimsy as straw.

I must rest, she said, angling her body toward the beckoning azure sea.

Good idea, Featherflies huffed, landing in the water and bobbing about like a duck. *We may as well rest when it's hot out. And I'm starving. Ooh. It's one of those tasty silver fish.* He ducked his head into the water, and Adelaide was grateful for the temporary silence.

She landed in the sea, the water hissing as it hit her scales. Waves rocked from her and crashed into Featherflies, sending him tumbling into the water.

After she'd eaten enough fish to silence the pangs in her belly, she laid her neck on top of the water and closed her eyes.

It wasn't the most relaxing rest; the waves sometimes broke across her face, jolting her awake and causing her to sneeze at the salt, sparks erupting out of her nose. But when the sun sank into the water with a cheerful golden glow, Adelaide was ready to fly again.

She stretched out her wings and, after several attempts, launched into the air beside the two birds, leaving a trail of water droplets behind.

The days blended into each other like the sea and sky. The trio soared by moonlight, then filled up on fish and let the lapping of the breakers and the warmth of the sun lull them to sleep.

Adelaide could fly a little further each night, though her body creaked at the end of every flight like old women's bones. She longed to sleep on solid ground again without waking up every few moments to spew out saltwater.

The closer they flew to Niclond, the more Adelaide's body threatened to transform, usually when she thought about how easily the dragons would see the human beneath her scales. Then it was only a matter of time before she started falling toward the ocean.

The first time it happened, Featherflies hadn't even noticed; he'd just kept flying and talking.

Cyr had screeched and said, *You're glowing again.*

I know. It means I'm going to turn into a human.

Can you stop it?

I'm trying. She had been able to that time, but not the next evening.

Despite her best efforts, she'd been wondering what the dragon rulers would do to her if they found out that she had been part of the rebellion to overthrow Elias.

Adelaide had felt the flickering of her transformation's flames but had dropped into the sea before she could fight them.

In this form, the water was as chilly as the Lentiasa River in the spring. She came up, gasping and choking on the sharp tang of salt.

Can I do anything to help? Cyr asked as he flitted above her.

Featherflies had finally noticed something was wrong and came over to investigate. *What's wrong with her? Why is she no longer a fire-flyer?*

Adelaide's arms were already growing tired from trying to keep herself afloat. She was a good swimmer but didn't usually swim in her dress and cloak.

Be quiet, she said. Thankfully Featherflies listened.

Adelaide tried to think about her powerful wings, her sleek scales and tail, but the water splashing into her eyes and her aching muscles made it difficult to focus. Cyr's coaxing didn't help much either.

Finally, when her throat stung from all the salt she'd swallowed, and her legs felt as if they couldn't kick anymore, the welcome burn began. But Adelaide had been too weary to fly, so they'd had to miss the rest of that night's journey.

After that, Adelaide's body threatened to transform about once a night, and she started flying just above the water, so she'd have less distance to fall. Her terror probably made the unwelcome transformation worse, but she didn't know what else to do.

At least she managed mostly to remain in her shape; she'd only fallen into the sea once more, and it hadn't taken nearly as long to return to her dragon shape as it had the first time.

By dawn of the fourth day, Adelaide longed to reach the end of the journey so much that she hardly cared if the dragons roasted her. At least she'd have solid ground beneath her again and wouldn't have to constantly wage war in her mind and body.

Look, there's one of my friends, Whitewings. He stays on Niclond all the time. He was born there. Whitewings! Featherflies called out to another seagull flying toward them. Adelaide was too exhausted to greet the newcomer.

Cyr too must have been exhausted, for he sat on her head between her spikes instead of gliding beside her.

Featherflies soared off with his friend and never returned, but they didn't need him anymore. The waking sun revealed a green smudge on the horizon.

Two naked mountains covered in nothing but black rock—what she guessed were volcanoes—rose above the green mass. From above, the island was shaped like a turtle, the rounded part of the shell toward Adelaide.

She was too tired to think about what awaited her there; she was just relieved to have arrived. She and Cyr descended.

Chapter Thirteen

High-pitched chittering like birds squabbling woke Adelaide. Something furry brushed her cheek, and another pressed against her back scales, tickling her.

These creatures nearly pulled out all my feathers before I scared them away, Cyr grumbled. *And they keep making those awful sounds.*

Adelaide stood and shook, trying to shake off whatever creatures were making the tickling sensation. *What are they?*

I don't know. Some kind of four-legged creature that walks like a human.

Adelaide turned her neck. A fluffy, black creature with a long furry tail leapt off her back onto the sand. Mischievous tawny eyes glanced back at her. Then it made some high-pitched baby-like noises and scampered off toward the oddest trees she'd ever seen.

They had long, feather-like leaves instead of branches and large, shelled fruits that could probably knock out a human if they fell.

Thanks for bringing me, Richter. You may go now, a male voice said in her mind.

But I want to talk to the strange dragon and bird, a younger male voice responded. *I'm the one who found them, after all.*

There will be time for that later. Go tell everyone as I know you long to.

A dragon the color of melted butter was prodding a small cherry-colored dragon down the path away from them. After glancing at Adelaide once more, the smaller dragon left.

Those creatures you were wondering about are monkeys, the yellow dragon said as he walked toward them. *Annoying at times, but not dangerous, especially not to dragons.* His stomach, neck, and back spikes were the same shade as the feather-like leaves. He gazed at Adelaide and Cyr with violet eyes.

The dragon dipped his snout to the ground while the animals he called monkeys climbed onto him. At least four others already hung onto his spikes with their tails or feet.

May the sun always shine on your scales and the winds carry you straight. I am called Resse, Violeteyes, Sunheart, Truthwearer, Bearer of Smiles.

All those names are yours? Adelaide asked.

I don't have as many names as some, yet more than others. The dragon grinned, revealing sharp teeth, yet the expression looked more like a dog's than a terrifying beast's on his narrow snout. *You may just call me Resse, though.*

I'm Adelaide, she said, her lack of names a tattered, stained cloak compared to Resse's rich speech.

But Adelaide couldn't have come better prepared; the only dragon she knew had died before he could teach her anything. She just hoped she wouldn't accidentally offend Resse or the others.

The fire burned inside Adelaide, and she cursed. What horrible timing. If her words or lack thereof had seemed like a ratty cloak, what would her human form—all sweaty and stained from the journey—seem like to this dragon who had probably never seen one before?

Adelaide forced herself to focus on her dragon form, and mercifully, the flames abated.

And I'm Cyr, one of the grandest birds alive, the hawk announced.

I wouldn't go that far, she told him.

Welcome, Cyr and Adelaide, Resse said their names as if tasting an exotic fruit, *to Niclond, the current dwelling place of the dragons. Where have you two flown from?*

We're from Klinhun, and we come to seek the aid of the dragons.

You're from Klinhun? Resse leaned forward, his tail uncurling and curling at his feet. *How did you come here?*

Adelaide's stomach growled as if it might eat her. She hadn't eaten since the day before and had flown many miles since then.

Resse's chest erupted in laughter. *Forgive me. It appears you are ravenously hungry.*

And thirsty, Cyr added.

Of course. I'll get you some provisions, and then you can tell me your tale. He turned and, with the monkeys still clinging to him, disappeared into the trees.

Adelaide sat down to await his return. *What do you think of this Resse dragon?* She asked Cyr.

He seems nice enough, though small for a fire-flyer.

You've only seen two dragons in your life.

He rustled his feathers. *Perhaps, but it's true. Elias could have eaten him if he wished.*

But not I?

Perhaps once you learn to fly better.

Adelaide didn't argue because she knew it was true.

Resse returned with some kind of spotted cat in his jaws. *This is one of the tastier prey on the island, but there aren't many left. In fact, this might be the last. It was the first one I'd seen in a long time.* He placed the cat at her feet.

A monkey put a round shell filled with water on the sand next to it. Cyr soared down, and the monkey skittered away.

The only thing Adelaide had eaten as a dragon had been fish, and the warm, bloody scent of the cat made her mouth water. She devoured it without another thought, enjoying the crunch and snap of the bones.

Are you ready to tell your story now? Resse asked, his tail twitching.

Adelaide licked her snout, then her silvery talons where blood had splattered. *Actually, I need to tell it to the dragon who rules this land.*

Oh, yes. Of course. Resse stood. *I'll take you to Evengier, Swiftwings, Wiseheart, right away. I should have suggested so myself, but we don't get many visitors here—none, actually—so your presence surprised me.*

But answer me this, does your presence have anything to do with Kindheart, Healer of Brokenness, Giver of Life, Lightscales, or, his common name, Prince Elias? Or his mighty father, who has too many names to say, King Ganelon, Protector of All Dragons? Resse stared at her with his odd, violet eyes, and Adelaide could only nod.

Something in her look must have alarmed Resse, for his tail stilled, and he turned around. *Follow me, then.*

Cyr soared overhead as Adelaide followed Resse on a wide, sandy path strewn with decaying leaves and crushed pink and yellow blossoms. On either side of the path, the flowers curled around glossy, broad-leafed trees that cast them in watery shadows.

Adelaide wished Elias was the one walking ahead of her, pointing out butterflies and sharing about how the dragons had found the island and cleared the paths with fire. She wanted to see it all with his eyes. Had he ever played in those nearby trees that sprouted a round, green fruit? What did he think of the brilliant crimson and emerald birds darting above? Did he think they were annoying or beautiful?

It was hard to imagine him as a dragon in this wild, bright place. It seemed somehow wrong to be here without the one who had first told her about it with such fondness and who hadn't seen it in years.

Why did you stop? Resse asked, glancing back at her.

Warmth rushed into Adelaide's cheeks. She hadn't realized that she'd stopped as if waiting for Elias to join her or looking for him in the trees.

There's just a lot to take in, she said as she continued.

One of the monkeys on Resse's tail leapt onto a branch above them and disappeared in the foliage.

Why do those animals ride on you? Adelaide asked. *Don't they know you could eat them?*

When I was a hatchling, I came upon a baby without its mother. I gave it some fruit and kept it warm that night. The next morning it left and returned with friends. They looked hungry, so I gave them food, and they never left.

He picked one of the furry creatures off his back and tossed it in the air. *Prince Elias threatened almost daily to throw them into Flaming-Tongue, one of our island's volcanos.*

Adelaide burned like a coal at the mention of Elias. *You were friends with Prince Elias?* Thankfully, her mind's voice didn't reveal her desperation for memories of him.

Yes. We would frequently explore the island together before he and his father left. Resse sighed, steam rising from his nostrils. *I've missed him greatly. But at least I saw him a few times on Klinhun.*

You were the dragon-messenger then who carried messages between King Ganelon and the dragons?

Yes.

He seemed friendly and capable enough, if younger than she would have expected to carry important messages across the sea. This meant that besides the current ruling dragon, Resse was the only living dragon who knew that King Ganelon and Prince Elias had traveled to Klinhun and lived there as humans. The others believed they were exploring islands, looking for a better home.

She hoped the other dragons took the news of this necessary deception well and were as kind to newcomers as Resse.

They stopped beside a wind-ruffled lake. Ducks bobbed on its surface and a few white birds with long necks and short, orange beaks stood in the shallows.

To their left, another wide path led through some triangular-leafed trees.

That's the north trail, Resse told her, noticing her gaze. *And that's the Dragon Trail.* He nodded to the far end of the lake where another flower-littered path led into the trees. *It just leads to a rocky beach on the southwestern part of the island. This lake, Caldera, is the only one on Niclond, so it serves as the central place for all the paths through the jungle.*

Why are there so many paths if you can just fly?

Resse tilted his head. *You speak like a hatchling, but you have the body and voice of an older dragon.*

Heat flared, and before Adelaide could stop the transformation, she stood before him in her human form.

She stared at the grass at her feet, crossing her arms over her chest as if she was naked.

You're a human? Resse asked, aghast.

Obviously, she said curtly. *I haven't been a dragon for very long. Prince Elias made me one with a special potion.*

To calm down and give her time before she had to look at Resse's expression, Adelaide walked to the lake. She took several long draughts of the cool, sweet water.

To her surprise, Resse followed her, and when he spoke, his voice carried none of the disgust or derision that Adelaide had expected.

Please forgive me if I have upset you. I haven't seen many humans. It's wonderful that you can shift between the two species, for it will help bridge the gap between us that Prince Elias and his father always wanted closed.

Adelaide nodded, though the transformation had so far been more frustrating and burdensome than a gift.

I look forward to hearing the full story if you choose to give it, Resse said as a monkey leapt off him and ran toward the water.

First, though, I need to bathe. Adelaide turned her back on the dragon and his monkeys in order to focus. Thankfully, it only took two attempts to return to her dragon form.

Does it hurt when you change forms like that? Prince Elias said it did.

Adelaide nodded. Then, she dove into the lake to wash the itching salt off her scales.

When she resurfaced and landed with a stumble on the shore, Resse was still there, staring at her. She wished he wouldn't watch her; it made her more self-conscious than she already was.

How long have you been a dragon? he asked. *And where is Prince Elias? Why did he not accompany you here?*

Adelaide's tail twitched. If only Cyr could share the tale instead. That way she wouldn't have to wade back into the painful torment. She was already flinching at the thought, but she needed to. For Elias. It was the least she could do for him and the dragons. *I'll explain everything when I meet the current ruler of Niclond.*

Resse bobbed his head. *Evengier, Swiftwings. This way.* He led her around Caldera Lake to one of the many trails that plunged into the verdant landscape. *This is the East Trail. It leads to Black Beach, but we won't be going that far.*

What's Evengier like? Would he flame her the moment she opened her mouth? Or act curious and kind to her as Resse had?

Oh, you'll like him.

But Adelaide wondered if *he* would like *her.*

He's wise and listens to younger dragons. He's good friends with King Ganelon and has the same gift that I do. Resse puffed his chest out.

Which is what? Adelaide asked.

Truth.

Which means?

I speak only the truth and can tell when others aren't.

It sounded more like a curse than a gift. But Adelaide didn't even have a dragon gift, so she wasn't one to say.

As they walked through air that felt like a hand clamping down on Adelaide, she glimpsed flashes of color that seemed too bright and shiny to be natural and heard the fluttering of wings too big to belong to birds.

For being overpopulated, the dragons were making themselves scarce. Several times Adelaide and Resse passed clearings where large, porous black rocks sat piled together in a heap. When she asked what they were, Resse turned to look at her.

How little you know keeps surprising me. This is a dragon roost. Some like theirs covered up, some don't. Some prefer banana or palm tree fronds. Personally, I like moss.

So, this is where dragons sleep?

Yes, though some prefer sleeping in trees.

Adelaide had a difficult time picturing that. *And where do the dragons lay their eggs?*

On Nesting Island, which is to the northeast of Niclond. The females stay there with their eggs until they hatch, then they bring the hatchlings here to the main island.

Adelaide shook her head. It all seemed so bizarre. Had Elias truly grown up as a baby dragon on some rocky island? Even though she had seen him as a dragon several times, she still thought of him as human. If only he were here to show her, she might have an easier time believing it.

A short distance later, the trees opened up, or, more accurately, had been destroyed, creating a large clearing that led to cliffs overlooking the sea. They didn't appear to be as high as those in Dhalion and consisted of the same black, porous rock that Resse said the dragons like to make their roosts with.

Around the clearing's edges lay blackened trees and plants. Prickly ivy wound its way around the dead branches as if trying to reclaim the conquered land. Several fragile pink flowers popped up out of the ash in the middle of the clearing.

Adelaide sensed movement on her right and crouched.

A huge shape shifted in the shadow of the trees. Two legs the size of tree trunks but the color of pine needles stepped into the sunlight. Then a serpentine green neck towered up over the trees, casting Adelaide in shadow. Two tan spikes as long as Adelaide's human body curved back from its massive head. Smaller spikes sprouted from the corners of its mouth up to the top of its head.

It was the largest dragon Adelaide had ever seen, and probably double the size Elias had been. She felt like a puppy in the presence of a wolf and tried not to cower.

The creature's eyes gleamed like bronze and were as large as shields. Thankfully, they were aimed at Resse, not her.

Your stomach is full and your wings strong? The dragon's voice rumbled in her mind like thunder.

Yes, father. Resse inclined his head. *And yours?*

Adelaide turned to Resse. *The king of the dragons is your father? You forgot to mention that.* She thought that ironic since his gift was truth; apparently, it didn't mean he had to share everything.

Resse shrugged. *I didn't forget to mention it. I just didn't deem it important. And he's not technically the king of the dragons. King Ganelon, Sunscales, is.*

Not anymore, Adelaide made sure to think to herself, although they would learn the truth soon enough. Her heart clenched when she thought about the story she would have to tell and the reactions it might produce.

Yes, I am Evengier, Swiftwings, Wiseheart, Stealthystep, Leafscales, Ysoria's Mate, Resse's Sire, and ruler of Niclond in King Ganelon's stead. The more important question is: Who are you?

Chapter Fourteen

Evengier's huge, bronze eyes scrutinized Adelaide, stripping off her scales and pretentions to the uncertain human beneath. This was it. When she would be discovered as a fraud and either be destroyed in a puff of smoke or sent back to Klinhun.

Surely those ancient eyes could see that she had only been a dragon for a few short days, could see how difficult it was to even remain in this shape, and see all her actions that had led to the death of their prince.

Her head bowed with the weight of his gaze until her snout hung just above the burnt grass. *I am Adelaide, citizen of Klinhun and friend of Prince Elias. I was sent here by the prince himself to plead for your help.*

Richter found her and a hawk on the shore looking half-dead and came and told me, Resse added.

That's not how Adelaide would have described her first encounter with the island before the king, and she glared at Resse. He just smiled in his dog-like way.

How have you come to our island, and how did you know

Prince Elias? Evengier asked.

Adelaide lifted her head, relieved that Evengier hadn't immediately scorched her or sent her away. *It's a long story,* she warned. She wouldn't hold anything back; the dragons deserved the truth of how their rulers had died.

The great pine-green dragon nodded, sending a gust of air across Adelaide's face. *Please wait to begin. The elders will no doubt wish to hear your tale. I will call them now.*

Oh, here it comes. Resse lowered his head and placed his talons over his ear holes.

Before Adelaide could ask what he was doing, Evengier opened his mouth and roared.

The booming blast reverberated from Adelaide's head all the way to the end of her tail and continued to echo long after he shut his mouth. Her skull throbbed, and she touched her earholes to make sure they weren't bleeding. They weren't.

Everyone on the island, and probably a good distance away, would have heard that noise.

Forgive me. Evengier looked at her with concern. *I didn't realize you wouldn't know that I was about to roar.*

Adelaide barely nodded, afraid her head would roll off her body if she moved too much.

I tried warning you, Resse said.

Not much later, Adelaide heard large wings beating the air and smelled what she now realized was the scent of dragons: a mixture of smoke and something refreshing like spring rain.

Three dragons the same size as Evengier landed on either side of Adelaide at the edge of the clearing. Despite how large they were, they all landed with hardly a sound.

The three dragons lowered their heads and murmured greetings to Evengier. Soon, three others hovered in the air above the clearing, casting those on the ground in odd, whirring shadows.

A dragon with light blue scales spotted with patches of white like a sky peppered with clouds landed beside Evengier.

What is the matter, my flame? Have there been more squabbles? The blue-and-white dragon asked in a female voice, rubbing her head against Evengier's neck.

He stretched his head out in pleasure, and Adelaide glanced away from the intimate action. At least, to her it felt intimate; she had no idea what dragons considered romantic. Perhaps to them shooting fire at each other was the height of passion.

We have a visitor, Ysoria. Evengier tilted his head at Adelaide, and the female glanced at her with eyes the color of a cloudless sky.

Oh? How unusual. Where do you hail from, Silverscales?

All the dragons looked at Adelaide.

She kneaded the ground with her talons, her stomach churning like boiling soup. *I am Adelaide, a citizen of Klinhun, and I come here at the request of Prince Elias, Healer of Brokenness, Giver of Life,* she threw in because he deserved the titles. *But before I recount my tale, I must tell you that King Ganelon and Prince Elias are both dead.*

Silence—sudden and heavy—dropped onto the clearing.

Then all at once, hisses, growls, and gasps as sharp as talons ripped through the air.

Adelaide again held Elias in her hands, his life draining away with his blood. Her friend the cause of his death, her gifted dagger and words the tools.

Please go on with your tale, Evengier's rumbly thoughts pulled Adelaide back to the present.

She took a deep breath as the dragons around her calmed. *I am a human whom Prince Elias befriended as I traveled across Klinhun to overthrow King Ganelon. I believed them to be rulers oppressing my people, but I was wrong.*

What is this creature saying? A sunflower-yellow dragon asked. *Prince Elias and King Ganelon were never in Klinhun.*

The others agreed, but as Adelaide had expected, Evengier didn't look surprised. *Please,* he said with a growl, *let the newcomer finish her tale. Then all will be explained.*

As she spoke, Adelaide lost herself in the piney-green scales of Evengier's chest that became the pine trees under which Elias had taught her how to fish, the beautiful greenery of the castle at Dhalion, and the woods outside Manfred's house.

No one interrupted or made a noise during the telling until Adelaide mentioned King Ganelon's death. Then the dragons hissed at the same time like a snake, and several snapped their jaws. Adelaide jerked back, her heart flying.

When she spoke of Elias's murder, dragons growled, and a patch of grass to her right erupted in flames. At the mention of Manfred's traitorous deed, their rumble of roars caused her spikes to stand straight up, and a tree near her burst into flames.

When Adelaide finished sharing her story, she was an empty body without a heart or flesh. Just bones. She longed to fly away to search for her missing parts, but knew she wouldn't find them.

Ysoria gazed at the ground, her tail drooping. *How can King Ganelon and his son, two mighty and strong-hearted dragons, be dead and gone forever?*

They can't truly be dead, a female with a splash of gold on her muzzle said. *They weren't even in Klinhun. They went to look for more land for us to settle in. Yes, they have been gone a long time, but we have never doubted their return.*

Evengier sighed. *There is something I haven't told you for your own good.* He glanced at Ysoria, who prodded him on with her sky-eyes.

King Ganelon and Prince Elias didn't depart Niclond to search for a better home for us because they knew that there isn't one, just islands like this one.

Instead, years ago, King Ganelon discovered how to turn dragons into humans. So, he and Prince Elias went to Klinhun to rule as humans and try to earn the people's trust so that we could return to our true home and the humans we were created to protect. Resse has been staying in contact with King

Ganelon and his son these last few years.

Evengier looked at Resse, who lifted his head high. A monkey hopping up and down on his head ruined the sophisticated look.

After a long moment of silence only interrupted by the waves crashing on the rocks below, a bark-hued dragon said, *How did King Ganelon and Prince Elias turn into humans? Such a thing has never been done in our long history.*

Evengier raised one of his shoulders. *I do not know. He didn't share the information with me, but I know it was a sacrifice.*

How could you have kept this information from us with your gift being truth? A rainbow-scaled female asked.

Evengier turned solemn eyes on her. *I never lied to you, Durilda. King Ganelon told you himself that he was going to search for other uninhabited lands before he left. And Ysoria answered any questions that might have required twisting the truth.*

But why didn't you tell us? We're the elders, after all, the sharers of our past and wisdom for the future, a dragon with a missing back spike said, betrayal cutting through his words.

Evengier lowered his head so that it nearly touched the ground. *I wanted to, and it pained me greatly not to tell you, protectors of my wings. But King Ganelon made me promise to keep his whereabouts a secret. He didn't wish your hopes to be raised without firm evidence that things could change. And he didn't want there to be more fighting among us.*

He lifted his head. *I agreed. It is crucial in this difficult time that we remain close, closer than scales.*

After a long moment of tail-twitching silence, Ysoria asked, *Does everyone agree that Evengier and King Ganelon acted in the colony's best interest not to tell them about King Ganelon and Prince Elias's true whereabouts?*

Everyone, some grudgingly, murmured their assent, and Adelaide was surprised at how quickly they did, even with the few grumbles. If she had learned that she had been purposefully lied to about the location of her king, she would have been furious. But these were dragons and hopefully wiser than humans. That was one reason she was seeking their help, after all—so they would rule Klinhun better than the humans.

And do you recognize the truth of Evengier's words and believe all that he has said to be true? Ysoria asked.

More murmurs and nods of approval. Adelaide thought it an odd question since Evengier possessed the gift of truth and couldn't lie, but apparently the dragons wanted to be thorough.

Adelaide felt someone's gaze on her and turned to see a red dragon staring at her with orange eyes. *And you are sure this new dragon is telling the truth?*

Yes, Evengier said. *Besides, Resse has not seen or heard from King Ganelon or Prince Elias or even our human friend, Manfred, since before the Tartuk birds' migration south. She is the last one to have seen Prince Elias.*

Adelaide felt everyone's eyes on her, and she suppressed the desire to turn away.

Even though they seemed to believe Evengier, it would help her case if they believed her as well. So, despite all her instincts warning her not to, she closed her eyes and imagined her human body.

The pain came like a forest fire—sudden, consuming, devouring. She would never get used to this agony.

When the torment ceased and she opened her eyes, nine pairs of dragon eyes stared down at her. Adelaide felt as naked and weak as a newborn baby. She had never spent so long in her dragon form before, and her human body felt unusually thin and frail, her arms and legs too skinny. Her braid startled her when its end brushed against her back. She ignored the desire to wrap her arms around herself and stood as tall as possible.

Ysoria's snout lowered to Adelaide's eye level. Adelaide could have stuffed her entire body into one of those cavernous nostrils. *Oh. I didn't realize how small humans are.* Ysoria smiled without showing any teeth. *Welcome to Niclond, land of the dragons, little one. Forgive us if we frightened you and for not welcoming you properly. We have had much on our minds as of late.*

Please call me Adelaide. She was not inclined to be known as "little one"; she wasn't even as small as Resse in her dragon form.

Of course. Evengier nodded at her. *We are glad you're here.*

But not all of them were. A pale blue dragon with red spikes gazed at her with suspicion. *I cannot trust one who led our prince to his death and did not respect or honor him even when shown his goodness,* the dragon's deep voice whispered into her mind—hers alone since no one seemed to notice the exchange.

The dragon's words were teeth ripping into Adelaide's already-torn heart. *I will regret the way I treated Prince Elias for the rest of my life. His death is my fault, and I don't deserve the dragons' trust, but I do need your help.*

The dragon merely snorted at her, still squinting at her, as if weighing her value in his mind.

She would need to be careful while here in Niclond to show the dragons that she could be trusted.

Chapter Fifteen

Do all humans smell as bad as you? Resse asked, shaking his yellow snout at her.

Several of the dragons' bellies rumbled in laughter.

Adelaide wrapped her arms around herself. *Most of them, except for the nobles who can afford to buy sweet-smelling soap.*

The dragons continued to ogle her; she was probably the first human they had ever seen. Still, it made her feel like a pig at a market.

Then a male dragon said in a quavering tone, *So it's true then. King Ganelon and Prince Elias are dead.*

The dragons stilled. Adelaide was forgotten as the realization settled in their minds that their leader, protector, guide, and friend would never return.

He's dead!

The mighty King Ganelon ... dead. Prince Elias ... dead as well. Their thoughts flowed to other dragons on the island, whom Adelaide could hear spreading the news like sparks carried by the wind.

Our king is dead?

He's dead, never to return!

Prince Elias will never rule. He and his father fly in the eternal skies.

The entire colony of dragons was now linked together in their shared thoughts and emotions; the raw agony brought Adelaide to her knees.

There was a chorus of roars throughout the island, so loud and powerful that it shook the ground and threw Adelaide to the dirt. She covered her ears against the onslaught.

The sky darkened, and she glanced up to see hundreds of dragons of all shapes and sizes swarming over her—a rainbow of color and light, the sound of their wings deafening. It was an awesome and terrible sight, and she couldn't tear her gaze away.

So strong and fierce in form, yet so beautiful in their jeweled scales, in the curve of their necks, in the pain and love of their ancient eyes.

The sound of drumming wings overtook that of the pounding waves. The dragons linked tails and closed their eyes.

Resse stepped toward her, his tail curled around that of a lavender dragon's. *Those with the gift of understanding are showing us memories of King Ganelon and Prince Elias. Touch my scales, and you'll see them too.* He placed his leg close to Adelaide, and she touched the warm scales and closed her eyes.

Images flashed through her mind quicker than lightning in a thunderstorm. A solid gold dragon, whom she guessed was King Ganelon, dove with talons outstretched to a hog in the foliage. Then he rescued a young dragon stranded on a rock in a billowing sea as rain hammered down. The king lifted a tree trunk into the air with one of his legs, then spoke to a slightly smaller dragon—the daintiest one Adelaide had ever seen. Had that been his mate, Elias's mother?

Then a golden-red dragon Adelaide knew well featured in

the memories, and her heart thumped like the wings above her.

Elias—smaller than when she had known him—soared with dragons around a smoking mountain, dove into the sea with Resse, caught a hatchling as it fell out of a tree, and shot flame into the air with other dragons as part of some kind of contest.

And then, the last image the dragons had: King Ganelon and Prince Elias soaring off into a pink-and-orange sky that bid them farewell.

Adelaide clung to the images of Elias as if they were his hand, holding her tight. She'd never get to hear him explain those memories to her himself or know what he'd loved most about his mother. The pain was a deluge that threatened to drown her.

When the rush of memories stopped, Adelaide brushed her tears away. She cursed the dragons for showing her memories of Elias and stabbing her bleeding heart again but also thanked them for showing her this untamed, free part of him that was a gift more precious than his kiss.

The dragons then hummed music without words, a haunting and mellifluous melody that threatened to bring more tears to Adelaide's eyes. No one who heard it could believe these dragons were merely fierce, fire-breathing, human-killing creatures.

This is a nice sound. Cyr landed on Adelaide's shoulder, startling her.

Yes, she agreed.

Why are you a human now? There are no stone nests here.

This was the best way to show them I was telling the truth. I'll change back soon.

When the velvet-rich song ended, Evengier bellowed long and loud. Adelaide jumped, and Cyr ruffled his feathers. *There was no need for him to do that,* he said.

One by one, the dragons came over to Evengier and Ysoria and bowed and promised them their loyalty and service. The new king and queen returned their bows, then the dragons dispersed.

Weary of the stares, Adelaide turned back into a dragon, eliciting shocked gasps. With Cyr on her back, she slithered past Resse who spoke to the lavender female he'd linked tails with.

Adelaide must not have slithered quietly enough, for Resse said, *Oh. This is her now in her dragon form. Isn't it fascinating how she can switch into both? That ability will help our two species greatly. Adelaide, this is Esa, Caringclaws, Lightbreather, Scalemender.*

The lavender dragon dipped her head. *May the sun always shine on your scales and the wind carry you far.*

Um, thanks. You as well.

Esa blinked long eyelashes. *How long do you plan to stay here, Adelaide?*

Not long. I need to ask Evengier for help fighting against Klinhun's neighboring country, Gyndilad.

I remember Prince Elias saying how much he and the others didn't like those humans, Resse said. *I'm sure you will have better success than I have with my father on that subject.*

You've already asked him?

I've told him what Elias and King Ganelon often told me, that Klinhun was on the verge of fighting with Gyndilad. Why don't you speak to him now? Most everyone has left, and I'm sure he will listen to you since you were one of the last ones to see Elias. Resse pushed her with his head.

Adelaide growled. *There's no need for that. I'll go when I'm ready.*

Forgive me, Resse said, backing up. *I get a little over excited sometimes.*

Esa laughed.

Adelaide padded over to Evengier, who now lay with his head on Ysoria's back. Not a very kingly position, but perhaps dragons didn't need to worry about that because their very presence commanded respect.

King Evengier, I have a request to make of you, Adelaide

announced when she stood before him. She wasn't sure if she should bow or not, so she lowered her neck.

The mighty dragon lifted his head. *Oh? What is it, Adelaide, Silverscales?*

She dug her talons into the ground, hoping she wouldn't mess the words up or offend him accidentally. The fate of her kingdom rested on her shoulders, and she couldn't let its people down.

She swallowed a few times, wishing Elias's confident, comforting presence was beside her. *Klinhun, your true home, is soon to be attacked by the Gyndilians, a people of a neighboring country. And because we no longer have a king, we will be destroyed and overrun by them.*

These are the same humans who destroyed your town?

And sister, Adelaide thought to herself. But she merely nodded. *We need the dragons to return to Klinhun and protect us. But also to rule. It was Elias's dying wish to see the dragons and humans united once more.*

Evengier stood. *Can you promise that the humans would not attack our colony when we arrive? Resse has told me of this festival where everyone tells a corrupt story of how we murdered humans in Klinhun and that we left in disgrace and defeat.* He snapped his jaws and Adelaide shrank back.

I can't promise such a thing, but if I, who reviled even the thought of the existence of dragons, could learn to trust them, then others can too. It's what Elias and his father wanted, and you yourself said Klinhun is your true home.

It was. But it would take too long to gain the people's trust—time that we don't have. The food supply here is no longer enough to feed everyone, and the colony is growing frightened. Evengier gazed out at the sea, then turned back to Adelaide.

Now that King Ganelon is no longer returning, we have nothing to wait for. I've spoken to the elders, and we think it's better to forget Klinhun, however much it pains us, and move somewhere safer.

Where? Adelaide asked.

We are thinking of moving the colony to Neklosa.

Neklosa? It was the country neighboring Klinhun to the southwest. Adelaide didn't know much about it except that it was quite a bit smaller, warmer, and on peaceable terms with Klinhun, though it had never aided them in their skirmishes against Gyndilad.

She didn't know what the Neklosians thought of dragons or if they even believed in their existence.

You're thinking of moving the colony to Neklosa? Resse asked with wide eyes.

At a look from Ysoria, he lowered his head.

Neklosa has never attacked or threatened dragons, and they were friendly to us in the past when we lived in Klinhun, Evengier explained.

Adelaide's thoughts spun. *But you lived in Klinhun before anyone else. It's your home. If you go to Neklosa, you still won't be able to live or reign freely. The Neklosians have their own rulers. But the people in Klinhun need a leader, and who better to rule them than the dragons, who were created to rule them in the first place?*

Evengier narrowed his eyes and brought them so close to Adelaide that she could see specks of gold glimmering in them. *The Klinians forsook us after we protected them and taught them the way of truth for centuries.*

He glanced away. *I do not take delight in the thought of forsaking Klinhun, but it's best for the colony, which must always come first. The elders and I will send a group of scouts to the leaders of Neklosa to see if we can live peacefully with them.*

But you'll just be guests, Adelaide said, her tail lashing the ground, creating deep furrows. *Besides, Neklosa is smaller than Klinhun. It won't take long before the people feel the pressure of your company.*

At least we will have room to fly and food to eat without the fear of being attacked. And if they no longer take kindly to our presence, we can always fly across the sea to look for another land. He said the last with a frown as he gazed across the ocean.

Adelaide didn't believe there was land across the sea; no tales or people had ever come from there.

Mother, Resse said in a pleading tone, *Do you agree with Father?*

Although the decision pains me, I support your father. We must try to move to Neklosa before we starve or kill each other.

There's plenty of food in Klinhun, Adelaide reminded them. But both dragons' eyes were now closed.

Adelaide knew when she was being dismissed, but she would be back. She hadn't flown so far to be disregarded so easily. The dragons were her people's last hope.

Chapter Sixteen

Later that day, when Resse, Esa, and Adelaide returned to the main part of the island, they decided to hunt.

If the dragons are so short on food, why don't you eat those creatures climbing on you? Adelaide asked Resse.

Because they're my friends. Would you consider eating that hawk of yours?

When he's being annoying.

I'm never annoying, Cyr said from his spot on her neck, and Adelaide snorted.

Well, I don't think about eating my friends. And if anyone tried, I would flame them quicker than the flick of a tail.

Good to know, Adelaide said. *So, we can hunt anywhere on the island?*

Yes. Resse nodded. *Meet here with your prey before the sun sets.* He slipped into the jungle with hardly disturbing a frond.

Esa smiled at Adelaide and disappeared just as quietly in another direction.

Would you like me to hunt for you? Cyr asked.

Nay. I have to learn sometime.

Very well. May you catch much prey. Cyr launched into the sky.

Adelaide sighed, then searched the twilit forest, her heat vision beginning to cast the trees and plants in an unnatural, blue-tinged light as the sun set.

A yellow-glowing squirrel darted across the ground, and Adelaide followed. Her strides carried her to the animal just as it scampered up a tree. She snapped her jaws at the squirrel, but it scurried out of reach. She extended her wings to lift her after it, but they caught in some vines.

Adelaide contemplated catching some fish in the lake, but it was too far to reach before their appointed meeting time.

After watching for prey without seeing any, she walked back to their rendezvous spot where Esa was gobbling down a rabbit and Resse was licking his bloodied nostrils.

Did you already eat your prey? Resse asked.

Adelaide was about to agree, but her stomach snarled, giving her away.

Oh, do you not know how to hunt? Esa asked.

Adelaide couldn't meet her concerned gaze. She'd once been the leader of a rebellion, traveled across Klinhun on her own, and now couldn't even hunt for herself.

She fought the urge to kick a tree, which would only show them that she was a child or hatchling or whatever they called young dragons. *I've only been a dragon for a short time, and Elias died before he could teach me.*

Why had she worded it like that? As if it was Elias's fault that he'd died and left her alone. What a horrible thought.

We'll teach you. Esa glanced at Resse, who nodded.

We'll be the best teachers you've ever not had, Resse said, and Adelaide snorted.

He leapt nimbly onto a vine-woven branch. *Height is always good. And because the trees grow too close together here to see prey from the sky, it's always a good idea to find a large tree to perch in.* He nodded to another broad branch beside him. *Go on, try it.*

Adelaide crouched, sprang up, opened her wings, and teetered to the side as a vine wrapped around one of her wing joints. She jerked backward, ripped through the vine, and landed unsteadily on the ground.

Resse chuckled, and Adelaide glared at him.

There's so much growth down here that you should never open your wings all the way, Esa explained. *They'll just get caught on something. In fact, you don't even need them to get up there. It's not that far, and your legs are more powerful than you think.*

Adelaide sighed. She crouched again, this time keeping her wings shut against her sides. She sprang for the branch and landed easily; it was much easier than climbing trees.

The branch she landed on wasn't wide enough to fit her entire body, and she lay awkwardly along it like Resse.

Well done, Resse praised her, making her feel like a child. *Now use all your senses. Sight, hearing, smell—*

I know what they are, Adelaide snapped, her frustration and embarrassment leaking through.

Good, Resse said. *Now use them to find prey. You must be patient.*

Patience was a skill Adelaide lacked. She scanned the forest floor—a distance that would've made her human sensations dizzy but now didn't bother her.

She saw a lizard—far too small to be prey—extend an orange throat. A bright blue bird darted through the branches below her.

Adelaide shut her eyes and smelled rotting plants, damp moss, flowers of varying degrees of sweetness, and an acrid, unpleasant smell from hot springs near the path.

She heard a petal fall to the ground, birds whistling, chirping, squawking, and crying, the breathing of Resse beside her, and something moving in the grass.

Adelaide craned her neck to look over the limb and spotted a snake slinking through the sward.

Now, Resse said when the snake was nearly right below her.

Adelaide launched out of the tree, careful to keep her wings snug against her body and her tail from causing chaos. She wrapped her front claws around the snake and landed awkwardly on her back legs.

Good job. Esa walked up beside her.

Cyr landed on Adelaide's head. *Soon you might be able to catch as much prey as me.*

Just wait. After a few more hunts, I'll be so swift and stealthy, nothing on this island will be able to escape me.

The next morning, Adelaide almost fell off the limb she'd slept on but caught herself by opening her wings.

After making sure she was alright, Cyr screeched in laughter. When she threatened to eat him, he took off.

She met Resse where they'd eaten the day before.

A few dragons are about to leave for Neklosa to see if their rulers will agree to let us live there, he said.

Already?

Come on. Resse led Adelaide back to the cliff where she had spoken to Evengier and Ysoria.

Dragons of all sizes stood under the trees, hovered in the air, or perched on branches, the larger ones bending them almost in half.

A group of adult-sized dragons stood in the middle of the clearing speaking to Evengier and Ysoria, who sat where they had yesterday at the edge of the cliff.

Please don't do this, Adelaide begged, squeezing between two younger dragons. *The people of Klinhun need your help, and you need them. It's your home, you admitted as much yesterday.*

Evengier turned eyes as old and weary as wave-beaten rocks on her. *We have no other choice. I can't risk more deaths at the hands of the Klinians. King Ganelon's and Elias's deaths have torn the joy out of our flight.* His eyes closed, and Ysoria touched his neck with her snout.

We don't hate Klinians, as you may be thinking, Evengier continued. *We still care for them and always will, but we must move on.*

It's your home, Adelaide pleaded.

If only Elias were here, he'd make Evengier see sense. Why had she survived, and he hadn't?

We cannot risk it, fledgling. Ysoria's thoughts were a woeful whisper.

Evengier nodded to the group of dragons in the middle of the clearing, and as one, they leapt into the sky. *May the winds be kind to you on your journey. Return as swiftly as possible.*

We will, Evengier, Swiftwings, Wiseheart, Stealthystep, Ruler of Dragons, the group replied.

They soared over the sea, the sunlight scintillating off their scales. They banked right and disappeared around the cliff, taking Adelaide's hope with them.

Chapter Seventeen

While Adelaide waited for the scouting party to return, Resse, Esa, and some of their friends, Turquan and the brothers Picot and Papin, helped her hone her dragon skills.

Cyr attempted to help as well, but his flying and hunting advice was from the perspective of a small bird, so Adelaide mostly ignored his suggestions. When she practiced breathing fire, he always conveniently had to hunt or patrol the skies.

The green male dragon, Turquan, irritated Adelaide like a pesky gnat with all his absurd flirtations. She didn't take his comments seriously because Esa had told her that he did the same with all the females his age on the island—Adelaide was just the newest and most interesting female.

But when Turquan jested once about how hot she was as she flamed at a log, her patience snapped. She turned her fire on him, knowing from what the others had told her that it wouldn't seriously injure him.

Alright, alright. I'll stop teasing you, Turquan said as he hopped out of the reach of her flames, squeezing his eyes shut.

Thank you, she said coolly.

With her new friends' coaxing and single-minded devotion that was a little too single-minded at times, Adelaide became a deadly fire-breathing beast.

She could light a tree on fire as easily as snapping her wings open, soar straight through a deluge of rain, fly faster than Resse, and soar around the island twice without breathing hard.

She could hunt as stealthily as Cyr and hardly ever missed her prey. She was dangerous and now needed no weapons but her body.

There was still the not-so-small matter of turning into a human at the most inconvenient times. Everyone suggested different solutions: plants, exercise regimens, drinking the potion again, breathing exercises, but none of the ones she tried worked. Adelaide didn't tell her friends that the problem was in her mind.

In between her rigorous training sessions, Adelaide kept trying to persuade Evengier and Ysoria to help Klinhun. Sometimes just Evengier was there, sometimes just Ysoria, and sometimes neither.

If the latter happened, she waited until one of them appeared, trying not to gouge too-deep marks in the ground and resisting the temptation to hurl fireballs at the trees. Neither of the dragons changed their mind, but Adelaide struck up a friendship with Ysoria, who was curious about humans and never annoyed by her visits.

Adelaide told Ysoria about her life in Alesfirth and what had happened to Emma, which caused only small barbs of pain to pierce her heart.

Larger stabs came when she thought about the rest of her family. What would they think if they saw her now with smoke for breath, scales for skin, and wings for soaring? Would her brother scream and flee, her mother faint? Would her father grab a rock to throw at her? Adelaide couldn't predict their reactions, so she tried not to think about them.

Ysoria told her tales of dragons past and present, and how she had caught Evengier's eye.

I was about your size, Ysoria said, gazing out at the sea. *I was soaring over the ocean near Black Beach, looking for fish. Evengier, Ganelon, and Jeharrez were on the beach flaming at each other, as males tend to do.* She smiled, and Adelaide nodded, remembering many wrestling matches between Odo, Gunter, and Conrad.

When I dove toward a school of fish, I may have twisted more than necessary. Ysoria chuckled, sending a flock of yellow-spotted birds into the air.

After eating, I flew back to the shore to relax in the hot springs, but Evengier stopped me. He said to me, "Ysoria, you are the most beautiful and fiercest dragon on this island. Would you be my mate?"

I was flattered, of course, for I knew Evengier to be a powerful and kind male. But we females like to know the males are serious, so I soared around the island as quick as I could, flamed at him as he followed, ascended high into the clouds, and dove into the depths of the sea.

He was always there, and he caught up with me as I dove into the ocean, so I linked tail and neck with him. Ever since, we have been closer than scales.

Adelaide couldn't breathe, as if a horse had kicked her in the chest. She'd never have the future that Ysoria and Evengier had. She'd never soar with someone who knew all the moves she'd make, who'd nuzzle her neck when she was upset. Her future was full of cold beds and silent days.

Before meeting Elias, she'd been too caught up with justice and revenge to think much about marriage. Now she wanted the love strung between Evengier and Ysoria more than how much she'd thirsted for justice.

She supposed she could marry someone else, but the idea had as much temptation as rotten fruit. No, if she couldn't have Elias, she didn't want anyone.

Then Adelaide shook herself. What was she thinking? Even if Elias had lived, she wouldn't have deserved him. She, a peasant, marrying a king? And the king she had longed to overthrow? It was crazier than a one-footed goose.

Did you love him? Ysoria's voice was as tender as a mother's kiss, but the words still clawed into Adelaide's heart and ripped it out, piece by piece.

She lowered her head under the agony. *It matters not now.*

To distract herself from thinking about the future she couldn't have, Adelaide asked, *Who is this Jeharrez who was with King Ganelon and Evengier on the beach?*

Ysoria's tail lowered, and her eyes dimmed. *He once was Evengier's and Ganelon's good friend. He was also the brother of Ganelon's mate, Liliath. He was strangely possessive of her and didn't react well when Ganelon took her as mate. For some reason he blamed Ganelon for Liliath's death, although it was an accident.*

So Liliath was Elias's mother. Adelaide hadn't known her name. Had Elias known about Jeharrez's anger and blame?

But mostly Jeharrez is known for being the one who tried to take rule of the colony after King Ganelon left. When the elders confronted him, he left the island, Ysoria said.

We know not where he is now. Although I am sad that he's left, he was always causing trouble, so it's probably for the best that he's gone. Ysoria turned her raindrop-clear eyes on the horizon and Adelaide followed her gaze, wondering where a dragon the size of Evengier could hide.

Chapter Eighteen

The next morning, after Adelaide caught some fish at the lake, she couldn't help looking at her reflection. She'd seen herself as a dragon several times—while soaring over the sea near Klinhun when she had first transformed, as she flew to Niclond, and twice in the past few days as she drank here, but she still wasn't accustomed to the sight of her new body.

Oblong scales whiter than eggshells shimmered silver in the sunlight. White spikes sharper than any blacksmith's creations meandered down her spine to cover her whip-like tail. Leathery-white wings embedded with tiny scales stretched out as long as her body, and curved spikes sat atop her narrow, lethal head.

At least her eyes were still the same hazel color. Larger, but the same woodsy brown. The sight of them reassured her that she was the same Adelaide beneath all these scales.

But did she want to be the same Adelaide? The same one who had led young men to their deaths and who couldn't be a dragon longer than two days because of doubts that clung like shells to the rocks on the coast?

Admiring yourself? If you want to admire me or even be my mate, I would be greatly honored, Turquan said as he walked over. Apparently, his promise to stop teasing her had ended with her training.

There you are, Adelaide. Resse and Esa came over, accompanied by Picot and Papin—the brothers who had helped with her training. *We've been looking for you,* Resse said. *The scouting party has just returned from Neklosa.*

Adelaide's tail flicked. *When?*

Just now. Turquan and I were flying over the east side of the island and saw them. We met everyone else on the way to find you. Resse bounced on his feet. *Come on.*

Adelaide's heart beat in time with her wings as they flew to Caterwaul Cliffs where Evengier and Ysoria roosted. However selfish it sounded, she hoped the Neklosians had turned down the dragons' request so they would have to go to Klinhun and bring lasting peace to her people.

When the group reached the cliffs, there were so many dragons that she couldn't see the ground or any vegetation, just scales, spines, and tails of all colors and sizes.

Their group drifted in the air with several others. The drafts from their wings made it challenging to stay aloft, but Adelaide's training had made her stronger. For once, it was easy to remain a dragon, so eager was she to hear what the scouts would say.

She glanced down to where a crimson male with green and blue scales spoke to Evengier. He, Evengier, and Ysoria were surrounded by a group of dragons with drooping necks and tails, some of whom looked to be dozing on their feet. They must have been the scouts who had traveled to Neklosa.

Then, Your Highness, we landed in Neklosa at night, as you suggested, the crimson male was saying. *It took us awhile to find the buildings where the rulers lived, and even then, we weren't sure if it was the right place.*

There Ulia, Vane, and I landed on the roofs while Godichal and Lictina flew overhead as sentries. I tapped on the roof to get one of the human's attention. Two armed men came up.

They were frozen with fright at the sight of us, and one of them threw a sharpened stick at me. It fell to the roof, and before they could shoot more or run away, I hummed peaceful music while Ulia explained why we were there and that we wished to see the king.

It took the men a while to understand, or perhaps they were merely frightened, but finally one of them left to fetch their king. The other remained, watching warily, though he had put his weapon down. I was glad that my music worked on humans.

Soon the guard returned with the king and queen, both of whom were bewildered and frightened. The queen nearly fell over at the sight of us, but her mate held her up. As I continued humming, Ulia explained who we were, where we came from, and why we were there—everything we discussed with you beforehand about what we should say.

After much deliberation between the king and queen and another man, the king determined that we could stay in Neklosa as long as we needed to, on several conditions. We could remain as long as we protected the Neklosians from invading countries and didn't harm their people.

Humans almost always want something in return, Evengier muttered in their minds. Louder, he said to the speaker, *Continue your tale, Harchier.*

The dragon inclined his head. *There is not much more to say, Your Highness. The humans offered us their roofs to sleep on and any deer or other creature we found in their forests to eat, and the water in a nearby pond to refresh ourselves. No one disturbed us, though large crowds came to see us. Thankfully, no one tried to harm us.*

We left the next night. We had no trouble on the return flight and flew as swiftly as possible to bring the good news to you.

Evengier nodded. *Thank you for the account.* He looked at the other members of the scouting party. *Do you all confirm the veracity of Harchier's tale?*

We do, they thought as one.

Does anyone have anything else to add? Evengier asked.

Only this, a female with orange spikes said, *although Neklosa is not as full of bounty and as large as Klinhun, it is still a good place to live with forests and friendly people, at least as far as we could tell from our brief time there.*

Adelaide suppressed a growl at the female's unhelpful words.

Very well. Evengier raised his head, towering above those on the ground. *Elders, what think you of this tale?*

It would be foolish not to accept the Neklosians' hospitality when we are in such desperate need of it, a female said.

A male covered in patches of dark blue said, *I don't think we need to fear a trap. We could always fly away if we sensed danger.*

That is a good point, Nicaise. Evengier looked at a spring-green dragon with four red feet who stood with the scouting dragons. *The humans spoke the truth, Vane?*

He nodded. *They had no desire to deceive us.*

Evengier flicked his tail. *Good. Unexpected but good.* He glanced back at the largest dragons standing in a ring around the scouting party. *Do any of the other elders wish to speak?*

We must do what is best for our colony, Ysoria said.

Evengier gazed at his mate for several heartbeats, then turned to the thunder of dragons. *Very well. It is decided. Our colony shall leave for Neklosa in a fortnight.*

The dragons roared their approval, but Adelaide lowered her head, the burden of saving Klinhun back on her shoulders. As it settled on her like a cart heaped full of coal, she realized how ready and eager she had been to give this pressure and weight to someone else.

But she couldn't shirk this duty; Elias had given it to her, and it was the weight she'd gladly bear to make things better.

The dragons hadn't been the ones to shatter the hope for a better Klinhun in the first place.

Adelaide just couldn't think about what would happen if she failed, because then *she* would shatter.

Chapter Nineteen

Cyr, we're leaving, Adelaide said as she landed near Caldera Lake. *The dragons aren't going to help us.*

The hawk flew down from a moss-robed tree and landed on her tail. A fish dangled from his beak. *Why not?*

Because they are going to go hide out in Neklosa.

And we needed their help to defeat the Gyndilians?

Yes. Adelaide's tail struck a tree, the spines getting stuck. She thrust herself forward, growling. *But we'll just have to do it ourselves. Like always.*

She retrieved her satchel from where she'd kept it in the hollow of a tree these last few days.

You're forgetting that you have us, Resse's voice rolled into Adelaide's mind as he landed beside her, followed by Esa, Picot, and Turquan. The latter winked at her.

What are you doing here? She asked.

We're going with you to Klinhun, of course, Resse said.

You can't come. Your king forbids it. What will happen if he finds out? He's your father, Resse.

The yellow dragon arched his neck. *Yes, but I'm old enough to make my own decisions, especially when his seem short-sighted.*

But I'm sure he won't be happy to find out that you've left, Adelaide pointed out.

Nay, Resse said. *But he won't be around to do anything about it.*

Where's your brother? Adelaide asked Picot. She never saw one without the other.

Picot's tail coiled by his feet. *He doesn't want to leave the mate he's chosen in case another mate chooses her.*

I don't understand why he's so worried, Turquan said. *Letselina has cared for him since they were hatchlings.*

Picot shrugged. *He doesn't want to take the risk.*

Although I love females, Turquan smiled at Adelaide and Esa, *I wouldn't miss the opportunity to get off this tiny island even for the most beautiful female dragon who soared the skies.*

It'll be dangerous, Adelaide warned them. *You could be injured or even killed by humans.*

Turquan stretched his legs in the dirt. *We're not that easy to kill, Sweetscales, and you'll need our help.*

Adelaide shot sparks at Turquan; he just wrinkled his snout at her.

I'll be quicker alone, she said.

Esa frowned at her. *Wasn't the purpose of your visit to acquire the dragons' help?*

Yes.

Then why are you turning it down?

How could Adelaide tell her and the others that she didn't want them to end up like Elias, bleeding his life out for her mistakes, or Gunter, a murderer with her weapon in his hands? That she wasn't a good leader and didn't want this attempt to fail as miserably as the rebellion.

She could still remember standing before Elias and Berold in the throne room, where the fate of the boys from Alesfirth hung from her words, how Hubert's shoulders quivered under her hand, how she was the reason for his terror and the threat of death looming over them all.

How she couldn't face doing that all over again for these friends who had already helped her so much. What if Resse caught an arrow from an enemy? Or it was Esa who trembled with terror in the face of some dangerous position that Adelaide had led them into?

And who was *she* to lead them when she hardly knew anything about dragons and could barely remain one for longer than a day?

But at the dragons' offer there was also relief, sweet like the first raspberries of summer. Relief that she wouldn't have to fly into danger alone, relief that someone else would help carry this burden.

With these thoughts, though, came loathing at herself because the relief came at the expense of putting her friends in danger.

Adelaide couldn't say all this, so she said nothing.

Resse must have understood at least some of her thoughts, though, for he said, *Don't fret. I've been to Klinhun many times. We understand the risks, and we'll be careful.*

Creaking and crunching came from the trees on their right, and they turned toward the sounds.

A dragon with pale blue scales and red spikes emerged from the trees, his eyes narrowed at them. Adelaide's tail stiffened.

It was the dragon who had eyed her with suspicion during the meeting with the elders.

Chapter Twenty

I hear that you hatchlings are planning to travel to Klinhun on your own, the blue dragon said. *Is this correct?*

Another familiar dragon with brown and white spots joined the first.

Papin? What are you doing here? Picot asked in horror.

I'm sorry, Picot, but I couldn't let you disobey our king. Besides, how can five dragons take on an entire army? You'll be killed.

At least I'll be killed fighting for the people our ancestors protected rather than hiding out in Neklosa.

The blue-scaled dragon growled. *So, it's true, then. You are leaving to go to Klinhun?* He glared at Adelaide, and the heat of his gaze made her look away.

Yes, but it's not Adelaide's fault, Resse said. *Before you arrived, she was trying to convince us not to go. But we choose to protect the Klinians as our ancestors did.*

Now the blue dragon turned his narrowed gaze on Resse. *Does your father know?*

Resse glanced away. *Nay. He wouldn't let us go.*

Then he must have a good reason for it. Come, call off this foolhardy journey and help us prepare for the journey to Neklosa.

I'm sorry, Quabin, Redspikes, Problemsolver, but we cannot. We must help the Klinians, or their country is lost.

Quabin measured Resse's confident stance for a long moment, then the rest of them. Adelaide's scales tightened as she wondered what the elder dragon would do next. She doubted he would seriously injure the others, but didn't know if the dragons' loyalty to each other extended to her as well.

Very well, Quabin said with finality. *I will call your father and the other elders so they can try to talk some sense into you.*

He opened his mouth to roar, and Adelaide said to her friends, *Come on. We must leave before the others arrive and outnumber us.*

She shot into the sky as a roar bellowed below. It took her a few wingbeats to realize that only Turquan and Picot followed her. *Where are Resse and Esa?*

Picot and Turquan glanced around in confusion. *I thought they followed us,* Turquan said.

Adelaide told them to wait as she soared back down to the trees.

Below, Resse was clutching a monkey in his talons as Quabin stood on his tail, anchoring him to the ground. Esa was trying to plead with Quabin to let him go. Adelaide knew tenderhearted Esa would never hurt another creature unless she had to, and from what Elias had told her about the dragons, she doubted they would injure Esa and Resse.

Well, Adelaide had no such qualms. She was desperate. And what she had in mind wouldn't seriously hurt Quabin and might actually hurt her more. But it was the only idea she had.

As she dove toward the elder dragon, she told Resse and Esa, *Leave the monkey and go!*

Then she pummeled into Quabin's side like a fist, knocking

him off Resse and giving herself a mighty headache.

The force of her dive launched her into the trees. They toppled and fell onto her.

Groaning, she used her fire to incinerate the branches that entangled her. Then she shot out of the bracken toward her friends.

Sorry about that, she told Quabin as she flew over him and Papin, *but the Klinians need our help.*

Adelaide followed Resse and Esa toward the others, then they flew as fast as possible toward Klinhun.

That was close, she said, shaking some branches off her neck, which sent a stab of pain up through her head.

I'm sorry, Picot said. *I didn't realize Papin would tell an elder our plan.*

Esa's tail tapped his neck. *He loves you, but he also has a duty to his colony and king.*

Resse shook his head, his tail drooping. *I can't believe I had to leave my monkeys behind. They'll wonder where I've gone.*

They wouldn't have survived on Klinhun anyway, Adelaide told him as Esa rubbed her head against his neck. *Aren't you more worried about what your father will do when he sees you again?*

No. He might chastise me, but he'll forgive me. The monkeys aren't as wise or forgiving.

Adelaide glanced back to see if the elders were pursuing them. She saw nothing but the fading shape of the island's volcanoes.

They won't pursue us, Turquan said, following her gaze.

How do you know?

They know that the only way to stop us now is by force, and they won't risk hurting us. We're on our own now.

Chapter Twenty-One

The return flight was much more enjoyable than the first. Adelaide's wings didn't wear out nearly as fast, and her body only transformed without her consent once. The dragons' rich songs and stories were more riveting than seagull chatter.

From far away and long ago we come,
with talons to protect and souls full of wisdom.

Always with the humans we have dwelled,
the virtues of justice and truth we have upheld.

Mighty King Vannes was the first we know,
conquering the wicked human Gunric, a great foe.
He created between man and dragon a bond of trust
that remained strong through many a tempest.

Next rose the just King Halibran,
teaching the humans for their life's short span,

while Queen Keina sheltered the lost,
dragon and human both without cost.

Powerful King Aloysius then reigned,
and for his peace and kindness to all he was famed.
But the serenity and peace were not to last.
Like a spark, envy and distrust spread fast.

Our fearsome forefathers fled
rather than see their human friends dead.
Some may say this was foolish,
but at least none can say that we are brutish.

Although power and strength throbs through our bodies,
our hearts hum with compassion and a desire to please.

So, with our fierce bodies do not be frightened or fooled,
it is with the strength of our souls that we have ruled.

Turquan's voice soared over the notes, perfect and peaceful, sending sweet contentment through Adelaide.

Is your gift music? She asked him.

Yes. Did I thrill you with my musical capabilities? I can also hum well.

Adelaide shook her head and looked at the lavender dragon. *What's yours, Esa?*

Healing. I can heal dragons with just a touch. Some can do it with merely a breath.

Adelaide nodded, remembering how Elias had healed her from more than mere physical wounds. Too bad Esa hadn't been around that day to heal him or that he couldn't have healed himself.

Adelaide turned to Picot. *What's yours?*

Understanding. I can share the past with others through memories if I touch them like what happened when we heard of King Ganelon and Prince Elias's death.

After a solemn silence of remembering, Esa turned her indigo gaze on Adelaide. *What's your gift?*

Adelaide frowned. *I don't know. I don't think I have one.*

I'm sure you do. All dragons have a gift.

But I'm also a human.

I doubt that matters. I'm sure your gift is just sleeping inside you, Esa reassured her. *It will no doubt manifest itself when you need it.*

Did the humans in the past who turned into dragons have gifts? Adelaide asked.

We believe so, although the stories are a bit unclear, as the human-dragons already had so many unusual abilities, Picot explained.

Why do you need these things called gifts if you can fly? Cyr launched off Adelaide's head and streaked through the wispy whiteness of a cloud.

Good point. Adelaide sped after him, using her sense of smell to find him. But she couldn't help feeling that possessing one of these special gifts was essential to being a dragon and she wouldn't truly be one without it.

She wasn't sure why she craved that so much, though. She was a human first and foremost, and her loyalty lay with them above anyone else. She could fly, flame, and roar like a dragon. Why couldn't that be good enough?

On the third morning of their journey, Adelaide spotted a brown speck on the horizon—a seed drifting through the sky of the sea—which she took to be the coastline of Klinhun.

All the eagerness she'd felt about being back in Klinhun evaporated. Too soon, she'd have to put those she loved at risk. Again. Her stomach burbled as if she'd eaten too many caramels at the Fire Festival.

Picot stretched out his neck. *Is that it? Klinhun?*

I can't believe we are this close to our homeland. Esa flicked her tail, her indigo eyes wide.

I wonder what the female humans are like. Turquan glanced at Adelaide. *Are they all as fierce and fiery as you? If so, I might settle for a human mate.*

Adelaide wasn't sure if she should be offended or flattered by his words.

A human mate? Picot's jaw fell open as he surveyed Turquan.

None of you will be disappointed—by the land, I mean, not the females. Resse flew in a tight circle above them. *I've only seen a small portion of the land, but what I saw was magnificent. There's so much space to fly. The forests are bursting with animals to eat, and the mountains are full of caves to live in. The humans are curious creatures and greatly in need of our help.*

Adelaide could now make out the white, sheer cliffs of Dhalion and the castle that stood like a glistening crown atop the cliffs' head, its sapphire-blue tiles glinting in the morning sun.

A few storm-scarred boats bobbed in the waves where the land sloped down to the water. But her eyes kept wandering back to the fortress, the place that had held both the home and end of the one she'd loved.

What's that large, brown sculpted rock sitting on top of the cliff? Turquan stared at the stronghold.

That's the castle where King Ganelon and Prince Elias lived, Resse explained.

Adelaide glanced back at her friends. *Wait here until it's dark, then once it's safe, I'll return and bring you to shore.*

Is that when you will introduce us to your friends? Esa asked.

Adelaide hadn't thought much about what she would do with her dragon friends when she arrived in Klinhun; she had been preoccupied with just getting them there and what to do about the impending war.

Not only would she need to introduce the dragons to her friends from Alesfirth, she would need to present them to Berold. Easy as throwing a dagger at a tree blindfolded.

She had the desperate desire to flee, to leave the task to someone else. But she couldn't, and the humans and dragons would have to work together if they were going to save their country.

So, Adelaide took a deep breath, reminding herself that Elias had believed in her and that these dragons did too.

Yes. I'll introduce you to them once it's dark, so not every-one will see you. But right now, I must prepare them. She had to make sure that Conrad and the others were doing well. And think of a way to approach Berold without being arrested. Her tail spiraled down at the thought.

Very well. We'll wait here. Resse landed in the sun-sprin-kled water with a large splash. The others followed, looking like brilliantly colored seabirds bobbing on the waves.

Hurry back, Silverscales. Turquan winked, and Adelaide glared at him before turning and soaring toward Dhalion.

It's good to be back, Cyr said as he glided beside her. *All the rain on the island made my feathers heavy. And despite having that rule not to eat birds, some of the dragons looked at me like they wanted to eat me.*

I wouldn't have let them. Adelaide surveyed the approach-ing shore. *I missed Klinhun too, but we still have lots of work to do.*

At least we're not alone.

Adelaide still wasn't sure if that was a good thing or not, so she just grunted.

When she could make out silhouettes of men in the bob-bing boats below, she landed in the water and morphed into a human.

The once-gentle lapping of the sea became hands trying

to pull her into its mouth. The slight annoying itchiness of the saltwater now burned her eyes and made her cough and splutter. Her dress dragged her down, and she kicked furiously to stay above the relentless waves.

She'd forgotten how weak and fragile her human body was. How had Elias managed to remain human for as long as he had?

Catch this, Cyr. She tossed him her satchel, and he caught it in his talons. Now her arms were free to help keep her afloat.

You look like a dying fish, Cyr observed. *Do you need help?*

I don't think there's anything you can do. Adelaide concentrated on moving toward the shore, which suddenly seemed impossibly far away. She could no longer reach it with just a few thrust of her wings.

And how would she keep from being dashed to pieces against those massive, hungry-for-desolation boulders on her left?

Nonetheless, Adelaide kept her gaze on the sandy beach and swam for shore, glad she had swum nearly every day in the Lentiasa River during the summers with Emma, Conrad, and Gunter.

The thought of her once-best friend sent claws ripping into her heart. Even if she found and forgave him, they'd never be able to laugh as lightheartedly as they had on those summer afternoons with nothing but sunlight and smiles between them.

Adelaide would never again be able to see him without seeing him standing behind Elias's prone form. She'd never be able to glimpse him now without remembering her own part. The easy friendship they once had would be gone.

The thought was enough to drown her. And why not? Why not let the water just take her into its cool, quiet depths where nothing could hurt her or her loved ones?

She saw Elias's stern gaze in her mind and remembered the dragons waiting for her on the waves. And Odo ... she had to keep fighting so Odo could have a better future.

Adelaide thrust her arms out and sucked in air, but her muscles burned. She still had about a stone's throw to go.

"Oh, my. What are you doing out in the water by yourself, lass?" A barnacle-encrusted boat drifted beside her, and a man with mahogany skin and tousled grey hair leaned over the side.

"Well, I …" Adelaide thought frantically for a good excuse, "my handkerchief flew into the water, and I went to get it, but the water carried me out."

"It's a good thing I saw you then. Come on." He reached out a wrinkled hand toward her, and she grasped it, pulling herself into the boat.

I'm glad you made it. I thought about pulling you out by your hair, Cyr said from above her.

I don't think that would have worked very well.

Cyr soared close to her head, making the man cry out, then flew toward the shore. *Now that I know you're safe, I'm going to hunt.*

Be careful.

You too.

Adelaide returned her attention to the man who still stared after Cyr. "What a mighty fine-looking bird." He turned back and grabbed the oars. "So, what's your name?"

Adelaide undid her soaking braid and combed her fingers through the black strands. "Emma." She wasn't sure if Berold was still looking for her, so it was best to keep her identity a secret until she met the swordmaster on her own terms.

He nodded. "Please, sit." He gestured behind her, and she sat on a plank of wood between two pails of fish. Water in the bottom of the boat sloshed over her boots.

"You must be more careful. There are many dangerous currents out here. Even I have to keep my wits about me, and I've fished here for thirty-four winters."

Adelaide nodded. "I will. Thanks for helping me."

As they drew near the beach, Adelaide realized that the stalls she had once walked through, marveling at the mounds of fruit, spices, and silks, were barren. No one sold anything in the market, and even up by the houses, the streets were deserted.

But shouts, the stomping of boots, and the clanging of metal on metal resounded from the castle grounds up to her right. Helmets, chain mail, and swords flashed in the sun.

"What's happening?" She asked the fisherman.

The dinghy's hull slid onto the sand, and the man dropped the oars. He scrutinized her. "I take it you haven't been here long, lass?"

"Nay. I just arrived this morning with my family from the outskirts of Fernohn. We don't get much news there."

The man's face sagged as he gazed at the shapes of men training above. "The word is that the Gyndilians are amassing on our borders by the hundreds and will begin invading our northern border any day now."

Adelaide stood, her heart pounding as loud as the waves on the rocks. "Truly?"

When the man glanced back at her, his eyes were a hundred years old. "That's not the worst of it." He wiped a hand across his brow. "I hear that the Gyndilians have captured the town of Alesfirth."

Chapter Twenty-Two

Gunter landed on trembling legs. When he was certain that he wouldn't topple over, he stretched his arms. He had never ridden horses much in Alesfirth, and now he had ridden one nonstop for more than a month. His legs and rear were not happy with him.

"Welcome to the town of Neikurn, runt." Baldwin bumped into him on his way to tie up his mount. "It's fairer than any of your mountain towns, I'm sure."

The Gyndilian town didn't strike Gunter as anything special. It consisted of flat, wooden buildings clumped together among a grove of evergreens between two crisp-cold mountains crowned with snow.

Men and women went about their business in the cool duskiness of a spring evening. Soldiers in black-and-silver chain mail chatted to each other in groups or watched the people around them with stern expressions.

"Ah." Leofric stretched. "It's good to be around our own people again. I'm going to drink myself to sleep tonight, I will."

Gunter's captors had discarded their peasant clothes as soon as they had escaped the outpost on Klinhun's border. They now wore shiny black boots and brightly colored tunics embedded in the right shoulder with a raven holding a sword in its talons, the emblem of Gyndilad. Their swords hung proudly out of silver girdles, proclaiming to everyone that they were knights.

"Don't forget we're leaving at dawn for the Master's camp," Dunstan reminded Leofric. "If you're not ready, we'll leave without you, and you can deal with the consequences."

"You're always so uptight, Dunstan." Ligulf chewed on a piece of grass. "When we return to Brandorf, it will be all work and no women. Come on, Leofric."

The brothers disappeared into the tavern and boisterous singing slipped through the open door.

"So, the great knights of Gyndilad have returned." A man with a bushy black beard walked toward them.

"Good-evening, Goddard." Baldwin nodded to the man.

"Where have you been this time?" Goddard's eyes flickered to Gunter.

"Klinhun." Baldwin's smirk belied his carefree attitude.

"Oh?" Goddard's eyebrows rose, and he glanced again at Gunter. "Doing what?"

"We're not allowed to give you that information, as you well know," Dunstan replied, lancing Baldwin with a look.

Baldwin scowled at him, then turned back to Goddard. "That's right. The Master forbade us to share the information with anyone." But the way Baldwin chewed the inside of his cheek and kept glancing at Dunstan made Gunter think that Baldwin wished very much to gloat about his secret mission. It wouldn't take much ale to slosh the truth out of him.

Dunstan mounted his horse. "It's been a pleasure seeing you, Goddard, but since I haven't seen my wife and daughter since before the first of winter, I'd like to—"

"Wait," Goddard held up a hand. "Have you heard the news about Alesfirth?"

Gunter gripped his cloak so hard that his hands turned red. He felt Dunstan's and Baldwin's gazes on him.

"What news?" Dunstan asked, and Baldwin stepped so close to Gunter that the man's shoulder brushed his. Gunter fought the urge to step away.

"Our men have taken the town. About a fortnight ago now. A messenger came and told us a few days ago. There was little resistance, apparently." He stroked his beard. "It'll only be a matter of time now, I reckon, before King Aethelmaer rules all of Klinhun."

Gunter again saw the glint of blades and the river of crimson running through the streets of Alesfirth. He smelled smoke as Gyndilians burned the town.

Ashes and bile coated his mouth; Adelaide's scream rose over the clamor of fighting. But this time, it was Elysande's empty blue eyes staring up at him, not Emma's. And it was his wail that rent the air, not his friend's.

"Gunter, Gunter," someone said from faraway. A hand shook him, and Gunter blinked. He was looking at Dunstan's blue eyes, not Elysande's. *She and Mother are alive. Conrad and Father would have taken care of them,* he told himself. Unless they had been … but no, he couldn't think about that.

"This one's a little mad," Baldwin told Goddard, who was staring at him.

The man took a step back.

"Much has happened while we've been gone," Dunstan said. "I'm happy to hear of Alesfirth's capture. Pray, tell me, how many were killed in the fight?"

Goddard tore his eyes off Gunter. "I'm not certain, but I believe only about a dozen of our men were killed. A few more were wounded."

"How many Klinians were killed?" Gunter asked, his voice creaking.

Goddard frowned. "That I'm less certain of. Can't have been more than a score. Several were captured to be servants and soldiers." He narrowed his eyes at Gunter. "Why do you ask?"

"He's from there," Baldwin replied, "but now he works for us."

"Ah. Very good. Keep a watchful eye on the rabble."

Baldwin placed a firm hand on Gunter's shoulder. "We do."

"And now, I'll take the prisoner with me." Dunstan glanced at Gunter. "Come along. You'll be staying with me tonight."

"With you and your family?" Baldwin stuttered. "Certainly, you don't want this pig reeking up your house on your one night with your family. Nay," Baldwin's grip tightened on Gunter's shoulder, and he bit his tongue to keep from crying out, "he can stay with the men and I at the inn. We'll keep a good watch on him. He won't escape."

"No, he won't." Dunstan pierced Gunter with a look as if reminding him of his failed attempt to flee and how pointless it was to try. "And I have complete faith that you could take care of him, Baldwin. But I wish for him to meet my family. He must be as tired of looking at your faces as I am."

"You want him to meet your family?" Baldwin's mouth opened so large that a whole apple could fit inside, and Goddard rubbed his beard.

"Yes, I do. We'll meet you and the others here at dawn." Dunstan prodded Gunter with his eyes. "Come on. I'm anxious to get home." He urged his horse down the muddy road.

Gunter remounted—which was the last thing he wanted to do—and followed Dunstan, leaving the two men staring after them.

"Why do you want me to meet your family?"

"Because I want you to see another side of Gyndilad besides fighting and boasting knights. And perhaps because I feel sorry for you. You seem to be a good man and should be married by now, not taken from your home to serve your enemy. Alas, fortune seems to favor Gyndilad right now."

Gunter didn't know what to think of Dunstan's treatment of him. It was more than he'd expected from any Gyndilian.

The man saw him not as an enemy to be scorned, but as a man to be listened to and respected. It made Gunter want to treat Dunstan the same way.

They halted in front of a two-story cedar house flanked on either side by fir trees. Red and yellow flowers grew in bushes in front of the house. The cleanliness and size of the place took Gunter by surprise because hardly anyone in Klinhun had two-story houses. At least not in Alesfirth or Dhalion.

Dunstan stared at the house for a long moment, rubbing his beard, then said, "Come on. Let's clean and stable the horses. They deserve a rest."

Dunstan led him behind the house to another smaller, wooden building where they fed and groomed the horses.

"When was the last time you saw your family?" Gunter asked as they walked back to the house.

"Too long." Dunstan yanked the door open. "Ailith? Are you home? Elgiva?"

"Papa!" A high-pitched squeal splintered the silence. A girl no more than three winters old, with curly brown hair, streaked through the room and clobbered Dunstan's legs. "Papa! Papa!"

The knight knelt and picked the girl up. He tossed her into the air, and she shrieked in delight.

"How I've missed you, Elgiva." Dunstan held her close. "Can you wrestle bears yet?"

The girl giggled and threw her arms around him. Dunstan smiled, a rare sight.

"You're home." A woman with hair the same color as her daughter's stood in the doorway to another room. Dunstan set down his daughter to hug his wife and kissed her so long that Gunter glanced away.

The family reunion made him thirst so much for his own that his knees quivered; he thought he might drop to the ground like a sack of turnips.

Would he ever play hide-and-catch again with Elysande? Or hear his mother cluck her tongue at him for stealing stray bits of food? Wrestle with Conrad after dinner or walk with his father through the fields?

"Papa, papa." The little girl had noticed Gunter; she pulled on her father's trousers and pointed at him.

Dunstan picked her up and turned to Gunter. "This, my fair Ailith, is Gunter." He placed an arm around his wife. "He is a prisoner from Klinhun. We're taking him to the Master."

She nodded at him, her eyes sad. "Welcome, Gunter. I'm sorry that you've come to our home for such a horrible reason."

Gunter blinked. He hadn't expected empathy from the wife of a Gyndilian soldier. But since Dunstan didn't treat him as an enemy, he shouldn't be surprised that his wife didn't either.

"Thank you, Lady Ailith, for letting me into your home. I know it's not the best time, since you haven't seen your husband in a long while. It's nice, though, not to have to sleep outside."

Ailith smiled, then turned to her husband. "How long are you staying this time, dear?"

His grin vanished. "We must leave at dawn."

The woman's eyes filled with tears, and Gunter turned his attention to an embroidery of a boar hunt that covered the back wall. He tried to block out their conversation, but when Ailith mentioned Alesfirth, his attention snapped back to the couple.

"Yes, I know," Dunstan said, glancing at Gunter. "Goddard told us outside the tavern."

"Well, I'm glad you didn't bring Baldwin and those two brothers with you," Ailith said. "I can't handle their company or their stink. Speaking of which ..." She stepped away from him. "You are in desperate need of a bath, my dear."

"Oh, am I?"

Ailith looked at Gunter. "And you probably would like one as well?"

"Yes, please." They hadn't bathed for at least five days, when they had come across a stream in the mountains.

After they washed in tubs behind the house, Gunter dressed in some clothes Dunstan loaned him which were much too big, but at least they were clean.

Ailith's cooking tempted Gunter to stay forever, especially after so many meals of stale bread and cheese. He tried not to devour the mushroom-stuffed mutton, fleecy white bread, and roasted carrots too fast. He didn't succeed.

As they ate, Dustan explained where they'd been and what he'd been doing the last few months. When he mentioned they had been to Dhalion, Ailith's hand froze on her piece of bread.

"Dhalion? What were you doing there?"

"Gunter was part of a rebellion to overthrow the king and was supposed to meet them there." Dunstan told her all that had happened since Gunter's capture up to their arrival in Neikurn.

When he finished, Ailith turned to Gunter. "So, you're the one responsible for the king of Klinhun's death?"

When she put it like that, so open and straightforward, the full responsibility of what he'd done crashed down on him like a blacksmith's hammer. Would it be his fault then, when and if Klinhun fell to Gyndilad? When all he loved was taken from him by the Gyndilians?

At the time, he'd only been thinking of stopping the prince from talking to Adelaide, from stealing his family's hard-earned goods and money. But what if it had caused a worse evil to befall the land—the Gyndilians killing his family and friends?

Gunter nearly choked on his bite of mutton as he considered the consequences of throwing that dagger at King Elias's back. He coughed and said in a strangled voice, "Yes."

The woman laid a hand on his arm, and he glanced up, startled. "You must be very brave to go through this ordeal."

Gunter shook his head, no longer sure if he had done the right thing by killing Elias. "Murdering someone's not brave."

"Not always." Ailith chose her words carefully. "But standing up for your countrymen is brave. And entering a country that is at war with your own most definitely is."

Gunter grunted. "I didn't have a choice in the matter."

"Mayhap not." Ailith removed her hand, but her words still soothed him. "But I can tell you haven't given in to despair despite all that you've gone through. Continue to hold onto hope and keep fighting for your people. The Master will no doubt show you mercy since you upheld your bargain."

She took a sip of wine. "I know you must miss your home and family terribly, but know that not everyone in Gyndilad wishes to conquer the world. Many of us wish for peace between the two countries and hold no grudge against Klinhun."

Ailith held her goblet up to him, and Gunter did likewise. Perhaps the Gyndilians weren't so bad after all.

Gunter slept in the stable even though Ailith said he could sleep by the fire. He wanted to give the family privacy and didn't want to wake them with his nightmares. It was a good thing he did, for they came like wolves hunting sheep.

He dreamed that he stood on the cliff where he had killed King Elias except that Dunstan, not the king, knelt before him.

Gunter aimed a dagger at his heart.

"Kill him!" Baldwin roared from somewhere.

Gunter thrust his dagger into Dunstan's chest, and he fell over, groaning.

"No!" Ailith screamed. Then their daughter, Elgiva, ran over, wailing. She turned into Gunter's sister, pounding him with tiny fists.

The deeper boom of fists on the door woke Gunter. He bolted upright, sweating and trembling.

The door opened, and a sliver of moonlight slipped in. "It's just me," Dunstan said. "It's time to leave."

While Gunter gathered his scant belongings, Dunstan said, "I'm surprised you didn't try to flee."

"I wouldn't know how to get home from here," Gunter said, and Dunstan nodded. Of course, that wouldn't have stopped Adelaide.

Perhaps the real reason Gunter hadn't fled was that he'd been too afraid to try, afraid of getting lost, of real wolves hunting him, Gyndilians shooting arrows at him, and a hundred other possibilities.

And he hadn't wanted to bring trouble on Dunstan and Ailith who had been so kind to him. That last may have seemed a paltry excuse to any Klinian, but it made Gunter less ashamed for not having tried to escape in the night.

After Ailith and Dunstan said their goodbyes, Ailith turned to him. "Farewell, Gunter. I'm glad I got to meet a Klinian despite what's happening between our countries. Remember what I said about bravery. True strength lies on the inside, not the outside. I'm sure you'll need it in the coming days."

Chapter Twenty-Three

Three days later, Baldwin stopped the group on a grassy plain. The mountains they'd traversed jutted up behind them.

"We should blindfold the runt since we're nearing the Master's camp." Baldwin dismounted and marched toward Gunter. "Dismount, filthy worm." He licked his rotten teeth as if he could taste Gunter's terror and enjoyed it. Then he grabbed Gunter's horse's reins. "Go on."

Gunter thought briefly about tackling Baldwin—something that Adelaide would do. The others would pin Gunter down before he could do much damage to the man, but at least he could face the mountain lion, the Master, with pride, knowing he'd done everything he could to escape.

But Baldwin's bulk towered over Gunter as he leered at him. Gunter had never won a fight before. They had only ever brought him bruised skin and bruised pride. He might as well save his energy for when he did face the mountain lion.

Although, what could a rabbit do before a lion? Nothing but flee, and he wasn't even courageous enough to do that. All he could do was sit and cower.

No wonder Adelaide hadn't wanted anything to do with him. Women needed men who could protect them or at least stand next to them side-by-side as they faced danger, not men who lay down in the dirt with their hands over their eyes.

Gunter dismounted onto trembling legs.

"There's no need to blindfold him," Dunstan said. "He doesn't know where we are."

"He might, and we can't take the risk if he escapes. He's a prisoner, and it would do well to remember that." Baldwin pulled out a too-familiar strip of cloth and tied it tightly against Gunter's eyes so that he saw nothing but a dim light around the edges.

Baldwin helped him mount, nearly pushing him off the horse on the other side. Gunter grasped the horse's mane before he could topple over. His fingers shook no matter how much he tried to still them.

"I'll hold his horse," Dunstan announced, and Gunter relaxed his grip on the mane. The man would do his best to not let any harm come to him.

Gunter wished he could thank the man somehow; even such a small thing made facing the mountain lion a little more bearable.

"Fine. Let's go," Baldwin said. "We should reach Brandorf by sundown."

After a long, exhausting ride, someone ripped off Gunter's blindfold. He blinked in the fading light of the sun. The familiar haphazard wooden-and-stone buildings of the Master's camp surrounded them.

Despair sucked at Gunter, pulling him down like the icy, murky waters of the Lentiasa River when he'd almost drowned as a boy. Then, Conrad's sure hand had pulled him out until Gunter's feet touched mud. But now no one could save him except himself.

He looked behind him to the south, where somewhere

Alesfirth lay, possibly smoking and in ruins. It seemed to point an accusatory finger at him, wondering why he let others bully him and didn't come help. The finger looked a lot like Adelaide's.

Gunter turned away, sickened by his own inaction. It was almost a relief to follow Baldwin into the camp.

Black-and-silver-uniformed Gyndilians called out greetings to Gunter's captors. Nearly all of them stared at Gunter, and he hunched in his seat.

After handing their mounts over to the stableman, they strode toward the building where Gunter's fate would once again be decided.

The glassy eyes of the boar, deer, and bear heads lining the walls inside the Master's house stared at Gunter as if they knew he would soon share a similar fate.

The group stopped in front of a table where the Master sat writing on a piece of parchment. Gunter wondered if the man ever left the table; it had been the only place he'd seen him on his prior stay here after the Gyndilians had kidnapped him on his way to find Adelaide.

Then, he'd made a deal with the Master to overthrow or kill King Ganelon in exchange for his freedom and no war.

And here he was, still a captive, and Alesfirth attacked. Again.

A dog with droopy skin sitting beside the Master barked, and Gunter jumped. The Master stroked the dog above its scarred left eye. Unlike his dog, the Master didn't need a scar to make himself look rough; his haggard, mustached face did that.

Baldwin clutched Gunter's arm; did he think Gunter would try to attack the man or flee when a guard stood to their right and another outside the door?

"Master," Baldwin said in a voice greasier than a smoked hog, "our mission was a success, and we have brought the prisoner."

There was only the scritch of the quill on the parchment.

Leofric and Ligulf exchanged a nervous glance.

When Gunter thought he might wet himself from the suspense, the Master laid his quill down and turned eyes the color of river silt on them.

"Welcome back to Gyndilad. I know the mission was a success because Dunstan wrote a letter and sent it to me by pigeon weeks ago. I expected the words to be in your hand, Baldwin, since you were the one who was supposed to lead this mission."

Baldwin's face flushed. "I did everything else, Master. Dunstan wished to write the—"

The Master waved a ringed hand, silencing the knight. "That's enough, Baldwin. You're just embarrassing yourself and annoying me with your paltry excuses."

Baldwin glanced down, clenching his sword hilt.

The Master straightened his parchment. "I alerted King Aethelmaer of the accomplishments of your mission as soon as I received your missive, and he was, as can be expected, much pleased. He wished to make you all commanders, although you will still answer directly to me.

"Now, Dunstan wrote, declaring that the Klinian filth," the Master said and sent a look of pure loathing at Gunter, "killed the king of Klinhun, but surely that is incorrect. Come, tell me who actually killed the king that he may be properly rewarded."

He raised up a finger. "But do not lie, or you will spend a week in the cellars with neither food nor drink."

Silent and still, the men resembled the motionless forms of the knights in the rug they stood on.

"Come, don't be modest. I have other duties to attend to." The Master's voice had a sharp edge. As if sensing his displeasure, the dog growled.

Dunstan stepped forward. "Sire, my letter spoke truth. Gunter, the Klinian, did indeed kill King Elias."

The Master stared at Gunter for several thunderings of his

heart, scowling so much that his eyes sank beneath his bushy eyebrows. He turned to the others. "Is this true?"

They grudgingly nodded.

"Explain, Dunstan," the Master commanded and placed his boots on the table.

After Dunstan recounted the events in Dhalion, the Master gazed at Gunter like a man scrutinizing whether or not to butcher a sheep. Gunter was sweating a rainstorm and could hardly hear anything over the thumping of his heart.

"Well, I must say, I'm surprised. I didn't think you'd hold up your end of the bargain."

"You didn't hold up your end." For a moment Gunter wished for the dagger Adelaide had given him, then remembered all the blood pouring from King Elias's wound and swallowed bile.

The Master returned his attention to the knights. "Baldwin, Leofric, and Ligulf, you may return home to Weitzen. I want you back here in ten days ready to work. Dunstan," he turned to the man, "I suppose you have seen your family in Neikurn on the way here?"

"Yes, Master."

"Good. Then you will remain here. I need your help."

Dunstan inclined his head. "As you wish."

"Leave, the rest of you." The Master waved his hand at the other three. Before departing, Baldwin glared at Dunstan, no doubt jealous of his position of honor. But Gunter knew that Dunstan would much rather return home than remain here.

"I suppose I won't kill you, then." Although the Master didn't look at Gunter, it was clear from his disappointment that he was talking about him.

The man sighed and patted his dog's head. "For some reason, King Aethelmaer believes you will make a good knight, despite my descriptions of your scrawniness and infatuation of your country. Merely killing a king doesn't make you a good fighter or a fighter at all, for that matter. Still, orders are orders."

The Master stroked his mustache and turned to Dunstan. "Take the prisoner to a cell and tell Heward not to give him food or water until he shoots something at the range. He doesn't need to hit the target, but he needs to aim for it."

"Yes, Master." Dunstan bowed.

At first, Gunter just stared at the man who had destroyed his life with just a few words not once but twice. Then he clenched his tunic.

In the journey to stay alive and return home, he'd given parts of himself away that he'd never get back, but he wouldn't give this part of himself away. He might not be brave like Adelaide, and he might have opened the door for the Gyndilians to attack his people, but he refused to become what they wanted: a weapon sharpened to kill his family and friends.

So, with the same determination that Gunter used to plunge a spade into the frost-hard ground, he said, "I'd rather die than fight for you."

"That can be arranged," the Master said with a smile.

Then, quicker than a diving falcon, he unsheathed his sword and launched himself over the table at Gunter. "I can always tell King Aethelmaer that you died on the way here, being so scrawny and sickly. It will be a pleasure to rid Gyndilad of you. So, which will it be?"

The cold silver of the sword bit into Gunter's throat, and he trembled. Was he strong enough to die for what he believed in for his parents, for Adelaide, for Klinhun?

Chapter Twenty-Four

Berold surveyed the knights on the castle grounds who had just arrived from Kildare. There was only a few dozen, most of whom didn't know how to march in a straight line, let alone how to plunge a sword into a man to kill him. To them, Gyndilians were people to be feared, not fought.

As soon as the messenger from Alesfirth, exhausted and covered in dirt and dried blood, had recovered enough to tell him that the Gyndilians had attacked, killed Lord Lambert, and captured the town, Berold had sent messengers to the nearest towns—Kildare, Lenast, and Fernohn—begging for knights.

So far, Kildare was the only one that had responded. The others were too busy squabbling for power now that King Elias was dead.

Berold shunted the familiar pain aside; he didn't have time to grieve his friend's death.

He watched the new soldiers parry swords with the Dhalion knights. The latter always won, for they had more training.

But even with all that training, they had failed to protect

Elias. *Berold* had failed. If only he had done something more about Adelaide or followed Elias that day, despite the man's command. Why hadn't Berold gotten rid of the girl when he had the chance?

Guilt was a shadow he couldn't shake, no matter how hard he tried.

"Sire!" Rolf, one of his commanders, yelled, pointing behind him.

Berold turned, his hand reaching instinctively for his sword, but someone punched him in the face before he could unsheathe it, knocking him back.

A man with blond hair and green eyes, whom he vaguely recalled from Adelaide's rebellion, lunged toward him, hands in claws as if to strangle him.

Berold leapt to the side and freed his sword from its scabbard.

The man came to a stop near the edge of the cliff, his face a mask of contorted rage. He grabbed a bowl-sized rock, probably to smash Berold's face with.

But as the man bent to pick up the rock, the swordmaster darted forward, quick on his feet from all his sword-fighting practice, and plunged the hilt into the man's breast just as he stood.

The momentum of Berold's thrust carried him off the cliff after the man.

Wind whistled past Berold's ears, and the sea lunged closer and closer. A jagged rock lay directly below him, ready to crush him to pieces.

With him dead, the Gyndilians would undoubtedly prevail, for how could the Klinian knights defeat their enemies without both a king and a swordmaster?

And then Berold wasn't thinking about Klinhun but about how much it would hurt to land on that sharp rock and what would happen when his life ended.

"Umph." Something squeezed Berold, squishing all his air out.

But he was still alive. In fact, the sea and rock were getting farther away.

Berold glanced up to see what had saved him: white, flat-like stones placed intricately together stretched above him. What in the world?

The thing dropped him hard onto the grass in front of the castle where he'd been training the knights. He rolled and eventually stopped, coughing up dirt and grass.

He turned to see his savior or slayer, wishing he had his sword.

His breath left in a rush.

At the edge of the cliff sat a white dragon, glittering silver where the sun struck it, almost blinding him. Giant, clawed legs supported a massive, almost-feline body, its oddly human hazel eyes staring at him.

The knights behind him were as silent as morning fog.

"Come any closer, and I will kill you," Berold said in a quivering voice. Then, louder, he said, "Somebody get me a sword!"

"Here, sire." Rolf placed the hilt of a sword in his hand. For the first time since Berold learned swordplay, the weapon shook in his hands, and it had nothing to do with the unfamiliar weapon.

The dragon's mouth opened, revealing teeth sharper than a sword and just as long.

Oh, I am so frightened by that, great swordmaster, a familiar voice said in his mind.

Berold jerked back in surprise.

The dragon closed its eyes and began to glow like a candle lit from inside until he couldn't see the creature anymore, just a nimbus of light. It shrank until it was no larger than him.

The glow suddenly stopped, and there stood Adelaide in a filthy peasant dress. Her hawk landed on her shoulder and stared at him with penetrating amber eyes.

Chapter Twenty-Five

"Now, since I just saved your life," Adelaide said, "it follows that you won't throw me in jail or kill me." She hadn't necessarily wanted to save the life of the man who'd thrown her in prison, but it seemed she hardly ever got what she wanted.

After learning from the fisherman that Alesfirth had been attacked, a war had ensued within Adelaide. Not with swords and daggers, but with thoughts and desires. She yearned—no *needed*—to see her family for herself, to make sure they were alive. If any of them had been killed ... She had slumped against the terrible thought.

Yet Adelaide couldn't just fly off to Alesfirth; her dragon friends awaited her arrival, and what about Conrad and the others? She needed to make sure they too were alive and well.

Too many people needed her, and the desires to help them all were the harsh clash of swords, a tug-of-war for her heart.

In the end, reason had won out. She was already in Dhalion, and there was nothing immediate she could do for her family. She'd be spotted if she flew for Alesfirth right then, and all her plans would be ruined. Again.

As soon as she had made her decision, she had spotted movement on the cliff where the castle sat. A man in a green tunic, who could only be Berold, fought someone. Was that Talbot?

They both fell off the cliff.

Only for the briefest moment did Adelaide contemplate letting Berold die. But Elias had been his friend, and Berold was the best person to lead their army against the Gyndilians.

So, she had rescued him.

"Who ...? How ...?" Berold now spluttered, staring at her while clutching his sword.

Cyr, tell our friends to meet us here, she told the hawk.

These humans won't kill you? He eyed the crowd of knights who stared at Adelaide with shock.

Nay. But if they try, I can take care of myself.

Still, let me know if they try to attack you. Cyr took off toward the sea.

"Now, first things first," Adelaide said. "The dragons never fought the people of Klinhun. They left instead of staying and fighting the humans whom they loved."

Cries of disbelief rose from the knights, and Adelaide rubbed her head.

"Adelaide?" Conrad pushed through some knights toward her. The others from Alesfirth followed him.

"Who let you out?" Berold demanded. "Someone, take these men back inside."

"Were you a dragon?" Hubert asked with wide eyes.

Adelaide nodded. "Yes. I'll explain in a moment. Berold, if you lock these boys up again or harm them or any of my friends, I will turn back into a dragon and throw you off the cliff myself." She narrowed her eyes at him.

Berold loomed over her, but she didn't fear him now, not with the knowledge of her family potentially dead. Besides, she could turn him into ash too easily.

Berold sheathed his sword, nearly missing his scabbard. He shook his head at the knights approaching her friends, and they stopped. He glanced back at Adelaide. "Very well. But you must explain everything, including why one of your men attacked me."

"I'm not responsible for the men from the rebellion. Most of them are grown men, and I've been away."

Berold opened his mouth, but Adelaide spoke first. "I need a drink before I say anything further."

After an awkward pause, Berold barked a command to a page, who disappeared and returned with a glass of wine.

Adelaide emptied the glass and gave the cup back to the boy. Then she spoke in a voice loud enough for all the knights to hear, "King Elias and his father were dragons." She spoke over their gasps. "They hid their identity because they knew how dragons are treated in this land. King Elias gave me the Gift of Dragons, which caused me to turn into one at will. I have spent the last fortnight on the island where they live trying to convince them to help us fight the Gyndilians."

No one spoke or hardly breathed, as if Adelaide's words had turned them into stone. Then a man said, "She's daft."

Others shouted insults and questions. But she didn't need to convince them all, just their commander. She turned back to Berold, who looked as if he'd been slapped. "I'm sure you noticed strange things about Elias and his father."

He stared off into the distance. "Why didn't he tell me if it was so? We were best friends."

"I don't know. It is a great weight to bear. But we can't think about that now. Berold, we need the dragons' help, as you well know."

He turned to her. "Would they help us? How many are there?"

Several knights cried out, pointing to a spot behind Adelaide. She turned to see the almost-too-bright-to-look-at shapes of Resse, Esa, Picot, and Turquan gliding toward them.

The knights near the edge of the cliff backed away as the

dragons descended. They landed on the cliff edge with a reverberating thud that knocked Hubert and a few knights over.

"I introduce to you my friends, Resse, Esa, Picot, and Turquan, whom I met on Niclond, the island where they live," Adelaide announced. Each dragon inclined its head when she spoke its name.

Thank you, Cyr, she told him when he landed on her shoulder. He nipped at her hair.

May the sun always shine on you, fair people of Klinhun, Resse said. *King Ganelon and Prince Elias were our king and prince as well. They were mighty dragons and beloved friends. We shall always mourn their parting of this world.* He dipped his head. *We have come to help you vanquish your enemies and regain our homeland.*

"*Your* home?" Someone in the crowd was brave or foolish enough to shout. "Klinhun is *our* home. You killed our ancestors. This country belongs to *us.*"

Adelaide ground her teeth. The speaker probably hailed from a part of Klinhun that hadn't heard the stories that Elias and his father had told about dragons.

I'm sorry you think we killed your ancestors, for we would never do such a thing, Esa said in soothing tones. *We have only come to help.*

Why are these humans so shiny? Are they wearing some odd form of dragon-scales? Turquan bent his head to sniff a knight who quailed beneath him.

It's called armor, Resse told him. *It's made of metal.*

"How do these dragons plan on helping us? Are there more of them?" His hand on his sword hilt, Berold peered behind the dragons as if expecting to see more drop out of the sky. If only that were true.

"They can fight." The dragons nodded at Adelaide's words. "There are many more, but the rest have unfortunately decided to harbor in Neklosa. The island where they live has become too crowded and is close to running out of food. Berold," she said gravely, and he turned his gaze back to her, "they can help us, and they will."

She lowered her voice. "Prince Elias made me promise before he died that I would reunite the dragons and humans. We cannot win this fight without them. Swear to me that you will let no harm come to them and that they will be allowed to do all they can to restore peace to our land."

Berold rocked back and forth on his heels, scrutinizing her.

"Elias trusted me. Why can't you?"

He shook his head, eyes tortured. "I saw you staring at his dead body in the sea the same day you were surrounded by men shouting to kill him."

Adelaide squeezed her eyes shut, trying not to see Elias's body, but her hands felt sticky as if coated with his blood, as if her whole body was coated with it and everyone in the kingdom knew.

Opening her eyes didn't help, because Berold's tormented gaze was a sharp reminder of what she'd done.

Adelaide's voice was ragged when she spoke. "I made many mistakes where Prince Elias was concerned, and although I wish I could undo them all, I can't. I can only make it up to him by fulfilling my promise to help Klinhun and the dragons. They're our last and only chance to save this country that he cared so much about."

If that speech doesn't convince him, I'm not sure anything would, Turquan said to the dragons and Adelaide.

She glared at him.

Berold followed her gaze to the dragons. "They won't hurt my men or anyone else?"

"Nay. They're good, as good as Elias was." Her voice choked, and she swallowed.

"Do they expect any form of payment?" Always the practical one.

Adelaide raised an eyebrow at the dragons.

Resse shook his head, and Turquan snorted. *What do they*

have that we'd want? Besides perhaps some females, he said.

Adelaide rolled her eyes and turned back to Berold. "Regaining their home will be payment enough." She didn't mention that one of the dragons, Evengier—if he could be persuaded to give up his Neklosa plan—would most likely rule Alesfirth. They could tackle that challenge if they survived long enough to deal with it.

Berold's eyes darted from her to the dragons, his hand clenching his sword hilt. Then he sighed. "Very well, since it's what Elias wanted. But I'll be watching them and you."

"And I'll be watching you. Now announce it to everyone, as well as the good news that the charges against me have been dropped."

He glared at her. "Who is in command here?"

"Who can turn into a dragon?"

He muttered something and faced the crowd. "Knights of Klinhun, these dragons are our friends and under my protection. They, too, desire peace in this country. Whoever harms them or even gets too close to them without permission from me or this woman," he said and jerked a thumb at Adelaide, "will face death by hanging. Is that clear?"

The men nodded, and a few stepped away from the creatures.

He just scared them even more. They can't hurt us, Esa murmured, and Adelaide patted her leg.

"And all the charges against this woman—"

"My name's Adelaide," she muttered.

"—are dropped. She is a free, innocent citizen," Berold said, as if pulling a tooth. "Now, attend to your duties. We have a war to prepare for."

He turned to Adelaide. "So, if you didn't kill Elias, then who did?"

"As I told you before, it was Gunter, one of my friends from Alesfirth."

"That scrawny man with hair like a rooster's feathers?"

"That's my brother you're discussing," Conrad said as he walked up. He turned to Adelaide. "I'm sorry. You told me to watch Talbot, but as soon as they let us out to train with the knights, he disappeared. I think he was the one who tried killing this man." He nodded to Berold.

Adelaide squeezed his arm. "It's not your fault."

"You two can reminisce later," Berold said. "First, I want to know, was it your brother who killed King Elias?" He studied Conrad, who was as tall and muscular as him due to all his work in the fields. "And you're a peasant, are you not?"

Conrad balled his fists. "Why does that matter?"

Before the two men could throw punches, Adelaide stepped forward. "Berold, I need some provisions and clean garments as soon as possible. I would get them myself, but I'm not familiar with the layout of the castle."

"What are you doing, Adelaide?" Conrad peered at her with the same expression he had often worn when they were younger, and she would announce that they all should play a game. Her games had usually ended with someone getting into trouble.

"Do you know what has happened to Alesfirth?"

"No, what?"

"Berold will tell you."

The swordmaster scowled at her, but she just searched through her satchel to make sure she had everything she needed.

"It's been captured by the Gyndilians. Several days ago. As far as we know, only a score of people have been killed or taken captive to Gyndilad."

Conrad didn't move or blink, and the others from Alesfirth gripped each other's arms and gaped at Berold. Adelaide's heart bled for them, especially because she knew all their families.

"Why didn't you send aid? Why didn't you help?" Conrad asked.

Berold rubbed his face, and for the first time, Adelaide noticed the scruff on his usually clean-shaven face and the dark circles under his eyes. It couldn't be easy running a country, preparing for war, and mourning your best friend all at the same time. And now she was beginning to pity him. How annoying.

"I'm only one man, and the attack was unexpected," Berold said with a sigh.

"Even though it's been attacked before," Adelaide added.

"Which is why we wouldn't think it would be attacked again. By the time we heard of the assault, it was too late to do anything. We can't retake the town now because the scant knights we have are needed to defend Dhalion or march to Gyndilad."

Conrad sagged against Aldy, and Hubert said with tears in his eyes, "What about my mama? Is she safe? Is my pappy okay?"

Berold stared at the ground, scuffing the dirt with his boot.

Adelaide placed her hands on Hubert's and his brother, Bodin's, shoulders. "I'm going to Alesfirth to see if our families are alive. I'll come back and let you know."

Hubert hugged her, erasing any doubt that Adelaide was doing the right thing.

"I'll come with you," Conrad said.

"And I," the others from the rebellion said, including Rohesia.

Her friends' loyalty warmed her heart. "I wish you could, but it will be too dangerous. I'm faster alone, and you're needed here to prepare for battle."

"It's too dangerous for you to go alone," Conrad protested.

Resse stepped forward. *I'll fly with you.*

I'm older than you, so I'll go, Turquan said.

Adelaide shook her head. "I appreciate all of your offers, but you must stay here to train and fight. It will be difficult to hide one dragon, let alone two. I shall go alone."

And you'll have me, Cyr added. Adelaide nodded. That would make things easier.

A shrill neighing came from the other side of the cliff, and the hair at the back of Adelaide's neck stood up.

"I need those provisions, Berold. Please," Adelaide reminded him.

With a stiff jaw and jerky movements, Berold turned and strode toward the main part of the castle.

Adelaide hurried to the heart-tearing animal cries.

"Where are you going?" Conrad asked.

Humans are strange, Turquan mused.

Adelaide ignored them and continued toward the pasture beside the stable.

Like a piece of night, mysterious and mad, a black horse raced up and down the pasture as if looking for something it had lost.

"I miss him too, Starflare," Adelaide murmured as she leaned over the fence.

The mare's ears flickered in her direction, but she continued galloping, sending tufts of grass and mud flying, her dark eyes whirling.

Adelaide could clearly see Elias, confident and princely in a red cloak astride the shadowy horse and hear his tender murmurings as he groomed Starflare.

Perhaps, if Adelaide had reacted sooner to Elias's kindness, she would have told him of the rebellion, and he would still be alive to ride his beloved horse, to soar into the sky to defend the kingdom he loved, to smile at Adelaide with those sky-mirror eyes.

She sagged against the fence, the grief and guilt a weight not even a dragon could stand beneath. She wished that she, too, could pound the ground into submission and scream her frustration at the sky instead of acting like everything was fine when she was crumbling inside.

Chapter Twenty-Six

Berold watched the young woman who had just saved his life, had turned from a dragon into a human, claimed his best friend was a fire-breathing beast, commanded and then threatened him, march away with her hawk on her shoulder.

He felt like pulling all his hair out at the lunacy of what had happened. He yanked his hands away from his head and realized that he was too close to his desire: strands of sandy-brown hair clung to his hands. He let a salt-tinged breeze sweep them away as he stared at the four dragons who took up nearly all the open area on the cliff.

What was he supposed to do with them? He hated to admit it, but Adelaide had been right. If any more people than those on the cliff knew the dragons were alive and back in Klinhun, they would rise up against them. That would mean war on two fronts, which would be like giving themselves to Gyndilad on a golden platter.

"I suppose you can't turn into humans?" Berold asked the dragons, trying to keep his voice steady as they gazed at him with simmering eyes.

The purple and the brown-and-white one shook their heads.

That is impossible, the yellow one said. At least, he thought it was the yellow one; the words seemed to float from him into Berold's mind.

He shook his head. It was eerie hearing a voice in a place that was supposed to be reserved for his thoughts alone.

"Very well. Go hide behind the castle wall in the forest and don't be seen." It felt odd giving orders to such mighty creatures, but this was his home, and the dragons didn't seem to mind.

They dipped their heads. The yellow one said, *If you need help for any reason, call for us or send someone to fetch us.*

Then, much quieter and more gracefully than he would have believed possible, the dragons sprang into the air, glided between the four castle spires—almost touching them with their bellies—and disappeared into the forest.

Berold watched them with awe. If he had an army like that, the Gyndilians and every other nation wouldn't even think about attacking them.

"Sire, the men are too distracted by those ... creatures to finish their drills," Rolf told him, gazing at the place in the forest where the dragons had landed with barely a rustle. "It's too bad that more of their kind didn't come."

"Indeed." Berold rubbed his hands. "Tell the men they're free to retire for the night. Make it clear that if they tell anyone about the dragons and what has just transpired, they will be thrown into the dungeon for a fortnight. I have ways of finding out." His friends among the men would tell him if anyone revealed the truth.

Rolf inclined his head. "Yes, sire."

"If we do not hear back from the other towns soon, we will march north to Gyndilad. That will be better than waiting for them to attack us."

"As you wish, sire." Rolf strode away.

As the men dispersed to their lodging for the night, Berold pondered the revelation that his best friend had been a dragon. He supposed it was possible; King Ganelon and Prince Elias had often behaved unusually and held somber discussions late at night.

On some of those nights, Berold had perceived the prince's window open, even on the chilliest of nights. Usually, the next morning Elias had shadows under his eyes and seemed barely able to hold his head up.

Berold had always attributed his friend's weariness to his discussions with his father, but perhaps on those nights his friend had been chasing the wind.

Elias and King Ganelon had had odd beliefs about dragons, believing—as Adelaide had said—that the creatures had never intentionally harmed a human. They'd even gone so far as to banish the original song about the dragons' destructive behavior that was sung every winter at Dhalion's Fire Festival.

If it was true that his best friend had been a dragon, why had he never told Berold? Berold would never have betrayed him; he didn't hate dragons as much as some in the country, and his brotherly love for Elias reached deeper than that.

Almost absentmindedly, Berold rubbed the scar on his hand that he had received seven years ago as a boy of twelve winters.

He had climbed the slimy rocks above the beach at Dhalion, glad to escape the dull duty of a page. If he had to clean another piece of armor, saddle one more horse, or fill one more goblet of wine, he'd take one of the knight's perfectly polished swords and run himself through with it.

Only one more winter. Then he could begin learning how to fight with those beautiful gleaming swords.

"It's a nice view up here, isn't it?"

Berold had jerked around to see a boy about his age with blue-grey eyes clambering up the rocks behind him.

"Who are you?" Berold asked.

"I'm Elias. Who are you?"

The page's jaw dropped. "Prince Elias?" His father had mentioned the new king and his son a few times, but Berold hadn't seen them yet—at least not that he knew of.

"Yes, and you are? I saw you brushing that striking paint horse the other day."

"I'm Berold Wishchard's son." Berold puffed up his chest. "He's a knight."

The prince leaned down to examine a seashell. "I haven't met him yet. Do you know what these are?"

Berold glanced at the wrinkly shells stuck to the rock. "No." He climbed higher. He reached out to the top of a rock with his hand, and it scraped him.

"Ow." Berold jerked back and slipped on the slimy rocks, but the prince grabbed him, steadying him before he could fall into the grumbling waves below.

"Thanks, Your Highness," he gasped and held his stinging hand close.

"Call me Elias. Can I see?" He gestured to Berold's hand.

The page showed the prince his hand. It bled steadily, dribbling down onto the rocks. Elias gingerly touched the injury, and Berold winced at the sting. The flow of blood slowed.

The prince frowned at the wound. Then he tore off a piece of his elaborate light-blue tunic and wrapped it around Berold's hand. "There. That should help."

"Thanks."

Elias smiled. "Of course. We're friends now, aren't we?"

Well, the boy had just saved his life and would probably rule over him one day, so Berold nodded. "And one day I will serve beside you as your knight."

Elias beamed. Then he bent down and sliced his hand on a rock near his feet.

"What are you doing?" Berold moved toward him.

"This will make it more official. Untie your hand and give it to me."

Berold did so, eyes flashing from his hand to Elias's matching wound.

Grasping Berold's palm lightly, their blood dripping as one onto the rocks below, Elias stated as if he were already the king, "I, Prince Elias, son of King Ganelon, promise to be your brother-in-arms and rule you to the best of my ability for as long as I live."

Berold didn't know what he was expected to say, but caught in the grandeur of the moment, he proclaimed, "And I, Berold Wishchard's son, promise to be your brother-in-arms and serve at your side as long as I live."

Elias smiled as he held up their hands to the sky. "And no one will dare stand up to us, Master Climbers of the Rocks!"

Their laughter rose over the crashing of the waves.

Berold's smile faded at the memory. Prince Elias a dragon? He supposed if anyone was one, it would've been the young prince, who could fly into a temper faster than a knight's footwork and hated being inside for more than a few moments. But why hadn't he told Berold, his brother-in-arms?

Well, it mattered little now. Berold strode across the grounds into the castle to plan an impossible battle.

Chapter Twenty-Seven

The food resembled raw pig entrails mixed with mud, but Gunter was so ravenous that he devoured the thick, lumpy broth in big gulps, barely swallowing.

"Whoa. Don't they feed you in Klinhun?" A Gyndilian knight with a scar on his forehead taunted Gunter from across the table.

Gunter didn't answer; he was too busy stuffing himself with the lukewarm stew. He had been stuck with only rats and flies for company the past four days in the same prison cell that he'd been thrown into before.

The tense moment with the Master had ended when Gunter said that he'd fight for the Gyndilians. What else could he do with a blade pressed against his neck? He apparently wasn't strong or selfless enough to die for those he loved.

Shame clung to him like the sweaty stink of the Gyndilians beside him. But he was still determined not to give in and to somehow find a way to escape and return home.

Every morning since he'd told the Master he'd fight, a knight had taken him to the target range to shoot a crossbow—the weapon that had killed so many people in Alesfirth—at a painted wooden circle stuck into a hay bale. Each time he had refused, and each time he had been escorted back to the cell with neither food nor water.

This morning, as he smelled the knights' morning meal when he walked by, he caved.

The crossbow had been awkward and too heavy in his hands, but his throat burned, and his chapped lips leaked blood. He doubted that even a river could quench his thirst.

He had briefly considered firing the weapon at his guard, but there were armed Gyndilians everywhere, and they would pounce on him faster than a cat on a mouse.

The arrow he'd shot had landed a pace away, sticking straight up in the dirt. But apparently it didn't matter how horrible his aim was, just that he'd shot at the target. His guard had taken him to the outside tables where the knights were eating and plopped a mug of water and a bowl of porridge in front of him.

Now that the contents were empty and Gunter's stomach gurgled happily, he thrust the bowl away, sick with himself and possibly with what he'd eaten.

He had taken the first step to become the weapon the Gyndilians wanted him to be. Just a few more steps would lead him to Alesfirth with a crossbow turned on those he loved.

"I'm surprised you were even able to hold the crossbow," a Gyndilian beside him said. The others guffawed, spewing bits of their much more appetizing meal of thick bread, creamy cheese, and roasted venison everywhere.

Gunter stood. He wished he could speak to Dunstan, but he'd only seen glimpses of the man on his way to the target fields.

"You can't let these men frighten you. They don't mean half of what they say." A knight came over, holding a plate of food.

"They don't frighten me." Gunter looked hard at the freckle-faced man who spoke without the guttural accents of the Gyndilians. "Where do you hail from?"

The man sat down and gulped his ale. "I was wondering when you'd ask." He set the cup down. "My name's Hardwin, and I hail from Klinhun, specifically Alesfirth."

"Truly?" Gunter didn't recall ever seeing the man before, but he ventured into town only for supplies or to run errands for his mother, so that meant little.

"Did you think you were the first Klinian we've picked up from Alesfirth?" A knight with crumbs in his sheep's-wool beard asked. "Most of the non-Gyndilian knights we take are from there. It's the closest Klinian village to us."

Why did the Gyndilians take men from Klinhun at all? Did they not have enough of their own people to fight for them? But other questions fought for dominance.

Gunter squeezed between a knight who gave him a dirty look and Hardwin. "But didn't you try to escape?" He asked the Klinian. "Don't you have a family?"

"Of course I did. I got this tooth knocked out when I heard they were taking me to Gyndilad." He pushed down his lip to expose a hole where a bottom front tooth should sit.

"I hear that he fought more than you, runt." A knight across from Gunter sneered at him. But he didn't know that Gunter had killed Klinhun's king. He probably wouldn't believe Gunter if he told him.

Gunter turned back to Hardwin and gripped the table as he leaned toward him. "So, you just gave up, then? You just gave them what they wanted? Became who they wanted you to be?"

Hardwin frowned. "I wouldn't say I gave up. I experienced another perspective." He stuffed some meat into his mouth. "I realized there was no point fighting them. I was just one man. And the Gyndilians keep my family safe while I do what they ask. If I don't, they'll kill them. I even get to see them once in a while."

He chewed, his gaze drifting away, probably to his family. "This privilege came in mighty handy when the Gyndilians attacked Alesfirth. Now I know for certain they're safe."

Like a splash of cold water on a spring morning, Gunter realized he could and would become this man if he wasn't careful. He could see himself wearing a black-and-silver uniform, sitting next to the Gyndilian knights like they were his family and shooting crossbows at the target (he couldn't see himself *hitting* the target; that took more imagination than he was capable of). And it would be easy to become a Gyndilian to protect his family. Or would he be protecting himself?

At least the Master didn't have Gunter's family. Not yet. "I haven't seen my family," Gunter said. "I don't even know if they're alive."

"I'm sure they are. The Gyndilians didn't kill many when they attacked Alesfirth this last time. What's more," Hardwin stuffed another chunk of meat in his mouth, "who's to say that King Elias would have made a better ruler than King Aethelmaer? He feeds, clothes, and takes care of my family and I in exchange for my loyalty. Isn't that what a true king is supposed to do?"

The man's words stumped Gunter. He knew there was more to a peaceful kingdom than that, but at the moment, he couldn't remember what it was.

Yes, he was on his way to becoming like this Hardwin man, and he didn't know how to stop it.

Chapter Twenty-Eight

"Well, what'd you find?" Adelaide asked Cyr as he spiraled above her. Her arms ached to sprout into wings to find out for herself what Alesfirth now looked like and if her parents were alive. But as it was daylight, that would be a reckless thing to do.

She'd been awaiting Cyr's return from Alesfirth all day. Hurling her dagger at a tree, washing herself in the familiar waters of the Lentiasa River, and pacing back and forth had not calmed her.

The large nest looks much the same, but quieter. Cyr landed on her shoulder. *Two males with shiny, black-colored skins were outside the gate holding some kind of weapon.*

Those must be Gyndilians. Adelaide twisted her braid around a finger. She didn't want to ask the next question, but had to know. *And the houses outside the town? Did you see anyone in them?* She swallowed. *What about mine?*

Cyr gazed at her with an unblinking amber eye. *All the nests outside the town are burned.*

Adelaide sagged against an oak. The house where she had learned how to make bread under her mother's watchful eye, where she used to sit in her father's lap, where she and Emma had made dolls out of straw, and where she had chased Odo was just … gone?

Cyr nipped her hair. *I hurt for it too. You healed me and kept me safe there.*

And my family? She didn't breathe as she waited for his answer.

I didn't see them, but they could be in the large nest.

Adelaide sighed, nodding. *Yes. I'm sure that's where they are.* Somehow, she would get them to safety. *Come on. Let's find them.*

No undulating waves of wind flowed through green wheat and no stalks of sweet corn towered over her. The fields were black and stiff, all the peasants' hard labor destroyed in the fire. It looked nothing like the place where she had grown up.

The acrid stench of smoke and charred wood climbed inside Adelaide's nose, and no matter how hard she rubbed it, the smell didn't leave. Stomping the dry, brittle grass felt good, as if she was stomping her worries into submission and had control over her life.

She walked until the familiar view of the untouched forest she'd seen every day came into view.

What is it? Cyr's head swiveled.

Adelaide leaned down and picked up a singed piece of wood from a pile and stared at it, then beside it at the charred heap of timber.

This pile of cinders and rubble couldn't be the place Adelaide had spent so much of her life making memories and mischief. She squatted down. Was this the fire they had always kept going, where they had spent every evening listening to Emma's stories? Were these charred pieces of wood their bed?

Adelaide couldn't tell. All the warmth and familiarity had burned in the fire. It wasn't her home. Not anymore.

It was our house, but now nothing is left but memories. Ash and sorrow coated her mouth.

And hopefully, your family, Cyr said gently. *I don't see any bones.*

Adelaide breathed a sigh of relief. *Good. Now let's see if we can find them.* She set her gaze on the fading light where Alesfirth sat and the Gyndilians ruled. They'd taken her sister and now her home.

Her fists clenched as a raging desire to burn the Gyndilians like they had burned her home roiled through her.

But if Adelaide acted on that desire, she'd become the kind of dragon that the Klinians believed in: violent, raging beasts.

Just having these desires showed that Adelaide wasn't worthy of the title "dragon."

Two torches blazed on either side of the wooden gate leading into Alesfirth. The light revealed two guards dressed in chain mail and black tunics, swords hanging from their waists and crossbows in their hands aimed at the ground—for now. On their heads they wore silver helmets with some kind of symbol that Adelaide couldn't make out in the deepening darkness.

Gyndilians. She seethed inside again but quenched the flames. She wasn't here for vengeance, just to find her parents and get them out of town.

Clutching her dagger, Adelaide snuck toward the far side of the gate, out of the guards' line of vision. She placed her feet carefully, barely breathing.

Her foot crunched some scorched grass, and she stiffened like spotted prey.

The men didn't glance at her, and Adelaide realized that they were deep in conversation. She treaded less carefully but still softly and stopped at the wooden wall just a little way down from the guards.

And you didn't see my family inside? Adelaide asked Cyr.

Nay. I only saw those shiny men moving around.

Very well. It'll just take awhile to search for them. She gazed at the two Gyndilians while contemplating the different plans she had concocted earlier that day while waiting for Cyr to return.

Distract them enough for me to slip by, she told him. *And make sure you're not caught.*

Of course not. I'm not a brainless sparrow.

I know. After you distract them, stay out of sight somewhere nearby. I'll need your help to escape once I find my family.

I'll do that. You don't get caught either.

Adelaide nodded and raised her arm. Cyr shot into the sleep-dark sky and dived at the two men—a blur of feathers, claws, and beak.

As the knights attempted to fight off the mass of frenzied feathers, Adelaide slipped past them into the slightly open gate.

If not for the lit tavern filled with uproarious laughter, the town would've been as still and somber as a winter night.

Adelaide slunk against the left wall away from the tavern. She listened for any noises to indicate where the peasants with burned homes might be kept.

She crept by too-quiet houses, pausing beside each one and peering into the cracks. She heard murmurs and saw families huddled on straw-dusted floors lit by candles, but none were hers.

She stopped twice in the shadows, barely breathing as Gyndilians walked past or stepped out of the tavern on the other side of the stone dais.

With each building that held no sign of her family, Adelaide's feet moved more slowly. She didn't want to reach the last place and find out that her parents weren't here, for that would probably mean they were dead. It was better to live with the thought that they were still alive than knowing they weren't.

Yet, she had to know. She soon reached the far end of town, near the ligneous Great Hall where light flickered in the shuttered windows and men's raucous laughter spilled out. The noise grated on her desperation, and she turned away, searching for anywhere her family could be.

There. Lord Lambert's stable squatted next to the hall. Of course. Why hadn't she thought of looking there sooner?

She slunk beneath the windows of the hall, then ducked into the stables.

Snores rumbled, and she neared five slumbering shadows on the floor. She leaned down to peer at them, and her gaze focused on the dark forms of her parents.

They looked older than she remembered; her mother's plaited brown hair had more streaks of grey, and wrinkles formed new roads down her father's face. How many of those had been caused by her sudden departure? How many nights had they stayed up wondering where she was?

Adelaide had basically forced them to lose two daughters. She hadn't thought of it like that at the time, but now her reckless actions made her want to vomit.

She didn't care if her father took a branch and hit her like when she'd been young and rebellious. She just wanted their familiar warmth around her again, to be small and safe in their arms, and not to have to worry about the fate of two species. She'd even let Odo tell her some of his horrible jokes and pretend to laugh at them.

Wait. Where *was* Odo? He didn't lie next to their parents.

Adelaide made another sweep of the stable, but he wasn't there. Just her parents and Gunter's family.

The thought of telling Gunter's parents about what he'd done made her want to dart out of the stable, but her parents anchored her in place.

She moved closer, hovering just above them. "Father. Mother. Wake up. It's me, Adelaide. I'm back."

Her mother, Galiena, opened her eyes. "What?" When her gaze landed on Adelaide, her eyes widened. She touched her daughter's face as if afraid it would vanish. "Adelaide, my dear, is that truly you?"

No blame or anger hid in her mother's gaze or movements, just shocked delight. Adelaide could bathe in its warmth all night.

She nodded. "Yes. I've come to take you somewhere safe." When had it become Adelaide's responsibility to protect her parents instead of the other way around? She supposed when she began the rebellion and left them to do what she thought was right.

Galiena sat up and nudged her husband. "Ferand, Adelaide's here. She's alive."

Her mother hugged her, sobbing, and Adelaide squeezed back—a child again where her mother's embrace was the summit of love and safety. Adelaide couldn't recall the last time she had hugged her mother; it must have been sometime before Emma had died.

"Adelaide? Thank the stars you're alive." Ferand hugged her. "But where have you been all this time?" He pulled back to look at her. "You left at night with no word except a lie to Odo."

Adelaide swallowed against the shame rising inside her. "I know. I shouldn't have done that. But now's not the time to explain. I'll tell you more once we're safely out of Alesfirth. But first, where's Odo?" She glanced around again for her brother's big ears and lanky form.

"He's ...they've ..." her mother glanced down, tears glistening on her sallow cheeks, taking sharp breaths to keep the sobs inside.

Adelaide glanced at her father. He, too, looked as if he might weep, and this alarmed her more than anything else she'd seen that day. The only time she remembered seeing him cry was when he had held Emma's broken body in his arms the day she had been murdered.

"Father, where's Odo?" Adelaide's voice was high and frail like a frightened child's.

Ferand choked out, "The Gyndilians took him."

Chapter Twenty-Nine

Grimbald, or the Master, as he preferred to be called, wiped the sweat off his brow. He was looking forward to a swig of ale and some roasted sausage. Os whined below him, and Grimbald reached down from his horse to pat the dog's head.

The knights marched up to the post that marked the starting point, aimed their crossbows at the target painted on the hay bale 500 paces away, shot, and marched back in line as the next group came to take their place.

He nodded when nearly all the knights' arrows sunk into the middle black dots painted on the targets. They would be ready to join King Aethelmaer's army soon in the march to Dhalion. Well, most of them.

Grimbald narrowed his eyes as the scrawny, sandy-haired Klinian ambled up—a piece of straw next to oak trees. The boy glanced at the target and flicked looks at the Gyndilians.

Even from Grimbald's location on the far side of the field, he could see the boy shaking. The Klinian released his arrow after the others had already shot. The missile missed the target by a good twenty paces, sinking into the grass in front of it.

The knights guffawed and called him names. Grimbald shook his head. This was the boy who had killed the king of Klinhun? It was a wonder such a feeble person could even hold a crossbow.

The Klinian kept his gaze straight ahead as he passed the jeering knights, his face the color of ripe strawberries. But not everyone was laughing. Dunstan walked over to the Klinian filth, and Grimbald tensed.

Dunstan spoke to the boy, and a look of relief passed over his face. Was that actually a smile on his ugly face? What had Dunstan said to him?

Grimbald clenched his reins at the sight of his best soldier making friends with their enemy. He couldn't afford for Dunstan to be distracted now with so much at stake.

He could punish Dunstan, but he was one of their best knights, and Grimbald didn't want him injured or weakened before entering battle. If only King Aethelmaer would let Grimbald kill the Klinian, then he'd be rid of this problem once and for all.

"Master," a voice spoke to his left.

"What?" Grimbald snarled and turned to glare at the person who had interrupted his contemplations.

"This just came for you from King Acthelmaer." One of the newer knights—Grimbald hadn't learned his name yet—handed him a letter.

He took the parchment and broke the seal of two swords crossed over a helmet. He read the letter written in the familiar lazy scrawl of the king's hand.

Swordmaster Grimbald, Chief Commander to the King,

Greetings from Weitzen. I hope the knights, especially the new ones from Alesfirth, are not giving you trouble and that you have made good use of the recent supply of weapons. How soon will the men be ready to meet the others? We must strike soon while the Klinians are panicked and distracted from the recent attack on Alesfirth. That was one of your cleverer ideas.

I am still not very surprised that a Klinian—even a weak one as you've described—was able to kill the king. I have seen stranger things in my life, as you know.

I saw Leofurn a few days ago, and she sends her love, as always. She says the children are well, although they miss their father. I have sent a letter from her. Soon this war will be over, and we can settle in that blessed land of Klinhun with our families and riches.

The main reason I am writing is to tell you that we need more recruits for experimentation. Please send them as soon as you can. Five to ten should suffice for this round. You may take people from Alesfirth, should you need to. I await your quick reply.

King Aethelmaer the Determined

147th King of Gyndilad

The Master's lips curled into a grin as he read the last paragraph. He knew at least one of the recruits that he would send for experimentation.

Chapter Thirty

King Aethelmaer still couldn't clean the stench of death and decay out of his nose. He'd had his page remove the clothes he'd worn during his meeting that afternoon with Jeharrez and now wore freshly laundered clothes, but the smell of rotting animals and fetid smoke clung to him.

Like many times before, he wondered why he had partnered with the dragon. Soon, though, it would find the right mixture, and the nightmare could end.

The memory of Aethelmaer's first encounter with the dragon arose too easily in the tent lit only by a guttering candle.

It had been night then as well, but not so dark that Aethelmaer felt held captive by the shadows of his past.

He had ridden his grey mare through the frost-covered Hinterkitten Forest to his friend's neighboring castle. His hands were nearly numb even in his fur gloves, and his breaths leaked puffs of white air. He looked forward to thawing out beside the fire, sipping a warm cup of currant wine, and consuming several meat pies.

He had much to discuss with his friend, including the attack on Alesfirth and his plans for the upcoming war, but it could wait until the morning. Now he merely longed to fill his belly with food and his body with warmth.

His mare skittered to the side, her ears flicking in every direction.

"Come on, Lightfeet. There's nothing out there." Despite his words, Aethelmaer's heart sped; he knew wolves roamed this forest. He should have brought some knights with him, but he had never had problems on this path before, and his friend's men would meet him when he was close.

Aethelmaer urged Lightfeet forward. She took a few tentative steps, then stopped, her eyes rolling, and her ears pricked forward.

A flash of orange light blazed over the king's head and landed in the dirt behind him.

Lightfeet squealed and shot forward.

His hands numb, Aethelmaer lost his grip on the reins and fell to the ground with a groan. He stood shakily, drew his sword, and stared at the shadows before him.

A shape darker than those of the trees and as large as a house detached itself and slithered closer.

Eyes like torches blazed from the top of the shadow. It looked like a—but no, that couldn't be. They were all gone or dead.

If you flee without listening to what I have to say, I will destroy you in one breath, a deep, raspy voice spoke in Aethelmaer's mind.

He stared at the fiery, unblinking eyes. Did the voice come from the creature?

Tremors racked Aethelmaer as the burning eyes crept closer, and he didn't think he could move if he wanted to.

A shaft of moonlight through the trees' branches revealed a long, gold-scaled snout and nostrils as large as his head. Two pointed horns sat on the beast's head and smaller spines stuck out of its face. Black-scaled legs thicker than a ship's mast supported the massive body that was partly hidden by trees.

You are the king here, yes? The dragon's gaze focused on Aethelmaer's hand. *Show me your ring. I've heard it will give me proof.*

The king was in no position to argue, so he fumbled with the glove on his right hand. When he finally managed to yank it off, he almost dropped it.

The dragon remained still and silent, staring at him, and he shook harder.

Aethelmaer held out the ring with the Gyndilian family crest inlaid on top, a raven clutching a sword in its talons.

The dragon slithered forward, and Aethelmaer leaned back, gagging. The creature smelled like raw meat left in the sun for a fortnight.

After gazing at the ring, the dragon stepped back and nodded. *Good. I am Jeharraz, Sunscales, Bearer of Memories, and I hear that you desire to defeat the southern country and claim it as your own.*

The king stared at the long snout because it was less terrifying to look at than the hungry flame of the creature's eyes. How did it know so much? And where had it come from? He'd thought the dragons were all dead now, either by the hands of the Klinians or extinction on whatever spit of land they'd fled to.

If you lie to me, Jeharraz growled, *I'll burn you to a crisp, then eat you.* He opened his mouth, and light smoldered behind teeth as long as Aethelmaer's arms. A rush of heat sucked at him.

The dragon shut its mouth, and Aethelmaer rubbed his watering eyes. He had to swallow several times before he could speak, and when he did, it was a whisper. "Yes, I'm planning to fight Klinhun." He cleared his throat. "We need their ports and other resources."

Good. You and I, King Aethelmaer, want the same thing, and we can get it much easier and faster if we work together.

I have some things to offer you that you shall no doubt want very much if, of course, you offer me something in return.

The eyes boiled him again. What could he have that a dragon wanted?

Chapter Thirty-One

Adelaide's heart splintered apart for the third time in just over a year. How much more painful news could she take before she completely shattered?

"Where did they take him?"

Ferand rubbed his eyes. "Back to Gyndilad. While they burned the fields and fought us, they took some of our children. Odo was in the field half a league from where I worked, and when we realized that the men galloping toward us were Gyndilians, it was too late.

"They grabbed him and some of the other boys and rode north. Then they started burning the fields and houses, and I had to make sure your mother was safe." His voice was pleading, as if asking her to forgive him, although the blame didn't lie with him.

She placed a hand on his. Odo, her baby brother with the too-wide ears and too-large curiosity was all alone in the land of their enemies. He must be terrified.

What was the good of possessing the armor of a squadron

of soldiers and the flames of a hundred fires if she couldn't even protect her family?

Adelaide straightened her shoulders; she would go after Odo. Hopefully, she wasn't too late. Surely, they wouldn't kidnap him just to kill him. "Why did they take him?"

Her father shrugged. "We don't know. Probably to sell him and the others as servants or workers. They took some girls too. One of the knights had compassion on Giles and told him the children would be taken to the capital, Weitzen."

Adelaide grimaced, remembering how close she had come to the same fate. Her heart bled for the kidnapped children, but she couldn't help them alright now. The only way was to defeat Gyndilad. But Odo, her own brother, on the other hand …

"My baby. My little boy." Galiena's sobs wrenched Adelaide out of her thoughts. "First Emma, and then you disappeared, and now my youngest. Will I ever see him again?"

Ferand drew his wife to him. "Shh. You will see him again, Galiena. Odo is alive, and we'll get him back."

Adelaide rubbed her mother's shoulder. "He's more valuable to them alive than dead. He's strong, and they'll want him alive to work their fields. Once I take you to safety, I'll find him and bring him back."

Adelaide was already forming a plan in her mind. After taking her parents to a nearby village, she would fly to Weitzen to find Odo. She didn't know where Weitzen was or how to get there, but that was a small matter.

"You will do no such thing." Ferand frowned at her. "You are not leaving us again. If anyone goes after Odo, it will be me."

Adelaide sighed. "We can discuss it later. First, we need to get out of here." She stood, and Ferand helped Galiena to her feet.

Her mother squeezed her arm. "I'm so glad you're alive and safe. Not knowing has been death."

"I'm glad you two are as well. I came as soon as I heard the news about Alesfirth's defeat."

"But where—"

"Not now, dear. We can talk later," Ferand told his wife. "Adelaide's right. We must leave before the Gyndilians hear us."

"Ferand, Galiena, what's happening?" A dark form stood, and Adelaide recognized the rich voice of Gunter's father, Raymond. "I thought I heard you speaking to someone. Has your daughter returned?"

Adelaide stepped forward. "Yes. I've come back to help my parents escape, and you must come with us."

Another shadow materialized, and Adelaide heard the rustle of fabric. "Have you seen Gunter and Conrad? How are they?" Gunter's mother, Kiona, asked with desperation.

Adelaide took a step away, as if she could flee the arrow that she would have to loose into Gunter's mother's heart. Why must so much of her words and actions bring pain? And if Gunter hadn't returned home, where was he? Perhaps he was still on his way. After all, he couldn't fly.

"I've seen them both. Conrad is well, but I don't know about Gunter." Adelaide turned to the door. "Come on. I'll explain everything once we're a good distance from the Gyndilians." She turned to her father. "Has Pinhurn been taken?"

"Nay. The Gyndilians haven't dared travel that far into Klinhun yet. The people of Pinhurn will be on their guard, having heard what happened here."

Adelaide nodded. That's where she would take them. The idea of leaving her family in a town that could be overthrown at any time scraped at her, but it was probably safer than Dhalion, the prize of the Gyndilians' war.

She led the way to the stable's door and peeped out. Seeing no sign of life, she beckoned the others to follow, then slipped into the warm night.

She pressed herself against the stable's wall as the adults creeped out. First came her father holding Galiena's hand. Then Conrad's parents, Kiona holding a sleeping Elysande.

Adelaide guided them along the dark spaces between and

behind buildings, grateful for the weak light shed by the fingernail moon.

As they slunk around the tavern and scuttled toward the gate in the wall, Adelaide contacted Cyr. *We're going to need your help again soon. Where are you?* She scanned the sky and top of the wall for his hawk-shaped shadow.

Soaring over the town. Did you find your parents?

Yes, and we're heading toward the gate now. She spotted him winging toward the front end of the town in a wide arc.

When I tell you, do what you did earlier to the guards. It seemed to have worked. But be careful since they'll be more alert. She hoped the gate was still open. If they were caught, the Gyndilians would probably tie them up or kill them.

Adelaide led the others forward. When they were about ten paces from the gate, she held her hand up for them to stop as they huddled together in the silhouette of the town's wall.

"Now what?" Her father breathed into her ear.

Adelaide startled. "Just wait."

Alright, Cyr. We're ready, she told the hawk.

A darker, starless piece of the sky streaked down to the other side of the gate. Yelps and gasps of pain erupted, and Adelaide trotted to the gate before anyone could help the guards.

She pushed against the thick wooden door and found it … locked. The Gyndilians must have realized their mistake after recovering from Cyr's first attack.

Adelaide pushed harder, with her whole body, but the gate still didn't budge.

"Move out of the way," Ferand said and strode up with Raymond.

They glanced at each other, nodded, and ran at the door. Realizing what they were going to do, Adelaide leapt out of the way.

Ferand wasn't the strongest man in Alesfirth, nor was Raymond, but they did have plenty of muscle from plowing fields for decades, and the gate had been built in a hurry to stymie the peasants' fear after the first attack. The Gyndilians hadn't reinforced it.

On the men's second attempt, the boards creaked and split. The men ripped off the broken pieces to create a ragged hole.

Are you coming? These humans taste bad, Cyr said.

Yes, Adelaide replied. *The gate was locked, so we had to break it.*

The men helped the women through the hole, and Adelaide pushed from behind, urging them to hurry. She flicked glances back to make sure no one was coming, and so far, no one was. But it would only be a matter of time; the destruction of the door hadn't been quiet.

"You next, Adelaide," Ferand said, pushing her toward the hole. She hoisted up her dress and climbed through, a jagged piece of wood scraping her head.

Cyr still fought with the Gyndilians, who attempted to dart around him to grab the women. Each time the guards reached for their crossbows or took a step toward them, Cyr bit their hands or raked his claws across their faces.

The men were making too much noise, and Cyr dropped uncomfortably close to the men's grasping hands; he was wearying.

Just keep at it until we're out of crossbow range, Adelaide told him.

Cyr shrieked in acknowledgment.

"Let's go," she called to the group and took off running.

The others followed, Raymond now carrying Elysande, who was awake and staring around with wide eyes. "Why are we running? Where're we going?"

"We're going to a safer town."

"But how will Con and Gunter find us?" Elysande asked.

Poor Elysande. How could she cope with the idea that one of her beloved brothers was a murderer? Adelaide wouldn't tell her, and Kiona would probably wait until she was older, once she herself knew the truth.

"They'll be able to find us," Raymond reassured Elysande. "They're smart. Now please stop talking."

When the others lagged behind, and Adelaide judged they were too far away to be shot, she slowed to a walk. A quick walk. No one followed them yet, but if the Gyndilians decided to, it wouldn't take them long to reach the group on horses. Adelaide longed to fly, but she couldn't carry all of them.

Cyr settled on her shoulder. His feathers stuck out at all angles like Gunter's hair, and his tail feathers drooped.

Well done. She stroked him.

He closed his eyes. *Don't ask me to do that again for a very long time. Or preferably never. Humans have much more persistence than squirrels and taste much worse.*

Adelaide smiled. *Hopefully you won't have to do it again. But you are a very brave hawk.*

He chirped in contentment.

"I'm proud of how you and your bird handled yourself back there." Ferand squeezed her arm.

My name's Cyr, the hawk murmured.

Adelaide's heart thrummed. At least she'd done one thing right. "Thank you."

"And now I hope you're going to explain where you've been this whole time and why you left with no explanation."

Adelaide didn't need light to see the anger and betrayal crackling in her mother's eyes. The warmth she'd felt a moment ago vanished.

"And I would like to know where my sons are." Kiona lengthened her stride to match theirs.

"Ade knows where Gunter and Con are?" Elysande turned large, luminescent eyes on her.

Adelaide flinched at the girl's gaze. She couldn't tell them the truth of Gunter, not here in front of his little sister. "Conrad is in Dhalion, and if Gunter's not here, then I don't know where he is."

"Why is Conrad in the King's City? And why isn't Gunter

with him?" Raymond asked.

They stopped in a copse of cottonwoods. Adelaide wanted to lie down and sleep for a hundred years. She would rather fight a horde of dragons than relate to her and Gunter's parents what she and their sons had done. Fighting dragons would only elicit physical pain; this would be emotional torment for everyone.

Adelaide leaned against a tree's coarse trunk, fiddling with the loose pieces of her braid. "After Emma ..." she swallowed and continued, "was killed, I, Gunter, Conrad, and some other people from Alesfirth began a rebellion to overthrow King Ganelon and Prince Elias. It was my idea."

Stunned silence, then the two women cried out at the same time.

"Excuse me?" Galiena yelped.

"Gunter and Conrad did what?"

Adelaide rubbed her head. If she hadn't stolen the daggers the day before the festival, she probably wouldn't have met Prince Elias, and he wouldn't have singled her out. He and his father would still be alive, ruling the kingdom justly.

Would Adelaide have married Gunter? She supposed they would have found happiness together, though it was hard to imagine. And what of the dragons? Would they have died slowly from starvation or still gone to Neklosa?

"We're waiting, dear," her mother prompted.

Taking a deep breath, Adelaide launched into her tale, speaking as if the events had happened to another person. And some of it felt that way. So much had occurred since those late-night meetings in the abandoned barn near Alesfirth that she hardly recognized that person.

When she came to the end of her tale, Elysande had fallen asleep, so Adelaide explained what Gunter had done to Elias. They deserved to know the truth, however much it would hurt.

"My kind-hearted Gunter? He would never, he could never ..." Kiona's voice trailed off incoherently. Raymond drew her close.

"It was my fault," Adelaide whispered, staring at the stars. "I was the one who started the rebellion and gave him the dagger. Without those ideas and the weapon, the opportunity would never have arisen."

A hand touched her arm, and Adelaide glanced up, surprised to find that it belonged to Raymond. "Perhaps, but he still made his decision, Adelaide. We don't blame you."

Kiona shook her head, tears slipping down her face.

"And you said that you don't know where he is now?" Raymond asked.

"No." Adelaide sagged further down the tree. "That was the last time I saw him. But Conrad is safe in Dhalion with the others. They're going to help fight the Gyndilians." Adelaide shouldn't have said that.

Kiona moaned like a bitter wind. "My boys. My boys are going to die. They're dead already."

Raymond drew her close. "They're not dead, nor will they die. They're strong. They'll survive."

The wounds Adelaide had inflicted on Gunter's family glared at her, and she had no way to heal them. She wasn't Elias. She caused pain instead of healing it.

She scrunched back into the tree's branches as if they could shield her from all the forms of heartbreak this night.

"And you've been in Dhalion all this time?" Galiena murmured.

"Yes."

"Doing what?" Her father asked.

Adelaide decided not to tell them about her transformation and trek to Niclond; her parents had enough to sift through, and she couldn't handle their horror. "I was making sure Berold and the other knights treated Conrad well and helped plan ways to fight the Gyndilians."

Galiena shook her head. "No. I don't want to hear any more talk of fighting or rebellions. You've done enough, Adelaide. Let the rulers take care of the Gyndilians."

"There are no rulers, Mother. Not anymore." Because of her.

"Let's not discuss this right now," Ferand said, lying on the grass. "It's late, and it's enough that Adelaide is here with us now."

"That's true," Galiena said, squeezing Adelaide's shoulder before lying down beside Ferand.

Despite Adelaide's exhaustion, her mind kept returning to the last few months and what she could have done differently to avoid causing so much despair. She stared at the shadows flickering in the trees as clouds swept across the sliver of moon.

Some of Elias's last words floated back to her: "Don't forget how to smile," and she attempted to do just that. It felt like a grimace.

How can I smile when you're not here and when my family's torn apart?

Chapter Thirty-Two

The group traveled to Pinhurn with as much celerity through the tree-sprinkled and night-darkened land as they could. They always traveled at night in case the Gyndilians decided to pursue them, as well as to hide from thieves.

Even though Adelaide traveled with people she loved, and her mother's bread-brown eyes lit up when they saw her each day, Adelaide couldn't help but yearn for the days when she had traveled this path with Elias, when she wasn't faced with her faults each time she looked at Gunter's parents.

And what was happening to Odo? It was hard to believe that the Gyndilians would treat him well after seeing the destruction they had inflicted on Alesfirth. Adelaide didn't talk anymore about her plans to find him. It would only cause her parents more pain.

At one point as they walked, Elysande asked Adelaide, "Can you sing a song? It'll help keep the shadows away." She glanced warily at the swaying trees.

Adelaide's voice was too raspy for singing. And remembering Elias and his songs made it hard to breathe, as if she would suffocate from missing him. But it was a small thing to give this girl who had lost so much.

Like a shy bird, the first song Elias had sung to Adelaide opened its wings in her mind. She hesitated to share it, but Elysande was gazing at her with expectant eyes, and no other song came to her.

> *"The grass is beaming,*
> *the sky is calling*
> *in my home Klinhun.*
>
> *The dragons stomp,*
> *the humans tromp*
> *in my home Klinhun.*
>
> *The wind whistles,*
> *the water ripples*
> *in my home Klinhun.*
>
> *The birds soar,*
> *the dragons roar,*
> *in my home Klinhun.*
>
> *Soon I will be there,*
> *in that land fair,*
> *in my home Klinhun."*

Her voice dropped to a whisper on the last stanza as she recalled Elias's autumn-honey voice erupting into the air, coaxing her to change her perspective.

"Where did you learn that, dear?" Her mother asked. Everyone's eyes were riveted on Adelaide.

She shrugged. "From a friend." She picked up her pace so

she wouldn't have to answer any more questions.

Not long after, Raymond and her father began discussing the impending war.

"Klinhun doesn't stand a chance without a king," Raymond said.

"I just don't understand why they captured Alesfirth instead of focusing on the northeastern side of the country," Ferand mused. "That would give them a straighter route to Dhalion. Unless they're going to use Alesfirth as some kind of outpost for their troops and work their way to Dhalion that way."

"They could," Raymond said doubtfully. "But it would take longer and cause more casualties than marching south past Fernohn into Dhalion." He rubbed his beard. "Perhaps they're using Alesfirth as a distraction while their real armies march toward the northeastern side of Klinhun."

Adelaide shivered and hoped that Berold and the knights would make their way to Gyndilad soon. The farther away the fight took place from Dhalion, the heart of Klinhun, the better.

How had Elias and his father endured it? With each passing day spent as a human, Adelaide's skin felt too tight, like a cocoon keeping her prisoner inside her own body.

She longed to stretch, to break free of the cocoon, to taste the wind with her tongue and wings. She watched Cyr with envy each time he took flight; her gaze wandered more and more to the unbroken sky.

Her skin was as hot as a blacksmith's forge, but when she touched it, it felt normal. The heat came from inside and seemed as if it would scorch her completely if she didn't let it out soon.

In the early grey hours before dawn, Galiena took Adelaide's hand. "You seem more at peace now than you did before you left us. It lightens me to see it."

Her mother's words startled Adelaide; she didn't feel at peace. She felt as if she was carrying a cart of eggs up a mountain and had to make sure none of them broke along the way. But her cargo was more precious: people's and dragon's lives. And everything was going wrong: the wheel broken, a raging river in front of her, an ice storm. Each day the cart grew heavier and her arms more tired. It was an important task, but she wasn't sure if she could complete it.

"What do you mean?" Adelaide asked.

Galiena's eyebrows knitted together. "It's difficult to explain. It's not necessarily that you're happier, but after Emma died, you shrunk in on yourself, not letting anyone in. But now you're starting to open back up and enjoy the world again. You seem less angry."

Her mother squeezed her hand, and Adelaide relished her mother's touch. She didn't know when or if she would have the opportunity to be this close to her again.

Eight days after leaving Alesfirth, the group arrived in the middle of the night at the gate of Pinhurn. Adelaide could barely make out the outlines of the Spearhead Mountains and the wink of moonlight on the lake past the village.

A knight in armor straightened at their approach. "What are all of you doing here so late?"

The knight beside him yawned.

"We have escaped from Alesfirth and seek shelter here," Ferand explained.

After searching through their satchels, the guards let them enter the town. Adelaide led the group to the stables.

As Kiona took Elysande to an empty corner of a stall and Adelaide's parents made themselves comfortable on the straw, she sidled over to Raymond.

When she had told Odo that she was leaving Alesfirth, it

had caused her parents much anxiety and grief. This time they would know where she was going, but her absence would still give them sleepless nights and haunted dreams.

She hated inflicting more wounds. But what else could she do? Odo needed her, and her parents wouldn't let her leave.

"I'm departing tonight," she whispered to Raymond. "Tell my parents I can find Odo faster on my own."

"But—"

"Tell them I'll return when we win this war. You all need to stay here where it's safe and try not to worry. I'll be fine." Probably.

Before Raymond could respond, Adelaide strode with a tight chest to her parents.

Her father gazed at her as she settled in the straw, and she wondered if he guessed her intentions. If so, he didn't say anything.

She made herself as comfortable as possible in the itchy hay and murmured, "good-night," to her parents. She stared at their sleeping forms, pondering if this would be the last time she'd see them. If so, would they remember her fondly or with frustration?

Emma wouldn't have caused their parents so much sorrow; there had been no room in her for such cruelty.

Adelaide stuffed her cloak in her mouth to keep her moan quiet as the absence of her sister came like a winter wind, slicing through her. *Oh, Emma, they need you. You would have taken good care of them.*

When the pain abated, she turned to face the wooden beams that let in shards of moonlight. *Cyr?*

Yes? His voice was close.

Where are you?

Above you outside. No one is around if you'd like to leave now.

She had told him her plan earlier. He hadn't understood why she'd want to leave her family so soon after finding them or why they couldn't all go search for Odo. To him, she was strong enough to carry both families.

After memorizing her parents' sleep-smoothed faces and apologizing silently to them, she grabbed her satchel and slipped out of the barn.

Adelaide nodded at the guards as she walked by, and they nodded back. When the gate disappeared behind a bend in the road, she walked into the forest.

She closed her eyes and transformed, relishing the strength of her muscles and the heat emanating from her stomach and spreading through her body.

Adelaide leapt into the air, her burdens shrinking the higher she flew.

After dipping and diving on the air currents until she felt home again in this body, she soared away to save her brother.

Chapter Thirty-Three

This is so much better than walking. Adelaide stretched her silvery wings as far as they could reach, scraping a boulder on the peak beside her.

Humans should have wings too, Cyr said from where he flew on her left.

Perhaps, but they'd probably misuse them, especially if they could breathe fire. She imagined an army of Gyndilians who could change into dragons and shivered at the destruction they would wreak.

She and Cyr flew near the Gyndilian border, enjoying the taste of pine and cool mountain streams rushing by on the wind.

Orange lights winked in the darkness below.

What are those? Adelaide squinted at the lights.

What? Cyr said from atop her head.

Those lights below us on the far side of that row of mountains.

I don't see any lights, Cyr grumbled.

I'm going to fly closer to them. Adelaide pulled her wings in and leaned forward, veering past a peak swathed in snow.

She zoomed out from behind the mountain and dipped in the air when she realized what the lights were.

Torches. Those must be Gyndilians. There were scores and scores of the torches fluttering intermittently on the ground like fireflies—too many to count.

She couldn't see the knights from this high and didn't want to soar closer and risk being spotted, but what else could those lights mean? Klinhun didn't have that many soldiers ready for war. And they wouldn't have made it this far north yet.

They were doomed; this vast army would wipe out the smaller Klinhun host in only a few days.

The fire raced down Adelaide's body, and she closed her eyes, focusing on the familiar weight of her wings. She would *not* fall here.

What does that mean? Cyr asked, leaping into the sky for a better view.

Adelaide's body stopped glowing, and she gazed at the lights, wondering again with horror at how many Gyndilian soldiers were hidden in the pockets of darkness among the specks of light.

It means that Odo will have to wait a little longer to be rescued. We have to tell Berold about this army.

Chapter Thirty-Four

Adelaide landed on the cliff so hard she jarred her legs and back. She curled up across from Dhalion's castle, her tail resting against her cheek scales. She didn't bother transforming; she'd probably crumble if she did.

She had flown from the Spearhead Mountains to Dhalion in two days, barely stopping to rest. She had even soared during the day, flying high enough to look like a hovering bird and being careful not to sneeze out any flames.

She had to tell Berold about the Gyndilian force, but not until she had a good doze. The ground was wondrously soft and stable, and her muscles melted into it ...

We have visitors, Cyr warned from dream-far away.

Good day Adelaide, Silverscales. I hope the sun smiled on your journey.

Adelaide groaned at Resse's cheery voice. *Go away. I'm sleeping.*

You'd think she'd be more glad to see us since we're helping save her country, Turquan said.

We're glad you returned safely and are sorry to disturb you. But now that these males have woken you, how's your family? Esa asked.

Adelaide sighed and stretched, creating long furrows in the grass that would've made her farmer father proud. She sat up and looked at her four dragon friends lounging close by.

When Adelaide's gaze landed on Resse, she laughed.

Fluffy chipmunks scampered over his buttery-yellow scales and green spikes, chittering at each other.

I see that you found some new friends, Resse.

His mouth pulled into a toothy grin. *I gave them a few nuts and now they won't leave me alone.*

Cyr clicked his beak from atop Adelaide's head. *They look delicious.*

Resse squinted at him. *I won't take it kindly if you try to eat one of my friends.* He gently picked one off his back and tickled its white belly with a talon—it was impressive that he didn't spear the thing—and put it back, where it scampered around his spikes.

Adelaide didn't understand why the creatures weren't terrified of him; perhaps they could sense his soft heart. Or perhaps they were just desperate for an easy meal.

Well, I'm glad you've returned, Turquan said. *It's been a bit dull around here. Did you happen to see any exceptional human females?*

Adelaide glanced around and noticed for the first time how deserted the castle grounds were. No one practiced archery or swordplay on the lawn, no horses neighed, nor did any men shout orders. And oddest of all, Berold hadn't come out to demand a report, nor had Conrad come to ask about his family.

Where is everyone?

They left two days ago to march to Gyndilad. We remained here to wait for you, Picot, the taciturn brown-and-white dragon, said.

Adelaide nodded, relieved that the army had left, but would

it be soon enough to reach the Gyndilian army before it began wreaking havoc on Klinhun?

Ignoring her throbbing muscles and the hollowness of her belly, she stood. *Please tell Berold that I saw an army of Gyndilians marching along the border of our countries to the east of the Spearheads toward Fernohn. There were at least 500 knights. It was hard to make out an exact estimate because it was night, and I didn't want to venture too close.*

Resse cocked his head. *Why don't you tell Berold yourself?*

I must find my brother. He's been captured by the Gyndilians and taken to their capital.

The dragons hissed.

Oh, and tell Conrad that his family is safe with mine in Pinhurn. Adelaide unfurled her wings, trying to ignore their protests from her recent flight.

Nay, Adelaide. Esa placed a lavender-scaled foot on Adelaide's silver one. *You should tell them yourself, for they will have questions that we can't answer. And you must rest and eat. You will be no help to your brother if you die from exhaustion before you even reach him.*

Adelaide tugged in her wings, seeing the prudence of Esa's words. She would like to hear Berold's plan and talk to Conrad herself. It wouldn't take very long to catch up to them. But most of all, she craved a nap. *Very well. We'll leave after I eat and have a brief rest.*

I'll get you some food. With two leaps, Resse disappeared into the forest.

One deer, three pigeons, two rabbits—one of which Cyr gladly finished for her—and a long nap later, the five dragons sprang into the indigo sky.

Thunder rumbled in the distance, and lightning lit up the sculpted clouds ahead of them.

The company stayed well away from the storm, soaring beneath the mountainous clouds, keeping their eyes trained on the ground for any sign of the Klinian army.

Did all the men from Alesfirth join the army? Adelaide asked.

I'm not sure. There was a group of males and a female with that man you call Conrad, Resse answered.

What about Hubert? He's a small boy with blond hair and gaps in his teeth. The thought of the boy younger than her brother going into battle sent tremors through Adelaide's tail. It would be her fault if he died.

He's fine. Turquan turned over, exposing his pale belly to the clouds. *He's staying with a family in Dhalion.*

How do you know that?

I arranged it with Conrad and the boy's brother.

Turquan's interest in Hubert surprised her; besides his jesting about women, he was usually less inclined to interact with humans than the other dragons.

He and the boy bonded while you were away, Esa explained.

Turquan snorted, sending a puff of steam whooshing into the sky. *I'm not sure 'bonded' is the right word. I let him clamber onto me like Resse does with his rodents, and he scratched between my scales. He's a good boy.*

He played with me nearly as much as he did with you, Resse said from behind them. *And I didn't almost knock him over with my tail.*

But he liked it, didn't he?

Perhaps the dragons did have a natural inclination to protect humans.

When they glided by the orange heat print of Manfred's house, Adelaide tensed.

Esa swung her neck around. *What is it?*

The flames in Adelaide's stomach raced into her throat, begging to be let out. This was the man who had taken Elias's father from him, who had caused him so much pain.

The man who lives in that house killed Elias's father. Flames tickled the back of her throat, and it took all her control not to unleash them on Manfred's house.

King Ganelon? Esa glanced down at the house.

Yes, Adelaide hissed.

Why? Esa sounded more perplexed than angry.

It doesn't make sense, but Manfred said that he poisoned King Ganelon to supposedly save him from the pain he faced in a human body and that the humans weren't ready for the dragons to return. Sparks leapt from Adelaide's mouth, and her tail whipped against her side.

He shouldn't have taken matters into his own hands. He didn't have the right. Poor King Ganelon.

Adelaide gazed at Esa's face, her eyelids lowered in sorrow. *You're not upset that Manfred betrayed and killed your king?*

Resse soared up on Adelaide's other side, and Cyr grumbled as he had to drop out of the way of the dragon. *Of course Esa's angry. She loved King Ganelon as much as we all did.*

Esa dipped her head in agreement.

Then why do neither of you want to burn his house down?

Vengeance is not our way, Picot piped up from behind. *It leads only to a never-ending cycle of violence and bloodshed. We would become what the humans feared we were.*

Adelaide's flames and fury evaporated, replaced with horror. She had wanted to destroy the home and the man whom Elias had loved as a dear friend.

And then she was plummeting to the ground.

Chapter Thirty-Five

Before Adelaide could even try to transform back, talons snatched her out of the air. Her stomach heaved as the world spun. Closing her eyes did little to help the whirling, helpless sensation.

I got you, Resse said.

Please put me on the ground, Adelaide said, her cheeks flaming in embarrassment.

Resse did, gently.

Once her stomach stopped heaving, she said, *I'll be off then.* She marched into the trees, Cyr soaring above, asking if she was alright.

Leaving like this, she'd be spared the pain of her friends choosing not to follow her and the embarrassment of them telling her that she was a horrible leader not worth following. *She* wouldn't want to follow someone into battle who couldn't even control their own body.

Did the fall addle her brain? Turquan said from behind her.

Adelaide, where are you going? Esa's gently perplexed voice undid her.

Adelaide leaned against a tree, rubbing her eyes. She would *not* cry in front of them after already humiliating herself.

I obviously can't control my dragon form or my rage, so I'm in no position to lead you. You may return to Niclond.

Turquan snorted. *This is our land, if you remember, and we're going to protect it.*

No leader is perfect. Esa came over, her breath warm on Adelaide's back. *Not even King Ganelon or Prince Elias were.*

Adelaide found that hard to believe, although Elias had mentioned having a temper. She'd only seen glimpses of it when she'd pushed him too far, but then it had been deserved.

I remember once when King Ganelon kept Prince Elias grounded for a week because he had flown so fast that his flight had uprooted several trees which fell on some dragons, Resse said, laughing.

Adelaide turned around. "Truly?"

He nodded.

And you were the one who was making him fly so fast because you two were racing across the island, right? Esa eyed Resse.

His buttery scales turned a sunrise pink. *You remember that?*

And Esa here, Turquan's tail poked her in the side, *took forever to learn how to breathe fire.*

Adelaide turned to her. *How long?*

Five years. Then Esa poked Turquan in the chest. *And you have dozens of scorch marks from every single female on the island.*

And they look mighty fine, too. He nodded in satisfaction.

And I'm bad at being around other dragons, Picot said, gazing at his feet. *I just can't seem to think of the right things to say.*

But you have an amazing memory and are very intelligent, Adelaide told him.

Picot bowed under the compliment.

The point is, Resse said, *that we all have flaws. But we learn to overcome them or accept them. We don't want to leave you just because you're not perfect. That's not what good friends do.*

Esa nudged her shoulder. *You'll learn how to overcome this. You've done so much already. It'll just take time.*

Adelaide had doubts, but her friends had given her hope again, and her body felt as light as a windblown leaf. She nodded. "Thank you."

Ready to fly? Cyr asked.

Adelaide breathed a sigh, using her friends' confident gazes and encouraging nods like handholds to climb out of the tree of her worries. *Yes. Let's find that army and warn them of the Gyndilians.*

Not much later, they stopped flying near the star-splattered Wymar River where six dozen leather tents sat interspersed amid the forest. A few fires blazed and popped.

Adelaide's heart clenched at the small size of the Klinian force. They would be slaughtered by the Gyndilians, but at least this way, with her news, they would know what they were marching into.

Ready to land? Adelaide tucked her wings in for a dive.

The middle of a forest isn't a good place to land, Picot said. *Aim for that small clearing to the right of the river instead. There are fewer trees to break.*

And we won't frighten all the humans, Resse added.

Adelaide shifted her tail and aimed her body toward the clearing. The grassy field was too small for them all to land in at the same time, so they took turns.

She closed her eyes against the voice in her head that told her she would never be able to land in that tiny place.

You can do it, Silverscales, Esa said from below. *You've landed in small places like this before.*

The others offered their encouragement, and Cyr said, *I'll be with you.*

Their voices drowned out the voice of her doubt, and she followed Resse. She nearly wiped out a tree on the edge of the clearing, but she managed to land.

Well done, Esa said, grinning.

Adelaide smiled back, wondering why such a little accomplishment had the power to lift her so high.

I'll go find Berold and Conrad. I'll return here when I've finished telling them about the Gyndilians. Adelaide closed her eyes, preparing to transform.

I'll go with you, Resse said. *I'd like to see what's happening, and my gift of seeing lies may be helpful.*

They walked through the forest until they reached the nearest fire where a man in chain mail stood. When he noticed Adelaide, he stalked forward, his hand on his sword hilt.

"Who are you?" His gaze lingered on Resse's pie-sized eyes.

"I'm Adelaide, a fellow Klinian and friend of the dragons. Please fetch Berold and a man from Alesfirth named Conrad. I must speak to them."

The man scowled. "How do I know you're telling the truth and not a spy from our enemies?"

Resse took a step closer into the firelight, revealing his serpentine neck and spiked head. *Because she is telling the truth.*

The knight gaped at him, his lips moving, but no sound came out. Then he managed to whisper, "Wait here," before darting away. He nearly fell into the fire in his haste.

Adelaide sat on a boulder. *Well done.*

Resse laid down, his neck stretching out toward the flames, and examined her with an eye that reflected the fire's glow. *I didn't mean to frighten him.*

Well, you didn't succeed.

Resse sighed, his breath mingling with the fire's smoke. *I'll be glad when the humans trust us once more.*

Hopefully it won't take too long. We need to work together in this fight.

Adelaide tried not to look at Resse, for his stretched-out form reminded her of another dragon that would lie beside the fire at night.

"Adelaide, you've returned. How's my family?" Conrad rounded the fire toward her, barely giving Resse a second glance. The others from Alesfirth walked behind him, darting wide-eyed glances at the dragon, who had lifted his head at their approach.

Conrad hugged her, his eyes bright with hope. She was grateful that she didn't have to snuff it out this time.

"They're well, though they miss you. I took them out of Alesfirth with my family, and they're now safe in Pinhurn."

Conrad breathed a sigh of relief, but his eyebrows didn't smooth out. "And my brother?"

Adelaide glanced at the fire's soothing dance. If only the difficulties in her life could mingle and weave so fluidly. "I didn't see him."

"And my family, Adelaide? Did you see them?" One of the other boys piped up.

Adelaide regarded Rohesia's and the young men's dirty faces lit with the same eagerness that had shone in Conrad's. She glanced away, frustrated with herself for not spending more time in Alesfirth searching for their families. The news of Odo's kidnapping had chased all other thoughts out of her mind.

"I didn't see any of your families. I'm sorry. There was no time to look, but I'm sure they're fine." An assurance as weak as a starving peasant, and she owed them more.

Their shoulders dropped, and Adelaide promised herself that she would bring hope to these boys and Rohesia again, real hope that would materialize into something lasting.

Of course, last time she'd tried something like that, it had ended in disaster. They were probably better off without her, but it was too late now. She had taken responsibility for them and would see them to the end one way or another.

"What's Alesfirth like now with the Gyndilians ruling?" Bodin, Hubert's brother, asked.

"I wasn't there long. But some of the fields are burned, and all the peasants are living in the village."

As the group discussed this disturbing news, Adelaide leaned toward Conrad and murmured, "They took Odo to the capital of Gyndilad. I'm going to find him and bring him back."

Conrad frowned. "How do you plan on doing that?"

"I don't know, but—"

"You sent for me?" Berold said in an agitated voice, striding toward them.

Before she could reply, he stopped in front of her. "I'll have you know that I'm the commander of this force and will be giving the commands. You are still just a peasant."

Adelaide stood, hands on her hips. "Perhaps, but one with scales who can breathe fire if I choose."

Berold crossed his arms and glowered at her. "So, what do you have to say that is so important?"

Her friends had stopped talking to watch the exchange.

"The other dragons and I just arrived from Dhalion. Gyndilad has indeed taken Alesfirth captive. They've burned the surrounding fields and all the villagers are living in town guarded by soldiers. For what purpose, I don't know.

"The Gyndilians have also taken some of the young people from Alesfirth to their capital, Weitzen."

Berold kicked a rock toward the fire and pulled his sword halfway out of its scabbard, then let it slide back. "There's nothing we can do about those in Gyndilad right now."

His reply had been similar to Adelaide's response. But regardless of what he thought, she'd go after Odo. Berold wasn't her commander, and Odo was her brother. She wouldn't let them kill or harm him as they had Emma.

"I wonder if Alesfirth is their base now, and if they'll strike from there," Berold mused, stroking his stubble.

"The Gyndilians aren't going to invade Klinhun from Alesfirth. Or at least, not right away. That town could just be a diversion," Adelaide said, remembering her father's and Raymond's discussions.

Berold's hand paused on his chin. "Oh? And what makes you say that?"

"As Cyr and I flew over the Spearheads on our—"

"Flew?" The knight who had gone after Berold stared at her.

"Yes, flew." She waved a hand at him, keeping her gaze on the swordmaster. "In the Spearheads, near the Gyndilian border, Cyr and I saw some lights, so we went to investigate. The lights turned out to be the torches of an army, probably at least 500 knights. I couldn't make out the exact number in the dark without risking exposure."

Berold paced around the fire, pulling his sword in and out. "Well, so much for our plan to surprise them at the border. Now it will be more like standing our ground. Five hundred, did you say? We barely have 200."

He turned back to her. "How long ago did you see them and where exactly?"

"About three days ago now on our border in the middle of the Spearheads."

"That's near one of our outposts. I wonder if they're going to take it or pass it by. We don't have the time or men to aid them now. Oh, if only the towns had sent me more men," Berold moaned, resuming his pacing.

"We're doomed to death or capture." Rohesia put a hand to her forehead.

Adelaide knew how the young woman felt. How many times had she wanted to give up? Just this very night she'd wanted to pass on the leadership to someone else.

But she had to encourage the others as the dragons had encouraged her earlier. "It may seem like we're doomed, but there's always hope. What happened to our saying, 'for our families, for our people, and for our futures'? Never give up, no matter what."

"We'll still march north to the border as before, but at a quicker pace," Berold said.

He turned to the knight beside him. "Tell Tanored and Aufrid to scout ahead on horseback to the border and return with any news. They are to leave immediately. Then gather the other commanders and meet at my tent. We have much planning to do."

The knight nodded and darted away.

Berold glanced at Adelaide. "We will need the dragons' help."

You shall have it, Resse said, startling the men, who backed away, their gazes riveted on his eyes that glowed as if they had sucked out all the flames from the fire.

Berold nodded. "You will indubitably wish to listen to our talk of strategy."

Of course. And we will offer our protection as you march north.

"You and the others will," Adelaide clarified. "I'm going to Weitzen to find my brother."

Conrad stepped toward her. "You can't go alone into Gyndilad. They'll catch you before you can even find out where they've taken Odo."

He speaks wisely, Silverscales, Resse said. *I will go with you.*

"Very well. We shall leave tomorrow night, since this one is mostly past."

"Do what you wish, since you will anyway," Berold said. "Just don't take all the dragons with you." He strode away, and Adelaide suppressed the childish urge to stick her tongue out at his back.

"Why must you leave so soon, Adelaide?" Conrad persisted. "I'm sure the Gyndilians won't hurt Odo. Besides, you just returned from a long trip and should rest. At least stay with us until we reach Fernohn. It will give you time to train with the dragons for the upcoming battle."

Conrad gazed at her with pleading eyes, and Adelaide hesitated. She was still drained even after the previous day's long nap, and the thought of another brutally long, swift flight made her body ache. If she kept up like this, there wouldn't be anything left of her to help Odo.

Fernohn might be on the way to where she believed Weitzen was, which reminded her that she needed to look at a map of Gyndilad before she left. It wouldn't do Odo any good if she got lost.

"Please, Adelaide. I've lost Emma and possibly Gunter, and I don't wish to lose you as well," Conrad said in his older brother tone that he had used to try to sway her and Gunter from doing something foolhardy. This time it worked.

"Fine." She sighed. "I'll travel with the army as far as Fernohn, then if Resse agrees, we will leave to find and rescue my brother."

That sounds like a good plan to me, Resse agreed.

"As long as the Gyndilian army doesn't find us first," Sayer said.

Chapter Thirty-Six

Gunter held the crossbow to his shoulder. His arms and fingers no longer trembled, but the iron-and-wooden weapon remained awkward in his grip just like the sword, spear, axe, club, hammer, and ball and chain that the knights had forced him to practice with.

The ball and chain had been the worst. He'd gotten it stuck in a fence post, and when he had yanked it out, it had cut through another soldier's armor, earning him two days without food and water, even though it had been an accident.

"Good," Dunstan called out from somewhere behind Gunter. "Now that you've put in the lock, aim at your target, and press the lever to release the arrow. Remember, it's much easier than using a longbow."

It may have been easier, but it was heavier, and Gunter's muscle had wasted away from his time in the cell without food.

"And don't forget to keep your eyes on the target."

Right now, the target was just a red circle painted on a hay bale at the end of the field, but in a few days, it could be a friend or family member.

No, he would not let that happen. He would leave before they forced him to shoot an arrow at Conrad or Adelaide. He could always turn the weapon on the Gyndilians, though he'd already failed once to choose death over his family's safety, so he could again.

"Concentrate," Dunstan said.

Gunter took a deep breath, stared at the red circle, and pressed the lever. The bolt zoomed past the target, bounced off a tree trunk and landed with a clatter at the tree's knobby-kneed roots.

"Well, at least you hit something that time." Dunstan walked over to him. "I think you're getting better."

"And it didn't stick in the ground." Gunter's pride dulled as he thought about what getting better meant.

"It'll be fine." Dunstan placed a hand on his shoulder. "I'll make sure you're not sent to Alesfirth and that you're in the back whenever we fight. You won't have to kill anyone."

"You don't know that." Gunter shrugged off Dunstan's hand. "You might not be there. And I want to go to Alesfirth to see if my family's alive."

Dunstan nodded and leaned against a post. "But if you keep this up, then you won't need to worry about it. All the knights you'd be fighting would scatter, afraid of flying projectiles."

Gunter chuckled. Dunstan's jesting often pulled him out of his foul moods. He appreciated these private lessons with the knight; it was the only time they could speak freely, and it allowed Gunter to escape his dark thoughts and the darker gazes of the Gyndilians.

"How's your wife and daughter?" Gunter asked.

Dunstan ran a hand across his forehead. "I just received a letter from Ailith. She's doing well. Sewing and gardening mostly. She sends you greetings."

Gunter saw past the man's serene expression to the worry in his cobalt eyes and tight shoulders and knew that he missed his wife and daughter greatly. Probably as much as Gunter missed his family.

"Ready for some sword fighting?" Dunstan drew out his black-hilted sword.

Gunter groaned. "I still have bruises from the last time we fought."

"Then you must fight harder and smarter."

Hoofbeats thudded toward them, and they glanced over to see a knight riding toward them.

"Sire Dunstan, the Master has a message for you." The man held out a folded piece of parchment sealed with red wax.

Dunstan slid his sword back into its scabbard and took the letter. "Thank you, Edwin." He read the note, then looked up at Gunter, his face as white as the paper.

The look sliced Gunter in half. "What is it?" He took a step forward, as if to look at the letter, which was foolish since he couldn't read.

Dunstan swallowed and folded the piece of parchment. He didn't answer or look at Gunter. "You may return to your duties, Edwin."

"The Master wishes me to escort the prisoner to the house."

Dunstan put the piece of paper in his pocket and gestured forward. "Lead on, then."

The messenger set off at a walk toward the Master's house. Gunter had hoped he'd never have to set foot in there again. He tried, without success, to still the trembling of his fingers against the crossbow that he held.

"Give that to me before you drop it or hurt yourself." Dunstan reached for the bow, and Gunter gladly relinquished it.

The sorrow filling the knight's eyes made Gunter's heart and feet stutter. "What is it?"

"The Master has decided to take you and some other Klinians north for experimentation," Dunstan whispered.

Gunter's hands rained with sweat, but not from the summer warmth. He had heard that dreaded word on his first visit here. "Experimentation? For what?"

"I'm not sure. Something to help with the war. But—" Dunstan shook his head and gazed at the messenger's horse.

"But what?"

Dunstan sighed and pushed a lock of damp hair off his forehead. "I don't know what the experimentation entails, but we never see the men who are taken for it again."

Gunter's mouth went dry. Should he try to flee?

As if sensing his thoughts, Dunstan leaned toward him and murmured, "I would have helped you escape if I had known the Master had planned this. But it's too late now. They would catch you and know that I helped you." He held up the letter.

Gunter's shoulders slumped. What would his parents think when he didn't return? Who would comfort Elysande when she had nightmares or help Conrad plow the field when his father's bones ached? And Adelaide ... would he ever have the chance to explain himself to her? To hear pride in her voice instead of that terrible scream?

They stopped in front of the building that held all Gunter's fears. Would the Master loom over him for the rest of his life— however short that may be?

A cart attached to two horses blocked the way up the steps. Nine men ranging from Odo's age to that of his father's huddled in the cart between sacks of provisions, their expressions morose. He recognized a few from home, though he didn't know them well.

Two knights sat on the horses attached to the cart, two stood on either side, and two more stood behind, all with crossbows cocked and ready to shoot.

"Where are they taking us?" Gunter asked Dunstan.

The man surveyed the men and knights. "I'm not sure. Maybe to the Kalte Mountains."

"Is that far?"

Dunstan nodded. "A fortnight or so ride away."

"Thank you, men, for your contribution to Gyndilad, your

future home." The Master stood on the top step of the building, his arms brandished wide, his droopy-faced dog beside him. "May you have a safe and swift journey." He nodded at Dunstan.

"You must join the others." Dunstan placed a hand on Gunter's shoulder. "You will make it through this." His eyes were blue fire. "You may not be physically strong, but your heart is, and that's what matters."

"Thank you," Gunter whispered, warmth settling over him like bathwater. He had made an unlikely friend in Dunstan—a speck of light in this dark place. The man's belief in him inspired Gunter to boldly meet his fate, not run, or sit and cower. Perhaps that was the best way to repay him for his kindness.

"Don't start kissing. Your wife would be jealous," the Master called from the steps.

"Take this as a reminder that not everyone in Gyndilad is full of hatred and that some of us are fighting for you." Dunstan pressed something smooth and soft into Gunter's hand and nudged him away.

The only sign of Dunstan's anxiety was the tapping of his index finger on the crossbow. He had become a Gyndilian knight once more.

Gunter walked to the cart, holding tightly to the cloth Dunstan had given him.

"Hurry up," one of the knights barked at him.

Gunter hauled himself over the side of the wagon. He settled between a young blond-haired boy and a man his own age. The cart surged forward, and Gunter rolled into the boy.

"Sorry," he muttered.

The boy said nothing.

Gunter opened his dirt-encrusted hand to see what Dunstan had given him. It was a silky blue handkerchief, probably belonging to Dunstan's wife, Ailith. Gunter's rough fingers chafed it, and afraid he would dirty it, he stuffed it into his trousers.

He glanced back, trying to convey all his gratitude in a look to his friend.

The man nodded once, then the wagon turned around the building, and Gunter's only friend in the country disappeared as the wagon pulled him like an executioner to his fate.

Chapter Thirty-Seven

The journey passed in a haze of heat, sweat, and stifling silence. The men spent eight days squished together in the cart like tomatoes in a barrel, staring morosely at the flat land scattered with sparse pine trees and hazy smudges of mountains to the east.

In Weitzen, a city that sat on a grassy hill jutting out of the forest like a busy, angry anthill, Gunter was tempted to slip into the crowds and find his way to Alesfirth, but the guards watched them like hawks.

A few days later, in the evening at the edge of the forest, the wagon rolled to a stop at a town called Gindar. It looked more like a hideaway for outlaws than a town. The buildings were just slabs of pine nailed together. Cracked mugs and bits of cloth were strewn across the ground.

"We're almost there, men. Then the real fun begins," a knight said while stretching next to his horse.

The other knights grabbed some rope and tied each Klinian's arms and legs together, then stuffed a gag into their mouths.

"Why are you tying us up? No one's tried to escape," a man said while watching the Gyndilians tie up the boy.

"Not yet." A knight grabbed the man's arms and tied them behind his back. Then they began moving again.

Gunter's body trembled like wind-shaken leaves. This was it, then. The end.

He'd meet it with his body bound and terror in his eyes—a pig for slaughter—rather than fighting to his last breath as Adelaide would have done in his place.

Gunter's tremors increased when he realized that he'd never see her again, never have the chance to tell her how he wished he had never killed the king. That it was perhaps the most cowardly thing he'd done because he'd done it out of jealous rage, not for the good of their people.

Although that rage had been his own, it had been sowed by Adelaide's own fury. A sudden thought shook him more than his imminent death. What if Adelaide wasn't as brave as he'd thought? What if she'd begun the rebellion just to avenge Emma?

How he longed to return to life before Emma's death, when the days were still difficult but much simpler, when Ade would come over with apples and stay to talk. When they would dangle their feet in the Lentiasa River and splash each other.

Oh, why had he let her talk him into the rebellion and then tried to find her by himself? It had only led to broken dreams and stone-sharp regrets.

The wagon rolled to a stop at the base of a mountain; its bulk blocked out the few stars that peered through the evening sky. A yawning darkness in the mountain gaped at them, and Gunter clenched his cloak tight.

Would his life end in such a dark place? Somehow it seemed fitting for him.

"So, which of you wants to go first?" The knights surveyed them.

What an absurd question. No one in their right mind would

volunteer to step into that darkness where who knew what awaited them.

"Remember, the Master wanted the one who killed King Elias to go first as a special honor," a knight said, grinning gruesomely.

Gunter hunched down as if that would keep him from being seen.

The Klinians looked at each other with wide eyes. They hadn't known that the man who had killed the king was with them. Had they even known that their king was dead?

Gunter tried not to make eye contact as if they would see his failures and hand him over to the guards, which was ridiculous, because the knights knew who he was.

"Ah, yes. How could I forget? Grab him while I make the all-clear signal." A knight turned to the gash in the mountain and whistled three high notes.

Hands yanked Gunter's arms, and knowing it was futile, yet desperate not to enter that terrible darkness, he squirmed. But like a worm stuck on a hook, it did no good. The knights hauled him over the side of the cart to the ground.

He would have fallen—his legs were trembling so much—if one of the Gyndilians hadn't held his arm. They cut through the bonds on his legs. But the guard's grasp on his arm didn't give him a chance to flee. He wouldn't have made it far anyway on his wobbly legs.

A rumbling shook the earth and vibrated all the way up to Gunter's teeth. Boulders fell from the top of the mountain to the ground, sending a cloud of dirt into his eyes. He coughed and blinked, then turned his gaze to the cave.

A spurt of fire shot at them, and Gunter ducked. He didn't need to, for the flames ended before they reached him, but he could feel their heat cracking his skin.

His guard yanked him to his feet, and Gunter looked back at the cave. He gasped into his gag.

A giant scaled beast towered in front of the cave, the last

rays of the sun illuminating its black-and-gold neck and face shielded with spikes.

It couldn't be, but there was only one word for the creature. *Dragon.*

Chapter Thirty-Eight

Gunter had believed all the dragons dead or gone long ago. Now his mind blanked as he stared at the creature that stared back with such hate-filled eyes that Gunter could feel it like flames. He shrank against the knight who held him.

This one's first then? A raspy male voice echoed in Gunter's mind. He winced at the invasion.

"Yes, Lord Jeharrez," a knight responded in a creaky voice. "He's the one who killed the Klinian king."

Very good. Wait out here with the rest. The dragon's scorching golden eyes turned once more on Gunter, crushing him into an ant.

Get into the cave, the creature commanded.

Gunter couldn't move. His limbs had become ice.

If you don't go into the cave, I'll burn you to death right now.

Heat and smoke washed over Gunter, and he coughed. He took an unsteady step forward as the knight pushed him from behind. He fell onto the ground.

The beast growled. *Get him up.*

Someone yanked Gunter to his feet, and he took small, hobbling steps to the cave, his eyes on the ground so he wouldn't have to look at the beast that came closer with every step.

Two ... three ... four ... five ...

On the twelfth step, Gunter reached the cold confines of the cave. He lifted his gaze and saw only darkness.

The dragon thrust his snake-like head inside, and Gunter backed up until he felt smooth stone behind him.

The creature moved into the cave until only a thin seam of light remained around his body. His neck towered somewhere above Gunter, his eyes burning like death.

Turn around so I can undo your bindings, the raspy voice said.

He was going to free him? Gunter turned to face the rock, his skin feverish. Something sharp—probably one of the creature's talons—sliced through the bonds on his hands. Gunter removed the gag in his mouth and turned around, not wanting his back to the dragon.

Since you killed the king of Klinhun, I will show you some of the reasons why I'm doing what I am. I honor strength and courage, as all dragons do.

Gunter would have laughed if he hadn't been so terrified. Strength and courage? Those were the very attributes he lacked. He hadn't even tried to escape once he entered the Master's camp, and he'd given in easily to becoming a weapon for the Gyndilians.

But the dragon didn't know that. It just knew that he had killed King Elias.

Something hard touched Gunter's head, but he didn't have time to wonder what it was. Images more real than his own memories flickered through his mind.

A small orange dragon lay dead on the grass, its pale blue eyes staring at the sky, a sword lodged between its leg and belly. An adult dragon stood next to it, weeping with a bowed head.

Then, men yielding spears shouted for the dragons to leave. They called them demons, a curse to Klinhun.

Another dragon appeared, this one small and shrouded in green foliage. The bones in its face jutted out sharply, and grey scales littered the ground like pebbles, leaving the creature bald and vulnerable.

Along with the images came emotions—betrayal, sorrow, rage—so deep and powerful that their waves drowned Gunter. They became all he had known, all he knew, and all he would know. His self—his own memories and longings—were battered by the stronger emotions and memories until they would be swept away completely, and these new memories would become his identity.

Gunter tried to pull himself out of the sea, but each time he remembered who he was, another wave thrust him back down. He couldn't take anymore. He'd claw his heart out just to stop the intense, overwhelming emotions.

While watching a group of dragons keening at a cave-black sky, he cried out, "Stop! Stop. Please. I can't take anymore."

The images and with them, the drowning emotions, stopped. Gunter remembered who he was, Elysande and Conrad's brother, a broken, but human man.

He became aware again of his surroundings. He was kneeling on the ground, gasping, his hands over streaming eyes. He struggled up.

You're weaker than I thought, the dragon said in disgust. *That was only a tiny amount of the sorrow that my kind has suffered at the hands of the humans. And I must live in that suffering every day of my long life.* He roared, and Gunter covered his ears. Dirt rained down on his head.

Drink this. Something—a mug—appeared in the air in front of him, gripped in a large claw. *It will make you stronger.*

"What is it?" Gunter asked, gazing at the cup with suspicion.

Drink it, or you will die. The beast growled, and Gunter believed him.

He thought of Adelaide, Conrad, Elysande, his parents, Dunstan, and Ailith with her handkerchief and kind words. She and Dunstan had thought him strong and brave. But he wasn't. He was weak and terrified, too terrified to fight for those he loved.

Perhaps this liquid would make him strong, strong enough to finally be able to protect those he loved, or at least to be worthy of them. At the worst it would kill him, and then he would be free from the Gyndilians once and for all.

Gunter's hand shook so much that it took him two tries to grasp the drink. When he did, some of the liquid sloshed onto his arm, and it sizzled.

Gasping, he wiped the burning liquid onto his tunic. Then, with the dragon's gaze on him, he gulped down the drink.

Fire raced down Gunter's throat and through this body. He was a coal, a branch on fire.

He opened his mouth to scream, but nothing came out.

Chapter Thirty-Nine

Armies moved slowly, like a large, fat caterpillar. And they looked like one as well, at least from the sky.

Adelaide, if the Gyndilians attacked our army with trebuchets, what would you do? Picot asked as the dragons flew over the men glinting in their chain mail and the fluttering gold-and-blue banners.

Although it was day, the dragons flew far and high enough away that hopefully any curious civilians would take them for birds. The army marched faster by daylight, and the knights needed to get used to the dragons' presence if they were going to fight together.

The Klinian knights still gave the scaled creatures a wide berth when they landed, casting them awed, terrified gazes, and speaking about them as if the dragons couldn't hear.

The knights hardly spoke to Adelaide, and when they did, they kept their eyes downcast, their hands on their weapons. She tried not to let their distrust bother her, but sometimes it did. Would she not belong anywhere? Not with the humans or with the dragons?

At least no one had fled the army or attacked the dragons. Not yet at least.

Well, Adelaide? What would you do? Picot prodded.

The Gyndilians won't be using trebuchets because neither army will be trying to break into a castle.

Picot whipped his tail. *Well, just in case they do.*

Adelaide sighed. She understood the reason for his barrage of questions, and she enjoyed the swerving maneuvers they practiced, but she couldn't stop her thoughts from soaring toward her brother and wondering what he had suffered or was suffering. She knew what it was like to be kidnapped.

Only her promise to Conrad kept her here. But as soon as they reached Fernohn, she'd leave.

I'd burn all the trebuchets while another dragon distracted the knights. And I'd fly high enough so that none of their arrows could penetrate my scale joints or eyes.

Picot nodded. *Good.* Since he had the gift of sharing memories, he used those from when the dragons had protected the humans to guide their lessons.

Do you know yet what your gift is? Picot asked. *It might help us in the coming fight.*

Nay. She'd forgotten all about it in the search for her parents and in the news of her brother's kidnapping.

I hope your gift is music. Nothing under the sky is more pleasant. Turquan hummed a high-pitched song filled with sunlight and smiles that instantly put Adelaide at ease.

She surveyed her friends. *How long did it take you to find yours?*

Less than a day, Turquan said. *I began singing shortly after I hatched.*

Now that just sounded odd. A singing baby dragon? How would it even know any songs?

I didn't know about mine until I could fly and get in trouble with my nest mates, Resse said, grinning. *I could never lie about what I'd done.*

Mine took longer to figure out, a few years, Picot explained. *Everyone learns about theirs in different ways.*

Cyr glided toward them. He had been hunting in the forest below. He flapped furiously, and before she could ask what was wrong, he said, *Humans with weapons are sneaking toward the large moving nests on wheels.*

The dragons looked down. Sure enough, a group of motley-dressed men holding daggers and bows stalked toward the supply wagons that ambled slowly at the rear of the army.

Resse's tail drooped. *We haven't done a very good job of protecting the humans.*

Those humans must be desperate to attack an army in daylight, Turquan mused.

Adelaide agreed; she had been that desperate and hungry before.

There's a bit of cover for them though, due to those trees, Picot said, nodding to a grove of maples that the first two supply wagons were about to pass beneath.

Before she could decide what to do, the wagons and four of the robbers disappeared beneath the trees. The robbers didn't reappear on the other side.

Stop them while I warn the others, she said.

Like perfectly aimed arrows, the dragons darted down to the copse of trees.

Adelaide raced to the fatter part of the worm, and several men cried out at her arrival. At what she deemed a close enough distance, she thought, *There are thirty armed men about to attack the supply wagons. We're going to fight them off.* She whirled around and flew back to the others.

Try not to hurt them. Just scare them off. Resse's voice floated to her as she soared nearer. Then she heard shouting and a roar.

Adelaide swerved around a maple, arriving at the tail of the worm. The dragons stood squeezed between the trees, glaring at the fleeing ruffians.

And don't return, or we'll burn you to a lump of ash in one breath! Turquan yelled after them.

We'll be watching better than we did today, Resse said just to the dragons.

Adelaide growled at the thieves, disappointed that she hadn't been there to help frighten them off.

Once the vagabonds had disappeared into the forest, the dragons turned their gazes on the scene before them. One wagon was missing two of its back wheels, and bags of flour had rolled off and splattered on the ground, dusting the grass and dirt with white as if it had snowed.

A knight lay on the ground with a terrified expression as Esa hovered over him, the tip of a talon resting lightly on his shoulder. A broken arrow covered in blood lay beside him.

Adelaide's nose wrinkled at the sharp scent of human blood and the fear of the knights who stood around watching with shocked expressions.

"What's it doing?" one of the knights whispered to a man beside him, staring at Esa.

Her name is Esa, and she's healing your friend, Adelaide said. She had never seen Esa heal before, but what else could she be doing?

The lavender dragon backed away slowly as the once-injured man sat up and gaped at the tear in his tunic where his skin was now smooth and whole.

"That's ... that's remarkable," he murmured while prodding his skin.

"What's happening here?" Berold rode up, his blue-speckled eyes sweeping across the knights, dragons, and once-injured man. As his horse neared the dragons, it balked and rolled its eyes.

Turquan hummed a light, lolling lullaby, and the horse stilled at once. The smell of fear, both human and animal, dissipated.

Adelaide explained what had happened, and the dragons

supplied how they had frightened off the thieves.

"Thank you for your help. More damage would have occurred if you had not flown down," Berold said once they finished.

It is our delight to serve alongside you, Berold of the Sword. Resse bowed to him, as did the others.

"Berold of the Sword?" The knight said with a quirked eyebrow.

Don't let it make you haughtier than you already are, Adelaide told him. *They might not roast you, but I still might.*

He eyed her. "Don't fret. I still remember that you saved my life." He peered into the trees where the thieves had disappeared. "It won't be good if these men talk about what happened. They won't speak about the dragons in a favorable light, and that's what we need."

"Who would believe them?" one of the knights asked.

We can't worry about that now, Adelaide said. *The people will either be ready for the truth when it comes or not.*

At least this incident cracked the ice between the knights and dragons. That night, more men than usual joined Adelaide and the people from her rebellion beside a crackling fire where the dragons lounged. Adelaide was in her human shape because she'd bathed in the river and wanted to help bridge the gap between the two.

The younger knights were the boldest in approaching her. They asked her everything from what it felt like to transform into a dragon (horribly painful) to what raw meat tasted like (delicious, as long as she was a dragon) and continued to zing off questions for her and the dragons like lightning bolts. It was as if they'd stored up all their questions the last few days, and now that they believed the dragons were on their side, the dam had broken.

"What's it like to fly?"

Adelaide listened carefully to Resse's response: *There are no words for it. It's freedom, delight, and peace all mingled together.*

Yes. That was it exactly, similar to what Elias had once said.

Adelaide wished to her bones that he could be here to see his dream take shape; it would have made him so proud.

"I still miss her," Conrad said from beside her.

For a wild moment, Adelaide thought he meant Elias. But of course not. Emma.

She, too, would have loved sitting here with her friends under the summer sky, watching two worlds combine like reflections on water.

"Me too." She would always miss her sister. Just like she would always miss Elias. It was a part of her.

Conrad hunched closer to the flames, holding his stomach as if he had the collywobbles. She couldn't fathom how much pain he had drowned in after Emma's murder, or how much it still haunted him. Adelaide had been too consumed with her own sorrow to notice anyone else's.

"You were going to marry her, weren't you?" she asked.

Conrad nodded, staring at the fire. "I was going to build a house first. I had already begun gathering the wood. Once I completed it, I was going to ask her."

"She would have said yes. She loved you." Adelaide remembered the way Emma's cheeks had tinged pink every time Conrad's name was mentioned, and how she had made excuses to visit his house.

Conrad clenched his stomach tighter. Perhaps talking about her sister would help him. That's what Elias had done for her, and it had soothed the ache.

"Remember the time Emma attempted to help a man who had fallen, and he yelled at her and called her a meddling fool? He almost took her arm off when he jerked around."

Conrad smiled, but it was taut. "She was so confused and disheartened that it took a bouquet of flowers and a swim in the river to cheer her up."

Turquan began humming, and a few of the knights and her friends swayed back and forth.

"I always admired her love of others," Conrad said. "Remember when she took some bread and cheese to that family with seven children who had just lost their father?"

Adelaide nodded, ashamed that she had longed to keep the bread and cheese for their family. Emma had been better than her in so many ways.

"I'm afraid of forgetting." Conrad met Adelaide's eyes.

"Me too. But sharing memories like this helps."

"Thanks." He stood. "I'm going to get some sleep."

As Conrad left, a sudden thought troubled Adelaide. Who would she discuss Elias with so that she didn't forget him? Most of the people from Alesfirth only knew him as a noble—just enough to distrust or hate him—and the other citizens only knew him as their king.

Resse, Esa, and the other dragons had only known him as a dragon and hadn't seen him since he came to Klinhun more than five years ago. Berold had only known him as a human, and the thought of talking to him in such a personal way made Adelaide feel like throwing up.

But Berold had known him as a human the best and most recently. It would be worth talking to him rather than letting her memories of Elias become a faraway dream.

And so, swallowing her pride and exhaustion, Adelaide made her way to the part of camp where Berold and the other commanders slept. If she didn't do it now, she never would.

Berold was still up, looking at maps by the light of a candle. He looked as if he could fall asleep at any moment.

There was no turning back now. Adelaide coughed to make her presence known.

The swordmaster glanced up and frowned. "What do you want?"

"I know it's hard to believe," Adelaide said as she settled into the chair across from him, "but I've actually just come to talk to you about Elias."

Berold let the map he was holding fall onto the table. "What about him?"

"Well," Adelaide tried to think of words that wouldn't reveal the desperation surging inside her, "you knew him much longer than I did, and I'd love to hear about his early days in the castle. And I can tell you the little I know about him as a dragon, if you wish."

She knew how painful it could be to unearth those precious memories, especially to someone you didn't like, so she expected Berold to turn her away in scorn.

Instead, after peering at her for a long moment, he sighed and leaned back. "What do you want to know?"

He must have been too tired to argue, or perhaps he thirsted to speak to someone about Elias just as much as she did.

They spoke long into the night, sharing memories. Berold had more to say but didn't seem to mind, losing himself in boyhood rompings with the young prince. He asked her quite a few questions about Elias as a dragon and her time on Niclond.

Although Adelaide and Berold weren't necessarily friends by the end of the night, they no longer loathed each other. Even in his death, Elias was bringing people together.

Chapter Forty

Several days later, the first ranks of the army reached Fernohn, and Adelaide felt like jumping into the Wymar River in joy and to cool off. Instead, she filled her waterskin, then returned to the army to say goodbye to her friends from Alesfirth.

"You still won't let me come with you?" Conrad asked.

"Nay." Adelaide shook her head, her braid whipping her cheek. "We're flying the whole way. And you need to stay here and watch over the others and make sure that Berold doesn't—"

"Harm the dragons in any way."

"I'm not worried about them. They can breathe fire. I was going to say make sure he doesn't do anything foolish."

Conrad dipped his head. "I'll do my best, Commander."

Adelaide turned to the others. "When are you all marching out?"

"In three days, after the army gathers more men and provisions," Aldy replied.

Adelaide nodded. "And you will engage the Gyndilian forces on the border?"

"That's where Berold and the other commanders believe the Gyndilians will be." Conrad swatted at some gnats buzzing by his face.

Adelaide gauged the expressions of the others at the news of the upcoming fight. Sayer and a few of the older boys' eyes lit up with excitement, but several of them, especially the younger ones, became pale.

Adelaide's heart clenched. These men were farmers and boys, not soldiers. They should be wooing women and preparing for the harvest instead of facing death. And *she* was the reason they were here. The reason they might never see their families again.

"You don't have to fight," she whispered. She raised her voice. "You could return to Dhalion or remain here until the fate of our country is decided. None of you have much fighting experience, and your families will be devastated if you don't come home."

Sayer clenched his jaw. "True, but if we don't win this war, we may not have families to return home to. You're the one who convinced us to stay and fight, after all."

Adelaide nodded, wondering if it had been the right thing.

Everard gripped the shoulders of the men on either side of him. "You did the right thing speaking those words. Our country needs us, and we aren't cowards. We will show all of Klinhun that the people of Alesfirth are just as important and courageous as any knight."

The others voiced their agreement. Then at Conrad's leading, they broke into the chant, "For our families! For our people! For our futures!"

Once, the chant would have warmed Adelaide with pride. Now it sickened her. Most of them probably wouldn't make it home, wouldn't marry, or see their parents again. How many of them would remain on the battlefield, cold and forgotten?

A vulture circled overhead, and she tried not to think about how some of them might become its food. She swallowed past the bile in her mouth.

Since Adelaide couldn't change their minds, she changed the subject. "What do you think of the dragons?"

"They're grand," Rohesia said. "I wish I could turn into one like you. Then I wouldn't have to be as afraid."

Adelaide still feared many things, but said nothing.

"How does that work exactly? I've been meaning to ask, but you haven't been around long enough to do so," Conrad said.

Adelaide shrugged. "I'm not sure. Elias gave me a potion he had made. I drank it, and then I turned into a dragon. It has something to do with love." According to Elias, only sacrificial love could transform a human into a dragon.

"Love?" One of the boys scoffed. "If a dragon loves a human, they automatically turn into a dragon?"

"Who'd want to love a fire-breathing beast anyway?"

"And why would a dragon love a human? Wouldn't it crush it?"

Conrad hissed at them to be quiet, but Adelaide jogged away from the blind, foolish boys toward the forest, not caring about the trees that scratched her face and the rocks that tripped her in the tear-blurred waning light.

She called to Cyr, *Are you ready to leave?*

Yes. I'm with the fire-flyers. We just hunted.

Adelaide scrambled deeper into the trees, rubbing her eyes until no trace of tears remained. She stopped when she spotted the dragons tearing into deer carcasses. Cyr perched on a tree, picking at a squirrel.

She looked at Resse. *Are you still willing to accompany me to Gyndilad?*

He stood, licking his scales. *It will be a great honor, Silverscales.*

Why did you ask him to go? I'm just as strong, and probably faster, Turquan said.

Because he's the one I can stand being around the longest and the one who's been around humans the most.

Fair enough, Turquan said before returning to his deer.

But you wouldn't have as good a time as you would if I went with you.

I'm not going for a good time. I'm going to rescue my brother.

The dragons followed her and Resse to the edge of the forest, and Cyr landed on her shoulder.

May your wings carry you straight and true, Picot said.

Watch over Conrad and the—

Humans from Alesfirth, Turquan finished. *We will, don't fret. We will protect them as we were made to do.*

I hope you find your brother, Esa said.

Thanks. So do I. Adelaide hugged her warm, smooth neck. *Be careful in the battle. Hurt as many of the Gyndilians for me as you can.*

Join us as soon as you're able. Turquan nudged Resse with his snout. *We'll need your excellent flying skills.*

Yes, you won't make it long without me.

So many goodbyes. Would Adelaide see these fun, wise friends again?

Don't fret, Silverscales. Picot nudged her side. *We'll see each other soon.* But he couldn't know that; no one could know for sure.

Chapter Forty-One

Adelaide enjoyed flying with Resse. He never probed too deeply into her thoughts, and a light-hearted smile always seemed to curl up his snout, though she knew he must miss Esa.

Surprisingly, the chipmunks remained on him during their long flights, curled up between his spines or hidden in his claws. The furry creatures always scampered off when they landed, but they never went far.

Have you ever accidentally killed one of them? Adelaide asked as they flew over the last stretch of the Nifmuir Desert, a massive empty expanse of sand hills that stretched into Findar. She was looking forward to leaving the open, parched land behind for the more familiar coolness of the mountains and better food than an occasional tough snake.

Nay. They squeak when I squeeze them too hard. But I have unintentionally burned a monkey.

A burst of light erupted below Resse.

What was that? Adelaide ducked under him to look for the source of the flash.

Another burst of orange light. Then another. Although she swept her eyes over the sand hills, she spotted nothing with her night vision, not even the small green spark of a lizard.

It looks like dragon fire, but it can't be. The others are far behind us, Resse said.

A low-pitched, agonized roar destroyed the night's silence.

Adelaide and Resse froze, hovering in the air.

Cyr landed on her head. *That didn't sound like any animal I know of.*

It was probably just a wounded mountain lion or something, Adelaide said, but didn't believe it. The roar was too wild and too wrong, like something was being tortured.

When she and Resse reached the spot where they had seen the eruptions of flame burst forth, all was still and quiet. Nothing moved on the desert sea below, and no bird or bug drifted in the sky.

Adelaide shivered. *Let's go. There's nothing here.*

After almost a fortnight of flying, a hill sprouting stone buildings and a giant, spear-like fortress materialized out of a sprawling forest. From Berold's description and the map she'd looked at when they'd talked about Elias, it had to be Weitzen, Gyndilad's capital. It was about twice the size of Dhalion, and somewhere in that rambling mass was her brother. Hopefully.

Adelaide gazed at the stars. From her dragon instincts, she knew they had about half of the night left. It would have to be enough time because she couldn't wait any longer.

Do you have a plan? Resse cocked his head at her.

Of course I do.

Truth is my gift, Silverscales. I know you're lying.

Adelaide sighed. *We'll just make it up as we go. I don't want to wait any longer to rescue Odo.*

Apparently, Resse didn't either because he didn't argue. Or

maybe he couldn't think of a plan either.

Adelaide focused on the buildings below. Where would Odo be? She didn't have time to peer through every window as she had in Alesfirth.

As she stared at the pointed fortress, demanding it to reveal her brother, a wooden structure just to the left of it pulsed with white light for a long moment, then faded.

What was that? The light was similar to the one she'd seen in Dhalion when she'd been searching for Conrad. Unlike dragon fire, it had been steady and serene, the color of moonlight.

What did you see? Resse's spines stiffened as he scoured the ground.

Cyr glided over their heads. *I didn't see anything.*

They hadn't seen it? It had glowed as bright as lightning. Odd. Well, the wooden building where the light had erupted was as good a place to begin looking as any.

Never mind, Adelaide said. *I'll sneak into the city as a human with Cyr. I think Odo might be in the wooden structure next to the fortress.*

Once I have Odo, I'll let you know, Resse, so you can create a distraction, and Cyr and I can escape with my brother. If all else fails, I'll transform and carry him away.

But they'll clearly see you, Resse pointed out.

Since we're already at war with the Gyndilians, it doesn't matter much if they see us. By the time someone lets their army know, they'll already be fighting our friends.

There were many loose threads in Adelaide's plan, but she couldn't think of anything better, and her heart was urging her to hurry.

How are you going to get inside as a human? Resse gazed down at the towering rock walls that encircled the city.

Adelaide glanced at the hawk circling above them. *Cyr and I are experts at that.*

His piercing eyes met hers. *I'm going to have to bite more humans, aren't I?*

Only if there's no other way to distract them.

Cyr clacked his beak and landed on her head.

I'll wait for you in the trees outside the wall, Resse said. *We'll still be able to communicate at that distance. Let me know at once if you are in any trouble.*

I will.

Where do you suggest we take your brother once we have him? Resse asked.

To Pinhurn, where my parents are. Then we can join our friends.

Resse's bone-white, arm-length teeth flashed in his dog-like smile. *They can't be having as much fun as we are.*

Adelaide grinned at the chipmunk crawling across his head. *Come on.*

They dove toward the forest on the outskirts of the city, the wind whistling past Adelaide's ear holes. A few moments later she emerged with leaves and dirt in her hair and tottering as if she'd had too much ale to drink, but fully human. Cyr perched on her shoulder.

You should probably fly overhead so the guards don't see you and ruin the surprise, she told him. She also didn't know if peasants had hawks in this country and didn't want to risk getting thrown in jail for stealing one.

I can see much better from up there anyway. He took off, his wings brushing her face.

As Adelaide neared the top of the hill where the three guards could easily spot her, he asked, *Now?*

Now.

Cyr dove, claws outstretched like he was about to snag prey. He emitted a shriek that sent Adelaide's already fleeing heart scrambling.

She dashed for the gate as the men's attention was jerked up at the manic bird. As Cyr struck, Adelaide darted past them.

She launched herself at the door.

And bounced back, her right shoulder throbbing in pain.

Of course. The gate was locked. This was Weitzen, the capital of Gyndilad, not a crumbled, forgotten town in the middle of nowhere.

Something tugged on the back of Adelaide's dress. One of the knights had grabbed her.

She jerked to the side, but the man held firm.

Then she heard a yelp, and the man's grip on her loosened. She glanced back to see Cyr attacking the man's face with his talons.

Thanks. Out of desperation, and before the man could seize her again, she hurled herself up the wooden gate, hanging onto the crossbeams with her arms and pushing against the timbers with her feet.

With much slipping, clawing, and gasping, Adelaide made it to the top. Most of the gate seemed to be in her hands, which stung and bled.

It was a good drop to the hard-packed ground on the other side, and three knights were rushing toward her from inside, pointing and shouting.

She should have thought this through more. But it was too late now. The guards on the outside were still wrestling with Cyr. If he was caught, it'd be her fault.

Telling herself that she had jumped from trees this tall, Adelaide took a breath and leapt.

She hit the ground with her feet and rolled. She stood gingerly on tingling legs; everything still seemed to work.

"What are you doing here?" One of the knights asked in a thick, guttural accent. He and the other two had stopped, no doubt wondering who would be so foolish to jump off a gate into the city in the middle of the night.

Adelaide didn't stay to chat. She bolted past them down the road, her gaze on the white spire. She couldn't outrun the men, but perhaps she could hide somewhere until they moved elsewhere.

She swerved around a cottage, leapt over a fallen barrel,

and ran around another house. She glanced up at the stone fortress that loomed closer—a grave marker for all those who had killed Emma and so many others.

Mistress! Cyr called. *They have me. They put something on my head so I can't see and tied something around my talons. But I'll find a way to escape, even if I must bite all these humans.*

She froze. They had caught Cyr—her loyal, annoying, faithful Cyr.

Chapter Forty-Two

Adelaide whirled around. *Where are you?*

I don't know. I can't see. But don't fret, I'm fiercer than they.

The knights would most likely take the hawk to the castle as a gift for their king. Adelaide could intercept them, take them by surprise.

She crept back along the houses, toward the road that traveled from the wall to the castle. But then, beside an empty market stall, she stopped.

What about Odo? She had to find and rescue him. But she couldn't just leave Cyr to be caged; he had rescued her in more ways than one and often helped her at great cost to himself without complaining.

"There you are." Hands yanked her arms and twisted them behind her. One of the three knights had caught up to her. No, two. Another one came up, aiming a crossbow at her chest.

"Why did you sneak into Weitzen? Are you a spy from Klinhun?" the man holding her arms asked.

"Let me go," Adelaide snarled, twisting. But the man's

hands were like chains.

"Come on, Osbert. We need to get back to our posts. King Aethelmaer will handle this whelp." The man beside her eyed her with distaste.

The knight named Osbert pulled her toward the road in the direction of the fortress. Adelaide attempted kicking him, but he moved out of the way. "None of that now. We won't hurt you if you just tell us the truth."

The other knight walked in front of them, glancing back at her as if making sure his prize goat didn't escape.

Adelaide's hands sweated and her heart pulsed as she remembered the rough hands of her kidnappers in the Tancred Forest. The terror of being trapped with nowhere to go, the desperation that fueled her violence. The ice in her skin that never melted, the taunts of Nick-Nose that coated her in filth.

No. Adelaide couldn't get lost in those memories. Odo and Cyr needed her.

She attempted to reach the dagger at her back, but the knight pulled her arms to the front of her body.

The other man sighed. "This is taking too long."

"Very well." Osbert grasped her shoulders and hefted her over his back.

Adelaide kicked against his stomach, but the man didn't even groan. It merely made her feel like a child throwing a tantrum. She would have rolled off, but the man had one arm clasped against her back, restraining her.

She could contact Resse, but his appearance would draw more attention, and they didn't even know where Odo was. She'd wait to contact Resse until she had no other choice.

Adelaide contemplated turning into a dragon. It'd get her out of this predicament, but then she'd have no element of surprise when she rescued Cyr and Odo. If she was in her dragon form, though, she could just demand that they hand her brother and hawk over, and they would be so terrified they would comply.

Before Adelaide could decide what to do, the Gyndilian in front of her had unlocked a door embedded in a squat building next to the castle. They entered a narrow, torch-lit hallway.

Water dripped somewhere nearby, and the whole place smelled like a cave, musty and damp. Adelaide couldn't transform now; she'd crush herself.

"I'll wait here." The knight who'd opened the door stood just inside it, his arms crossed.

Osbert stopped at another wooden door, this one strengthened with metal bars. At the possibility of being stuck inside another jail cell, Adelaide squirmed.

"Stop. You're not getting loose. We're just going to hold you here until King Aethelmaer tries you," Osbert said.

This didn't comfort Adelaide, and she continued attempting to writhe out of his grip.

"What's going on, Osbert?" A man with sleep-heavy eyes and unkempt hair stepped out of a door in the hall.

Osbert turned toward the man, causing Adelaide to face the hallway they had walked down.

"This lass climbed over the gate and ran through the village, but Alfruith and I found her not far from here. I'm not sure how she managed to get past the front guards, but there was quite a ruckus, so she might've had an accomplice." He shifted his weight. "Can you open the door? She's heavy."

Adelaide kicked him for that comment and felt slightly better when he grunted. There was a rattling of keys, a click, and the creaking of a door.

Osbert carried her into the room, and the prison guard yawned. Not very threatening. Perhaps she could somehow convince him to let her go?

The knight set her down in a straw-covered cell that smelled like sweat and urine. He shut the metal-barred door, and the guard locked it. The two men left, closing and locking the main door behind them. A torch beside it flickered, casting the small square room in a dim glow.

Adelaide leaned against the wall, the stone cold against her sweaty skin. She tried to think of ways to escape and find Cyr and Odo. She didn't want Resse hurt and couldn't think of a way that he could get her out without endangering himself. She'd tell him of her predicament if she couldn't think of another way out.

"Adelaide?" A man's voice murmured from the cell to her right.

Adelaide's breathing stopped.

She knew that voice. It had spoken healing and mercy to her; it had shown her light when all she had seen was darkness. But it couldn't be. That voice was gone; it would never speak again in this life.

Still, Adelaide turned to peer through the gloom.

Leaning against the bars separating the two cells, his hands wrapped tight around them and staring at her as if he would never stop, stood Elias.

Chapter Forty-Three

The battle was not going well.

Gyndilian soldiers stretched before the Klinians on the grassy plain north of the border like a swarm of angry flies. More had poured out of the tooth-sharp Nefar Mountains that morning.

"Would you like us to give the command for the dragons to attack?" Rolf asked, standing beside Berold on the outcropping of rock where he had set up his command tent. It gave him a good view of the grisly struggle below.

Berold rubbed his hands through his sweaty hair as he surveyed the Klinians toppling off horses, thrusting swords at the better trained Gyndilians, and spraying the grass and dirt with their blood.

The battle had just begun yesterday, but so many of their people already littered the ground like cut grass.

What would Elias think of him now? Berold had promised to be his brother-at-arms but hadn't protected him and now couldn't even protect the people that Elias had cared so much about.

"Sire?" Rolf inquired. "Our cavalry is nearly finished, and as you know, most of our archers were killed at that first trebuchet attack."

Berold grimaced at the remembrance of the fiery ball that had made a huge dent in their left flank and taken out too many archers. It was just like the Gyndilians to use weapons that had no place on a battlefield.

If the Klinians continued losing this many knights, they would have a new Gyndilian king by tomorrow night. Berold had known the Gyndilian army would be vast—they always had better armies—and Adelaide's information had warned him of the size.

But there had been nothing he could do except send messengers to the towns ordering—although it had felt more like begging—them to send more men. But he couldn't wait for them to arrive; the Gyndilians would overrun Klinhun if he didn't slow them down.

Berold cursed as he sifted through his options. "Have you moved the remaining archers to higher ground?"

"Yes, sire. They are now just to our left."

Berold glanced over to see several exhausted, bleeding men sitting in the dirt holding long bows. "Good. See that they have enough arrows. Have the squires make more if need be.

"And I want at least a dozen men, preferably men who can shoot, waiting in that valley where those Gyndilians came from. Tell them not to go until it's dark."

Rolf scratched his beard. "Good thinking, sire. And the dragons?"

Berold hated to use their secret weapon so soon, but if they didn't, the Gyndilians would crush them by morning.

"Tell them they may cause as much havoc and destruction as possible. But they are not, in any circumstances, to get themselves killed."

Rolf nodded and walked behind Berold to the trees where the dragons hid.

The swordmaster watched the men he'd trained for years and, just recently, laughed with over fires, fight valiantly. Their shrieks and groans pierced him like the swords and polearms they dodged.

Fear—for his men, his land, and himself—spilled over him like the men's blood on the ground. He gripped his sword, waiting for the opportune time to join them.

Wind buffeted Berold, tousling his hair and the tent behind him. He glanced up. The three dragons—Turquan, Esa, and the one that began with a *P*—soared over the Klinians, their scales shimmering in the afternoon sunlight.

As one, they roared. Berold's ears throbbed, and he felt the vibrations all the way to the soles of his feet. Both armies stopped fighting to gawk at the three massive, yet elegant creatures gliding overhead.

As the dragons dove toward the Gyndilians with their maws open, streams of fire gushing forth, the Gyndilians screamed and ran for cover.

The Klinians shouted with glee, and hope returned to Berold.

Perhaps dragons could save Klinhun after all.

Then something bright in the corner of his eye jerked his focus away from the dragons. He turned to where several Klinian knights were burning with odd, black-tinged fire. Had the dragons somehow turned on their own men by mistake?

But no. The green, brown, and purple dragons still spurted bouts of flame at the enemy, weaving back and forth across the sky. Then what ...?

A dark shape larger than a bird glided toward them from the Nefar Mountains. A plume of the same black-tinged fire descended on the Klinians.

There wasn't just one of the odd-shaped, fire-breathing

birds, but a dozen, all plunging straight for the Klinian army.

"Swords of Dhalion," Berold cursed. "They have dragons too!"

Chapter Forty-Four

Adelaide stared at the man's long, wavy brown hair, his thick beard, and light eyes that looked so much like Elias's, but couldn't be because Elias was dead. She had mourned him every day since the moment he had breathed his last in her arms. This must be a specter sent to haunt her for killing him.

"Adelaide? It's me, Elias. I'm alive." His voice sounded so real. It sounded like the man's who had spoken to her of mighty creatures with hearts larger than their claws and teeth, who had sung heart-soaring songs and spoken healing words.

Adelaide took a step closer.

His hands tightened on the bars. "I'm so sorry, Adelaide."

The man's words were absurd. If he was Elias, why should he be sorry? And where had he been this whole time? Why hadn't he come to her in Dhalion? Perhaps it wasn't truly him. The real Elias wouldn't have let her face so much despair all alone.

Adelaide stopped in front of him and touched the smooth, tanned skin of his cheek. He felt real.

He didn't move as she drew her finger down to the edge of his lips. His eyes remained on hers, as if trying to peer into her thoughts.

She tore her gaze from his and noticed a tear in the sleeve of his faded red tunic. She pulled open the cloth. There, on his arm was a white scar with a long line and another above it: the sign of a traitor. The brand that Elias had taken for her.

In that moment, Adelaide knew that this man was Elias, *her* Elias, who had pursued her even when she had planned to kill him.

She jolted away from him as a storm of emotions broke upon her: delight and honey-sweet relief that her prince was alive and well, anxiety about where he'd been all this time and why he looked like he might fall over at any moment. Then a volatile rage at not coming for her in Dhalion, for letting her mourn him these last months bubbled inside her.

"You were dead. I mourned for you. Where have you been?" Horror at what she'd said spilled over her, and she clamped her hand over her mouth.

What right had she to be angry with Elias when he'd treated her rebuffs with kindness and patience and loved her despite her faults?

Adelaide sunk to her knees, tears welling in her eyes. "I shouldn't have said that. I'm sorry. I'm not mad at you. I can't be mad at you."

He reached out and touched her shoulder. "You have a right to be angry with me." His voice was broken bones. "Words cannot express how sorry I am that I caused you pain, Adelaide. How can you ever forgive me?"

"There's nothing to forgive." Adelaide turned to memorize his face, those overcast or clear-sky eyes, the lips that smiled so easily. None now, which she'd have to remedy soon.

"I would never intentionally hurt you," Elias continued, his gaze pleading with her. "I didn't think I would survive. I didn't want you to have that hope and then see me die again. No, better that you had thought I had died than to suffer through the agony all over again."

She didn't care as much about his actual words than that his rich, autumn voice was filling the world again.

"When I came to, I was floating in the sea. I thought I had died."

Adelaide winced. "I threw you into the ocean. I thought you were dead and couldn't stand the sight of you up there on the cliff all alone and broken."

Elias took her hand and squeezed it. "I don't blame you for what you did. It makes sense under the circumstances.

"As I floated, I heard the cries of birds and their feathers tickling me. Then I passed out again. The next time I awoke, I was in a forest. The birds must have lifted me out of the water and deposited me there. It all felt like a dream. I don't remember much about that time, except my skin burning and being thirsty, always thirsty." He rubbed his throat as if he could still feel the dryness.

"Some of the birds must have pulled the dagger from my back and covered it with leaves to help it heal. They provided me with food and water."

If it hadn't been Elias telling the tale, Adelaide wouldn't have believed it. Even so, she still found it hard to accept. "Why would birds help you?"

"I befriended many while I lived at the castle. They were the only ones beside my father that I could share my true identity with. It sounds pitiful, and it is."

His lips turned up in an attempt at a smile, but it wasn't the one she missed. She couldn't return it. Elias hadn't had any siblings like her to keep her company as a child. She loved Cyr, but his companionship couldn't measure up to that of a human's or dragon's.

"I was thankful for my friendship with them when they restored me to health. I'll never say another bad thing about sparrows or any bird again."

"Don't let Cyr hear you say that. He greatly dislikes sparrows."

At the thought of the hawk, Adelaide contacted him. *Cyr, I've been imprisoned. And guess who is here with me?*

Who?

Prince Elias.

So, he was alive after all?

Adelaide frowned. *What do you mean? Did you think he could have survived?*

Nay. I knew he was badly wounded on the cliff, and it seemed doubtful he would live. And then, after I helped you escape from that stinky nest, you said he had died.

Well, Adelaide couldn't argue with that.

"At least I'm alive now, right?" Elias said.

"You heard that?"

"Enough to get the gist of what you two were saying."

"I wish I could have seen the birds lift you out of the ocean," Adelaide said, remembering her storm of grief. "It would have saved me a lot of pain. For Berold and I both."

"Berold thinks I'm dead too." It wasn't a question.

"Not only that, but he believes I killed you." Adelaide stared at his feet, which were covered in leather so tattered that some of his toes peeked through. He no longer looked like a noble in his threadbare, torn tunic and pants. What would she have thought of him if he had shown up at her house like this that fateful day? She probably wouldn't have spent so much time running away.

Elias tilted her chin up so that she met his gaze. "It's my fault that everyone thinks I'm dead, not yours or anyone else's. Alright? You didn't kill me."

Adelaide murmured her agreement, though her heart disagreed.

His gaze became so warm that it burned her face, and her heart tripped over itself. She never wanted to look away from those deep-as-the-sky eyes.

He let go of her chin, and Adelaide blinked, coming back to herself and swallowing disappointment.

"How did you end up here?" he asked.

"I'll tell you after you've finished your story. Mine's bound to be more interesting." She tried smiling and managed it this time.

Elias gave her the grin she longed for. "Oh, how I've missed you."

"I missed you too."

He kissed her nose, making Adelaide thrum, then continued his story. "With the help of the birds, I slowly recovered my strength and was thinking of returning to you and the castle when, on my first attempt to gather water for myself, I was captured by a group of ruffians near the Wymar River. I was still too weak to transform. Besides, if they saw my dragon form, it would have ruined all those years my father and I had worked to build respect."

Adelaide sucked in a breath at his news, clinging to his hand. "Were they the same as my kidnappers?"

Elias rubbed his beard. "I'm not sure. Were there six men and an older woman named Griselda?"

Adelaide nodded. She thought of the man who'd been her main guard and who had helped her escape. "Was there a thicker, silent man with them?"

"I don't recall such a man, but I was ill most of the time."

Adelaide hoped the man who had saved her life had left and that the kidnappers hadn't punished him for helping her. "Why were you ill?" she asked. "Was it due to your wound? How badly did they treat you?"

He gazed down at their entwined hands. "Adelaide, dearest, could you not hold my hand so tightly? I'd still like to use it once we escape."

Adelaide realized she was gripping it as tight as a hawk grips its prey. "Oh. I'm sorry." She let go. And he had called her dearest. Her heart had wings, but she didn't let it fly. There could be no future for them together.

"I'm not sure why I was ill," Elias continued. "I think the wound did get infected at one point, but, thankfully, the kidnappers let me wash it. They wouldn't receive anything from the Gyndilians if I died. They also gave me rancid food, which caused my stomach no end of trouble." He rubbed his too-thin stomach as if it still pained him.

Adelaide ached for all that he had suffered. Perhaps if she had checked to make sure that he was truly dead, he wouldn't have had to face all that misery. "If your gift is healing, why didn't you heal yourself?"

Elias sighed. "I couldn't, despite trying many times. I used to be able to before I drank the potion to become human. Perhaps that changed my gift so I can only heal other's wounds. Or perhaps I can only heal deeper wounds like grief and revenge." He gazed at her with such a tender expression that Adelaide couldn't hold it and glanced down at their hands.

"Or perhaps it was because I wasn't transforming, which took more strength than I could muster. I gave much thought to the potential loss of my gift during that foggy time, but arrived at no answers.

"In any case, I had to recuperate as a normal human. I finally did as we rode north of Pinhurn."

"Did the kidnappers bring you here?" Adelaide asked.

"Nay, they were commanded to deliver me over to the Gyndilians on the border near Alesfirth. And I blame what I did next on you, Adelaide, daughter of Alesfirth and seeker of justice."

"Me?"

"Yes." Elias grinned. "After all the time I spent with you, when I overhead my kidnappers say that the Gyndilians were fighting in Alesfirth, I longed to rush to their aid with no thought to myself."

"You would have done that anyway."

"Perhaps, but watching your bravery and loyalty to your

people has given me a desire to exhibit more of those characteristics."

Adelaide's cheeks flamed. "So, were you successful?" She doubted it since she had seen the Gyndilians ruling Alesfirth only a short time ago.

Elias picked up a piece of straw and watched it drift back to the ground. "Nay. I did escape that night from my kidnappers as we camped near the town, but just barely. It was nothing like one of your famed attempts."

"Of course not."

"Some birds in the area helped distract the guard while I slipped away on a horse I stole. The guard called for help, and they would have been upon me in an instant if more birds hadn't come and helped." He shook his head. "I owe them so much."

Adelaide smiled. "Birds can come in handy. Cyr's helped me get past several guards these last months."

Elias frowned at her. "I hope you haven't been doing too many foolhardy things without me to get you out of trouble."

Adelaide waved his concern away. "Not too many. But I want to hear what happened after you escaped."

"Well, by the time I reached Alesfirth, the fighting had ended, with the Gyndilians winning, as I'm sure you've heard by now. I didn't see you, though I asked everyone I could. That was another reason I had gone to Alesfirth—to see if you were there. I knew that if you had heard about the attack, you would have raced there."

"I did," Adelaide whispered, a sour taste in her mouth. "It was later, though, after they had already sent captives to Gyndilad."

Elias groaned and leaned back, his hands tightened into fists. "Oh, the winds of fate are blowing hard against us!" His hands dropped to his sides. "Well, we are together now. That's what matters."

Adelaide nodded, though she wished she had seen him in

Alesfirth. Not only would it have lifted her out of her grief, but they might have been able to help more people. "Did you see my family while you were there?"

"I arrived as the last peasants were being shepherded into town. I asked and looked around but saw them naught. Outside the village, some Gyndilians caught me because neither I nor my horse were strong enough to run or fight." He scooped up some straw and let it trickle to the floor. "I did see Odo, though."

"You did?" Adelaide grasped the bars. "How was he?"

"Terrified, of course. He was bound up with some other lads. I told him not to be afraid and that we would get out of this mess soon. That was the last time I saw him because I was taken out of Alesfirth and brought here."

Adelaide swallowed and released the bars. "He's the reason I'm here."

"I'm sure he's safe and healthy. He's a brave boy."

Adelaide nodded, trying to hope for the best. "What happened to you then?"

"I tried to escape on the way here, but I obviously didn't succeed. I had it in my mind that I could confront King Aethelmaer and defeat him single-handedly. See how you've changed me?"

"It seems like for the worse." She pulled her legs up. "Without my influence, you wouldn't have dared go to Alesfirth and wouldn't be caught."

Elias stretched out and touched her leg, the only part of her now within reach. "Nay, Adelaide. You're a good influence. You inspire me to take risks for my people."

"Which led to your imprisonment," she said and gestured at the cell walls, "where you can't do anything for your people. How is that a good thing? How is anything I've done the last year a good thing?" She laid her head on her knees, feeling as old and tired as a grandmother

Elias shuffled closer, and she longed for the warm comfort of his arms.

"Adelaide, dearest," the nickname made her uncurl her fingers, "you have made mistakes. And though your rebellion may not have begun from the purest intentions, you did long for justice and a better way of life for your people. You may not have gone about it in the best way, but because of your acceptance of me, I'm not dead and we are closer to having peace in this country and justice for peasants than we ever have."

"Because of me you died."

Elias shook his head, his voice as tender as spring growth. "No. Someone else threw that dagger at me. It had nothing to do with you."

Adelaide realized that he still didn't know who had killed him. "It was Gunter," she said into her legs.

"What?"

"Gunter killed you. With the dagger that *I* gave him." Tears leaked down her face, and something hot and sharp pressed against her chest.

"Why would he do that?"

"He was in my rebellion. He just got separated from the others somehow."

"Adelaide, look at me," Elias said gently.

She shook her head.

He sighed. "Adelaide, please look at me. I hope I haven't become that ugly in the months we've been apart."

She jerked her head up. "Of course you're not ugly."

"Then it won't pain you to look at me as I tell you that even though it may have been the dagger you gave Gunter that wounded me, it was Gunter, not you, who threw it." His eyes were a knife cutting to the deepest part of her, but they held no blame, no accusations. Just ... love. How was that possible after all she had done to him?

Chapter Forty-Five

"You did everything in your power to convince the people in your rebellion not to kill me," Elias said. "And they didn't. Now you're helping unify the dragons and humans."

Adelaide rested her head on her legs again. "I failed at that too. They wouldn't listen to me. Only Turquan, Resse, Esa, and Picot came with me. All the others are in Neklosa by now. They're not coming to help us."

Elias frowned, rubbing his beard. "Those foolish, haughty dragons. They deserve a good, long talking-to."

Then he gazed back at her and touched her leg again, his voice turning gentle and urgent. "It's not your fault, Adelaide. They didn't listen because they're stubborn and afraid. They probably wouldn't have listened to me either."

Adelaide doubted that; his words were like wind carrying a storm, powerful and changing.

"So, the Gyndilians don't know that you're the king?" She whispered in case the jailer decided to return.

Elias shook his head. "I'd probably be dead if they did. I

think they're going to try me as a spy, but I'm obviously not that dangerous, or they would have killed me already. Or maybe they just have a long list of criminals to judge."

"So," he leaned forward and propped his chin on his hand, "you made it to Niclond. What else have you been doing? Were you able to turn into a dragon?"

"Yes, but something must be wrong with me, because it doesn't always work." She glanced down at her boots.

"What do you mean?"

How to explain it? "Well, it only happens when I'm a dragon. Sometimes I'll have doubts, and my body begins to transform back into a human without me wanting it to."

"That sounds dangerous." His concern cracked her heart.

Adelaide nodded. "I've fallen a few times, but, thankfully, have been able to retain my form long enough to land. Resse caught me once."

Elias sucked in a sharp breath.

"Have you heard of anything like it happening before? It's never happened to you or anyone you know, has it?"

He shook his head. "Nay, but I've never known any humans who have been changed into dragons. Our stories don't mention it."

That was what she'd expected, but still, it was disappointing.

"Is there anything I can do to help? It might be my fault because that was the first time I made the potion. I'm so sorry if it is."

Adelaide reached out and squeezed his hand. "I doubt it's your fault."

"Well, I'll make sure when we're flying that nothing happens to you."

Adelaide smiled at his protectiveness that was as much a part of him as his scales and wings; this time she didn't try to fight it. She knew she needed it. "Thank you."

"I can't wait to see you in your dragon form and fly with you."

"We'll have to have a race," Adelaide said. "I'm sure I can beat you now."

Elias raised an eyebrow. "We'll have to see about that. So, what else have you been doing?"

"Trying to save our countries with little success."

The door rattled, and they both turned. The same man who had imprisoned Adelaide entered, carrying two clay bowls. For the first time, Adelaide realized that dawn's light seeped through a barred window across the room.

The guard set one of the bowls on the ground in front of Adelaide and pushed it toward her under the bar with his foot, then did the same with Elias.

Adelaide pulled the bowl toward her. Steam wafted off the top of the gruel. It scalded her tongue and was burnt and crunchy but felt good oozing into her empty stomach.

"Not bad, is it?" Elias asked once the man had left. "It does get a bit old, though, after eleven days."

"That's how long you've been here?"

"If I've been counting them right. But you were going to tell me what you've been doing."

Adelaide told him about her first flight and how Berold had locked her up when she returned.

"He did what?" Elias thundered, and Adelaide flinched at the menace in his scowl. He looked as fierce as a dragon.

"He locked me in the jail at the castle," Adelaide repeated. "He believed I killed you."

"And you let him lock you up?"

He knew her well indeed. "What did you have in mind that I do instead? Kill your best friend? Fly away? You had just died, and I had just transformed for the first time. I wasn't exactly in the best mental or emotional state." She didn't add that she had thought she'd deserved the punishment.

Elias tugged on his hair. "I can't believe he did that. He knew I loved you."

"He's never liked me," Adelaide reminded him. "And it

didn't help that he found me watching your supposedly dead body drift away in the sea. But I saved his life later, so he won't be locking me up anytime soon."

"You did what?"

Between sips of her gruel, Adelaide told Elias all that had happened since she had escaped from the tower in Dhalion. When she gently told him that Manfred had killed his father, Elias bent over as if the words had punched him, his bowl clattering to the ground.

"Why would he do such a thing?" Elias whispered.

"He said he couldn't stand to witness King Ganelon's pain anymore and that the people of Klinhun weren't ready for the dragons."

"They'll never be ready. At least, the nobles never will be. They're too blinded by their greed. That doesn't mean he had the right to kill my father." He hugged his arms to his chest, and Adelaide did her best to comfort him, though she didn't have much practice. Emma had always been the comforter.

"I know. I'm sorry," she murmured, patting his arm. "I'll go with you to pursue vengeance on him, if you wish."

Elias glanced up at her with wet eyes. "No, Adelaide. That's not the way of the Rulers of the Air. We pursue love, justice, and wisdom. Never vengeance. Manfred's fate shall be decided by justice, not in a storm of rage."

Adelaide shrank into herself. She had known as much, so why had she let the words out? There were too many stains on her to deserve this man.

The thought made her want to cry forever because she wanted him in her life. Being apart from him for so long had made her realize how much she longed for a life with him.

"So, what happened next?" Elias asked, not noticing the agony inside her. He picked his bowl up.

Adelaide rubbed her burning eyes and proceeded with her tale. When she mentioned again that Evengier and Ysoria had refused to help the Klinians, his face hardened. "I had expected more from them. I suppose fear can incapacitate even the wisest of dragons," he muttered.

When she came to the end of her tale, Elias leaned back, his now-empty bowl on the ground. "Whew," he whistled, "you've been busy."

Adelaide drained the last lump of her gruel and set the bowl down. Weariness from her tale seeped into her, and she longed for some water.

Elias looked up at the walls confining them and stood. "Well, are you ready to leave? I'll lose my sanity if I remain in here another day."

Adelaide stood and stretched. "Do you have any plans?"

"Of course not. You're the expert at escaping difficult situations."

She rolled her eyes and turned away from him so she wouldn't be distracted. *Resse?* She shouted mentally in the direction of the trees where he hopefully still waited.

Elias rubbed his forehead. "Ow. Any dragon or bird within a ten-mile radius would have heard that."

Adelaide flinched. "Well, there hasn't been much time for proper training. And it doesn't matter as long as no humans heard it."

"Yes, you'd need to speak directly—" His words were drowned out by Resse's mental holler.

Adelaide! Where are you? What's happened? I contemplated contacting you many times, but thought you would do so first if you were in trouble.

I'm in a jail cell in a building at the front of the fortress. Cyr has been captured too. Could you create a diversion or get us out somehow without harming yourself? It's too risky for me to transform. She glanced at Elias, who stood listening with a thoughtful expression. *Oh, and Elias is here with me.*

Chapter Forty-Six

King Elias? How is that possible? You told us he was dead.

It's true, Resse, Elias said. *We'll explain everything once we're out of here.*

King Elias, Kindheart! It's a joy to hear your voice. I'm soaring over now.

"I hope he doesn't do anything too foolish," Adelaide said, thinking of Resse's fervor.

"He won't. He has a good mind and makes use of it. He has to since he was the one who flew between our people all those years."

Adelaide nodded and pushed against the metal bar. It groaned but didn't budge.

"I've already attempted that and about ten other ways of escaping this place." Elias's gaze flicked around his cell.

As they pondered other options for escape, a ripping sound erupted above them. Talons cut through the ceiling above Elias's cell, and he darted to the far side as a chunk of rock plummeted to where he had just stood. A stream of water poured in after the rock; it must be raining outside.

Resse? Adelaide asked, stupefied.

Move to the side so I don't hurt you. This is the only way I could think of to get you out quickly.

Adelaide moved to the far wall of her cell, protecting her head with her hands as the ceiling cracked and crashed down on them.

When the clattering stopped, Adelaide turned to face the pile of wet rubble in her cell. A long gash stretched from half-way above Elias's cell to hers.

Take Adelaide first, Elias said, moving toward the identical pile of stone in his chamber.

The door to the prison banged open as Resse thrust his snout through the hole he had made in Adelaide's cell. Just his window-sized nostrils were visible.

The jailor gasped and darted back out.

Hurry, Silverscales. The humans out here are throwing poky things at me. Resse stretched down his scaled snout further so that it hovered just above the rubble. *I can't come any closer, or I might get stuck. I can see why you want out so badly. This place is smaller than a bird's nest and stinks worse than dragon's breath.*

Adelaide ran toward Resse's snout, jumped off one of the pieces of stone, and launched herself onto his muzzle. She slipped down the slick scales.

Resse tried to lift her up, but she was still falling. At the last moment, she grasped the sides of his nostrils and pulled herself up.

Ouch. Please be careful. I only have the two nostrils.

Sorry, Adelaide muttered as he lifted her slowly up out of the prison and into the air.

Raindrops struck Adelaide and sent shivers down her arms. She leaped up between Resse's eyes toward the spike on top of his head, grabbed it, then pulled herself around into a sitting position at the base of his neck between two spikes.

A spear whizzed by, barely missing her leg.

Resse snaked his head into the hole that opened into Elias's cell. After a moment in which Adelaide had to dodge two more spears and three arrows from the few brave knights on the ground, Resse pulled his head back up.

Elias clung to his snout, then scrambled up to the top of his head and wove between the spikes until he reached Adelaide.

"Should we turn into dragons?" she asked.

He shook his head as he sat between the spikes above her. "It'll take too long, and we don't want them to know that Klinhun has three dragons."

Where's your brother, Adelaide? Resse asked. *If I stay here much longer, the ground will collapse beneath us.*

Indeed, cracks in the roof already stretched from his four clawed feet all the way to the edges. His wings beat the air as he tried to keep most of his weight airborne.

On the other side of the castle, in a separate building. At least, that was where the light had flashed. They didn't have time for her to be wrong. *You can take us to the building, then go hide while we look for him and Cyr. You can pick us up once we have them.*

I'll look for Cyr while you look for your brother. It won't take as long, and I know his scent, Resse said.

Very well, Adelaide agreed.

Resse leapt over the hole he had created.

"Hold on!" Elias yelled.

Adelaide gripped the spike in front of her, wishing it was Elias's waist. This definitely wasn't as comfortable as riding Starflare.

With a few more jolts, they were airborne, and Adelaide's arms relaxed. If she hadn't flown with her own wings, she would have believed that this kind of flying was freedom.

Resse soared over gawking peasants, then tucked his wings in as they neared the building on the other side of the castle gates that had lit up the night before.

I'll land in front of it.

That'll take too long. We can jump off, Adelaide said. Before Resse could respond, Adelaide lowered herself to his knee joint with the help of the neck spike.

Then she stepped onto his claw and jumped the short distance to the ground. She rolled and ran for the oak door, hoping it wasn't locked.

A thud resounded behind her, and Adelaide turned to see Elias landing on his feet. He sprinted toward her. "Please don't do something like that again without telling me," he gasped.

"Come on." She turned and ran for the door, knowing they didn't have long before the men who had shot at them showed up. A large, brightly colored dragon made sneaking around impossible.

I'll go find Cyr, Resse said, his whipping wings making a slapping sound in the rain. *I'll meet you back here, preferably outside.*

Adelaide yanked on the door and breathed a sigh of relief when it opened.

Her and Elias's boots squeaked on the floor. Torches on either side of the door revealed a wide room with two straw pallets beside a smoldering fire.

"Odo?" Adelaide whispered, though it was clear no one was in the room.

"Open the other door. It might lead to the inside of the castle." Elias nodded to an oak door at the far end of the room.

Adelaide passed the fire and makeshift beds. The door was locked. She groaned and pulled on her braid. "Do you think there's another entrance to the castle that would be open?" Without waiting for an answer, she marched back to the outer door.

"Adelaide, wait."

She turned to Elias. "What is it? We don't have time—"

He placed a finger to his lips and pointed to the locked door. It rattled, and Elias pulled her down behind one of the straw pallets.

The door whooshed open, and Adelaide crawled forward to see who it was.

Even in the dim light from the dying fire and the guttering torches, Adelaide recognized those large, round ears and that thick, straight hair.

"Odo!" She cried, standing.

He started back in surprise. "Adelaide?"

"Yes. We've come to rescue you."

"Adelaide!" He darted toward her, and she hugged him, patting the black-and-silver uniform he wore. He'd grown so tall—the top of his head now reached her chin. In the quick glance she swept over him, he didn't appear to be hurt or emaciated.

"Morning, Odo. It's good to see you again, though it would be even more enjoyable if we were in Klinhun," Elias said, grinning.

"Prince Elias?" Odo looked at him. "You escaped the Gyndilians then?"

"King Elias now," Adelaide said.

"Sorry." Odo's ears burned. "King Elias."

Elias ruffled the boy's hair. "As I told you in Alesfirth, you may call me Elias. And yes, I did. I'll explain more when we're not running for our lives."

"Come on." Adelaide grasped Odo's hand and pulled him toward the door that led outside.

Elias held the door open, and they dashed out.

"Halt where you are, and we won't shoot. That boy belongs to King Aethelmaer," a man pointing a crossbow at them near the main gate said.

Nine other men stood on either side of him, all aiming crossbows at them.

Chapter Forty-Seven

Adelaide dragged Odo behind her. "He belongs to no one except his family. He's my brother."

Elias stepped in front of Adelaide. She tried to step up beside him, but he held her shoulders back. "Nay. I can't let you get hurt."

"And you think I want to watch you die a second time?" Her voice rose as the memory of his death flashed through her mind.

"No one's going to die," he murmured. "I can transform."

"As can I."

Elias opened his mouth, but an ear-splitting roar boomed over the pounding of the rain.

Resse landed in front of them with a jolt. Odo stumbled behind her.

Several men yelled; Adelaide hoped most had fled.

Something wet and dark landed on her shoulder. *Cyr!* She stroked his feathers. *Resse found you.*

And you. I was going to look for you once I escaped, you

know. He nipped her hair.

I know. And I missed you too.

Hurry. I don't want to scorch them. Resse's worried voice filled her mind.

Elias already sat on his friend, holding out his hand to Odo, who stared at Resse with shock. His face was the color of eggshells.

"He's a friend. Come on." Adelaide pushed her brother toward the dragon, and with Elias's help from above, he managed to climb onto Resse's neck.

Then Adelaide scrambled up and sat behind her brother.

"Hold on to the spine in front of you," Adelaide said, and Odo grabbed it.

With another roar and a jet of fire shot over the guards' heads, Resse sprang into the air. His three riders leaned forward, gripping his spikes. He flew up through the blanket of clouds into a balmy blue sky above.

Elias let out a roar of triumph as if *he* was the one flying them to safety and glanced back at Adelaide. "We did it. Though I shouldn't have doubted with you there."

"You did help a little."

Odo gazed around with wide eyes, and Adelaide squeezed his arm. Cyr flew beside them, wondering why Adelaide and Elias weren't flying.

Soon, she promised him, just thankful to have those she loved safe with her.

When Adelaide's bottom started to become numb, Resse landed with a jaw-clenching jolt in a meadow ringed with thorny, blue evergreens on the edge of what had to be the Hinterkitten Forest.

A mockingbird warbled somewhere nearby, and although it wasn't raining here, the trees dripped and puddles lay beneath their overhanging branches.

Elias helped the wide-eyed Odo to the ground and then Adelaide. As he chatted with Resse, Odo turned to Adelaide and whispered, "I thought you hated the prince. And why are you friends with dragons?"

Adelaide gazed at Elias's too slim, yet confident form as he stood beside Resse's violet eye. Her heart sang at his presence. "He's a good man, although he can be annoying at times. As for the dragons, I'll explain later. It's a long story."

"What about you?" She pulled on one of his ears like she had when they were younger. "How are you holding up?"

"Other than riding on a living, breathing dragon?"

Who can also speak into your mind, Resse said, gazing past Elias to Odo.

The boy stared at the dragon as he lay down and pulled in his wings.

"How do you do that?" Odo asked. "Where did you come from? Why are you here? Are there more of you?"

Elias laughed and sat down in the dewy grass with his back against Resse.

"Before Resse answers your questions, you must first tell me about how you were captured and what you've been doing all this time." Adelaide pulled Odo down to the ground next to her and stretched her legs out beside Elias's.

"As long as you tell me where you've been and how you've made friends with dragons," Odo told her.

"And then you must tell me where you've been, King Elias." Resse angled his head so he could gaze at them with one of his eyes.

"It appears we'll be here for a while," Elias said.

Odo rubbed his hand down Resse's scales. "I was working out in the fields with some other boys from Alesfirth. In the chaos of the fighting and burning of the fields, two Gyndilians grabbed me. They took me into Alesfirth with some other boys and girls. We had to sit outside without anything to eat or drink the whole day. If we moved, the Gyndilians yelled or spat at us." He shivered.

"The next day I saw King Elias, and he asked me not to tell

anyone who he was, so I didn't."

Elias nodded at Odo. "I appreciate that greatly."

The boy's ears reddened. His earthy-brown eyes met Adelaide's. "They took me to Weitzen, where I had to wait on the nobles, run errands, and muck the pig pens." He grimaced. "That was the worst, all stinky and gross. But they treated me well overall and fed me."

"I'm glad to hear that, but I'm more glad that you're with us now." Adelaide hugged him, then gave him her half-filled animal skin.

I'm going to hunt, Cyr said, taking flight. *All this talking makes me hungry.*

Get enough for us too, please, Adelaide said.

Resse's green-spiked tail flicked on the ground. *I'll help him. That will make it go faster.*

Cyr gave a sharp cry and disappeared above the trees.

Resse stretched like a cat, and Adelaide pulled Odo away from him as the dragon stood.

"What's he doing?" Odo asked.

Adelaide realized he hadn't heard anything they'd said because they'd kept the conversation within their own minds. Odo wouldn't have been able to understand Cyr anyway. "Going to hunt," she explained.

Resse opened his leathery, yellow wings. He took several running leaps, stretched his wings their full width, and leapt into the air—a golden leaf brilliant against the blue sky.

Odo gasped as he watched Resse's departing shape.

"Would you like to hear how I met him?" Adelaide asked her brother.

He turned his wide eyes on her and nodded. He listened with rapt attention, especially to the parts about her transformation and her time on Niclond. Elias listened attentively as well, although he had just heard the same story.

When Adelaide finished, she leaned back, her throat scratchy and her stomach growling.

Odo gawked at her, and she laughed at his expression. "So, you can turn into a dragon whenever you want?" he asked.

"Yes," she said, knowing what he'd ask next.

"Can you do it now?"

"I'd like to see that as well," Elias said, sitting up.

Adelaide glanced down, fiddling with her braid. What if Elias thought she was ugly as a dragon? What if he could still see her poor, peasant plainness and left her for good?

But she'd have to transform around him sometime.

She closed her eyes on Odo's and Elias's expectant faces and dwelled on the tautness of her wings as they carried her on the wind's river, the strength of her barbed tail, the protection of her scales that rustled over her like armor.

Adelaide noticed the refreshing scent of spring rain first, then, when she opened her eyes, the beauty of Elias's face. His eyes couldn't be described as just a shade of blue-grey. They were the sky on a stormy day, the sea raging against itself, fresh steel ready for forging into a weapon.

And they were looking at her as if he was the dragon and she his sky. The heat from his gaze blazed from the tip of her snout to the end of her tail. She never wanted to look away.

"You are a stunning creature, Adelaide," he murmured. "The name Silverscales is not worthy for one such as you. You should be called Moonscales or Starscales." He placed a hand on her snout, and she leaned into the touch, closing her eyes.

"You're huge!" Odo shouted, and Adelaide jerked her eyes open, remembering that they weren't alone.

Elias's gaze promised her many more tender moments in the future, and Adelaide's heart thrummed. But then she remembered that there wasn't supposed to be a future for them, and her tail drooped.

Odo stepped close to her. "Can I touch you?"

Adelaide nodded and lowered her neck to him.

He placed a trembling hand on her scales. "Whoa. You're warm."

It's the heat from my belly.

"It still sounds like you in my head," he said. "Can you blow fire like that other dragon?" Odo looked at her as if all his dreams would come true if she said yes.

His name's Resse, and of course I can. I wouldn't be worthy of the name dragon if I couldn't.

"Yes, you would," Elias argued.

Adelaide stretched out her head into the cloudless sky. She opened her jaws, took a deep breath, and blew out with all her strength.

A stream of orange and white flames shot past her throat and teeth—tickling them—into the sky. After a moment, she cut off the flame with her tongue.

"That was the neatest thing I've ever seen." Odo bounced on his feet.

"Nicely done," Elias said. "I see that the others taught you well. I wish I could have been there to do it. I should've—"

Stop. It's not your fault that you weren't there.

"Does it hurt when you breathe fire? How do you change into a dragon? Can I?"

After gazing at Elias a moment longer, Adelaide turned to her brother. *It doesn't hurt because my mouth and teeth are coated with something that protects them.* That's what Picot had told her, at least. *I'm not sure how the transformation works, and no, you can't change into one.*

She lay on the grass and wrapped her tail around her, careful not to accidentally hit Odo with it, who still stood beside her.

"Why not? If you can be a dragon, so can I."

It's not that easy, and it's a painful process. Elias knows more about it than I do.

Elias put his hand on Adelaide's head. "As your sister said, it's a complicated process, and it does hurt. A dragon and human both have to give one another something valuable in order to transform, and at least one of them must love the other sacrificially for the process to work."

"Love?" Odo made a face as if he'd eaten a rotten apple. "Why?"

"Perhaps because it's the most powerful force in the world."

That quieted the boy, but only for a moment. "Can I climb on you, Adelaide?"

I suppose, but be gentle.

Odo's feet pattered on her leg and then her side, and she laughed. *Quick, that tickles.*

With a grunt, Odo pulled himself up behind her neck. "Whoa. Everything's so high up here. I'd be even taller if you'd stand up."

Sorry, but I'm too comfortable for that. She laid her head on the ground, and Elias rubbed circles on her snout.

She sighed. *That feels nice. And it's pretty brave of you, considering I wanted to kill you only just a few months ago.*

He grinned. "True, but I don't think you'd burn the only living king when we're at war."

Probably not.

The motion soothed Adelaide, and she relaxed—truly relaxed—for the first time since she thought Elias had died. Even though her friends were fighting a war and the future of their country was still unknown, here, in this moment, she could enjoy that Elias and her brother were safe.

"King Elias, are you a dragon as well?" Odo asked.

"Very astute of you. Would you like to see?" He stopped rubbing Adelaide's head, and she wished Odo had kept his mouth closed.

"Yes! Do you look like Adelaide?"

"I'm nowhere near as beautiful as she." He stood and took several steps back. "It's been much too long since I've changed."

He closed his eyes, and a glowing light cocooned him, growing until it consumed him. The light faded, and there stood Elias the dragon.

Adelaide had forgotten how majestic he was, or perhaps

she could see his grandeur better in this body. His golden legs and sides glimmered like sun's summer rays, and his back, neck, and tail shimmered a vibrant scarlet.

A pleasant musky, cedar-smoky scent emanated from him.

Adelaide stood, almost without knowing she did, every muscle in her massive body tight and fiery as she gazed at his now-blue eyes. She stretched out her neck to his thicker, higher one and sniffed. The scent swallowed her.

Do I smell nice? He asked teasingly.

Adelaide huffed and took a step back, hoping she wasn't blushing.

You smell nice to me too, Adelaide Starscales.

Now not just his scent swallowed her, but his eyes also. She could easily, happily drown in those depths for the rest of her life.

"You're bigger than Adelaide!" Odo said from Adelaide's back, interrupting the spell cast on them.

Elias took a step toward the boy, his scales rustling like wind through branches. *Males usually are larger than females.*

But I can probably fly faster than you, Adelaide told him.

The sound of wings beating the air overhead was followed by the thud of two deer as Resse dropped them on the ground. *I see that you're now in your true shape, King Elias.* Resse landed and bowed to Elias, then launched himself at him, his mouth in a snarl.

Adelaide growled at the sight of anyone—even a friend—attacking Elias. She crouched to the ground, ready to pounce.

Elias leapt out of the way and grabbed Resse's smaller neck.

"They're just playing ... I think," Odo said in a quivering voice.

Adelaide huffed, keeping her eyes on the tumbling, growling dragons. She did her best to stay out of their way—aware of the fragile human on her back.

It was a good thing they were far from civilization, or the Gyndilians would be upon them at any moment from all the growls, snarls, and crashing of the two creatures.

Well, I'm going to eat before my stomach eats me, she said to the immature dragons.

Giving the wrestling dragons a wide berth, Adelaide walked toward a deer carcass.

"I'm not eating *that*," Odo said.

You won't have to eat it raw, she told him. She sent a thin beam of fire to roast the carcass. The scent of burning fat and smoking meat made her mouth water. Once the fire burnt itself out, she tore off one of the legs and nudged it to the side. *Here.*

Odo crawled off her and gingerly picked at the still-smoking meat.

Adelaide tore her carcass in half and swallowed one of the chunks whole, enjoying the crunch and crack of bones.

Odo frowned. "That's disgusting."

You don't have to watch.

Next time we'll have to fight in the air, Resse said, walking over to Adelaide and Odo with a lighter step than usual.

Why? I'm even better than you at fly-fighting. Elias stopped in front of Adelaide, his eyes as light as the sky above. *I'm glad you saved some for us. I know how much you love food.*

Adelaide scrunched her face at him and then heard more than felt Cyr land on her head. *I caught my prey before the yellow fire-flyer did,* he thought.

Resse looked up from his deer, blood smeared across his scales. *Yes, because it was a squirrel.*

Once everyone finished eating, and night crept into the cool mountain air, Adelaide announced she was going to the stream to bathe.

Why? Your tongue works just as well. Resse licked the scales on his chest as if to show her how to do it. Elias too was cleaning one of his feet with his tongue.

Adelaide shook her head. *I need more than a licking, and I've already heard Elias's tale.*

She walked off in the direction of a bubbling brook.

Be careful, Elias said.

She turned back to him—a shimmering orange shape in her night vision. *I am a dragon now, you know.*

And any creature that looks at you would flee with fright.

Adelaide took that as a compliment.

Chapter Forty-Eight

"Ow. Adelaide, you're crushing me."

Adelaide jerked back the wing that she'd covered Odo with the night before to keep him warm.

He sat up and blinked. "I'm hungry."

Adelaide wouldn't need to eat for another few days if she remained a dragon. *There might be some meat left from last night.*

Across from Adelaide, Elias stretched and stood. *Good morning, fairest of all dragons.*

Heat crawled across Adelaide's scales. *Good morning.* She could get used to being greeted every morning by those sea-deep eyes. No, she couldn't.

"Where's Resse?" Odo asked.

Right here. The dragon's buttery neck emerged from beneath the trees as he strode toward them. *I just went to drink some water.* About half a dozen chipmunks scurried along his body, and Adelaide and Elias shared an amused look.

Now what are we going to do? Resse sat beside them. *We*

shall need your help with the Gyndilians, King Elias.

I'd like to help, Elias said. The sun struck his scales so that they glowed like the heart of a fire. He glanced at Odo, who gnawed on a piece of bone they must have missed last night.

The words Adelaide needed to say scorched her like embers. *You should go to the dragons in Neklosa and order them to help us against the Gyndilians.*

She didn't want to say farewell to Elias again so soon—what if this time was truly the last time she'd see him? The thought paralyzed her, and she fought to keep herself from begging him to stay with her always.

Oh, I should? Will you ever stop giving orders? Elias spoke lightly, but Adelaide sensed a sorrow churning beneath the surface of his words that matched her own.

Probably not. She hoped he couldn't hear or sense her own emotions, but the way he gazed at her—as if he longed to pull her close and never let go—told her otherwise.

Odo, would you like to feel my wings? They're soft but strong, Resse said.

Odo scrambled over to the dragon, and Adelaide thanked Resse for the distraction.

Only a soft slithering of scales let Adelaide know that Elias moved to stand beside her.

And what will you do while I'm flying to the dragons for help? He said in her mind alone, his voice as close as if it whispered in her ear.

She longed to lean into him, but that would only make their parting harder. *Fight the Gyndilians with the others, of course.*

And do you think I can let you do that, knowing that I could never see you again?

Adelaide met his blue-stone eyes. *Do you think I can let you fly away with the possibility of never seeing you again after just getting you back?* She blinked, and a tear the size of a cherry fell to the ground. *But this is the only way we can save our people.* She said it for both their benefit.

Elias wiped her tear away with his tail. *I will soar as quick as the winds to return to you, my love.*

I expect nothing else from you, my king. I will miss you each moment you're gone.

As will I.

Elias touched his snout to hers, breathing deeply. *I'm afraid that the dragons won't listen to me.* Shame shadowed the admission.

Adelaide leaned back to see him better. *Why? You are their king.*

Elias looked down at the grass. *I haven't lived with them for so long that I'm afraid I'm more human than dragon. And what if they prefer Evengier as their king to me?*

Adelaide wasn't used to comforting Elias; he'd always been the one to speak truth to her. In a way, it encouraged her that he needed comforting. It showed that he wasn't perfect.

Elias, she said gently but firmly, lifting his head with her snout so that he looked into her eyes. *You are the most deserving king—human and dragon—that I have ever known. You left everything to save your people.*

I didn't have much choice at the time, Elias muttered, and Adelaide growled at him.

You were willing to chase a revengeful, angry peasant who loathed you across the country for your people. You became what you weren't for them. If the dragons can't see your loyalty and love for them, then they don't deserve to have you as their ruler.

Elias gazed at Adelaide for a long moment, then rubbed his head against hers. His musky, cedar-smoky scent shot fire through her.

Thank you, Starscales. I needed to hear that.

It's the least I can do for all that you've done for me.

They stood there breathing each other in until Odo laughed at something Resse was doing.

What will we do about Odo? Elias pulled away and glanced at the boy darting around Resse's back, trying to grab a chipmunk.

Can you take him to my parents in Pinhurn since it's on your way south? He'll be safe there. The possibility of never teasing her brother again, never seeing those ears redden in embarrassment pushed more tears down her snout. Why was her life always full of goodbyes?

I'll see that he gets there safely. And you won't do anything rash without me, will you?

Adelaide tried to smile, but it faltered. *Whatever gave you that idea?*

He growled, and Adelaide sighed. *I will do what I need to, but won't be overly rash.*

Elias nodded. *I will see you again, Adelaide, my Starscales.* He touched her nose with his, and she shivered, longing to beg him to never leave her again.

Elias turned back to the others. *Odo, are you ready to fly?*

"Of course! Where are we going?"

I'm taking you to your parents in Pinhurn on my way to Neklosa.

Odo turned to her. "You're coming too, Adelaide?"

I wish. But I must go with Resse to help our friends fight the Gyndilians.

"Are they dragons too?"

Some of them. Adelaide glanced around for her satchel and nudged it toward Odo. *Find my animal skin in there and take it with you. I filled it up last night.* She wouldn't need it because she'd be flying as a dragon the entire way to the battle.

Odo clung to the pouch. "Will you be safe?"

Adelaide blew warm breath on him, ruffling his hair. Before she could reply, Resse said, *As safe as possible with me. Many things on earth and in the sky fear me.* He winked at Odo, and a chipmunk scrambled over his head.

Truly terrifying, Cyr said as he landed on Adelaide's head. Elias snorted.

With a pat on Adelaide's foot, Odo climbed up Elias. "Can I tell Mother and Father that you're a dragon now? They'll be so excited."

Adelaide doubted they'd feel excitement. More like shocked and heartbroken. *I suppose. But only tell them and no one else.*

Odo nodded solemnly. "I won't."

As Adelaide watched her brother sitting on Elias's back, and Elias preparing to soar away, her tail whipped through the air like a tree in a gale.

He will be fine, Elias reassured her.

And you?

I didn't die the first time, did I?

Adelaide growled. How could she bear to be separated from him again?

I will return to you, and with aid, he vowed. Then he turned toward Resse. Adelaide couldn't hear their conversation.

It's sad that Elias is leaving again so soon, Cyr said.

At his voice, Adelaide had an idea. It would break her into even more pieces, but at least Elias wouldn't be alone while traveling to Neklosa. *Cyr, I want you to go with Elias.*

Why? Cyr squawked. *Do you not want me to fight beside you in this great battle?*

Of course I do. Adelaide's tail drooped. *But I'll be with Resse and the other dragons. Elias will be alone until he finds the colony. And even then, they may not return with him.*

Cyr ruffled his feathers. *I would do anything for you, mistress.*

I know, she said. *And I, for you. Go with Elias to protect him. As you know, he matters greatly to me. I know you can handle this important task.* Her heart ripped as Cyr settled on her snout; she couldn't remember the last time they'd been apart for more than a few days.

Cyr pierced her with his amber eyes. *I'll go, but know that I listen for your whistle alone.*

More tears threatened to spill down Adelaide's cheeks. She

blinked them away. *I'll miss you too. You're the fiercest bird I know.*

Cyr tapped his beak against her snout, then hovered over Elias.

He stared at her. *Are you sure?*

She nodded. *Yes. Now go before I change my mind.*

Very well. Stay safe, and may the wind carry you far, Elias told her and Resse, his gaze lingering on hers.

May the sun stay warm on your scales, King Elias, Resse said, bowing.

"Farewell, Adelaide. See you soon!" Odo called as Elias tore his gaze from hers and leapt into the air. His blood-red wings stretched out beside him, reminding her of the last time she had said farewell. Would this be their last?

Elias keened as he soared away; Cyr gazed at her with helpless hatchling eyes again before following.

Fly quickly back to me, Adelaide said as the three disappeared into the clouds.

Chapter Forty-Nine

Resse attempted to keep Adelaide's spirits up with songs and stories on their journey to Gyndilad's southern border. But Cyr and Elias's absence pulsed inside her like dying coals, singeing everything.

The closer they flew to their friends and their unknown fate, the less Resse sang and spoke.

Once, as they neared the Dandorn River that meandered south of the Hinterkitten Forest, a wind sprang up from the Nefar Mountains that buffeted them so strongly, they had to descend or have their wings ripped off.

Adelaide persuaded Resse to continue on the ground, though it took much longer. When the sun's golden head rose, they curled up, wing-weary, beneath some trees until the safety of night enveloped them.

Sometimes they had to fly during the day, far up in the thin, bird-less air because there was nowhere to hide but in too-short grass or thistle-filled shrubs. Adelaide longed for the day when all this secrecy would dissipate like the long shadows of night.

Soon the two wove through the bare peaks of the southern range of the Nefar Mountains, and Adelaide's scales itched with filth and anxiety.

Do you hear or see anything? Adelaide asked as they soared over a boulder-strewn ravine.

Nay, Resse said without irritation, even though she'd asked him this about a dozen times over the past two nights. *Oh, wait. I think I saw a bear down there.*

Adelaide sighed, steam hissing from her nostrils. *You know that's not what I mean.*

I know. And you should know that I would tell you immediately if I had seen anything of the Klinian or Gyndilian armies.

I can't believe the Gyndilians would march over such treacherous terrain. Adelaide glanced down at the vertical cliffs and ravines crisscrossed with streams and loose rocks. It reminded her of the Spearheads, and she was thankful that she and Resse didn't have to cross the mountains on foot.

So, what's your plan once we come to the battle?

Adelaide squeezed her talons. *To crush and burn as many Gyndilians as possible.*

Resse looked at her. *Don't you think that's a bit ... rash?*

No. We must use the element of surprise while we have it.

True, but it sounds like something a hatchling would do.

Adelaide growled.

Which you aren't, of course. But surprise only lasts so long. What are you going to do once it's been lost?

Keep attacking.

Yes, but we should cover each other so that none of the knights will pierce our wings or trap us. Resse then reminded her of some of the offensive maneuvers they'd practiced on the way to Fernohn. She listened, though her missing of Elias and Cyr made her want to give the Gyndilians shards of this agony.

As the sky lightened to the color of ashes, the cry of ravens and the rasping of vultures pierced the silence.

Then the stench of blood, so much blood, inundated her. The rusty, wrong scent of human blood caused her nose to burn. Then there was smoke and tar, rotting flesh and sweat. The biting scent of fear overlaid everything, and Adelaide's stomach quivered.

We must be getting close. She tried to see past the mountains to get a glimpse of the battle. She heard no sounds of fighting. Did that mean they'd already lost? Had Conrad, Esa, Turquan, and Picot all been killed?

Adelaide, Resse's mental call yanked her attention, *look.*

She followed his gaze down to a valley where a group of men and tents huddled beside a stream. Their black tunics and the Gyndilian crest on the two flags near the tents sent a flood of fury through Adelaide. They were the ones who'd murdered her sister and sent Adelaide on a journey ending in anguish for so many people. They were the reason Gunter was lost and Odo had been captured.

Because of them, she didn't have a home and the people of Alesfirth had to cower like terrified rabbits in their own town. Because of them, she might never see Elias or any of her loved ones again.

It was too much. The agony rose until it burst its banks like a torrential flood, and Adelaide had to let it out.

She opened her maw and sent an inferno blazing at their tents and flags. Screams shattered the silence, and the burning scent of humans thrust up her nose.

Adelaide froze in horror, stopping the flow of flames. What had she done? Those people were threatening her country, yes, but they themselves hadn't killed her sister or sent her after Ganelon and Elias. Adelaide had done that herself.

She was turning into the beasts that the Klinians were so afraid of, that Elias was trying so hard to change their beliefs about. She'd never deserve him. Never.

She heaved, but only sparks came out.

Why did you do that, Adelaide? Resse asked. *They weren't attacking us or our people.*

I wanted them to feel a tiny bit of the heartache they had brought me. But you're right, they weren't attacking us. Forgive me.

Resse nudged her with his snout. *Rage is a dragon's worst enemy, and you have more reasons than most for giving in. You must master it before it masters you, which I'm sure you'll learn to do. You are forgiven.*

The screams followed Adelaide as she soared after Resse. She doubted they'd ever leave her.

On the other side of the mountains, the battlefield was a swamp of blood; puddles dotted the grass. Swords and shields were almost as numerous as the dead, and body parts, as well as dead horses, were flung everywhere.

Adelaide heaved again, longing to gather all her loved ones and take them far from here. But death would just follow them.

There were more gold-and-blue uniforms on the dead and dying than black and silver, which didn't surprise her, but the sight still sent tremors through her.

She and Resse soared over the battlefield that was now a graveyard, and Adelaide tried not to search for familiar faces. She would know soon who was alive and didn't want the image of their mangled bodies imprinted in her mind forever.

They winged toward the gold-and-azure flags of Klinhun on a ridge overlooking the blood-splattered field.

As Adelaide and Resse descended toward a swath of grass near a forest, horses squealed, and knights yelped and darted away.

Adelaide! Resse! Several inner voices shouted, and Esa, Picot, and Turquan slithered out of the trees toward them.

Adelaide's heart smiled at the sight of her friends alive and well. They each touched heads with one another.

You look as stunning as ever, Silverscales. Turquan opened his jaw in a partial smile.

And you are as irritating as ever.

It's good that you've returned, Picot said. *The fight isn't going well.*

Before Adelaide could ask for more details, Resse's voice leapt into their minds, *We saw as much. But first, I must tell you that King Elias is alive.* His tail flicked back and forth against his side.

The others gaped at him.

"What's going on here?" Berold strode up with Conrad and another man Adelaide didn't recognize.

The three men stopped a few paces away, and instead of frowning at her like he once might have done, Berold just said, "I'm glad to see that you've returned, Adelaide, Resse." His beard lay untamed against his face, purple moons outlined his eyes, and he stank of fear. She realized how terrible his job must be. How many of his comrades and friends had he sent to their deaths?

Thank you. I'm glad we can aid in the fight. Their conversation was as formal as two rulers from different countries meeting, but at least the hostility had evaporated.

"It's good to see you are well," Conrad said, almost as exhausted and filthy looking as Berold. "Did you find your brother?"

She nodded. *He's safe. And how are the others from Alesfirth?*

"Sayer had a fairly bad arrow wound, but Esa healed him."

Adelaide inclined her head to the lavender dragon who hummed deep in her belly. *It was my pleasure.*

Adelaide glanced back at Berold. *And how goes the fighting?* She hoped he'd tell her something different than what she'd seen on the battlefield.

Berold gazed past them down to the bloody swamp. "We're at a standstill now and have been since the day before yesterday." He glanced at the man beside him. "We believe the Gyndilians are waiting for supplies."

How many men have we lost? Resse asked.

"Too many, although Esa has healed and saved many that would be dead otherwise."

Resse touched his snout to Esa's.

Don't tell Berold about King Elias being alive, Adelaide told the dragons. *It'll only distract him, and Elias might not return in time to help.* She hoped with all her scales that wasn't the case, but she didn't want to raise Berold's and the other's hopes just to watch them blow away.

Berold spoke before her friends could reply. "The dragons have helped tremendously, but the Gyndilians still possess a much vaster army with better weapons, more supplies, and superior-trained men."

Why don't we attack while they aren't attacking us? Adelaide asked.

"They would expect that, and we just don't have the means to—"

A raspy roar filled the air, then another and another until a chaotic chorus of sounds battered Adelaide. The roars were rougher than the rumbling ones of dragons, and her spikes stiffened at the unnatural noise.

Several men nearby shouted, and Berold looked over at the far side of the battlefield, his face bone-white.

Adelaide glanced over too and gasped.

Thirty or so creatures—Adelaide had no name for them—circled the field in the air on thin, leathery, charcoal-colored wings. They had no scales, but charcoal-grey skin, arms and legs that stretched into sharp black talons, and tails that ended in sharp barbs.

But the worst thing about them was their heads: round and human-like, complete with hair and eyes. A burnt sewage smell floated about them, and Adelaide gagged.

What are they? She asked, repulsed by the circling vulture-like creatures.

Abominations, Turquan growled.

One of the creatures broke off from the others and blew a trail of fire at the already smoking field. It was wispy compared to theirs, but it still managed to catch some of the remaining pieces of grass on fire.

It appears that they have attempted to do what Elias did—to turn a human into a dragon—but have done it horribly wrong, Picot said, watching the creatures with deep sadness.

Who would do such a thing? And how do they even know how? Adelaide asked.

I don't know, but there are many evil people in the world, Esa said. *King Aethelmaer must have found out somehow or is working with someone who knows.*

Can they be killed? Adelaide asked.

Yes, but not easily, Turquan answered. *Their skin is tough. They are impervious to our flames unless we use a steady stream all at once. Their wings and faces are their weakest parts. But there are many of them, too many.*

Many of them also kill themselves once they're captured. Esa smelled of sorrow and regret.

Resse rubbed his head against her neck.

Perhaps we should attack them? It galled Adelaide, but she looked at Berold for permission. Elias wasn't even there to see how well they were getting along.

Berold looked at her, then at the creatures that now flew dangerously close, bolder at the lack of action on the Klinians' part. "I suppose you'll have to because we can't afford to let our lines so far back get hit. We'll join you in a counteroffensive on the ground with what remaining forces we have." He barked a command to the man beside him.

Should we wait until the knights are ready? Adelaide asked, forcing herself not to launch into the air at the offending creatures.

"They are already in battle formation, sire," the man beside Berold said.

Berold nodded. "Good. Then you dragons can go now. And

Adelaide," he looked as if he'd rather pull out a tooth than say what he was going to, "thank you." He didn't need to explain; Adelaide knew he was grateful for how she had deferred to his leadership.

It's what Elias would have wanted. And you are the leader of the army, she said to him alone. Then she turned to the dragons. *Ready?*

They nodded and launched into the sky.

Turquan flew to her left with Picot beside him, and Resse and Esa soared to Adelaide's right. They were as fierce and dangerous as a bonfire. Adelaide wouldn't want to fight along-side anyone else—except Elias and Cyr—but she couldn't think about them now.

What's the plan? Picot asked as they soared closer to the vulture-like creatures.

Let's split up and come at them from different angles, Turquan said. *It's worked well in the past.*

Esa, will you fly with me? Resse glanced at her.

She assented, and they split up. Turquan flew to the top of the whirling mass, Picot to the left, Resse and Esa to the right. Adelaide soared beneath the horde of grey, dodging their bursts of fire. When some hit her, it tickled.

Halfway through the mass, she turned around, facing the creatures, and roared a great bout of flame at them, attempt-ing to divide them. Most ignored the fire, so Adelaide used her other weapons.

She bit into backs, tails, and necks—anything charcoal grey—crunching until she heard bones break. She swiped at them with her tail, knocking them into each other and sending them somersaulting away. She grabbed them with her claws and hurled them to the ground, ignoring their cries and the nasty taste of their too-thick, yellow-tinged blood.

With their larger, more powerful bodies, the dragons soon diminished the ranks of the weaker creatures.

One soared at her, claws extended, and she swerved. She

hit it with her tail, sending it spinning away. As she watched it tumble through the air before it righted itself, there was something familiar about it that scratched at the back of her mind.

A slash at her leg brought her back to the battle. She opened her maw and poured out flames on a creature that had bitten down on her arm. It fell to the ground.

She caught sight of the creature that had pulled on her curiosity. She dove toward it, staring at the messy brown hair that stood straight up like feathers. Like the hair of someone she knew.

Adelaide almost didn't want to find out, panic teetering inside her, but she had to know.

As she soared close enough to see into the creature's face, horror spilled and tumbled over her.

Gunter?

Chapter Fifty

Gunter was the wood that the fiery rage from the dragon's memories devoured. It was a fire that never went out, consuming what Gunter had been.

He had stopped trying to fight his way through the raging sea of memories and emotions that had returned when he'd drunk the liquid the dragon had given him. They became *his* memories.

Once-powerful dragons stuck with arrows like pigs, a land he had fought to protect for years disappearing while the people he'd loved, protected, and sacrificed for cheered as he and the others left. The cries of hatchlings that didn't have enough to eat, his own unending hunger. King Ganelon stealing his sister for a mate, the pit of darkness when she died.

The dragon had been right; these memories gave him strength. Strength to fight the larger dragons who would let the humans rule—the humans who had betrayed them.

Gunter? A familiar voice tugged at the frail human memories buried so deep that he'd almost forgotten them. He froze in surprise, but the voice was soon burned up by the fire.

The creature that once was Gunter roared, burning his throat, and soared away as the flames licked up his soul.

◆ ◆ ◆

Adelaide stared after the creature. No matter how much she wished she could deny it, it had been Gunter. His eyes were no longer a light, carefree blue, but a vivid red. They gazed past her as if he didn't know her, but his face had otherwise been the same.

Oh, what had they done to him—to her best friend who had climbed trees with her, made faces at her when she'd been irritating, and caught frogs with her, Odo, and Emma on summer evenings?

She tried to think of a way to help him.

Adelaide, they're leaving, and it's pointless to follow. Come on, Resse said, stopping beside her. *You're not hurt, are you?*

Not in the way he meant, so she shook her head.

Good. Come on.

Adelaide numbly followed Resse back to the camp, unable to eradicate Gunter's lost red gaze out of her mind.

"Nicely done," Berold said as they landed on the ground behind his tent.

"Adelaide, are you alright?" Conrad asked.

She couldn't face him now; she didn't have the words to tell him what she'd seen. Would she ever?

She stalked toward the woods and entered as far as her bulk allowed. Then she curled up, her tail spikes a barrier between her and the world.

As she closed her eyes, she heard Turquan tell Resse, *Those creatures always flee before we can fully eliminate them. Then they return with more than the previous day. First there were only ten of them, then fifteen. The next day there were twenty and now thirty. Next, there will probably be forty-five or even fifty.*

But there weren't fifty of the creatures. There were hundreds.

Chapter Fifty-One

Elias was an arrow released from a bow, soaring with one goal in mind: to find the dragons, convince them to help, and return to Adelaide as soon as possible.

The green plains of Neklosa unfurled beneath him like parchment. He scanned the land for marks of dragons: piles of dung, scattered scales, burnt wood or earth, their smoky scent. But nothing so far.

He flew faster than he ever had, his wings and body groaning with each flap. But it still wasn't fast enough. With every scale, he ached to be with Adelaide and his people who were dying to protect Klinhun—as he should be doing.

At least Odo was safe. Elias had watched the boy enter Pinhurn a few days ago to find his parents. Odo had begged him nearly the entire flight to let him stay with Elias. But the boy was safer where he was.

Do you see anything? Elias asked Cyr. He had better senses than the hawk, but his thoughts distracted him, and two pairs of eyes were better than one.

Nay. Just human nests and fields.

Elias sighed. Hopefully, Adelaide and his friends would still be alive by the time he returned.

As he neared a shimmering lake, he noticed shapes larger than birds soaring over the water. *Cyr, do you see those shapes over the lake? Do you think they're dragons?*

I see them, the bird said. *But they're too far away for me to be certain what they are.*

Elias flew closer, and when the sun struck one of the creatures, light scintillated off in an array of blues and greens. Elias projected his thoughts to the dragon. *Hail. I am King Elias, Kindheart, Healer of Brokenness, Giver of Life, Lightscales, and son of King Ganelon, former king of the dragons. Please gather Evengier and the elders. I must speak to them immediately.*

The dragon froze, hovering in midair. *King Elias? You're alive! I will tell Evengier now.* He soared away, and Elias landed on the lake's shore to wait.

As the crowd of dragons around Elias grew, so did his anxiety. Despite Adelaide's words, he still felt as if he was shrinking into a hatchling under their curious gazes. He hadn't been around this many dragons in so long. What if he said something too human and they all laughed? Or worse, what if he couldn't think of the right words to convince them to go with him to Klinhun?

Even though by dragon law he was their rightful king, they could still choose to obey Evengier rather than him.

Prince, or, I suppose I should say, King Elias. A mighty pine-green dragon that made Elias feel like a puppy landed in front of him. *It is good to see you. We all thought you were dead and mourned for you.*

Yes, I'm sorry, but I was unable to return to Niclond. I was ill, and a band of thieves captured me. Only recently did I escape.

Evengier nodded. *I am glad that you're not dead, and I am pleased to return the rulership of the dragons back to you now that you have returned.* Evengier bowed to Elias, and he exhaled in relief.

The first difficulty—Evengier recognizing his authority after being gone so long—was overcome. But the climb to gaining their help had just begun.

The crowd of dragons surrounding them bowed, and Elias wished his father was there to see his son trying to follow in his footsteps.

Pray, tell us more about what has befallen you since you and your father left and how you are alive, Evengier said. *And how you became friends with a female human and turned her into one of us.*

Or more than friends, Ysoria said in Elias and Evengier's minds, coming up to stand beside her mate.

Elias was too tense to smile at Ysoria's remark; he just nodded at her. *There will be time for that story later. Right now, our homeland and the people we once loved and lived alongside are in dire need of our help.*

Evengier leaned back. *Yes, Adelaide Silverscales said as much when she came to Niclond. But why would we endanger our people to help those who cast us aside and could do so again?*

Several of the elders, who stood in a tight ring around Evengier and Elias, nodded. Elias clenched his teeth to keep from growling.

How can we not do otherwise? He made sure his thoughts reached into the minds of all the dragons, glad they couldn't see the trembling human boy beneath his scales. *Isn't what makes us dragons helping those in need whether they care about us or not? Will we forsake those we were created to help just so we can be safe and comfortable?* He nodded at the lush lands rolling around them.

A few elders twitched uneasily.

We are not humans who look out only for ourselves and our own. We are dragons, protectors of Klinhun and all that resides there. Will you show the world your bravery by standing with me in defending the land we once claimed, or will you hide here, in a land not your own, helping no one but yourself?

Chapter Fifty-Two

Nothing happened on the battlefield for two days but watching and waiting. Adelaide mostly slept, recovering from her flight, but her sleep was riddled with the faces of Gunter and Elias. Gunter's had blood-red eyes and dagger-sharp teeth, and Elias's body was broken and bleeding.

The other dragons paced, hunted, and took turns patrolling the skies.

On the eve of the third day, the abominations returned.

There are more of those loathsome creatures flying this way—about a hundred, Turquan said loud enough to threaten Adelaide with a headache.

She glanced up from the deer haunch she'd been devouring. Turquan streaked toward them.

There are more coming, he said as he landed with a thud beside Picot, whose jaws dripped blood from his own meal.

"How many?" Berold called as he rode toward them.

Probably well-nigh five hundred.

Berold cursed and whirled his horse around, shouting, "Fenrick, Lucas, Conrad, I need you!"

Adelaide stared at the sky above the field. A rushing sound like the heartbeat of a river filled her ears, the sound of many—too many—beating wings. She tensed.

Hundreds of the ugly grey creatures swarmed out of the valley that Adelaide and Resse had soared through just days ago. They winged straight at the Klinian army, their identical crimson eyes saturated in rage.

Adelaide searched each face for Gunter's, but there were too many, and they kept shoving and thrusting each other, making it difficult to keep one in focus.

"You all know what to do," Berold said from behind them. "We'll tackle the ground forces while you attack those in the air. Fight hard and keep your wits about you, and we might have a chance at winning this."

They didn't. Everyone—dragon and human—knew it. The horde of creatures in the sky would be enough to send any man running for his life and dragon shaking in fear. But there was also a great number of Gyndilians flowing through the gap toward their war-weary allies at the far end of the field like water set loose from a dam.

Adelaide's stomach swooped as the new troops formed ranks to face them. Elias and the others had better fly faster than the wind if they were to arrive before the Gyndilians killed them all.

Berold turned to face the ragged Klinians as they clanked into position. "People of Klinhun, we may be smaller, but we fight for our lands, our homes, and our futures!" He yelled from his horse at the front of the army.

A half-hearted cheer rose from the men.

You don't have to fight alone. We, the rulers of the skies and protectors of Klinhun, give you our wings, flames, teeth, and claws until our enemies flee in fear! Resse cried for all to hear.

A much louder cheer rose from the ranks.

Adelaide turned and growled in surprise at how close the abominations had come. They hung just a few wingbeats away, their faces ravenous. It was time to end the talking and begin the fighting.

For Klinhun! Adelaide shouted as she took off into the grey-choked sky.

The men and dragons roared as one.

Shall we do what we did last time? Resse asked from beside Adelaide.

Yes, but this time let's switch our positions, Turquan said. *You and Esa, come at them from beneath, I'll come from the top, Picot from the left flank, and Adelaide from the right.*

Their faces seem to be the most vulnerable part, so aim for those, Picot added.

Just don't kill one that has spikey hair, a scruffy brown beard, and a smaller body than the others. I know him, Adelaide said.

The others only had time to murmur their assent before they separated for the attack.

Adelaide didn't fight as vehemently as before now that she knew some of the creatures had once been people from Klinhun. She looked at every face before she attacked and called Gunter's name with her mind.

She spotted him once but lost sight of him; he never responded to her calls. She would have to capture him somehow. And after that, she wasn't sure. She'd try to bring the lost boy inside back.

But there were so many of the deformed creatures. For each one she tore in half, hurled to the ground, or cut the wings off, at least two others tore her own wings, flamed at her face, and clawed her body.

Twice Adelaide had to find Esa to heal cuts on her wings that made it nigh impossible to fly because of the pain.

The clash of sword on sword and men's and horses' screams joined the din of thrashing wings, snarls, growls, ripping skin, and the jarring of bodies. Adelaide and her friends fought until their wings burned, their throats rasped, and blood—theirs and their enemies'—coated their scales and dripped into their eyes.

Then they kept fighting.

The King of Gyndilad is here, Picot said as the light dimmed.

Where? Adelaide asked as she clamped her teeth on a deformed creature's neck and shook it until it stopped moving.

On a horse toward the back of their army.

Adelaide spun around. As she rose above the swarm, she noticed the fight wasn't going well on the ground. She hadn't expected victory, but the sight of so many men clothed in gold and blue lying in pools of their own blood lodged a painful splinter in her heart.

Berold cut through men as if they were grass, inspiring courage in those who saw him. But a horde of Gyndilians lay in wait near the mountains, and only about a hundred Klinians, divided into three ranks, awaited the command to help their countrymen.

At this rate, it would be a miracle if they survived until dawn. *Hurry, Elias, hurry,* Adelaide murmured.

Do you see the king, Adelaide?

Oh, yes. She was supposed to be looking for the King of Gyndilad. Adelaide peered down past the ranks of Gyndilians to the back of their force.

A fat man with a black beard sat on a dappled grey horse near the forest abutting the mountains. He wore the finest tunic she'd ever seen, held a shield emblazoned with the diving raven of Gyndilad, and a helmet so shiny that it couldn't have ever seen battle. He spoke to a man with shaggy hair pulled back. A dog stood next to the man.

Adelaide had no doubt that the pudgy man in his unspoiled armor was the king. This was not just a person following orders, but the very man who had ordered the destruction of her home, the death of her sister, and the abduction of her brother.

She roared, startling an abomination that was trying to

surprise her from beneath.

We must kill Gyndilad's king, Adelaide said to her friends.

How? Esa asked. *Archers stand in front of him. Besides, these half-creatures probably won't let us get near him.*

We have to try. If they killed the king, then all this madness would end. And perhaps this mountain-heavy burden could finally be lifted off Adelaide.

She kicked at the creature reaching for her, sending it tumbling back. She brought down her wings, aiming for the king who sat so nonchalantly on his horse.

A mass of the half-creatures surrounded her, attacking from every angle, so thick that she couldn't move or see.

She and her friends were forced to back away, killing the creatures from afar.

As the sun slipped behind the mountains, covering the field in a blue bruise of light, Esa said, *I think I saw that human-creature you mentioned.*

Adelaide blew fire at an abomination that attacked her. At Esa's words, talons gripped her heart, tearing her in two directions. Should she continue toward the Gyndilian king or Gunter?

Gunter was her best friend and needed her help. And the swarm of repulsive creatures wasn't dissipating anytime soon.

Adelaide swung her tail, swinging her body around as she searched for Esa. She spotted her soaring behind and above the two armies, fighting one of the creatures head-on while attempting to throw one off her back.

Adelaide twisted through the melee, grabbed the creature on Esa's back, and tossed it as far as she could.

Thanks, Esa said as she flung the other creature through the air with her teeth.

Of course. Adelaide licked some blood running down her face as she searched the skies. *Where did you see him?*

On the west side of the field. He was shooting fire at me. I grabbed him, tossed him away, and he glided higher up.

Adelaide soared toward a lone shape in the sky.

Gunter, it's me, Adelaide. I know you're still in there, she crooned to the creature with spikey hair.

A cut oozed on his shoulder, but it didn't look deep. He watched her with those eerie red eyes as she eased closer.

She stopped a wing's length away, staring at him with one eye as the other watched for danger to her left. *Gunter, it's me, Adelaide. I'm a dragon now, well, sometimes. I can change when I want to. Elias made me like this.*

A shiver went up his spine, and his eyes contracted. He turned and disappeared into the mass of half-human creatures.

Perhaps she shouldn't have spoken Elias's name; maybe it had caused bad memories to flare. But at least he hadn't attacked her.

Still, Adelaide couldn't help wondering if the boy who loved swimming in the Lentiasa River and picking flowers with his little sister no longer existed.

Chapter Fifty-Three

The flames kept burning the creature that had been Gunter, but there was also that voice that was so familiar. Had it betrayed him and the dragons too? No, it couldn't have. It belonged to a dragon.

The name came like a butterfly: fragile and gentle. Adelaide.

His surprise pushed him out of the waves that tried sucking him down. Adelaide was here and a dragon? King Elias had made her one?

Fury threatened to push him back down into the raging sea, but something in his claw stopped him. Something soft and silky. With much effort, as if trying to pull out a weed, he remembered a Gyndilian man with a kind heart and a woman with warm words who had told him he was brave.

Gunter didn't have the bravery and strength that Adelaide had. He didn't know if he wanted her version of bravery anymore, if it even *was* bravery. But he would not be what the Gyndilians wanted him to be. Jeharrez's strength wasn't strength, it was just violence and cruelty.

It was time to see what kind of strength Gunter had.

Clinging to the handkerchief and forcing himself to think about Elysande's blue eyes and Conrad's hand on his shoulder to stay above the waves, Gunter flew toward the other creatures who were suffering like him.

302

Chapter Fifty-Four

Adelaide and the dragons attempted to snap up a few moments of sleep, but the clashes on the battlefield and the roars of half-human creatures made it impossible.

Not able to endure the thought of the Klinians being slaughtered while they did nothing, the dragons and Adelaide drank from a nearby stream and swooped back into the terror-rent sky.

I'm not sure about anyone else, Turquan said as the sky swept into the yawning-grey light of dawn, *but I can't fight much longer. My wings feel like they're made of rocks.*

And you're the one who said earlier that you could take down half these abominations by yourself, Resse said as he chased a creature through the air. *But I agree with you. We need a break.*

Adelaide's wings burned every time she beat them, and her throat ached from spurting out flames. The dragons had severely diminished the horde of creatures, but there were still hundreds, many of them new and fresh, that had flown out of the mountains just a short while ago.

She hadn't seen Gunter, alive or dead, since last evening, and her stomach gnawed on itself in worry. Had he been killed?

Perhaps we should—

A loud bugling behind them cut Picot off.

Adelaide turned and saw a golden-red dragon soaring toward them, the first rays of the sun bouncing off his scales and dazzling her eyes.

Elias. Something inside Adelaide that had wound up when he'd left, unbent; anything seemed possible now.

She soared toward him as quickly as she could on her weary wings.

Adelaide. Elias touched her nose, and his scent flamed her inner fire. *It's good to see you.*

And you.

King Elias? So, you are *alive,* Turquan said, drifting over. *How?*

We'll discuss it later. Now, we have a war to win! He roared and dove at the repulsive creatures, which had stopped fighting to stare at him.

As he moved, the sky behind him came alive in a storm of color and movement as hundreds of dragons—*real* dragons— dove out of the clouds to clash with the enemy.

Adelaide's heart surged as what looked like all the dragons from Niclond roared and rushed at their enemies like a waterfall of pure power and rainbow beauty.

She thought she recognized the pine-green scales of Evengier and the sky-blue ones of Ysoria, who winked at her as she zoomed by.

You did it, Elias! Adelaide said. *Why did you even doubt?*

I just reminded them what being a dragon truly means. He brushed her shoulder with his snout, and Adelaide melted.

Which is?

Helping those in need.

Adelaide nodded. *That's exactly what you did for me.*

He pulled away and scrutinized her. *You're bleeding. I could try to heal you.*

They're only surface wounds. Let's worry about them after we finish off the Gyndilians. Adelaide lunged at an abomination flying toward Elias and sunk her teeth into its belly.

Elias batted another away with his tail.

Thanks, he said as Adelaide spat out the foul creature's blood.

A swarm of birds—hawks, eagles, falcons, and even a few owls—blotted out the rising sun as they coasted over the trees and then dove under the gawking half-breeds at the Gyndilian army.

That bird of yours has just as reckless ideas as you do and is just as determined. Elias's teeth gleamed in a grin.

Cyr? He did that?

Did someone say my name? The hawk asked, flapping up between them.

I'm glad to see you alive. Adelaide blew air at him as he landed on her snout. *I guess you don't need me as you once did.*

I'll always need your companionship.

Aw. And I'll always need yours. She scratched his back with a talon. *Good idea with the birds.*

Thanks. Cyr shuffled. *I'm just glad you survived without me.*

I wish we could stay here and chat, Elias said, *but the others need our help.*

Of course. Adelaide soared after him toward the churning mass where the dragons collided with the abominations. She ached to sleep, but the sight of Elias, Cyr, and the other dragons had lit her with energy.

Don't get killed, Cyr said as he flew off toward the birds attacking the Gyndilians. Many of the soldiers had fled at the sight of the dragons and birds, but there were still several hundred left.

Adelaide spotted Conrad yanking his sword out of a fallen

Gyndilian and cleaning it on the grass. Toward the front of the Klinian army, nearly right at the door of the Gyndilian camp, Berold fought the Gyndilian knight with long hair and a worm-like mustache who had stood by the king earlier. They both handled their sword as if it were a third arm.

Adelaide, watch out! Elias called.

She glanced up in time to see one of the creatures diving at her from above, its claws outstretched and its face twisted in fury.

Elias grabbed its tail in his jaws and hurled it away.

Thanks, Adelaide said, her heart thumping.

She fought beside him, then wrestled her way past the abominations to where King Aethelmaer had sat. This was the perfect time, while the dragons destroyed the abominations and the birds distracted the army, to stop him.

Where are you going, Adelaide? Elias's thoughts rippled with concern.

To find King Aethelmaer.

What will you do with him when you find him?

She shrugged. She'd like to kill the king, but didn't think that would please Elias. *Capture him, I suppose.*

Be careful. He's sure to be well guarded.

I won't go alone. She glanced around at her friends. *I'll take Resse and Turquan if they're willing.*

I'm coming too, Elias said.

Adelaide rolled past the wispy flames of the abominations. *You need to lead the dragons in the air.* Although she felt safest beside him, she didn't want him close to danger. He was too valuable, not only to her, but to the humans and dragons. They couldn't risk losing him again.

I'll be back soon, she said. *Keep the Gyndilians and those nasty creatures focused on the fighting.*

Very well, Elias sighed. *But if I so much as sniff that you're in trouble, I'll come for you.*

His comment lifted her wings, but she only said, *Keep yourself safe.*

Adelaide asked Resse and Turquan for help, and they flew over. Resse shot glances behind him where Esa fought alongside a blue-green dragon.

She'll be fine, Adelaide reassured him. *There are plenty others now to help.*

He assented and followed her and Turquan.

I can't see the king, Resse said as they neared the Gyndilian side of the battle.

He must be hiding around here somewhere. And he calls himself a king. Turquan shook his head.

Adelaide stared down at the camp that looked so miniscule and unthreatening from this height. A few Gyndilians stood watching the fight, and the dappled horse the king had sat on the previous day cropped grass nearby. But there was no sign of the king himself.

He must be in one of the tents, Adelaide said.

They all looked the same, probably to disguise which one was the king's.

Which one? There are dozens, and even though these are our enemies, I don't like the thought of flaming the humans inside while they have no ability to fight back, Turquan said.

At the sound of flapping wings, Adelaide glanced up. About a dozen grey creatures winged toward them.

Of all the apples! They didn't have much time. She glanced back at the camp, wondering which tent hid King Aethelmaer.

The tent farthest from them, near the trees climbing up to a ravine, lit up like sunlight striking the surface of water.

Scales of light! Turquan said. *What is that?*

Resse turned to Adelaide, his violet eyes wide. *Did you do that?*

Adelaide was as stunned as them. She had done it again—the thing that had happened with Odo in Gyndilad and while looking for Conrad in Alesfirth. But why were they able to see it now, when last time Resse and Cyr hadn't been able to? Because she had wanted, *needed* them to?

An explosion of fire stung Adelaide's eyes, and she hissed. The grey creatures were upon them.

Before Adelaide and her friends could retaliate, an abomination plummeted into those attacking them.

Remember those you love, it told them. *Fight.*

The voice was familiar. Yes, that was Gunter's ruffled hair. What was he doing?

The grey creatures were trying to figure that out too as they hovered in midair, staring at him.

Is that your friend? Resse asked Adelaide. *What's he doing?*

I don't know. Maybe he's trying to get them to stop fighting.

Gunter flew between the abominations, telling them to remember their loved ones and Klinhun. His message must have sunk in—at least for some of them—because about half a dozen flew away.

I wonder where they'll go, Turquan mused. *No one will accept them like that.*

Gunter turned his crimson eyes on Adelaide, and her heart warmed at the recognition in them. *What are you trying to do, Ade? I can help.*

We're trying to find King Aethelmaer. But you've done enough, Gunter. I'm so sorry for what happened to you. She reached out a talon as if to touch him. She didn't know what she'd do; she just wanted assurance that he was here, alive and the Gunter she remembered. But, of course he wasn't the same.

I haven't done near enough.

Before Adelaide could respond, an air-ripping roar, louder than any Adelaide had heard, erupted as if the earth itself was shouting. The wind from the sound buffeted her wings, and she plummeted to the ground.

So much anguish and hatred burst through the sound that her soul shivered. She shrank against the ground, longing to fly far, far away.

When the sound faded, Adelaide lifted her head and wished she hadn't.

Chapter Fifty-Five

A huge dragon, vaster even than Evengier, landed on a rocky incline above the Gyndilian camp, sending an avalanche of boulders toward the dumbstruck army.

The dragon's gold spikes thrust out of its head and back like spikes on a ball and chain. The golden scales on its stomach and sneering face didn't glow in the sun as if they were dead, and everywhere else its scales were as black as winter darkness. Its neck stretched as long as one of the spires on the castle in Dhalion.

It gazed down at them with red-lined golden eyes, its massive tail flicking back and forth as if about to pounce.

Adelaide trembled. How could they possibly destroy such a beast? Perhaps if all the dragons attacked at once ...

The dragon shot forth a blazing plume of fire at the sky, and Adelaide's scaled face flushed from the heat. It wouldn't take much of that fire to melt her wings.

Jeharrez, Elias's voice hissed loud in her mind. She turned and saw him hovering in the air above the dragons and their foes.

The name reminded her of the dragon that Ysoria had told her about, the one who had risen up against Evengier and been forced to leave the island. But that didn't explain why Elias was calling its attention to himself.

Jeharrez grinned, exposing teeth as long as his legs, and Elias glared at him. This was the dragon who had attacked Evengier while Elias and his father had lived in Klinhun. But Elias had had no idea that the traitor had found his way to Gyndilad and teamed up with King Aethelmaer.

It's so nice of you to join us, especially since you brought your friends. Jeharrez's voice was raspy as if he had a cold. *I'm disappointed your father couldn't join us, though.*

Elias growled.

I will help you destroy him, Evengier told Elias.

He nodded at him, then swung his head back to Jeharrez. *Did you do this to them?* He nodded at a nearby part-dragon creature.

Of course. They are my dragon army. You have killed and wounded many of them, but I will create more.

Why are you doing this? Elias asked in revulsion.

Jeharrez crouched and set his gaze on the knights who looked away from the malice in his glare. *To destroy all the humans for forcing us out of our home, which we had possessed long before any of them.*

That was centuries ago, Adelaide said, and Elias ground his teeth. Why must she always put herself in danger? *You can't kill all the humans just because their ancestors treated them horribly one time.*

Jeharrez sneered at her. *And what's to stop them from doing it again? Humans are fickle, weak creatures who defile this land with their greed and selfishness. They don't deserve our protection or even to live here anymore. Dragons are the ones who should rule and populate the land.* His tail thumped against the ground, knocking down some trees.

And you turned your back on the dragons by letting yourself become a human. Jeharrez scowled at Elias. *I will never understand why you would want to, but at least it'll make you easier to kill.*

Elias narrowed his eyes at the traitor. *I didn't turn my back on the dragons. I became a human to help them. Yes, humans can be greedy and selfish, but they can also be brave and loyal,* he thought of Adelaide, *especially when we help them. But dragons also have the capacity to betray. You yourself attacked Evengier, whom my father, King Ganelon, placed in charge.*

Jeharrez's black talons dug into the earth. *We had to starve on that tiny island while you and your father fled here to get fat.*

We didn't flee. Elias knew there was no reasoning with Jeharrez, but the dragon's words reached in and unearthed all his doubts and weaknesses. *My father and I came to Klinhun to try to earn the humans' trust so we could show them our true selves and rule again.*

You neglected to tell us this, and it was taking much too long. I had to pull the truth out of your truth-loving friend. He smirked at Resse, who shrank to the ground.

Elias's stomach plummeted to his tail. *You knew my father and I were in Klinhun as humans?*

Jeharrez exposed his teeth. *You shouldn't tell your secrets to those who can only speak truth.*

Elias glanced at Resse, who sank even lower to the ground, curling in on himself. *Forgive me, Elias. He kept asking me where you and King Ganelon were, and I wouldn't say, but then he asked in a way that I couldn't lie. But I didn't tell him that you and King Ganelon were humans.*

Elias sighed. *It matters not now.* He turned his gaze back

to the beast whose eyes glowed like pulsing coals.

I guessed that you and your father had learned how to turn yourselves into humans, for why else would you be able to live here so long? You betrayed us for them. Jeharrez growled.

But it actually worked out, because it gave me the idea to create an army of dragons from the humans. With them, not only could I kill the humans and return this land to the dragons, but I could also kill your father, whose love for the humans made him weak.

Snarls ripped through the dragons' throats at the mention of King Ganelon, and Elias's fire warmed his throat, ready to stream out and destroy this traitor.

Unfortunately, I didn't have the opportunity to kill King Ganelon. But at least now I can kill you. Jeharrez's eyes glittered, and he arched his spine-lined back.

Why do you hate him and me so much? Elias couldn't help asking as he swallowed his flames. Soon he would have his opportunity.

King Ganelon took my nest-mate away.

That was not the answer Elias was expecting. *He took her as his mate. That's what dragons do.*

He couldn't protect her! Jeharrez snarled. *He let her die because he was weak. And he nearly did the same to the dragons by waiting on the narcissistic, traitorous humans to love us.*

And you won't change your mind and join us in fighting the Gyndilians? Elias asked, though by the rage in the dragon's glare, he knew the answer.

Nay. The Gyndilians are my backs to step on to destroy the humans. Your love for them makes you unfit to rule the dragons.

Then, Jeharrez, you have betrayed your king and your people. All the wrath of the dragons will be upon you, Elias proclaimed.

He dived at the gold-and-black beast, his talons extended.

Chapter Fifty-Six

Adelaide watched as Elias flew straight at the larger dragon. His eyes were narrowed into slits, and nothing about him looked familiar. The kind prince had disappeared, a wrathful dragon taking his place.

But Adelaide was not afraid. She knew that Elias would never hurt her or anyone she loved. She was more concerned about his combat flying skills; how much did he know? Jeharrez could knock him away with just a swipe of those colossal claws.

Elias swerved around a plume of Jeharrez's fire. She should go help, but King Aethelmaer was still alive. And to be so close to the man who had ravished her town and had her sister slain and not do anything burned her more than fire.

The king now stood outside the tent, which no longer glowed from whatever she had done to it. With wide eyes, he watched the dragons fighting.

Before Adelaide could take advantage of his distraction, Gunter soared down and bathed the king in fire.

Arrows twanged and pierced his not-as-tough-as-dragon skin, and he screamed in agony.

Never had she heard him sound so much in pain nor so human.

Adelaide burned the Gyndilians surrounding him, the stink of scorching flesh filling her nostrils. Some of the abominations flew down and killed the Gyndilians. Gunter's words must have convinced them to do so, to remember who they were.

Arrows bounced off Adelaide's scales, and she swiped her tail, knocking over several approaching Gyndilians.

Gunter, are you alright? she asked as she landed beside him. Then she turned into a human.

He didn't look good; blood was pouring from his wounds, and he breathed shallowly.

"I'm so, so sorry," she murmured, tears pouring down her face. "It's my fault this happened."

"No," Gunter said, his voice weak. "I was selfish and killed Elias. I'm sorry I wasn't braver. I'm sorry I wasn't brave enough for you."

Adelaide stared at him, hardly comprehending his words. "Is that what you think? That I didn't want you because you weren't brave?" A hysterical sound half between a sob and a laugh erupted out of her as she held his head in her lap. "You're the bravest person I know. You stood by me in my search for justice and you left Alesfirth on your own to find me. You killed King Aethelmaer. I'm sorry I didn't make that clearer to you. You're like a brother to me, Gunter."

Blood dribbled down his mouth as he tried to say something.

Adelaide put her head against his. "I'm not losing you again, Gunter. I won't allow it." She turned and said to Turquan, Resse, anyone, "Get Esa. Someone, get Esa, please." Sobs choked her, and she turned back to Gunter, who was smiling at her. What was there to smile about?

"I'm glad I got to see you once more before I leave." He coughed. "And that Elias is alive. Tell him I'm sorry."

A roar of pain ripped through the air, reminding Adelaide that someone else she loved was in danger. She couldn't do anything now for Gunter. But maybe she could for Elias. She couldn't lose them both.

"You tell him yourself, Gunter. Hold on until I return, alright?" Adelaide squeezed his arm.

Gunter just blinked at her, and the only way Adelaide could tear herself away from him was by thinking about Elias's pain.

"Get Esa to help him," she told Resse, then transformed. She took off into the sky.

Evengier lay beneath Jeharrez and Elias, breathing shallowly, several cuts on his side. Ysoria flew down to Evengier, who must have recently fallen after helping Elias fight Jeharrez. Perhaps that was why Elias had roared in pain.

She hoped it was, though buckets of blood poured off his neck.

The sight of it incensed her, and the fire in her stomach spread to every part of her so that her scales felt like simmering embers.

She roared out a blasting pillar of flame as she lunged toward the huge dragon.

Elias, hovering over Jeharrez, glanced up at her. *Adelaide, you're glowing.* His wonder-filled voice broke through her fury-hazed mind.

But she didn't have time to puzzle out what he meant as she soared at Jeharrez. Elias sunk his teeth into the dragon's neck while gazing at Adelaide with squinted eyes.

Jeharrez screamed, and before he could knock Elias off, Adelaide plunged under him and grabbed his neck from below. Blood spurted onto her face, blinding her, but she held on, even when Jeharrez spun upside down to shake them off.

Finally, when Adelaide's jaw ached with the effort of holding on, and her snout was covered with blood, Jeharrez's growls ceased, and his breathing slowed. He sank to the ground and landed with a thud.

Adelaide stepped away, licking the blood off her snout so she could see. Elias walked toward her, his golden scales splattered with crimson, the wound on his neck weeping red drops.

She stepped close to him, touching his leg with hers, reassuring herself that he was safe. *Are you alright? You need to have that wound closed by a healer.*

I will. He gazed at her with concern. *And you? There's blood all over you.*

It's Jeharrez's.

Elias gazed down at the dead dragon. *His gift was understanding, and King Aloysius, the king before my father, gave him the memories of the humans' betrayal. It was probably too much pain combined with the death of his nest mate, my mother. She was one of the few dragons who truly loved him.*

One of Jeharrez's golden eyes stared up at the sky. It still seemed to spark with anger, but it didn't move.

Come, we must go see if Gunter's alright, Adelaide said. *He was injured as he attacked King Aethelmaer.*

Elias followed her to the place where Resse and Esa stood. Gunter was still—too still.

Adelaide transformed and ran over to him. "Esa, can't you heal him?"

The dragon shook her head, her tail drooping. *He's lost too much blood. He's ... gone.*

Gunter stared up at the sky, still in his half-dragon form. Adelaide wished she could return him to his original body, but didn't know how.

She leaned over him, expecting his red-tinged eyes to focus on her, but they remained still and empty. Gunter was gone, already soaring in skies she couldn't reach.

Adelaide had been mourning him ever since he had attacked Elias. The Gunter who listened to her harebrained schemes and never told her she was crazy, who was willing to risk his life to travel with her across the countryside—that man had somehow disappeared when the dagger was thrown at Elias.

But now, in this field of gore and death, she'd found him again. Only to lose him in her grand fight for freedom and peace.

"Bring Conrad here, please," she told Elias in a choked voice. Talons were ripping her into tiny pieces.

Adelaide didn't hear him leave; everything felt far away as if the shock of Gunter's death cut her off from the rest of the world.

She noticed something clenched in his hand. It was a silk handkerchief stained with dirt and blood. Where had he gotten such a thing? But it didn't matter; it had been important to him, so she would value it. Perhaps it had been the thing that had kept him sane through his ordeal.

Adelaide clutched the piece of cloth to her chest and gazed at Gunter's grimy, peaceful face. He was dead, and it was her fault.

She shouldn't have told him about the rebellion, shouldn't have given him that dagger. Another life ruined because of her. Would she ever stop feeling the pain-lashing effects of her mistakes?

Adelaide sank until her head touched Gunter's too cold, too hard chest and murmured apologies as if saying them enough would bring her friend back.

And then she wasn't the only one murmuring and mourning the once-happy, sweet Gunter. Conrad sat near, holding his brother's head, tears streaming down his face as he wailed, "My brother! No, you can't die. You can't."

Adelaide had mourned for so many: Emma, Elias, and now Gunter, that she felt like a shadow, an ephemeral breeze cast this way and that in the storms of loss. An apple with no core because it had been cut out of her.

As she wondered how she would go on, Elias was there. He

held her close, his comfort familiar and strong. Resse's breath blew warm against the back of her neck, and Adelaide remembered that she was not alone.

318

Chapter Fifty-Seven

When Adelaide's eyes dried, the stars twinkled in the sky-ceiling.

Elias said softly, "What would you like to do with his body?" He drew away from her but kept a firm grip on her hand, for which she was thankful. Without it, she felt like she might float away.

Conrad stared down at Gunter's odd-shaped form, the living brother's eyes glowing silver in the twilight. "Bury him, I suppose. It's what we would do in Alesfirth. But not here."

He glanced around at the slain men and dragons and the living stumbling around, looking for friends or family. His gaze settled on the trees at the Klinian side of the field. "We'll do it over there."

Elias and Conrad carried Gunter while Adelaide walked alongside them. Resse, Picot, Esa, and Turquan walked beside them like guards.

As they neared the trees, Berold came up, his eyes wide and disbelieving. "Elias, it is you. You're alive. And a dragon.

I thought I heard your voice, but ..." He frowned. "You have much explaining to do."

"Yes, but now isn't the time. I'll come and explain everything to you later. Make sure the men and dragons are getting along and resting. Our work is far from over."

Berold nodded, then saw Gunter and frowned. "What are you doing with that thing?"

"It's not a thing," Adelaide snapped. "It's Gunter, one of my best friends."

"You have odd friends."

"And I'm one of those friends," Elias reminded him wearily. "I'll come speak to you soon."

Berold nodded and walked away.

At the edge of the forest, Conrad set down Gunter's body. "This will do."

Since they didn't have shovels, the dragons created a hole in the dirt with their talons. Conrad and Elias placed Gunter gently in the dirt, folding his wings awkwardly so they'd fit.

"Rest well, little brother," Conrad murmured, with a hint of tears in his voice. "Our family will know of your courage. I'm sorry I was too late to help you." He rubbed his eyes.

I knew you not, human friend, but you flew well there at the end, fighting for us, and for that I am thankful, Resse said, and the other dragons murmured their agreement.

"I hold no grudge against you for trying to kill me," Elias said as he gazed at Gunter's pale form. "You were a friend of Adelaide's, so you must have been a good man."

Adelaide stepped forward. "You were my best friend, and I still hold you in the highest regard, as I ever have. I won't forget you, and I'm so sorry this happened." Her eyes filled with tears.

Elias took her hand and pulled her close. "It's not your fault, Adelaide."

She leaned against him, trying to believe his words.

Turquan began humming, then words joined the oozing-slow, winter-solemn music.

"Leaves are falling,
light is fading,
the sun is calling.

The sun is setting,
stars are winking,
the moon is shining.

Flowers are fading,
birds are sleeping,
the clouds are parting.

For you will leave us now,
For you will lead the way home,
and so we sing farewell."

Farewell, the dragons, including Elias, whispered as one.

"Farewell, brother," Conrad said, his face contorted in pain.

"Farewell, Gunter," Adelaide murmured, her heart still somewhere on the battlefield.

Just as the dragons were about to sweep the pile of dirt over Gunter's body, a man stepped up. "Do you mind if I say a few words?" He had a cut on one side of his face, and a sword clinked against his Gyndilian armor.

Adelaide stiffened. "Who are you?"

"My name's Dunstan. I'm—or was—a commander of the Gyndilian army but also a friend of Gunter's."

The man stared down at Gunter with so much sorrow that Adelaide's heart thawed toward him. Perhaps he had been a friend to Gunter these last few months.

"Sure," Conrad said, "but make it quick."

Dunstan nodded and stepped up to the hole. "I'm glad to have known you, Gunter, if only for a short time. I couldn't give you your freedom, but at least you have it now. May your soul find its way to light." He held up his right hand in a fist to his heart and bowed his head, then stepped back.

The dragons swept the dirt into the hole, burying Gunter to this world, but not to Adelaide. She wouldn't forget him. She would let the reminder of their mistakes motivate her to live better.

"I must go see Berold. He deserves an explanation," Elias said once the grave had been covered.

We'll go with you, Resse said.

The other healers probably need my help, Esa added.

Elias looked at Adelaide. "And you?"

"I'd like to stay here for a while." She darted a glance at the man called Dunstan who now sat on the edge of Gunter's grave. She wanted to hear what he had to say about her friend.

"Will you be alright?"

"Yes."

Elias's brow didn't smooth out, as if deciding whether she truly would be fine.

"I'll stay here a bit longer as well, Your Highness," Conrad said. "I'll make sure she gets back to the camp safely."

"Very well. If you need anything, Adelaide, just let me know." He gazed at her a moment longer, squeezed her hand, then walked with the others back to the camp.

Adelaide felt cold and alone without his warm, steady presence. She sat beside the Gyndilian man, and Conrad sat on her other side.

"So, how did you know Gunter?" Adelaide asked.

The man launched into a story almost as unbelievable as the dragons sleeping around them.

Just a few seasons ago, Adelaide wouldn't have believed that her friend, so self-conscious and tenderhearted, could have made a deal with one of the Gyndilian leaders, attacked Prince Elias, and become friends with a Gyndilian knight. But neither was she the same cynical young woman who had hated all nobility when she left Alesfirth last winter.

"That's the handkerchief from my wife that I gave Gunter

before he left the Master's camp." Dunstan nodded at the cloth Adelaide didn't realize she was twisting in her hands.

"Oh. You can have it back then." She held it out to him.

Dunstan shook his head. "You knew him better than I did. Hopefully, it will bring back good remembrances. Now, if you'll excuse me, I'd like to make sure that they're treating my men well and get some sleep." He stood and walked past the Klinian tents.

"I can't believe Gunter did all that. It's surprising he survived as long as he did," Conrad said, gazing at his knees.

Adelaide gazed at the handkerchief. "He was a brave man."

Chapter Fifty-Eight

The next morning, as Adelaide stared at a biscuit, trying to will herself to eat it, Elias turned to her from where they sat at their encampment. "At least one good thing has come out of this battle. We now know what your gift is."

Adelaide glanced at him, startled. "We do?"

"Light." He grinned. "You were glowing like a dagger of light as you flew toward Jeharrez, and you lit up King Aethelmaer's tent, didn't you?"

Adelaide shrugged. "I suppose so. I also did it in Weitzen and Dhalion."

But they didn't have long to talk about her gift because Elias was pulled away to discuss important political matters.

Adelaide would have been bored the next two days if she hadn't learned that she could heal the abominations.

It was Esa's idea. Adelaide was sitting on a stump beside Gunter's grave, feeling useless and lost. Not only did she mourn her best friend, but she wasn't sure what she was supposed to do now that she had saved her people. Who was she if not a fighter for justice?

She couldn't help Esa heal, and Elias's meetings with Dunstan, the new king of Gyndilad, and Berold didn't concern her. Berold had killed the man that Dunstan had called the Master, and King Aethelmaer had no known living relatives, so Dunstan was appointed king. At least temporarily.

Adelaide, I need your help, Esa said, ambling over.

"With what?"

The other healers and I can fix the abominations' bodies, but we can't return them to their normal human state. There's too much darkness inside them.

"What can I do about it? I'm not a healer."

No, but your gift is light. So, you might be able to chase the darkness out of their minds like you did with your friend. Esa gazed at Gunter's grave.

"I probably just got his attention because I knew him."

It wouldn't hurt to try. Esa turned and walked toward the vulture-infested battlefield.

Without anything better to do than mope, Adelaide transformed and followed Esa. The scents of the battle were too sharp in this nose, and she fought back the desire to vomit. She considered turning back into a human, but since her gift was part of the dragon side of her, it would probably work better in this form. If it worked at all.

Esa stopped at the edge of the blood-soaked field where some of the half-dragon, half-human creatures lay. A few dragons walked among them, murmuring or humming calming tunes.

The creatures were either insensible or moaning in agony, twitching and writhing. Adelaide wanted to flee from their despair, but if there was even the slightest possibility that she could heal them, most of whom were probably Klinians, shouldn't she try?

Let's start with this one. Esa pointed a talon at a writhing abomination that looked the same as the others. *I've already healed his wounds, so there's nothing wrong with him physically, but he acts as if he's being tortured.* Esa's tail dropped to the ground with the sound of defeat.

Adelaide walked over. *What should I do?*

Esa eyed her. *I'm not sure. How did you use your gift before?*

Adelaide shrugged, thinking back to when the light had shown her what she wanted it to in Dhalion, Weitzen, and here on the battlefield. *I just concentrated on what I wanted.*

Start there then. Esa turned her gaze back to the abomination.

Sighing, Adelaide stared at the creature. What did she want? She wanted the creature to stop being in pain, to find the peace that Elias had given her. She wanted all the rage in its clenched talons and crimson eyes to disappear.

And then she was no longer looking at a writhing half-dragon, half-human creature but at herself crossing the land with a dagger in her clenched hands and fury in her eyes. *Be calm,* she told herself, told the creature. *Get out of the darkness.*

A brilliant white light shot out of her scales and hit the creature. It screeched louder than before, and for a horrible moment, Adelaide thought she was burning it.

But when the light disappeared, there was not a burnt creature, but a human man crying.

Adelaide would have thought it had never been the abomination if the man hadn't kneeled at her feet and murmured over and over again, "Oh, thank you, dragon. Thank you for leading me out of those terrible memories."

I knew you could do it, Esa told her smugly.

Healing the abominations took a lot of energy, but it also gave Adelaide purpose. She just wished she'd been able to heal Gunter.

"You never stop amazing me," Elias told her that evening around the fire after she'd explained what she'd done. "You're as much of a healer now as me, maybe more so."

Adelaide wiped chicken grease off her chin. "But what will we do with the men?"

"Take them back to their families. If there are any Gyndilians, Dunstan can take them back with him. He seems to be a good man and, if the Gyndilians will have him, a good king."

Adelaide glanced up and noticed Berold frowning at his bread as if it had just deeply insulted him. "What did that bread do to you?"

"I'll be remaining in Gyndilad as an ambassador." He ripped the bread apart while looking at Elias.

"Most people would deem that an honor," Adelaide said.

Berold glanced at her. "Perhaps, but it's not my home, and I was just reunited with my brother-in-arms after believing he was dead for many weeks."

"Well, you weren't the only one."

"At least you'll return home with him," Berold said.

Yes, but what then? Adelaide tried not to think too much about what would happen when they returned to Klinhun; she knew what she must do, but it hurt too much to think about.

"You won't be alone, Berold. I'll have some men remain here with you and will return frequently for visits and meetings." Elias clapped his shoulder. "And I'm sure the women are just as fine here as in Klinhun."

Turquan, sitting nearby, snorted in laughter.

Early the next morning, Elias made an announcement to the dragons and knights. He gave it as a dragon so that everyone could hear his voice in their minds. Pride soared in Adelaide at the sight of him standing as a dragon before his people—both species.

Today we depart as one for Dhalion to begin the long process of peace and healing. Our friends, family, and countrymen have not been here to see us fighting together. So, it is up to us to show them that we can be one. Dragons, he gazed out at the shimmering creatures standing amidst the crowd, *the time for hiding is over. It is time to reclaim our home and become the humans' protectors once more.*

The dragons roared. A few men standing nearby winced.

Humans, Elias continued, dropping his gaze to the war-weary men who looked at him with wary admiration. *It's time to come alongside the dragons with your knowledge and fervor. May no one in Klinhun be oppressed while we are here.* The men shouted, and Adelaide joined in.

Good. Now we can leave this stinking place, Cyr said as the men lined up and the dragons took to the air.

Adelaide agreed with the hawk, then said to Elias, "Nice speech."

He grinned. *Thanks. I was up most of the night worrying about what to say.*

"You mean the words don't just come to you on the spot?"

Never. He transformed and peered into Adelaide's eyes. "How are you?"

"Fine."

"No, you're not. You just fought in your first battle and buried your best friend, not to mention all the things that happened before that."

Berold rode up on a chestnut accompanied by other knights. He dismounted, and he and Elias hugged. "Be careful in Dhalion," Berold said. "You won't have the best swordsman in Klinhun to keep you safe anymore."

"True, but I am a dragon."

"Oh, yes. That will take some getting used to."

"And I'll have the fiercest, most beautiful woman by my side." Elias grasped Adelaide's hand and pulled her to him.

Did he mean what she thought he meant? She trembled but pushed away her glee. It couldn't be; he was the king, and she was the daughter of a farmer.

"You're the best peasant I've known," Berold said, looking at her. "I won't forget that you saved my life. Keep an eye on Elias for me, and I might forget that you're a peasant."

Adelaide smiled, although she couldn't promise him anything. "And you're not the worst noble I've met. Perhaps I'll forget you are one if you never lock me up again."

"Yes, Berold, you shouldn't have done that. Adelaide would never have killed me," Elias said.

Berold swung into his saddle. "I didn't know that at the time."

"Be careful, Berold." Elias laid a hand on his horse's neck. "The Gyndilians won't be happy that their king is dead. Hopefully, they'll take well to Dunstan's rule. I'll send more men and come myself once things between the dragons and humans are settled in Klinhun."

"I look forward to it." Berold and his men rode away, and Elias swung his gaze to Adelaide.

"Ready?"

"Of course." She missed her family with every thud of her heart.

Chapter Fifty-Nine

Adelaide flew above Elias at the front of the knights. He rode a stocky, brown horse that he had taken from the Gyndilians. She knew from overhearing his mutterings that morning as he groomed the horse that he missed Starflare.

He had told her that he would much rather fly at her side than ride, but the men needed their human king at the moment, and someone needed to remain on the ground to protect them. Even so, she still longed to test her strength and speed against his. Perhaps they could before Adelaide had to leave. No, she wasn't thinking about that.

The dragons were all in good spirits, humming, singing, and talking about the humans' peculiarities and how much Klinhun had changed from their tales or memories. They didn't seem worried about what the citizens would think of them.

I'd like to explore the Spearhead Mountains sometime. Turquan gave the jagged mountains on their right an appreciative look. *And then I'd like to find that boy Hubert and settle down near his family.*

You've given up your dreams of a fine female then? Adelaide teased.

Turquan huffed smoke. *Of course not. I've just resigned myself to wait a little longer.*

If they're real, I'd like to visit those caves made of gems that used to be one of our ancestors' nesting sites, Esa said, her eyes sparkling.

They're real. I've seen them. Adelaide remembered Elias sharing about the dragons and how she had fled. Oh, how things had changed.

Something in the corner of Adelaide's vision moved. She glanced down. Below them were the dark eyes of the mines of Fernohn. Men stood around the mountain, throwing rocks and pieces of wood at the dragons and shouting.

"Dragons!"

"They're real!"

"Run to the village and warn everyone. Grab weapons."

A few coal-dusted men ran to the village. Some stood staring at the dragons, and many threw anything they could get their hands on. The items either didn't make it all the way up or bounced off the dragons' scales and fell back onto the men.

"I am King Elias," Elias shouted as he rode up on his horse. "These dragons are our friends and allies. We have just returned from fighting the Gyndilians alongside them, so please stop throwing things at them."

"King Elias?" One of the men said, fingering a dagger. "You're supposed to be dead."

"It's a long story, but I never died. These dragons," he gestured up to where they hovered in the air, "just helped us defeat King Aethelmaer."

The man scoffed. "Sure. And now they're here to kill us. Dragons don't think, they just act."

The man threw a rock which hit a young dragon in the face. More people from the village had gathered, gawking at the dragons. A few fired arrows at them.

Adelaide dove down and landed beside Elias, causing his horse to nearly throw him off. The villagers stepped back, some crying out in alarm.

It's true, what he says. And he's the king, so I would listen to him if I were you, Adelaide said, then transformed.

The villagers stared at her in a mixture of confusion, awe, and fear.

"You're the maiden who was with the prince when he helped after one of our mines exploded," a woman said.

Peering into the crowd, Adelaide recognized the tavern owner who had given her a drink and told her about the good deeds of Elias and his father when she first came to Fernohn.

Adelaide nodded. "That's me. Just like last time, we mean no harm."

Elias placed a hand on her shoulder. "Dragons have returned to Klinhun in peace," he announced. "They are good, and they are welcome here. Any of these knights behind me can vouch for the help they have provided on the battlefield against the Gyndilians."

The knights nodded.

Elias dismounted. "Before I tell you everything that has happened, I must show you one thing." He closed his eyes, the familiar glow emanating from him, then he emerged in all his golden-crimson glory.

Adelaide watched the crowd. They gasped and cried out in alarm as they stared at him.

I am King Elias, king of the dragons, he said into everyone's mind. *I have always been a dragon, but I haven't always been a human.*

He then explained how the dragons had left Klinhun rather than fight the humans. He told the rest in a steady, commanding voice, all the way up until the recent battle.

The villagers' gazes never wandered off his regal scales, and their brows wrinkled in confusion or mouths gaped in shock during the telling.

So, Elias said at the end of his tale, *the dragons have returned to Klinhun. As their king, I attest that our only desire is to protect the citizens of this land and call it home once more. Do you choose to accept our reign and presence here?*

None could dare refuse or challenge Elias as his blazing eyes stared at them from above, and his spiked tail hung over them like a club. A few nodded, and some murmured their assent.

Good. Then I need some of the best and quickest riders in Fernohn to step forward.

After a moment, five men came to the front of the crowd.

Elias turned a solemn eye upon them. *You are to ride as fast as you can to the largest villages in Klinhun: Dhalion, Pinhurn, Kildare, and Alesfirth. Tell everyone what you have heard, that the Klinians have defeated King Aethelmaer of Gyndilad with King Elias's help and that of the dragons.*

Tell them that the dragons are here to restore a peaceful reign with me as king. Show them these as proof. Wincing, he tore off four of his beautiful golden scales.

"Elias—" Adelaide said.

They will grow back.

The men darted up and took the scales from Elias's talons as if afraid he might attack them.

Now go, as quickly as you can, Elias told the riders. *Make sure to let everyone know that if they harm or attempt to harm a dragon, they will stand trial and their very life may be forfeit.*

The men scrambled away at Elias's fierce gaze.

And now we begin to make amends, Elias announced to all.

Adelaide, the other dragons, and some of the knights remained in Fernohn for a few days, helping build mines, lifting timber, moving boulders, and a myriad of other things that the villagers needed done.

Adelaide understood Elias's reasoning for the work: even after just two days of laboring alongside the dragons and watching them serve their village for nothing in return, the townsfolk thawed and a few even touched the dragons—with permission, of course.

But Adelaide grew frustrated with the labor. She longed to see her family and restore her home to what it had once been. Gyndilians probably still poisoned it with their presence.

She would miss the dragons, and, of course, Elias. But no, she still couldn't think about that; her heart threatened to split apart each time she considered another separation from him.

On the eve of their last night in Fernohn, Turquan told tales to eager little ones, dragons and humans, about when he had almost fallen into a volcano on Niclond.

A touch on Adelaide's shoulder startled her. She glanced up to see Elias standing near.

"I'd like to speak with you, if you don't mind." He walked off in the direction of the Wymar River.

Here it came then, the time for more goodbyes.

Repressing the longing to beg him to sit with her by the fire forever, she stood and followed him.

"You didn't wait for a reply," Adelaide said as she caught up to Elias beneath some evergreens on the bank of the rushing, moonlit river. "What if I hadn't come?"

He turned to her, his eyes glinting in the pearled light. "But you did." He scuffed his boot in the dirt.

After a moment trying to ignore her writhing stomach, Adelaide asked, "So, what did you want to talk about?"

Elias clenched the hem of his tunic. "Much has happened to us both, Adelaide, and I know that you're still grieving Gunter."

Adelaide flinched at his name.

"But all that's happened has just served to make my decision truer and more final, and I can't wait anymore." He pulled his hair.

He was going to ask her. He truly was.

She swallowed and tried to lighten the mood. "Just say it, Elias, before you pull all your hair out."

One of his fingers traced her lips that was drawn into a tight smile, and she shivered, longing for more.

"I shall never forget when I first saw you smile. It was so beautiful, so unexpected on such a hard, troubled face. I promised myself to woo it out of you every chance I could."

He stepped closer, his eyes silver in the moonlight, capturing her like a net. His warm, large hand was an anchor. "Will you be my wife, Adelaide? Will you give me the opportunity to make you smile for the rest of our lives? You are a courageous, loyal, lovely woman and dragon, and there's no one I'd rather live and rule beside than you, Adelaide, Starscales."

Even though he had hinted at the proposal, and she thought it was coming, hearing his words and the love wrapped around each one still took all the breath from her.

She wanted to roar, to shout with joy that Elias had chosen her—Adelaide—out of all the maidens and dragons to be his forever.

But even now, in the moonlight, she could see the paler, shinier scar tissue of the burn he had taken for her.

And saying yes would mean that Adelaide would be queen. She didn't belong in a fancy castle. She was a peasant who owned nothing more than her dress and the dagger still wrapped tight in her girdle.

The differences surrounding her and Elias rose like mountains between them. He was a king, and she was a farmer's daughter who had tried to kill him.

Adelaide took a step back, forcing Elias to drop her hand. "I want to say yes, Elias, I do." She blinked back tears. "I care about you, but that's why I have to say no. I've done so much to hurt you." She glanced at his scar again. "And I'm just a peasant. You deserve so much more." She tasted bitter salt in her mouth.

Elias's face twisted, and Adelaide loathed herself for hurting him more. "Adelaide, you've always been more than a peasant to me. You are brave, passionate, and don't need jewels or land to be happy or beautiful. You sacrificed so much to help your friends and people.

"And we all make mistakes. We will continue to make them and forgive each other."

She took another step back. "I'm sorry, Elias," she whispered before turning. With each step away, her heart urged her to return and let him hold her until the snow fell and thawed again.

"I will find you and ask again, Adelaide. I care too deeply to let you go," Elias called after her.

Chapter Sixty

It had been easy, almost too easy, to overthrow the Gyndilians in Alesfirth.

Adelaide, Resse, and Esa had roared as they soared over the village. When Adelaide had spewed out flames overhead, the Gyndilians scattered like a flock of spooked ravens.

Esa and Resse lingered long enough to make sure that none of the villagers attacked her, then they flew off to help the king (Adelaide refused to think his name; it hurt too much) quell the few foolish humans who were trying to attack the dragons. Then they would find a nesting place for the eggs that Turquan and some other dragons would bring over from Niclond.

Adelaide missed them. To keep herself from thinking about them and a certain king, she hurled herself into rebuilding villagers' homes that had burned in the Gyndilians' fire.

She was grateful Cyr was with her or she might have flown to Dhalion out of boredom and loneliness. As it was, the king's last words clung to her, and she throbbed at missing him.

Adelaide had mostly finished rebuilding her family's house

by the time they returned with Gunter's parents.

She sat outside the new thatch house eating some bread and having a rather one-sided conversation with Cyr when she spotted three figures tromping over the tender new shoots that fought through the charred earth.

"Adelaide!" Odo called, waving.

She stood, and Cyr flew to the top of the cottage. "How was your trip?"

"Good." Galiena hugged her. "We returned with Gunter's parents. They might come over soon to ask you about their sons."

Adelaide cringed. How could she tell them about Gunter? Would they even believe her? Hopefully, Conrad could help them through their pain when he finished aiding the king sort out matters in Dhalion.

"How are you?" Ferand squeezed her shoulder, then peered up at the cottage, shielding his eyes from the sun. "That looks good. Who did it?"

"Me."

Ferand frowned. "Who helped you?"

"No one." She ignored Cyr's insulted exclamation as she contemplated how much Odo had told her parents. She glanced at him.

"I told them everything. Can I ride on you today? It was fun riding on King Elias, but he was in such a hurry that it wasn't very comfortable."

"I'm not a horse," she told him.

Galiena gasped. "So, it's true? You're a … you're now a …" she faltered into silence.

In response, Adelaide transformed. Once the heat calmed to a simmer, she opened her eyes.

Her father's mouth was as large as a moon, and her mother's skin was as pale as clouds.

"How long?" Ferand asked in a quaking voice.

Adelaide frowned. She hadn't kept good track of the days

with everything that had happened. *Not long after Elias was crowned king. I can tell you the whole story if you'd like.*

◆ ◆ ◆

Time and dragons slowly brought peace to the land. A mated dragon pair came to reside and rule near Alesfirth, helping where they could and listening to grievances. Others soon lived outside the town, entertaining villagers with stories and aerial acrobatics.

The townsfolk eventually stopped looking for or gripping weapons whenever a dragon came near, but it would still be a long time before they completely trusted them.

Old and new songs about the dragons sprouted, and crowds gathered to hear them singing in their rich voices that rumbled to the skies.

Galiena stopped gasping whenever Adelaide transformed, and her father took advantage of her strength to give her a seemingly unending list of tasks. She occasionally let Odo ride her when he wasn't being annoying

Although a long, hard-fought-for peace was enveloping the land like a tender embrace, Adelaide didn't feel at peace.

Her home, which had at one time been enough, now seemed to choke her with its smallness.

She spent much of her time flying with Cyr in a sky blue enough to drink, where no one stared at her, and her failures were forgotten—where she felt free.

But whenever she landed, the smallness of the place and the king's absence crushed her. Every day she hoped he would come, and every day she got irritated at herself for wishing such a thing.

So, she took to the skies, where everything was just the breeze caressing her face, the swooshing of wings, the taste of clouds and sunlight.

Chapter Sixty-One

When burning-fire leaves rained to the ground, and the mornings became as crisp as apples, he came.

Adelaide sat near the fire inside her house with her family, regaling them with the story of how she had rescued Berold's life, when a knock sounded on the door.

Galiena's eyebrows rose. "Are we expecting anyone, Ferand?"

He shook his head. "I guess it could be Darfin's son bringing the bridle, but I wasn't expecting him for another day or two."

"I'll get it." Adelaide stood, wiped straw off her new brown dress, and opened the door.

Elias stood there in his flaming red cloak, grinning. Starflare nibbled on the grass behind him, and she was struck by the similarity of the first time he'd come to her door, and she'd closed it in his face.

"Good day, fair maiden." He bowed to her. "Will you speak with me this time instead of shutting the door on me?"

Adelaide stepped out, closing the door behind her. Only then did she realize that he hadn't come alone. Resse, Turquan, Picot, Esa, Conrad, Berold, and even Manfred were there, standing in the trees.

"What are you all doing here?" She flicked a piece of straw out of her hair, suddenly aware that she must stink of smoke and chickens.

Elias rubbed his hair, which was longer than she remembered. Dark bruises yawned under his eyes, but otherwise he looked the same as when she'd left. "Please go get your dagger, Adelaide."

"Why?"

"I'll tell you in a moment."

Adelaide went back inside, ignored the curious gazes of her family, and retrieved the dagger out of the satchel that she hadn't touched since returning home. She drew out the too-familiar weapon that had seen everything.

Back outside, Adelaide handed the weapon to Elias, glad to be rid of it.

"I know you love me, but your guilt is holding you back. You're drowning in it," Elias said.

In one swift motion, he broke the dagger in two while breaking her with his gaze. "You are free, Adelaide. You made some mistakes, but you don't have to let them imprison you. I forgave you long ago, and I am sure Gunter never blamed you for anything that happened. Now you just have to rest in that forgiveness."

He tossed the pieces of dagger into a clump of trees past Starflare.

"Why are all of them here?" She gestured at the crowd.

Elias grinned. "To help you find a way out." He glanced behind him and nodded. "It's time."

Resse stepped forward and said, *I am Resse, Truthspeaker, Esa's mate. Among many other things, I once intentionally set fire to my friend Turquan's foot. But I am forgiven and loved.*

He stepped back to join the others.

Conrad stepped forward next. "I am Conrad, son of Raymond, and I allowed my brother to leave on his own and didn't go looking for him." He swallowed, and Adelaide longed to squeeze his arm. "But I am forgiven and loved." He stepped back.

Manfred was next. "I am Manfred, son of Barlek, and I killed King Ganelon." He looked at the ground, tears glistening in his gaze.

Elias placed a hand on the man's shoulder.

Manfred met Elias's gaze. "I am forgiven and loved."

Elias nodded at him, and Manfred returned to the others.

Berold stepped up next. "I am Berold, Wishchard's son, and I once hated peasants and acted appalling to them." He nodded at Adelaide. "But I am forgiven and loved."

Elias patted his back.

The others all did the same, saying one mistake that they had made and that they were forgiven and loved. Adelaide wanted to hug them all tight to herself and never let go.

Finally, Elias stepped close to Adelaide and took her hand. "I am Elias, son of Ganelon and king of Klinhun. I wasn't there for my love when she needed me most. Am I forgiven?" Tears pooled in his beautiful eyes.

"Of course," Adelaide whispered, her voice rough. "And I love you."

He kissed her cheek, his lips softer than petals.

When he drew back, he said, "It's your turn, Adelaide."

She took a deep breath, clinging to Elias's hand. "I am Adelaide, Ferand's daughter. I started a rebellion to overthrow the king that led to the death of a dear friend and almost to the death of the king of Klinhun."

He squeezed her hand and then asked the others loudly, "Is she forgiven?"

"We forgive you," they shouted as one, and Adelaide felt herself begin to unclench for the first time since Elias's body lay bleeding on the cliff. She could see sunlight bursting through the clouds of the days ahead.

"And is she loved?" Elias asked.

"She is loved," everyone shouted, including Adelaide's family behind her.

And she felt it—the love pouring from them like a fresh spring rain, saturating her heart so something beautiful could grow.

Elias took Adelaide's other hand. "Join me, Adelaide. Let go of it all. Be the excellent queen and dragon that I know you will be."

"What if I hurt you again?" Her eyes flickered to the scar beneath his tunic.

"Then I will forgive you. And when I hurt you, you will forgive me. We will learn together." He brushed his lips against her hand. "Please consent to be my wife, Adelaide, fairest of maidens and dragons. You know best what this country needs, and I can't imagine ruling or living without you by my side."

Adelaide couldn't say no to a man with such hopeful eyes, nor he who held her hand so tight as if she might flee. But she was no longer tempted to. She knew his tender, strong heart, knew that she had his forgiveness as well as those of her friends who watched with delight.

Adelaide's grin stretched all the way to her toes as she let herself believe in their love. "I suppose I consent, King Elias. Just let me have everything my way, and I won't attempt to kill you."

Elias's grin outshone the sun, and everyone shouted or roared.

Adelaide stepped closer to Elias and said to her brother, "It looks as if you will get to live at the castle after all."

Chapter Sixty-Two

On the coldest night of the year, dragons and humans gathered around a crackling, blazing bonfire in Dhalion and throughout Klinhun. Next to Adelaide, Elias, her husband and king, sang the end and beginning of the story of the dragons in his golden voice as the other dragons hummed along.

"When time first breathed and woke
men and dragons walked in Klinhun side-by-side.
The dragons' protection sheltered the land like a cloak,
and by the humans' gratefulness the two were unified.

Then darkness by lies seeped inside man's mind,
and they turned on their protectors and friends.
The dragons left for another home to find,
to keep their trust and eventually make amends.

But darkness crept into the land,
tarnishing the character of the dragons,

so that broken was the peaceful strand
of trust that they had held in their talons.

Humans struggled without their peaceful protectors
as greed grew in the dragons' empty spaces.
But one who remembered the stories of his ancestors
met a woman made from fire and ashes.

Together with allies in another land they faced
the lies and darkness in the form of a dragon.
In destroying him, human and dragon embraced
so that peace shines here once more as a beacon."

They let the fire burn until dawn, the brightness of the dragons' flames lighting the land with hope.

Acknowledgements

It's bittersweet that Adelaide and Elias's story is over (at least for now). I'm so thankful to my King and Savior, Jesus, for giving me this story to share with the world, which is only a frail shadow of the greater story of His love and forgiveness.

To my beta readers for this project: Amy, Anjali, and Mary Louise, many thanks for helping make this book better and for all your encouragement as I wondered if anyone would like it. Your excitement got me through some difficult times.

And, of course, I'm so grateful to the team at Atmosphere Press: my editor Alex (what a surprise and delight to work with you again!), Ronaldo's team of cover design wizards (didn't they do a fabulous job?!), and my copy editors who can spot a misplaced comma a mile away. It's always a pleasure to work with you, and I've enjoyed our partnership as we brought Adelaide's story to life together.

My alpha reader and the love of my life whom I forced to read portions of this book at least twice, you're sweeter than a mountain of chocolate and more precious than Gollum's ring.

I must give a huge thanks to my family in Texas who rallied around the first book and organized a wonderful book signing that made me feel like a real author. Your support in telling everyone you know about my baby means the world to me!

And last, but definitely not least, thank you a million times, reader, for all your love and support of Adelaide and Elias. Thank you for following their tale to its conclusion; I hope you enjoyed spending time with them. See you in the next book!

Want more from Adelaide and Elias's world? Sign up for Rachel's monthly newsletter at the link below and receive a deleted scene from *The Gift of Dragons* as well as other goodies and sneak peeks!

About Atmosphere Press

Founded in 2015, Atmosphere Press was built on the principles of Honesty, Transparency, Professionalism, Kindness, and Making Your Book Awesome. As an ethical and author-friendly hybrid press, we stay true to that founding mission today.

If you're a reader, enter our giveaway for a free book here:

SCAN TO ENTER
BOOK GIVEAWAY

If you're a writer, submit your manuscript for consideration here:

SCAN TO SUBMIT
MANUSCRIPT

And always feel free to visit Atmosphere Press and our authors online at atmospherepress.com. See you there soon!

About the Author

Rachel A. Greco dreams of being a dragon but has settled instead for being an author, which is almost as fun. Her short story, *Fairy Light,* won an honorable mention in the Writer's Digest Annual Writing Competition, and several of her other short stories have been published. When not writing, she can be found reading, kayaking, or dancing with elves in the forests of her North Carolina home.

Visit her website for all things fantasy and bookish at **www.rachelagreco.com**. You can also find her on Instagram and TikTok at **@rachelagrecoauthor**. Come say hi and talk about dragons!